MW01075670

In loving memory of Henry Duncan Spens Goodsir

and all the men who perished

on the Franklin Expedition

1845-1848

You will never be forgotten.

Copyright © 2020 by Jennifer Reinfried and Changed Fate Press

First edition February 2020.

Cover design by Evelyne Paniez.
www.secretdartiste.be

Published by Changed Fate Press
www.changedfate.com

The past is always present.

FOREWORD

In May of 1845, their sails billowing with high hopes, Her Majesty's ships "Erebus" and "Terror" departed from Greenhithe on the Thames under the command of the veteran Arctic explorer Sir John Franklin. They were meant to discover the long-sought Northwest Passage across the top of North America, but their expedition ended up at quite a different destination – that "undiscovered country from whose bourn no traveler returns" – death.

Not a single one of the one hundred and twenty-eight men who sailed with Franklin survived to tell their tale, and more than a century and a half of searches has turned up only a scattering of enigmatic clues: three graves, a few stone cairns, some skeletons in a boat, and equipment scattered on the ground, including chronometers, a sextant, some spoons and forks, nails, and fragments of sailcloth. Franklin's ships were finally found – the "Erebus" in 2014 and the "Terror" in 2016 – but even then, the ultimate reasons for the expedition's demise remain uncertain.

Into that uncertainty have leapt two kinds of writers – historians, such as myself, who have sought to sift the evidence and connect the scattered objects, and writers of fiction, who have deployed the power of the human imagination to reconstruct what may have happened. Among the latter have been a good many writers of note, from Jules Verne to Margaret Atwood; by my account, the Franklin disaster has inspired no fewer than two dozen novels over the past few decades, not to mention numerous books of poetry, an Australian musical, and a German opera.

Most recently, in 2018, AMC presented a ten-part television series, *The Terror*, based on Dan Simmons's novel of the same name, which was in turn inspired by the Franklin story. Simmons added an element of horror – a mysterious spirit animal in the form of a twenty-foot high polar bear – but thanks to showrunner David Kajganich, the show also featured a remarkably accurate reconstruction of the ships, the men, and their daily struggles. The intense realism of the production, indeed, made the supernatural element all the more powerful.

It's a similar admixture of carefully researched fact with speculative and alternative histories that lies at the core of Jennifer

Reinfried's *In Eternity*. Within her world, we have not only an alternative past in which the expedition's naturalist Harry Goodsir meets a different fate, but a different future in which his altered fate takes on new significance. The inhabitants of this altered future, driven underground by a biological cataclysm of man's own making, discover in Goodsir a scientist who, though caught himself in a struggle to survive, may hold the key to the ultimate survival of all mankind.

It is a changed fate indeed for a man whose work involved the careful cataloguing of the natural world, and who – in part because of his wonderful portrayal by the actor Paul Ready in *The Terror* television series – has become increasingly central to the way we imagine the Franklin disaster, and to understanding the ideals and aspirations which lay behind its audacious goals.

Having worked with Ms. Reinfried, along with Mr. Michael Tracy – who is Harry's closest living relation – on the backgrounds of Harry's life story, I'm confident that this remarkably well-researched book possesses that same alchemy between the details of history and the purposes of our imagination that has brought so many writers over the years to that distant shore where, nearly two centuries ago, the boldest explorers of their day met their fate amidst the ice.

Dr. Russell Potter
January 2020

INTRODUCTION

As one of the last surviving members of the once illustrious medical and scientific family of the Goodsirs of Largo, Fife, it gives me great pleasure to introduce this book specifically on my kinsman, Dr. Harry D.S. Goodsir, Assistant Surgeon and Naturalist on board HMS *Erebus* of the ill-fated Franklin expedition.

When *Erebus* and *Terror* were encased in the icy grip of the Arctic waters and the long encampment began, one can only imagine the utter fear and panic that set in on the minds of the officers and crew. No one knew where they were, which would erase the likelihood of an immediate search and rescue. It was a fact that no doubt was on each crew member's mind. The subsequent southerly death march with an anticipated goal of reaching the Back River, though along desolate lands, at least gave the crew a chance of survival. They began their slow, painful, march in extreme temperatures moving ever so slowly in death's icy grip. During these long days and months, death was probably welcomed. As for Harry, he may have been one of the last to perish near the Peffer River in the southernmost part of the island.

Jennifer Reinfried has taken this story further to remarkably capture Harry's triumphs, defeats, and achievements, and ultimately seizes upon the fear, despair, desperation, and pure horror facing him and the crews of the *Erebus* and *Terror* in a captivating fictional narrative. She has ultimately broken new ground and has gone beyond the historical evidence and into speculation, which is, in my opinion, intriguing.

This is a gripping, imaginative account. Be sure you leave a light on.

Michael T. Tracy
November 2019

In Eternity

Book One of Harry Goodsir's Changed Fate Trilogy

THE END

One

Annie
2017

The metal strings of the Les Paul bit hard into the pads of my fingertips. I watched the gathering crowd, trailing my guitar pick down and letting an open chord ring. The sound soothed the uneasy sensation that had settled over me since I'd arrived for our show.

A few people shuffled a bit closer to the stage. Eager to start, I glanced over at Ryan, hunched over the top of his bass amp. His hand flew over a crumpled white paper, scribbling with a brown Sharpie. I squinted past the bright stage lights, searching for his still absent younger brother.

Dennis leaned forward on a stool across the room. He was chatting up a bartender with lips painted a harsh red. She shot him a disinterested glance and handed over a round tray of drinks. He held it high and wove through the crowd. I caught his eye and jerked my chin at his drum throne.

"Here, Annie." Ryan slid my copy of our set list across the stage using the toe of his sneaker. I peered down, fingering the fretboard of my guitar while trying to decipher his crappy handwriting through a faint shoe print.

Dennis hopped up on stage, grinning over the tray of three waters and three dangerously full shot glasses.

He lowered it beside his drum kit and glanced around for his worn sticks. "Ryan, you're not gonna change first?"

His brother shook his head, slipping the pad of one thumb down the bass' strings. "Left work in a rush and forgot my clothes. I'll be fine in scrubs."

"Just grab a shirt from our merch bin," I suggested. "It's in the van out back."

He snorted. "Who am I, Eddie Van Halen? I'm not wearing our own band shirt during a show."

"Well, I'm sure some of the girls here will dig your adorable matching threads." Dennis stretched and slipped his cell in the front pocket of his jeans.

Ryan chugged back a few mouthfuls of water. "No one's gonna come near this stage once we start. These lights are hot as hell. The sweat is gonna be brutal."

"This will help us smell even worse." Dennis lifted two of the shots he'd brought. "Jamo. Annie's favorite."

I grinned and grabbed the closest one. We clinked the shots together and knocked the warm whiskey back. The liquor's heat settled with the restless feeling in my stomach.

"Guys, let's rock." I shook out my hands and rolled my shoulders. Tossing back my chopped red hair, I twisted the amp's volume knob. A thudding echo came from Ryan's big bass amp; he was ready.

Dennis dropped behind his kit. He clacked his drumsticks together three times, then slammed them down onto the Mylar membranes. Ryan and I started in time, cranking out the first notes of "I Melt with You."

I stepped on my overdrive pedal. We sped up the song, playing it harsher and more raw than the original. Leaning into my mic, I let myself get lost in the lyrics, effortlessly keeping up with the quickened tempo. I didn't notice the crowd, didn't pay attention to the sweat already forming at my temples and along my back. All I felt was a lightness, a sense of floating.

Nothing else mattered when the music flowed. Not the master's thesis draft due in two days. Not the worry I'd had over my dad's upcoming hip surgery. Not even the shitbag who'd stood me up for our third date the night before. Only the chords held any sort of importance now.

We transitioned into Jet's "Are You Gonna Be My Girl" with barely a pause between. I let a chord ring out while

Ryan's fingers plucked out the song's opening bass line. The deep thrum echoed through the bar and beat hard against my chest.

Dennis came in on the snare. People I didn't know cheered from just past the stage, their eyes bright and faces flushed. I lunged forward, lifting my guitar high in anticipation. Ryan yelled into his mic and we were off. The crowd sang along as he took the lead on lyrics.

People surged forward, bumping into each other, spilling drinks to the floor and along the front of the stage. No one cared, no one fought, but I did shuffle back to avoid having beer-soaked Chuck Taylors the rest of the night.

Halfway through the song, the crowd shifted to the right in a harsh ripple. Three men were flung against the stage. One flailed and his hand caught my mic stand, pulling it with him as he went down. I leapt back, the whine of feedback harsh in my ears.

The fallen man looked up at me, dazed. I didn't have time to pick up my mic. I jumped left, sharing Ryan's instead and glaring at the crowd.

No one watched us any longer.

All eyes were turned to stare at something behind the stage. I glanced over my shoulder without missing a note and squinted to the bar's open front door.

The gruff doorman I'd nodded at when I arrived held up a swaying woman. Blood stained the side of her face.

I stopped playing, dropping my pick and reaching for Ryan. "Dude, stop," I shouted.

He shot an irritated glance at me. He slapped the strings on his bass, letting them hang in the air. "I said, are you gonna be—"

A scream, long and sudden, overlapped the quickly dying song.

I whipped off my guitar, propping it against Ryan's amp. My thudding heart suddenly beat with a new, faster tempo.

"The hell?" Dennis stood. He clutched both sticks in one hand and stared at the bloodied woman.

Shouts sounded. Footsteps slapped along the sticky floor. Somewhere a glass dropped, shattering. Ryan finally turned toward the front door. At the sight of the injured woman, he tore off his bass and let it topple to the stage. Its thud was heightened by the amp. Feedback screeched through my skull. I slapped my palms over my ears. I quickly unplugged my amp and Ryan's, cutting out the protests of the discarded instruments, then ran over to the PA system and yanked its cord from the socket.

Above the din of the confused crowd came an inhuman, high-pitched wail full of hate and rage. My stomach flipped, as if I was falling from a great height. The haunting sound continued. It blended with loud screams of horror. What the hell was happening outside?

Dennis had vanished into the panicked crowd. By the door, Ryan crouched low next to the horrified bouncer and he was shouting something, using a fistful of small napkins to wipe the blood from the shaken woman's cheek.

I shoved aside my sweat-dampened hair, its ends tickling the back of my neck. I had no idea what to do.

Dennis appeared at my side, his face slick. "We should get out back."

I nodded, but paused, my eyes on his brother.

Ryan was shoved over by three people barreling through the open door. All three were screaming and also covered in bright red blood. He tried to stand only to be jostled aside again.

Pandemonium swelled. A fleeing girl passed, her elbow driving hard into my stomach. I gasped deeply and stumbled. Dennis took my hand and pulled me to the side wall, away from the stage and the screaming, undulating crowd.

I couldn't breathe. I couldn't see straight. All I heard was screaming and the continuous, horrific wailing. A balding man fell into me. I collided into Dennis and we both crashed against the wall.

"They're killing people!" The man's spittle flew through the air.

Ryan appeared, pushing the man aside and pulling me and Dennis to our feet. His face was white with horror. Together, we stared back at the bar's front door.

A cloud of thick, roiling smoke poured in through the open door. It smothered anyone that got too close. Skeletal faces swarmed in its midst. Horrific, wraithlike creatures clawed their way into the bar along the walls and floor, their sharpened fingers gouging wood and tile. Their jaws hung loose and impossibly low. They had no eyes.

The heart-stopping, piercing howls I'd heard flowed from the open mouths of the creatures. The things flew forward in the air, swirls of mist where their legs should be. They reached out for the panicked people trying desperately to escape. Claws sliced through flesh with ease. Blood coated the floor, the stage, and now our instruments.

We turned and ran. I hit the back door first. It swung wide and I burst into the cool Nevada night air. Dennis collided into a confused group of people who'd gone out for a smoke during our set.

"What the hell's going on?" one cried out.

"Somebody call the cops," he panted. One of the female smokers stared at him, blue eyes lined with heavy black mascara. She pulled her phone out and quickly swiped its screen; a short, rail-thin man with buck teeth stood next to her, already holding his own phone to one ear. I slapped a hand over my pockets before realizing I'd left my cell next to Ryan's on his amp.

I turned and eyed the nearby tree line. "We need to hide."

"No, we need to run." Ryan pelted toward our van nestled between two other vehicles in the back lot.

A car to his right lurched forward with a kick of stone and dirt. The red-lipped bartender trembled behind the wheel. When she saw Ryan, she swerved to the right, her mouth open in muted shock.

"Shit!" Ryan jumped back and fell hard on his side.

Dennis rushed to his brother. I grabbed one of the smokers who'd been about to peek through the back door. I slammed it shut and pulled her away. "Don't. Something's in there. Killing people."

Ryan wiped gravel from his palms and let Dennis help him to his feet. They stared at the retreating car. The driver almost made it to the street before the monsters caught her.

Three wraith creatures flew around the bar from the front and swarmed the retreating car. They flooded in through the open back window. The woman's horrified screams filled the air.

She swerved again in a desperate attempt to get away from the monsters. Seconds later, the front of her car slammed against a tree trunk and stopped. Ryan started toward the wreck.

"What are you doing?" Dennis chased after his brother. "You'll draw those things right to us!"

"I can't...we can't..." Ryan stopped, digging his fingers into his short, dark hair. "I have to help her."

Two of the smokers bolted, running into the nearby woods without a backward glance.

I started to follow. "Ryan, we have to get out of here!"

The bartender in the car let out an agonized scream that joined the wails of the wraiths. They pulled her out from the vehicle, their sharp claws embedded deep in her flesh. She begged for help with a voice scratched and raw. Her cries quickly morphed to howls of pain. Ryan started toward her again, but Dennis held him back.

"We can't help her." I came back and helped restrain him. "Ryan, those things will come for us next."

Despite our efforts to look away, it was impossible not to see the young woman suspended in the air above her car, among the undulating cloud of monsters. She thrashed and writhed in agony. The bright red paint on her lips matched the color of flesh that was torn from her face and arms as the horrific creatures flayed her alive.

Her screeches petered out. The wraiths dropped her body and flew around in a wide arc.

Dennis dry heaved, clamping a hand tight over his mouth. He turned toward our van, shoving a hand in his pocket for the keys.

"No." I grabbed his wrist. "They're coming."

Together we ran, the three of us joining the passing ranks of horrified, screaming people. We fled toward the woods. Before we could reach the trees, the cloud of monsters poured out of the back door. Illuminated by the bright, bare bulbs along the side of the building, the slaughter began again.

"Spread out! Get down!" Ryan gestured wildly at scattering people, but raw panic had taken over common sense. More screams filled the night. Instead of hiding, everyone continued to stampede into the woods. They barreled past trees and into low hanging branches. People fell on roots jutting high or into thick bushes, crushing newly grown spring leaves.

Wraiths swooped low over the widening crowd. Handfuls swooped low, taking out two or three people each time with grotesque sounds of tearing flesh.

"Annie," Dennis breathed. He pushed me away from the massacre in the trees. "Toward the front."

We swerved and changed direction. Ryan, just behind us, dug into his pocket, pulling the key to his Jeep free.

"Bet you're glad I was late now," he rasped.

"I'll never complain about it again." My head pounded in time with my running feet. The three of us came to a quick halt against the side of the bar. I pressed close to the wall, praying the monsters didn't come back this way. Clouds drifted over the moon and stars but the bare bulbs along the wide building still shone bright.

"We can barely see those things in the dark." Dennis looked wildly around. The screams and cries of people were beginning to lessen, but the creatures' wailing still rang.

"Fuck, fuck, fuck." Ryan inhaled sharply, counted to three, then quickly stuck his head around the corner to eye the front lot. "Okay. I can see the Jeep."

"Are there any...any of those things?" Dennis shoved a shaking hand through his damp hair, then wiped it on his black *Pontypool* shirt.

"No. I mean, I don't think so. Some of the lights out front broke. I can't tell."

I let my eyes shut for a moment. "We have to try."

Dennis, nodding, squeezed my hand.

"On three, then." Ryan lowered into a slight crouch, his body tensing. "One."

Mimicking him, Dennis let go of me and wiped both palms on his thighs.

"Two."

The wails grew louder; I nearly bolted forward in fear.

"Three!"

We sprinted around to the front, quiet and quick, aiming for Ryan's huge silver Jeep Wrangler. He pressed a button on his key fob and headlights flashed once, twice.

Certain a clawed creature would snatch me up, I stumbled and nearly fell. Ryan reached the Jeep first, glancing over one shoulder while his fingers slipped over the driver's door handle.

I braved my fear and jogged around to the passenger side, watching the dark shadows for any movement. Dennis clambered into the back seat while his brother leapt in behind the wheel.

A loud screech echoed. I dove into the vehicle and slammed the door. A handful of wraiths pulled up short just outside of my window, skeletal faces mere inches from mine.

Ryan's hands shook. He struggled to get the key into the ignition. His tremors were made worse when the few remaining lights along the front of the bar were suddenly blotted out.

"Fucking go!" Dennis shouted from the back seat.

The Jeep rocked on its wheels. I shoved away from the window where hanging skeletal maws gaped and snapped.

Ryan twisted the key and the engine surged to life and the Jeep's headlights illuminated the front of the bar. Creatures poured out from the open door and surrounded us. They scratched at the windows, their claws clacking and scraping the glass.

"Oh, God, we're gonna die." Dennis whimpered, securing his seatbelt while shying away from his own window. "We're gonna die, we're gonna die."

"No, we're fuckin' not." Ryan slammed the Jeep into gear. It shot forward through the cloud of wraiths. Their haunting wails switched to screams of rage. Their claws dug into the metal and plastic of the Jeep, but the creatures quickly slid off and fell away.

More light flared to life. Through the churning mist of the creatures, I could just make out other survivors driving over the curb. The cloud of wraiths broke apart, leaving us with a smaller, yet still deadly group.

I stared through the windshield, gripping my seatbelt tight. "They can't get in through the cracks."

"But they're smoke." Dennis reached forward and gripped the back of Ryan's seat, knuckles white.

"They're still solid enough to claw shit up."

"What the hell are they? Where did they come from?"

"Don't know." Ryan cranked the wheel hard to the left and we bounced out of the gravel parking lot. "Don't really care right now."

Two of the fleeing cars collided with each other in a loud slam. The wraiths still chasing us shifted and dissipated to go after the slower prey.

Dennis stared at me. "You have blood on your face."

My stomach surged. I reached up, just noticing the taut, sticky feel of my cheek.

Ryan risked a glance over. "Are you hurt?"

He sped away from the bar and the people we were unable to help. The horrors quickly disappeared in the Jeep's side mirror.

My fingers found a tender spot on my right temple. "I must have hit my head. Probably when that asshole pushed us."

"Annie," Dennis said. "That asshole's dead now."

"Oh, God. I'm sorry. I didn't mean to…" My words trailed off. Tears burned in my eyes and my stomach churned with nausea.

Dennis sat up straight and dug into his front pocket. My heart leapt at the sight of his cell phone. He started swiping at its screen with both thumbs.

"Call Mom." Ryan glanced into the rearview mirror. "Tell her what happened, that we're okay."

I stared at the phone, wishing I could snatch it away and call my own family. Dennis pressed it to his ear. For a few agonizingly slow seconds, the only sound was the road beneath our tires.

His eager expression quickly faltered. "Mom. Please call me back. Now."

He dropped his hand and tapped on the screen again.

"Let me try my parents." I twisted in the seat, reaching out.

"Uh, guys?" Dennis looked up from the screen. "It wasn't the only attack."

"What?" Ryan demanded, eyes still on the road.

"Yeah...the news says there's a lot of people dead. Other places in Nevada have been wiped out."

"Dennis." I held out my hand again. "Please."

He handed over, watching as I dialed the number I'd had memorized for almost a decade. I hit the green dial button and brought the phone to my ear.

It rang three times. "Come on...come on..."

"Annie?"

I gasped deep. "Dad? Oh, God, Dad. Are you and Mom okay?"

"Oh, Annie. We've been calling you. Alarms have been going off all over. The news says it's terrorists, that they attacked Nevada. Where are you? Are you hurt?"

"I'm fine." I wiped my nose on the sleeve of my shirt. "No. I mean, I'm not fine."

"Oh, honey. Are you somewhere safe?"

"We're driving. I'm with Ryan and Dennis. We were playing a show when it happened. We ran, but...a lot of people just died." My voice cracked.

"Annie, honey." My mother's voice filled my ear and I lost it. Tears fell freely. I wiped angrily at the drying blood on the side of my face.

"I just put you on speakerphone," my dad said. "What happened out there? Where are you exactly? Can you get somewhere safe to wait this out?"

"Just a sec, Dad." I fumbled with the cell, turning its speakerphone on as well.

"Annie?" My mom's words held clear fear. "Answer us. Can you get somewhere safe?"

Ryan spoke up. "Yeah, we can, Mrs. Ross. There's a place we can go."

"Where?" my father demanded.

"My mother worked at a lab in the forest just south of Mt. Irish. She showed me where it was just in case there was some kind of pandemic or global attack. She told me to take Dennis there in any type of emergency. Apparently, there's an underground bunker."

I shot a surprised look into the back seat. Dennis shook his head and shrugged.

"Good," my dad said, his voice echoing through the Jeep. "Annie, you stick with them. Protect each other and get to that place right away."

"What? No. I'm coming home."

"Don't you dare," my father said harshly. "The news says these attacks are spreading fast. It isn't safe to travel right now, especially across the country. Get underground with the Breckners and stay there until everything settles. Okay?"

I gritted my teeth and squeezed my eyes shut.

"It's too dangerous to try to get here, Annie," my mother cut in softly. "We're too far. Just get somewhere safe. Send us a—"

The phone cut out. Frantic, I hit redial, but the phone didn't ring; all I heard was dead air.

"What? What happened?" Dennis demanded. "Did the battery die?"

My grip tightened on the cell. "There's no signal."

"What? How? I always have coverage out here."

"I don't know, Dennis," I growled.

"Could the towers be down?"

Ryan took a sharp curve too fast but kept us on the dark road. "Already? Not possible."

"Try again, Annie." Dennis gestured at the phone.

I hit the green button again and pressed the cell to my ear, but all I heard was a slight hiss. "Nothing."

"It can't be a coincidence." Dennis leaned into another turn, straining against his seatbelt, then sat forward. "It's the things out there. Has to be."

"How?"

"I don't know! Maybe they have a way of interfering with signals or something."

"Holy shit!" Ryan swerved, just missing a car barreling out of the woods. We skidded along the road, with me cursing loudly the entire way. The Jeep halted near a shallow ravine between a low, metal guardrail and a flat ditch. Wherever the rogue car was heading, it was already gone.

I forced myself to release the death grip I had on the dash. "Ryan. Go."

He ignored me and flung the door wide. He climbed out of the Jeep, stalking away down the middle of the road.

"What in the hell is he doing?" Dennis unbuckled his seatbelt and hopped out of the vehicle to chase after his brother.

I tried the phone again with the same results. Pulling up the browser app only gave me a connection error. I glanced up through the windshield at Ryan. He took a few more long strides toward the woods, stopped, and screamed a long string of profanity at the nearby trees.

Dennis looked away. He dropped his head into one hand. His brother fell silent and slowly sat in the gravel along the side of the road.

I clenched my jaw and refrained from throwing the dead cell. I kept hearing the screams of people we left behind, kept smelling blood. My stomach wobbled yet again; I couldn't quell the rising lurch in my belly.

Flinging the door open, I got out of my seatbelt just before vomiting. Bile burned the back of my throat.

Suddenly at my side, Ryan pulled my short hair free of my face. "It's okay."

I wiped my mouth with the back of one fist. "No, it's not."

"We can't stop, guys." Dennis crouched a few feet away, averting his eyes. "Those things are still out there."

Ryan helped me to my numbed feet. "We just…left those people."

I squeezed his hand in gratitude. "I hate that we had to. It kills me. But what could we have done? We have no way of defending ourselves."

He nodded, casting a miserable glance back the way we'd come. "All right. Let's move."

Back in the Wrangler, we drove in total silence.

Hours passed without any sign of the monsters – or of any other survivors. I stared out the dusty windows as we made our way through Nevada, trying to scan the dark night sky.

Crashed cars littered highways. Ryan's grip tightened on the wheel harder with each passing corpse or empty vehicle in the street. The moon continued its ever-moving journey along the sky, but nothing other than us moved even as time stretched on. It was as if everything and everyone had been killed, leaving us in a dark, abandoned, bloodied world.

Sometime around four in the morning, I lost the ability to remain alert. Ryan still sat at the wheel, his back straight and eyes wide.

"We need to sleep." I shifted in the front seat, legs aching to be stretched.

"We are not pulling over. We're nearly there."

A snore sounded from the back seat where Dennis sat slumped to one side.

"They could attack again at any second and we wouldn't be able to see it coming."

"All the more reason to get there. We need cover. Shelter."

"There are plenty of houses around. I'm sure we could find one to stay in for the night. Or even other survivors."

He frowned at me. "No. We'll be safe at the lab, underground, with my mom."

I stared through the windshield, unable to prevent a wide yawn. My eyes drooped while I tried to scan the sky again. The terror of the night hadn't left me, but exhaustion now threatened to knock me out.

A large herd of deer shot across the road in a blur. Ryan cursed loudly and stomped on the brake.

Dennis woke with a yelp. We all were thrown against our belts. Ryan swerved, just avoiding three fawns that bolted back into the forest. The wheels of the Jeep bounced over the shoulder, up and along the steep side of the road. We tilted at a dangerous angle and twisted to the right, then my world tipped. We slammed against the ground, sliding in a screech of metal and stone.

I cried out as my head smacked against the window.

The moment the Jeep slid to a stop, Ryan was climbing up and out of the driver's seat. Perched on the vehicle's side, he heaved open the back door. "Dennis? Dennis!"

His brother hung in the seatbelt, gravity causing his hair and one arm to hang to the side. "Hey, whaddya know? I'm alive."

"Are you all right?"

Dennis let out a low grunt and tried to undo his belt. "I don't think anything's broken."

Ryan peered past him. Two shallow scrapes had cut open on the left shoulder of his scrubs and bled freely. "Annie?"

I took stock of my injuries. The side of my head hurt worse than it had before, but miraculously, the side window hadn't shattered; it had been the only thing that protected me from the dirt and gravel.

Giving Ryan a weak thumbs up, I unbuckled myself with trembling fingers, moving slowly. I made sure I could move every part of me before climbing up the way Ryan had.

The cool night air touched my sweat-slicked face. I pulled myself out of the ruined Jeep. Dennis appeared from the back door. He sat on the side with his legs dangling in the open door, letting his brother check his pupils and feel along the back of his skull. He only endured it a few seconds before he pushed away from his brother and dropped to the ground.

Ryan reached out and pulled my eyelids wide, sticking his face close to mine. "Dizziness? Nausea?"

"Clawing hunger that will make you turn on us and eat our brains?" Dennis called from the ground.

Ryan's lips pursed and he sat back.

"I'm fine. Just a headache." I slowly rose, crouching low, and picked my way down the Wrangler.

We stood in silence for a moment. Trembling. Listening.

Ryan cursed, softer this time. He climbed back up his ruined vehicle and dropped inside. I shared a look with Dennis. We could hear Ryan rummaging through shattered safety glass.

Moments later, he jumped back up and hauled himself out, his brother's phone and its long charger in one hand. "Screen's cracked to hell, but it still works."

"Can you tell how much further?" Dennis wiped his bleeding knuckles with the hem of his shirt.

Ryan stared down the dark road. He chewed his lower lip, thinking, then started to walk. "It was just up the damn road. We were so close."

We hurried forward in silence, ever aware of the darkness pressing in on all sides.

"Here." Ryan pointed toward a dark gap in the trees. "We turn off the road, go in here. It should be straight this way."

"Seriously?" I stared into the dark, very claustrophobic woods. "There's no path."

"We're going in along the side. It's the only way I know."

"Are you sure this is right?"

"Not everyone has your crappy sense of direction." He winced, shooting me an apologetic look. "Sorry, didn't mean to snap. I just remember the gash on that weird, old, gnarled tree."

Dennis and I followed his gaze. Ryan started into the woods before we could say anything.

I scrambled after him. "I thought you said this was a top-secret government lab. Not very top-secret if you bring your kids."

"She often chose family over the rules. And over work, unlike Dad. She took me here a couple of times. Well, not all the way, just made sure I knew how to get to this hidden path."

"She never told me any of this." Dennis tripped over a root and fell against a narrow tree.

"I'm older than you. I'm in charge."

"I'm twenty-eight," Dennis grumbled. He stepped over a tangle of roots laying across the side of the road. "I can take care of my damn self. And I say we should use the flashlight app, because I can't see shit."

Ryan shushed him. "We're not using the phone, not yet. We have to conserve its battery."

"What's the point if we can't make calls? With the Internet down, the damn thing's just a portable mirror."

Ryan sighed. "Just keep walking. We're almost there."

We advanced, weary and terrified, staying close to each other. Soon, we came to a tall electric fence that stretched into the dark. Ryan led us to the right. Dennis and I followed, keeping our distance.

After endless moments picking through the trees, we reached an abandoned guard shack.

"Don't touch anything." Ryan peeked into the shack's door and poked a button near the open frame. The gate swung open in silence.

We kept walking.

After about fifteen minutes of nothing but crunching gravel underfoot, I saw a glint of light through the trees. I stopped short.

"What's that?" I pointed but the light had vanished.

"Where?"

"I thought I saw something move."

Ryan squinted. "Slow. We approach slow."

He took the lead with careful steps. The trees began to thin and revealed a large clearing full of destruction.

We'd come across a building with its roof torn off. One wall lay in large concrete chunks that dug deep into the ground. Crushed trees spread away from the building beneath more concrete pieces. Moonlight glinted off of countless broken shards of glass, and metal pipes rose into the still night.

"Is this the place?" I asked in a whisper.

Ryan held an arm in front of us. "I think so."

"Do you think it's safe to get closer?"

Without responding, he stepped out of the trees, glancing all around. Dennis and I hurried to catch up.

Something unexpected to the left caught my eye. "Guys."

A few long mounds of dirt rose from the ground. They didn't seem very old.

Dennis stopped short. "Are those graves?"

"I don't know." Ryan looked at the dark sky, defeat etched in his eyes. "We can't focus on that. We need cover."

"Well, there's kind of no roof, so we really need to find this underground bunker." I stepped over concrete and rubble, carefully making my way into the destroyed building.

Dennis didn't respond. He stood rooted to the ground, staring at the mounds of dirt. His chest heaved up and down in a slow, careful motion. "Do you think Mom..."

"No," Ryan snapped. "She isn't."

"How do you know?"

"She's not dead." Ryan glared at him a moment then spun, stalking after me into the remains of the building.

Ryan and I picked our way through a long room full of dirt, glass, and what looked a lot like dried blood. Big tables spattered with old streaks of mud had been shoved to one side.

We found ourselves in a short hall. My shoe sent a long screwdriver clattering, startling us.

Ryan opened a door to reveal a large empty supply closet. He shut it softly. "No one's here, dead or alive."

A breeze picked up. It tickled my face and brought with it a sense of dread.

Dennis cried out somewhere.

I whirled. Ryan bolted past me and through the open back door.

"Over here!" his brother shouted.

We sprinted around the corner of the building. I followed close behind, narrowly shifting to the side to avoid an axe with its head buried in the dry ground.

Dennis stood a few paces away, near the tree line. His feet were planted next to a flat metal door. He leaned over and pulled on it, muscles straining. It opened to one side. "Guys, it's the bunker."

I stopped at the flat door, staring down into blackness. Grey concrete steps disappeared below.

"If it wasn't locked, maybe someone else is already down there." Ryan glanced back at the ruined building a few yards away. The wind picked up even more, echoing through the trees.

I couldn't see anything past a short set of concrete stairs. "What, they're just hanging out in the dark?'

Dennis hopped inside, using his phone for light. He stood on the top step and crouched. Ryan let out a low curse.

"Dude," I said. "We have no idea if it's safe."

Dennis glanced back up. "It's gotta be safer than out here."

I hesitated, then lowered next to him, shooting a sheepish glance up at Ryan. "He's right."

The three of us slowly made our way down into the bunker. Ryan slid his hand along a wall behind us. Dennis swung his phone back and forth, trying to see into a dark, narrow hall that stretched away from the entrance.

Sudden light flared all around.

"There's power," Ryan whispered, his hand near a switch.

Wind whistled over the opening above us. I went back up the stairs and peeked up at the dark sky dotted with winking stars. Branches swayed, their leaves rustling. I grabbed the long inner handle of the door and pulled.

The loud thud was followed by a sort of slurping suction. After a soft hiss, the door settled an inch lower above my head.

Ryan reached up and touched the underside of the thick metal door. "Did it just seal itself?"

I shoved my shoulder into the door, grunting. After the same sounds, it raised and opened a crack. I stepped back down the steps and watched the process again. "I think so."

"It's why Mom said to come here in an emergency." Dennis pocketed his phone and turned to stare down the now lit corridor. "I bet it's airtight. And if there's a generator, people could live down here if there was nuclear war. We should lock it."

I looked up at a large, complicated mechanism near the handle. Reaching out, I pushed up on a large lever, jumping at the loud clunking noises within the door.

"So those wraith things out there can't get in, then?" Ryan maneuvered around his brother, staring down the hall.

I stepped away from the bunker's entrance, still casting a look up toward the locked doors. "What if other people out there need to get in?"

The brothers exchanged a look.

"If even one of those creatures got in here, we'd be dead." Ryan sighed. "I want to help, I do, but I think we have to wait it out together down here. At least for now."

I nodded and stared up at the low ceiling just inches above our heads. "I don't think I could live down here."

"We should take a look around." Ryan was clearly eager to explore the sanctuary we'd discovered. He took a few steps forward. "There could be equipment. Food."

Dennis wrapped one arm around my shoulders. "You feel up for a gander?"

Despite everything, I snorted. "A gander, huh?'

"Mmhmm. A gander. A looksie. A peek around."

Even Ryan chuckled. "That's not even a thing."

I cast one more glance at the sealed entrance. "So, we look around and then what?"

He shrugged. "We wait for help to come."

THREE YEARS LATER

Two

Annie
2020

The impossible door loomed tall. Its flat, metal surface was covered in dents and multiple scratches from our countless attempts to get it open over the past three years. It mocked us from its place at the end of the back hall, still standing strong despite everything we'd done to try to get it open.

"God, I hate this door." I zipped my hoodie, trying to block out the constant underground chill that always lurked just beneath the heat we kept at seventy.

"Okay." Ryan pushed back his shaggy brown hair. He crossed his arms, staring at the computerized keypad to the right of the door. "The highlight of our long, boring days. What number are we on?"

Dennis squinted at the spiral notebook in one hand. Light wrinkles lined his eyes. With skin pallid from long years we'd spent underground, he looked a decade older than he was. "Uh. Six."

Ryan rubbed his face. "I don't have time for this, man."

"Try forty-two."

"Dammit. Give me the next code to try."

"Just try it. What's the worst that could happen?"

Ryan threw a hand in the air. "You know damn well it would waste yet another attempt at getting this thing open. If we had unlimited chances, I'd let you put in whatever the hell you want, but we don't. Now give me the next one to try and stop messing around."

I made a grab for the notebook, pulling it out of Dennis's hands. "I agree. I want to get this over with so we can make food."

Ryan's careful handwriting littered the page along with crossed out numbers, calculations, and scribbles. Near the bottom right corner was a long list of combinations we had yet to try.

"4380," Dennis said, peering over my shoulder.

His brother nodded, reaching toward the flat keypad.

"But I still think we need to try something new."

I lowered the notebook. "Why? Going in order like this takes forever, yes, but this way we're bound to not miss it."

Dennis snorted. "We haven't even gotten halfway there in three…*three*…years. Do you understand how much longer this is going to take?" He stared between Ryan and me, but we just stared back in silence.

He let out a long breath. "Okay, it's a four-digit code, which comes out to ten thousand different combinations."

"We've talked about this already, Dennis." I rubbed my neck again.

"I know. Like, the day we got here."

"No," Ryan stated. "The day we got here we were too tired. We explored the bunker, stuffed our faces, and passed out for hours."

"Fine. But if you figure in the remaining five thousand, six hundred, twenty-some days it would take to finish all of the possible combinations, we're going to go insane before we succeed. I just don't have it in me to come up with any more weird, new games to keep our minds busy, and I've already counted all the pock marks on the ceiling in my bedroom *and* the dining area. Twice."

I pushed past Ryan with a sigh and quickly tapped '4-3-8-0' into the keypad. I poked the small, rectangular button beneath and we all held our breath in silence, watching the light above the door flash yellow three times before turning a solid red.

Small block lettering appeared inside the wide rectangular submit button: *Four attempts remaining.*

I resisted the urge to punch the door and quickly typed in '4-3-8-1', submitting the new code with more force than I'd intended.

Yellow flashed three times, then red reigned.

Three attempts remaining.

"I'm just saying," Dennis piped up. "If our Mom was in charge at the lab, I guarantee she came up with something more meaningful to lock this thing."

4-3-8-2.

Submit.

Yellow, yellow, yellow, red.

Two attempts remaining.

I gripped the notebook tight, grinding my teeth. "Yeah, well, we tried everything we could think of. What other combinations exist that might have been meaningful to your family? Unless you've thought of something else the four of you used, like important dates you forgot, or passcodes, or…"

A thought tried to poke its way through my mind.

Ryan paced back and forth in the narrow hall, not looking at either of us. "We go in sequential order, as we've always done."

Dennis threw up his hands. "Great! We'll just be here another five years. So sorry I want to get creative and find out what the hell is so important on the other side of this door."

I turned away from the keypad with narrowed eyes, trying to think. "Guys…"

"Getting creative will waste attempts." Ryan rubbed his pale, drawn face, fingers scratching over his dark, two-day old stubble.

Dennis strode past me, approaching the keypad and glaring down at its glowing digital screen. "God, you're stubborn as hell."

"Don't touch it, man."

"Just let me open up the console. I told you, I can probably figure out a way to bypass the code if you just let me try."

Ryan laughed, incredulous. "Do you want to get locked out of this thing permanently?"

I pinched the bridge of my nose. "Guys, shut up, I think I just figured it out."

The bunker's lights flickered and went out, dipping us in solid darkness.

"Uh. Guys?" Dennis's voice moved a bit closer.

Fear spiking, I dropped the notebook. Thoughts of wraiths flooding inside sent my heart into a thudding mess. I forced myself to remain calm and lifted my hand, fingers brushing against someone's shoulder. "What the hell happened?"

"Shh." Ryan said. "Listen."

The only thing I could hear was my ragged breathing. I shuffled forward, lightly trailing my fingers along one wall and keeping the other hand in front of me. The bottom of my socks snagged on the bunker's concrete floor. "I don't hear a thing."

"That's the issue. I think the gennie's out. Dennis, did you remember to add more propane this morning?"

"Yes, Mom."

"All right." Ryan's voice was suddenly right next to me, his hand bumping my arm. "Grab hold of each other. Single file into the kitchen."

Not wanting to go first, I chewed my lip. "What if something's in there? Ryan, what if…"

"I'll get in front," he said in a firm voice. "Here, Annie, grab my shoulders and Dennis, you hold onto hers."

We slowly inched forward. I squinted into the stubborn darkness, horrified that something could reach out and tear my throat open at any moment.

Nothing attacked. We made it out of the back hallway and into the kitchen by touch alone. I felt along a short counter, fingers bumping into drawer handles. "Wait."

The first turned out to be the silverware drawer, but in the second, my fumbling brought out a lighter. I flicked it, relieved at the sudden dance of flame before my eyes.

"Oh, thank you." Ryan turned, glancing around the kitchen in the meager light.

I hurried after Dennis, accidentally bumping my hip into the protruding handle of the electric stove. Unable to shake the sensation of someone watching me, I quickly turned to check back the way we'd come, but the hallway remained empty. I carefully turned back, my flickering light illuminating Dennis's path.

"There's a flashlight by the generator." Ryan slipped the butcher knife free of its block. He jerked his chin, indicating I should go next, that he'd bring up the rear. We all stepped into the hall, checking corners carefully while I attempted to keep my hands steady. He started toward a door straight ahead, Dennis close behind, but I didn't move.

"I'm not bringing an open flame near propane," I said.

The brothers exchanged sheepish glances.

"What about the flashlights in the medical room?" Dennis asked in a hushed voice.

I nodded. Putting my back to the supply room door, I turned left, trying to ignore the suffocating darkness. I led the brothers away, stopping as I entered the main hall. Turning right, I hurried toward the bunker's entrance. My meager light flickered over the wall between the left and right hallways, lighting up our abundance of tally marks carved into the concrete.

"I feel like I'm in CSI." Dennis's voice cut into the silence, startling me.

Ryan shushed him, frowning. "Seriously?"

"What?" Dennis shot back. "No one's here. The door's still locked." He pointed above us.

Some of the tension dissipated from my neck and shoulders at the sight of our manual locks firmly in place. Dennis climbed the four stairs and pushed against the door as an added measure. It didn't budge.

"It's still locked tight," he said. "Nothing's come through there, not since our last supply run."

Ryan straightened, glancing back the way we'd come. "Come on. We need those lights."

He took the lead. I followed, cupping a hand around the little flame that had begun to shrink and sputter.

Reaching the first door on our right, Ryan pulled it open slowly and slipped inside. The motion nearly extinguished my little flame entirely. I grunted, shying away and nearly colliding with Dennis.

"I never realized just how ominous it is down here until now." He let out a fearful chuckle, turning haunted brown eyes to focus on me.

A beam of bright white light shot out of the medical room, followed by Ryan. Grateful, I extinguished the lighter and slipped it into my front pocket.

I eagerly accepted a second long, round flashlight. I shone it into our medical room, the beam playing over closed cabinets, organized bottles of medications we'd looted over the years, and underneath the flat metal exam table.

Ryan handed a third flashlight to Dennis, who turned it on, and trailed its beam into corners and down the dark hallway. Nothing moved. Everything was the same as before.

We turned our lights down the hallway, away from the bunker's entrance and toward our living quarters. We split up, quickly checking the bathroom and the four bedrooms. Nothing was out of the ordinary.

"Okay." Dennis rolled his shoulders. "Let's go check on the gennie."

We jogged back down the hall, passing into the silent dining area and stopping before the supply room door. Ryan pulled it open and shone his light inside, but it wasn't until all three of our beams pointed inward that I noticed the smoke puffing out of the generator's side. The distinct smell of burning plastic wafted over. Groaning, I pressed a hand over my mouth. Dennis pulled the front of his t-shirt over his nose and stepped into the supply room. "Ah, shit."

Standing nearly four feet tall and stretching nearly seven feet along the wall, the thing was a beast. It took up a third of the supply room and had been chugging away every day for six hours at a time for the three years we'd been trapped underground.

Ryan tugged at the generator's side hatch, coughing and wrinkling his nose. The panel popped free, releasing a blue-tinged plume of trapped smoke. Angling my light down, I peeked into the machine's innards, waving a hand back and forth to clear the air. "Can you fix it?"

"Dammit, Annie, I'm a nurse, not a mechanic." With a rare smile, Ryan rubbed the back of his neck and sighed.

"I think it's the control panel." Dennis stepped forward.

I again felt as if something was watching me. Raising my light, I swept my flashlight up, checking above our heads for hidden mist-like creatures but finding only the low concrete ceiling.

I dropped my hand, letting my beam trail across long rows of shelves on the left; the stacks of canned food seemed smaller in the dark. The room had been packed full of food when we'd first arrived. Now, endless stretches of empty shelves pricked worry in my mind. The brothers had just gone on a food run and already it seemed what we had left wouldn't sustain us for long.

"There's a fried wire." Dennis said, pulling my focus back to the generator. He grabbed a wrench from a nearby shelf of tools. "The plastic coating, that's what's smoking. I gotta get these wires off the battery."

"How do we fix it?" I asked, nerves heightening.

"Ultimately, we just need new wires. New connectors, too."

"Where do we get that from?"

"Amazon."

Ryan stared at the silent, still generator. "Any hardware store, I'd expect."

"Great. We have to go outside." Dennis twisted the wrench and pulled a wire free. "Again."

"Not you this time." His brother raised an eyebrow in my direction.

My heart skipped. "Me? Why me?"

Dennis grinned. "The ol' sledgehammer and I have a date with that door."

"Not after you nearly decapitated yourself last time we tried to force it open." Ryan scowled, shaking his head.

"I was joking."

Ryan started back the way we'd come, leaving the silent generator behind. "Dennis, you're the only one who has any remote idea how the gennie works, and how to fix it."

I chased after him. "Barely. None of us had even seen a generator until living down here. And your medical training is insanely important, so don't tell me who stays and goes."

"If something happens to Dennis, the gennie doesn't get fixed. Without the gennie, we'd have no power and our air would stop recycling. We'd be forced outside. He stays down here, and Annie, you come with me."

"Because I'm the expendable one."

Dennis closed the supply room door and jogged after us. "Look, the control panel's just a limited computer. Easy fix. If you guys get the wire and connectors, I'll be able to get it up and running again no problem."

"What, he's just supposed to sit down here in the dark by himself?" I demanded.

"We don't risk all of our lives at once." Ryan led us past the tallied wall and toward the bunker's entrance. "Same as always."

I scoffed. "Look, if we die out there, Dennis is stuck here by himself, losing air, and no way of knowing he's screwed. He should come with, just in case."

"He stays."

"Guys."' Dennis gave us both a soft shove toward the bunker entrance. "I'll be fine here. I'll open a can of SPAM and pass the time playing solitaire in my head."

Ryan gripped his brother's hand and pulled him into a tight hug. "If we're not back by sundown, something got us. In that case, you have my full permission to crack that panel open. But until then, don't touch that door."

Dennis smiled, but the flashlights easily picked up worry and fear in his eyes. "Don't get killed."

Three

Annie
2020

I stared open-mouthed at the desolation of our world. Bare, brittle tree branches stretched upward, all devoid of their leaves. A soft wind flitted past us, tossing dead grass into lazy ripples. Small rocks crunched beneath our shoes. Dry clumps of dirt exploded in muted puffs under my feet. The sky, cloudless, had a dusty feel to it; blue tinged with a slight orange. Above, the brilliant orb of the sun shone cheerily as if life hadn't been an endless, monotonous, want to blow-your-brains-out-with-boredom string of days bleeding into one another for three years. At least the sun felt glorious on my underexposed skin.

Ryan and I were the only living things around. The familiar rustling of animals rummaging through foliage was gone. No bugs flitted about. No birds sang. My throat tightened at the memory of sitting on the porch with my dad, listening to the mourning doves. He loved mimicking their coos. When he'd tried to get me to join, I'd just laugh, but now, I'd give anything to hear his voice join their calls again.

I turned in a slow circle. "Ryan, I knew it was dead out here, but…this is awful."

"Yeah," he said, his voice soft.

I scanned the sky for any dark, roiling clouds, pulling the shoulder straps of my backpack tighter. "I refuse to believe everyone is dead. How is that possible?"

Ryan didn't answer. He started to jog away, shooting me a glance over a shoulder. I followed after another quick glance at the sky.

We passed the destroyed remains of his mother's old lab and the now nearly flat mounds of dirt we'd seen upon first arriving. None of us had the stomach to unearth them.

"Those wraith things," he said, shaggy hair bouncing. "It's like they suck the life out of everything. For all we know, the whole world looks like this."

Keeping pace with him, I ducked beneath a branch as we entered the surrounding dead woods. "Impossible."

"Everything's dead, and nobody's come knocking on our door, not even once. If it had been three months, I might agree with you, but three years?"

"No." I pulled my hair, longer than it had ever been, into a ponytail, securing it with a rubber band from my wrist. "The world is way too big."

"Unless there were more wraiths released than we think. We have no idea." Ryan hopped over a large stone in his path. "We also have no way of finding out. We're totally isolated here, trapped. And we can't stay in the bunker much longer."

I shifted right, sidestepping around a bush that threatened to snag my ankles. "What do you mean? You and Dennis scored a ton of food on the last run. Yeah, it's getting low, but you said there was more."

He stopped so suddenly I nearly collided against his back. His face was flushed and sweat trickled down his temples. I glanced back the way we'd come but the ruined building was already out of sight. When he didn't speak right away, I grunted and bent at the waist, dusting off the bottoms of my pants.

Ryan pulled a dented metal water bottle from his own pack. He shook it once and took a small sip.

"Look," he said finally, holding up the metal bottle. "This works because the bunker has pipes hooked up to some sort of underground source we can't locate. Maybe that's what's behind the sealed door, I don't know. If we hadn't found the bunker, we'd have died a long time ago."

"Okay…"

Ryan gestured to the dead world around us. "On the few runs we've done, Dennis and I haven't found any fresh water nearby. We have no transportation, no clear direction to walk if we need to."

'Walk? Why would we walk?"

"Bottled water went bad long ago," he continued, his words picking up speed and his eyes widening. "And we'd only be able to carry so much."

"Ryan, stop. We have the bunker water."

"We do." He crossed his arms. "But as you know, canned fruit, anything citrus, has already gone bad."

I frowned. "Citrus? So?"

He nodded, dropping his gaze. "Canned veggies and meats last longer, yes, but only about three years."

I swallowed, stomach flipping. "Three years…"

"Annie, we're going to run out of edible food, and soon, we're gonna start getting sick. And listen. You hear that?" He held a hand to one ear. "No birds. No animals. The traps Dennis and I set last year remain untouched. Which means no fresh meat.

"Now, I've been careful about the vitamins, making sure we take some every few weeks. But if we don't find some fresh food in the next few months, we're all gonna start to get really sick."

"Why didn't you say something sooner?"

"I only realized it when I was taking inventory two days ago." He rubbed his eyes. "I needed to mull over our options before raising any alarm. Take stock of meds that have by now lost a lot of potency. I thought about looting a garden store, but even that won't work with the wraiths sucking the life out of everything."

I looked around at the dead flora. "We could still try."

"Yeah." He gave me a half smile. "We're gonna hit up the nearby town. It has an Ace Hardware. If we can get there, we can get some seeds and a couple grow lights. We might have life-sucking monsters flying around, but we at least still have electricity."

I grimaced. "Had. We need to replace that fried wire, first."

Ryan started to jog again. I followed him through the heat of the late morning, stopping only to catch our breath and take more sips from our water bottles.

The sky remained clear of clouds as well as wraiths that wanted to butcher us. The silence of the dead world around, however, was somehow more menacing than the threat of a possible attack. We kept a steady pace, hurrying forward, slightly hunched, with eyes always on the sky.

We crested a tall, sloping ridge. I stopped between two long dead plants. I bent, putting both hands on my knees, and peered down on a street surrounded by a smattering of buildings.

"Finally," I gasped. "That wasn't nearby at all."

Ryan wiped the back of one hand over his forehead and nodded. "A little under two hours' walk from us, give or take. There's still plenty to go through, but two people can only carry so much; Dennis and I just kept looting what was closest."

The steep decline forced my speed into a dangerous pace. Pumping my arms, I ran, enjoying the freedom of the open, empty world. My skin prickled. I risked another quick scan of the sky but saw nothing as I passed into the town. Empty buildings flew by until I slowed to a quick stride.

I breathed deeply, turning to watch Ryan approach, mouth turned downward. "Don't do that again, Annie. We need to stick together."

"Where's this hardware store?" I said, keeping my voice low. I glanced around at vacant windows and doorframes.

"Down the main street to the right. But…just don't look around too much."

Unsure if I was more uneasy from his words or his tone, I picked up my pace before I could fully catch my breath. I'd opened my mouth to ask for clarification when I saw the first dead body – at least, what was left of it. Crumpled along the sidewalk in front of a barber shop's shattered front windows, the corpse was barely recognizable. At some point it was clear the torso had burst or liquified, spilling what was inside along the concrete. All that remained of the innards was a flat, mushy lump and dark stain under the half-mummified, half-skeletal body.

"What the fuck?" I stumbled backwards, my upper lip curling. "Is that normal?"

Ryan glanced at the body with haunted eyes. "No. Not really. By now bodies should be fully decomposed, especially in the Nevada heat. It's still decomposing, just really slowly. No animals are around to pick at it. I'd think rain would have washed most of it away, but who knows how often storms have come through since we've been underground. I honestly don't know. I don't have enough facts."

We hurried down the street, making sure to glance around every corner and into every window. Nothing other than us moved.

Ryan let out a soft whoop when the hardware store came into view. Running up, we peered through the front windows for any sign of life but found none.

He jerked a thumb over his shoulder. "Come on. We're not splitting up."

The inside of the store reeked of something rotten. I'd barely made it three steps inside before I had to step over two other half-decomposed corpses. I kept my eyes averted to avoid burning too much detail of flesh and bone into my memory.

Wide tunnels of sunlight filtered through the dust-caked windows, illuminating our fresh footprints that overlapped much older, faded ones.

"Are these all from you and Dennis?" I whispered.

"Not sure. I think so. We never encountered anyone else on our runs."

"I remember. It's just…how can there not be more people that survived?"

Ryan was quiet a moment as we advanced further into the still and deserted store.

"Maybe there are," he said finally. "I don't know."

We quietly walked down deserted aisles. I held my pack open while Ryan collected packets of seeds, light bulbs, and grow lamps. At the last minute he hefted a long crowbar in one hand and added it to his own backpack.

"This is creepy." I glanced behind me. "Like being in a store after hours, but way, way worse. I keep expecting one of the corpses to get up and come at us."

"Definitely still not used to it," Ryan grunted. After scanning through a selection of wiring, he chose the size Dennis had described. We spent another five minutes looking for the connectors.

I stared around at all the abandoned items collecting dust. "Couldn't we use like, a lot of this stuff?"

"Sure." He handed my pack over. The muscles in my arms strained at the new weight. "But there's always only two of us, and a lot can get heavy. Besides, we gotta get back before it starts getting dark. No offense, but you're slower than Dennis."

I scoffed, shouldering the bulky backpack and pushing past him. Eager to leave the disgusting, dusty store, I shouldered the door open, stepping back into the heat and squinting at the sky. "There's plenty of daylight left."

He grinned at me. "I give you ten minutes before you want to switch packs."

"Challenge accepted."

After forty minutes of picking our way over the rough, dusty terrain, I grudgingly switched packs with Ryan. The pace I had initially found freeing was now grueling with the added weight. My lungs burned constantly, and I sweated more in two hours than I had in my entire life. My socks and tank were soaked through.

With the high sun beating down on us, our trip back was slower, peppered with additional water breaks.

"We're nearly back," Ryan panted, nodding at a tree line up ahead. "Just through there a bit."

"A bit." I let out a sarcastic laugh. "A bit, he says."

"What do you think's behind the impossible door?" Ryan asked suddenly. "I know we've all speculated, but really, what do you think it is?"

Grateful for a distraction from my burning lungs, I slowed. "I'm still leaning towards the water source. Maybe a well or something? The water's coming from somewhere."

He shook his head, shaggy brown hair plastered to his forehead and temples. "If it was something people might need, why make it so difficult to get to? It can't be anything someone would need to survive."

"Yeah, I guess so."

"But it's gotta be something huge." He shot me a rare smile. "Something that can help us. It has to be."

We hopped over a wide, low bush and entered the dead woods. "Yeah, but…what if it's not? What if it's, like, something dangerous? Why else lock it up?"

"That was the first thing you said when we found the door." He licked his dry lips and sped up slightly. "I trust your judgment, Annie. Always have. That damn door makes me uneasy."

We hurried through the trees in silence, lost in our own thoughts. I wiped my hands on my pants and made a face; I was impossibly caked with dust that seemed to find its way into every crease of my skin. I lunged over a dry, fallen log, wishing more than anything I could just lie down and sleep.

Ryan's backpack slapped against the small of his back. When we finally made it to the clearing, he suddenly stopped short. I collided against his back. I spun toward him but bit back sharp words when I saw his horrified eyes.

Ryan sprinted forward with a harsh cry, his sneakers slapping along the dry ground. My eyes locked on the bunker door where the dirt was gouged with a handful of long, deep claw marks.

Four

Annie
2020

I ran toward the bunker at full speed, unable to stop my mind from picturing Dennis torn to shreds. I leapt over rocks and dead brush. Ryan ran in front of me, his breath tearing in and out. We reached the damaged ground at the same time, both skidding to a stop in a great burst of dust.

Ryan yanked a metal chain from around his neck. He tried to get a grip on the small key, but his fingers were trembling too much. Hacking on a lungful of dust, I fell to my knees beside him.

"The door," I panted. "It's sealed. Maybe he's all right."

The panic on his face didn't lessen. He shoved a large key into the built-in outer lock.

Unable to curb my own anxiety, I pounded both my fists against the metal twice, then froze. The hair on the back of my neck rose. Someone was watching us.

Maybe what attacked the doors was still near.

I whirled. A small cluster of wraiths broke free of the tree line at the opposite end of the ruined building nearby. They shot forward, jaws dropping to hang impossibly wide.

"Ryan!" I screamed just as the inhuman wails of the creatures began.

Horror shone in his eyes. He scrambled backward across the door, boots thudding along its surface, and fell onto his back in the dirt.

I scrambled after him, dirt building up beneath my nails. With nowhere to run and the eyeless sockets of the wraiths focused on us, there was little we could do but cower. Biting back my defeat, I kicked both feet on the bunker door, praying Dennis was near.

Ryan and I clung to each other, laden packs weighing us down, and watched with horror as our death approached. The howling creatures stretched out clawed hands as they drew near, swarming past the demolished building. I let out a wordless scream and pulled Ryan closer.

With a clatter and a thud, the bunker door flew open.

"Holy shit!" Dennis spun on the stairs, jaw dropping at the sight of the wraiths.

I wasted no time. Pushing Ryan forward as hard as I could, we fell down the concrete steps. I choked on the dust we kicked up. I landed painfully on my backpack; something sharp gouged into my torso.

Ryan landed on his side with a grunt of pain. Dennis yanked the door shut, sealing us in total darkness. He scrambled for his flashlight and bashed the locks into place.

He leaped back down the steps, chest heaving. "Holy fuck, you guys, are you okay?"

"We are *never* going out there again!" I roared.

Ryan let out a strained moan. He still lay on the floor, face and arms caked with dirt, eyes squeezed shut. He gritted his teeth and reached down to his left ankle.

Dennis dropped down in an instant, flashlight clattering to the ground, hands hovering over his brother but not quite touching him. "What's wrong? What can I do? Ryan, tell me what to do."

"It just twisted under me." Ryan inhaled sharply. "I don't think anything's broken."

I turned to stare at the sealed door in the dark above me. "The wraiths were trying to get in."

"What?" Dennis's eyes widened.

"They tore up the ground around the bunker doors. Didn't you hear them?"

He paled, shaking his head and following my gaze. "I didn't hear a thing other than you pounding. I've been in the hall this whole time."

Ryan sat up, wincing. He tenderly massaged his left ankle, slowly turning it in circles. "Help me get my boot off."

His brother nodded and set to work on its laces.

I shook my head, still staring at the door above us. "If they were nearby, they could have come for Ryan and me at any moment. Why didn't they?"

"Thank God they didn't." Dennis helped his brother pull off his left boot.

"Annie's right." Ryan flexed his toes then rubbed his ankle again. "We were out there for hours. They could have killed us anytime."

"So they set a trap?" Dennis looked between us. "Bullshit."

Horror dawning in my mind, I nodded. "They knew you were down here. They must have wanted all of us, not just us two."

Ryan coughed and attempted to stand, putting some of his weight on Dennis's shoulder. "Or maybe they wanted to get inside."

I stepped forward, grabbing the pack Ryan had shrugged off. "We need to find out what the hell's behind that damned door."

We staggered toward the medical room, flashlight beams waving, but Ryan shook his head and leaned against the wall. He took a few tentative steps, limping but otherwise bearing his own weight.

"You need to lie down, man." Dennis paced behind his slowly advancing brother. "I'll get the gennie fixed, okay? Did you get the new wire?"

Ryan ignored him. "We need to check on the impossible door."

"We will," I said. "But right now, you need to put your leg up. We almost got slaughtered. Let Dennis and me take over. Please, Ryan, slow down."

He only hobbled faster. I cast a wary glance around the dark kitchen. Giving up, Dennis and I followed him into the back hallway and stopped at the tall metal door.

"The red light is out." Ryan leaned against a bare concrete wall.

"Because there's no power." Dennis aimed his flashlight at the control panel. "I could open it up now. Try to bypass the code."

Ryan shifted his weight to his right leg a bit more, jaw clenching. "Then why won't this damned door open? We've been punching codes in for years, and you're telling me that even losing power doesn't do the trick?"

I sighed and rubbed the tender spots in my lower back.

"Whatever's in there could help us," Ryan continued, his voice laced with frustration. "Maybe it's a weapon. One that could kill the wraiths. Those things, they know where we are. They can't get to us while we're in here; that much is clear, but they just laid a trap. I refuse to believe they're just gonna move on after nearly getting us in their claws."

I patted my dusty clothing, trying not to inhale the dirt that puffed free. "If there was a weapon in there against those things, then the people who'd been here would have known about them well before the end."

He nodded. "All the more reason to get inside, see what they were hiding."

Dennis lowered his flashlight. "Well, then I'll tear open the panel and try to get in that way."

"No," Ryan snapped. "We can't risk triggering any type of permanent shut down. Go fix the generator."

His brother grabbed the pack from my aching arms and jogged off into the dark without a word, his flashlight beam bouncing.

I switched my own light on. "Come on, Ryan. Get off that ankle."

"I'm staying right here until the power is on and we try the door again."

"God, you're stubborn. At least sit while he works."

Ryan scoffed but let me take some of his weight. With one of his arms around my shoulders, we slowly made our way back down the hall, away from the impossible door, and into the wide dining area. Dennis's mutterings echoed from the open supply room door across from us.

"Annie." Ryan lowered into a plastic chair and sighed in relief. "What was your idea earlier?"

"What idea?"

"For the codes. Before the power went out you said you might have figured it out."

I flushed, glad for the pressing darkness of the bunker. "It kind of all seems stupid now."

He made a circle with his injured ankle, sucking in a sharp breath through his teeth. "We have two more attempts at the door for today."

Chewing my lip, I crossed my arms. "I just thought that, well, you're a family of four. If your mom was using a code with personal meaning, she might, I don't know, maybe use your names."

Ryan's face softened. "We tried that when we started, remember? We did my name alphanumerically, but it didn't work. And I'm the only one with four letters in my name."

"No." I dropped into the chair next to him, my body singing in relief. "I mean, I just thought that maybe she used the first letter of each of your names. Claire, Duncan, Ryan, Dennis. C, D, R, D. Whatever that would be on a phone keypad."

He blinked at me, slowly extending his left leg before him on the ground. "Huh."

I shrugged. "It's a stretch, I know. Seems stupid now."

"I don't think it's stupid. What's stupid is demanding to go in numerical order for years when there are still thousands of combinations left and dwindling supplies."

I tried to keep my face impassive. "You were trying to help. Trying to keep order. And doing it, albeit a little harshly."

"As you love to point out, we Breckners are a stubborn bunch."

"Don't I know it. I'll get you some ice for the ankle."

"Annie." Ryan's face softened in the light of my flashlight. "Thanks for coming with. You're a badass."

I smiled and rose. "Same. I hope we never have to do that again."

Sudden light blinded me. I threw up a hand, squinting.

"He did it." Ryan let out a tired whoop of victory. "The little shit actually fixed the gennie."

Smiling, I squinted down at him, trying to see. "Stay here a minute so I can see if everything's okay."

I jogged across the dining area and toward the supply room.

"How is he?" Dennis popped out of the door.

"He's fine," I said. "Everything good here?"

He regarded me seriously. "It wasn't easy. Almost lost an arm. Both, actually."

I landed a playful punch against his shoulder. Turning, I called out to his brother. "Ryan, hold tight, I'll get that ice."

Dennis followed me toward the kitchen. "I really don't know about you, but I'm starving."

"Same. Maybe you can whip us up a nice steak dinner."

He grunted. "Don't joke. I miss steak so much. You have no idea what I'd give for a medium rare cut with a side of potatoes and green beans."

"Just two days ago, you spent an hour complaining about the potatoes and green beans."

Dennis gave me a crooked grin. We peeked into the back hallway to check on the impossible door. Sure enough, the little keypad was glowing.

"It's like it's just staring at us. Watching. Taunting us." Dennis narrowed his eyes. "Yeah, that's it. I'm gonna get the sledgehammer."

I snorted. "You know, we picked up a crowbar."

"Ooh, my plan of attack unfolds."

"We have two codes left," came Ryan's voice. He hobbled toward us, favoring his left leg.

"Stubborn Breckners," I muttered.

Dennis eyed his brother. "He's the worst patient."

"Oh, come on." I stifled a yawn. "We'll try the new codes tomorrow when the attempts start over."

Dennis turned away from the keypad with a grin. "Actually, the power failure reset it. We now have five again."

"That solves it." Ryan waved a hand. "Let's do this now, Annie. I didn't hobble all this way for nothing."

I glared at the tall, menacing door. "I hate you," I grumbled.

"Me or the door?"

I chuckled. "Fine. What order?"

"What are we doing?" Dennis asked.

"Try Mom, Dad, me, shithead." Ryan rubbed one eye. "So…that would be, what?"

I slowly twisted the end of my ponytail, thinking. "Letters on old phones always started with number two. Remember? Number one was always for voicemail. So that would be 2-

3-7-3, which we would have already tried. Damn, that means the only ones left would have to start with the seven. With you, Ryan."

Lifting my hand, I slowly punched in 7-2-3-3 and tapped the submit button. The three of us stared up at the light above the door.

Yellow, yellow, yellow.

Red.

Four attempts remaining.

"Well, damnit." I stepped back.

"Try again," Ryan urged, shifting his weight.

"Wait." Dennis reached out and grabbed my wrist before I could enter another number. He looked over his shoulder at his brother. "What about that dog Mom had when she was little? What was its name?"

"Before I was born?" Ryan blinked, perplexed. "Hell, I don't know. Sadie?"

"She loved that dog. Hung the little inked paw print in her study at home. It's probably still there." His mouth twitched and he turned back to the keypad.

Ryan didn't seem to notice. "Yeah. Was it Shelby? Crap, I don't remember."

"Got it." Dennis snapped his fingers. "Sage. Right?"

His brother just shrugged.

Dennis hesitated, then tapped in '7-2-4-3' on the keypad. He glanced back at us, his index finger hovering over the glowing submit button.

"Worth a try," I urged.

Dennis poked the panel and we all looked up again.

Yellow, yellow, yellow.

Green.

Five

Annie
2020

A soft beep filled the short hallway, followed by a series of deep, heavy thuds. The green light above us faded and the impossible door swung open.

"Holy hell. We defeated it." Dennis turned his wide brown eyes on me. "Do we just go in?"

I took in a long breath. "We go in. Slowly."

Ryan pushed off the wall, brow furrowed. "Shouldn't we take some sort of weapon?"

"Why?" Dennis chewed a thumbnail, eyeing the darkness beyond. "Nothing lives inside. Otherwise they would have come out long ago. Right? And if it's booby trapped, well, a crowbar won't save us."

Ryan limped forward, putting himself in between us and the door. We watched, bodies tensed, as he pulled it open the rest of the way.

A small room shrouded in darkness awaited. I swallowed, trying to quiet my inner dialogue, which was on high alert. Everything was deathly quiet. Ryan flipped a nearby switch; shadows flitted away as harsh light filled a small room.

It reminded me of my favorite professor's study blended with some sort of home office. I stepped inside, toward a long, wooden desk that lay to our right, a single old chair pushed close. Two tall bookcases packed full stood beyond the desk, and a bank of low metal filing cabinets stretched floor to ceiling to our left along the opposite wall. Directly across from the now defeated door was a smaller, nondescript one.

"Books? Files?" Dennis slowly shuffled past me, trailing his fingers along the desk and leaving long lines in the heavy dust. "That can't be all."

Ryan opened the small door across from us, revealing a large closet. "And, uh…coats."

"Why would they have coats?" I stood on my toes, peering over his shoulder at different colored parkas hanging in a neat order. Beneath each was a pair of heavy boots. Thick gloves and hats poked from the tops.

"Sure." Dennis glanced inside too. "Why not? I'm sure global warming will turn Nevada into the Arctic soon."

"Prepared for anything, I guess." Ryan let the closet door fall shut.

"We should go through this stuff." I nodded at the filing cabinets, but my gaze kept traveling back to the bookshelves by the desk.

Ryan shouldered past, gripping the handle of the closest drawer. He pulled, but it remained in place. He moved to a few others, yanking each. All were locked.

Frowning, I tried the drawers of the desk, jiggling the handles up and down, but they, too, resisted. "Why lock something if it's already sealed behind that door?"

"Maybe someone does live in here after all?" The sound of Dennis's tense words brought a chill down my spine. I turned to see him staring at another, smaller metal door that had been hidden behind tall file cabinets. Before we could protest, he yanked it open and peered inside.

I bit back a scolding comment and instead asked, "What's inside?"

"It's some sort of control room."

Ryan hobbled forward. I trailed behind the pair, entering the next room and raising my eyebrows in shock.

Dennis wandered over to a long table stacked with three small monitors, a keyboard lit with red light before them. A large, strange control panel with dozens of knobs, switches, and a big red button sat to the left of the monitors. Dennis felt along the front of the screens, looking for the power buttons, but found nothing. Grabbing one of two nearby rolling chairs, he sat, tapping keys at random. The screens remained dark.

Leaving him to figure out the electronics, I followed a still wandering Ryan. We ignored yet another metal door to our right and instead stepped up to a long window set into the far wall, past the control panel.

I cupped my hands, peering through the thick glass. It felt strange, almost like plastic. My breath fogged its surface. The space beyond was dark and menacing.

"This is giving me a bad feeling." I stepped back from the glass. "What if what we find in here is dangerous? I mean, why else would it be so heavily secured?"

Ryan rubbed his jaw, still staring into whatever lay beyond the window. "But it wasn't, though. I mean, if you had the code, you could waltz right in. Clearly it wasn't a threat if the people here could go inside whenever they wanted."

I crossed my arms and took a step away from the window. "Unless the people here were dangerous."

"You're saying my mom…?"

I looked away. "No, of course not. But…what if what they were working on here…got out?"

"Got out?"

We stared at each other in silence a moment.

"My mother did not create those monsters." Ryan's voice was low, harsh. His cheeks began to redden.

"I'm not saying she did, or that anyone did, not on purpose. Just…what if what's down here made those things? We thought we were going to find more food or a water supply, not something out of a weird science station or whatever. Should we really be messing with any of this?"

He stared hard at the concrete floor beneath our feet. "I understand what you're saying, but there's absolutely no way my mother was involved in the world's end. I refuse to believe that."

"Got it!" Dennis called out, breaking the tension. Grateful, I jogged back to find Dennis crawling out from beneath the control panel table.

We stared at the monitors as they slowly faded into focus.

"Wait," Dennis muttered. "That's outside. This place has cameras. Inside, too, see? That's the entrance. Oh, what the hell, even in the bedrooms?"

"Can we move them around?" I bent over the control panel but couldn't discern what any switches or knobs operated.

Dennis dropped back into the chair, wheeling forward and squinting at the screens. Flat light illuminated his already pale face; black and white images reflected in his eyes.

He clacked around on the keyboard for a few seconds with no success. "I don't think so. Let me mess around with this panel."

"Hold on." Ryan nodded at the dark window. "We need to figure out what else is in here first. And we stick together."

"You never let me do anything." Dennis rolled the chair back a few feet.

We approached the next metal door, all glancing into the dark room through the windows again as we went. Nothing moved.

The handle was cold to the touch. I twisted it and pulled, trying to shake an annoying sense of déjà vu. I flipped on a light switch, and again, my confused gaze met a sight I had not expected.

A long, narrow room stretched away from us, the concrete walls painted a bright white. A short platform, like a stage, stood to our left. I glanced past the window at a narrow section of tall shelving units. Cords and wires hung in haphazard fashion from the middle shelf, but the rest were nearly bare.

"This is weird." Dennis squeezed past, squinting into the bright room.

"Yep. Quite." I approached the far shelves. The brothers trailed behind. Our sneakers squeaked a rhythm on a clear layer of epoxy covering the grey floor.

The bundle of wires was all one connected unit. Each stuck out of a long, rectangular metal box. Two green lights shone steady beneath a long but blank digital display. Numbered buttons stuck out along the bottom of the strange box.

"One through nine…" Dennis tapped his chin, then scoffed. "Great. Another combo."

Ryan leaned forward, hands on his knees, and peered at the box. "I think it's something else. Look, there's more buttons. See the comma and apostrophe?"

I nodded. "And one with a little circle."

Dennis reached out and pressed the key labeled '1.' The digit illuminated in bright red to the far right of the display.

"Dammit, Dennis." Ryan slapped his brother's hand away. "What the hell is wrong with you?"

"What? We need to figure out what it does, don't we?"

"Ryan's right." I gave Dennis an apologetic glance. "We need to figure out what the hell all of this is. Why it was locked away. Until then, we shouldn't touch anything else."

I peeked around the other side of the shelving unit, expecting another door. The bright, thick walls were bare; we'd arrived at the end of the bunker.

"We should go back and look through those books," I said softly. "And the files. There have to be some answers in that room."

Ryan nodded. "Agreed. We go back to the study and work together to figure out just what the hell all of this is."

Following him back the way we'd come, we retraced our steps back into the control room.

"Why are you always bossing us around, dude?" Dennis grumbled, not looking at his brother.

"Because if you were in any sort of charge, all you'd be doing is listening to Annie's iPod on repeat and trying to come up with new Dungeons and Dragons levels."

Dennis snorted. "Levels, huh?"

Realizing a classic Breckner fight was near, I picked up the pace, hurrying back into the study once more. "I'll start with the books. Ryan, sit at the desk and get off that ankle. Try to open the desk drawers. Dennis, you tackle the filing cabinets."

"What the hell is so wrong about finding new ways to pass the time?" Dennis demanded. "What are we supposed to do down here for the next ten years, sit in the dark? Stare at the walls? All we've done is eat, sleep, try to crack the code, and once in a while, risk our lives for supplies outside."

"Not true. We have game nights."

"If I have to play Life or Mouse Trap one more fucking time, I'm just going to let the damn wraiths eat me," Dennis growled.

"You always win," I said, hoping to lighten the mood.

"This is the first new thing that's happened in years," he continued, ignoring me, "and you still find a way to suck the excitement out of it."

I sighed and stopped before the closest bookshelf, hoping the argument would peter out. Squinting, I tilted my head to one side.

Nearly all of the books were hardcover, and either some shade of icy blue, dirty white, or black. The titles, too, were all similar: *Franklin, Found. Their Final Frozen Days. Her Majesty's Ships: Erebus and Terror.* I glanced one shelf up to find more. *Franklin, Crozier, and Fitzjames. The Fateful Franklin Expedition: What Went Wrong?*

The bookshelf on the right all held works relating to a historic event called the Franklin Expedition. The one on the left held non-fiction works about life in the mid-19th century and some research journals. There were even a few stacks of historical fiction novels jammed in near the bottom.

"You never ask us our opinions." Dennis wiggled a desk drawer hard, which rattled in its frame. "It's always tell, tell, tell, never ask."

"What's the Franklin Expedition?" I raised my voice above his.

Neither brother looked over at me.

Ryan slammed the side of his fist against a filing cabinet in frustration. He began tugging at random drawers in quick succession. "And what would you be doing different, hmm? Other than typing codes in out of order, on a whim, or pushing buttons on a machine before knowing what it does?"

I rubbed a temple, trying to focus on the books before me. Along the top of one of the bookshelves, nearly hidden in the dim light, I found small coils of paper. Placing a foot on the lowest shelf, I tested its weight, hopped up, and pulled one of the rolls down. I dropped back to the floor and smoothed my find along the desk.

Curved and dotted lines decorated what I identified as a map of the mass of islands above Canada. Some were scrawled on, with a red X here and there.

Another roll of paper opened to reveal a large drawing of a place labeled King William Island. Again, red markings littered the margins. This particular map, however, showed a string of handwritten coordinates and a green X along the island's southeast coast.

Replacing the maps, I pushed my tangled, red mass of hair from my face and stepped back, contemplating the shelves once more. I stood on my toes and tried to peer along the top of the other bookshelf, but it seemed bare.

A loud thud made me jump. I glared at Dennis, who'd kicked the desk drawer he'd been struggling to open. "Will you two calm the hell down?"

Ryan backed away from the filing cabinets, threw his hands in the air, and limped out of the room.

"Why does he always have to be such a stubborn ass?" Dennis plopped down into the worn desk chair, tilting his head back and staring at the ceiling.

I knelt by the drawer he'd been yanking on. It had loosened considerably but still wouldn't open. Standing, I grinned at Dennis and kicked the drawer as he'd done, aiming just beneath the lock. The entire desk trembled. I kicked it again, and again, enjoying the release of my pent-up frustration. After a fifth kick, the wood finally splintered.

"Hell yeah, Annie!" Dennis pulled on the drawer's handle. With a crack, it finally broke free of its lock. He reached inside and dropped a small bundle onto the desk surface. He stared at it with clear disappointment. "That's it?"

I reached out and touched the soft fur of some sort of animal skin. Picking up the bundle, I turned it over in my hands to find flaps on the other side. I pulled them back, revealing a small, black book.

"Whoa." I breathed.

Dennis leaned back in the chair. "Another book."

"Go try the cabinets again or something." I pulled the book free. No title was etched into its spine. The covers were a soft, black leather, dull and faded with age.

Dennis shoved himself out of the chair and obliged, attacking the drawers of the filing cabinets with loud rattles. I sat on the desk's hard surface and slowly opened the book about a third of the way in.

I stared at small, neat handwriting.

> *It came again last night. Men cried out all around, their shouts echoing throughout HMS Erebus's wooden confines. Boots thudded along the deck above me, rousing my consciousness from the pathetically little sleep I'd been trying to obtain.*
>
> *I did not want to run out into the darkness. I wanted to bury into my blankets, hide from the endless frigid dampness, and just drift back off to sleep. But I could not. As the only one left on Erebus with medical experience, I had a duty to perform. Only the men's potential peril and need caused me to rise from my bed.*
>
> *Scrambling in the darkness, my fingers found the sleeve of my peacoat. Shivering in the icy air that constantly permeated through the frozen ship at all hours, I slipped my coat over my clothes. Sliding the little door open, I quickly snatched up my slops and ran from my tiny room.*

"Here, use this." Ryan suddenly reappeared, limping back into the small study. He tossed the crowbar we'd looted at his brother, who tried to catch it but missed. In a loud clatter, the tool skidded along the concrete floor. I squinted at the brittle pages of the journal in my hands, wondering why it was here instead of a museum.

Hunching over the little book, trying to block the grating sounds of metal on metal as Dennis tried to pry open the filing cabinet drawers, I turned back to the very beginning of the journal. There, on the first page, was another piece to the puzzle: "The Private Diary of H.D.S.G. 1845 - "

"What are you doing?" Ryan appeared next to me.

I showed him the page. "Trying to understand why there's a bunch of books down here on something called The Franklin Expedition."

"Sounds familiar."

Dennis grunted, levering the large crowbar back and forth. "Wasn't that on Nat Geo a few years back?"

I flipped back to the entry I'd been reading. "No idea. I didn't have cable. And I was studying American history. This is British Navy stuff."

He paused a moment, seemingly noticing the stacks of books for the first time. "There was a special on it. They'd just found one of the boats back in 2016."

"Boats?" Ryan pulled *Franklin, Found* from the shelf and began to flip through it.

Dennis yanked on the crowbar again. He wiped sweat from his forehead with one shoulder. "Yeah. A couple ships got stuck in the ice above Canada and everybody died."

I stared down at the journal. "Holy shit."

"Most is still speculation," Dennis continued. "Even after finding the wrecks, no one really knows what happened to them."

"Hey." I waved a hand at the hardcover book in Ryan's hands. "Look in the back. Is there any mention of the initials H.D.S.G.? Or is there a crew list?"

His eyes moved back and forth but shook his head. "I need more info."

Turning back to the journal, I kept reading, but this time out loud.

"No sooner had I left the sleeping quarters than a blast of horrifically frigid air hit me. I shivered in the depths of my slops. Lacking my Welsh wig, my ears quickly began to go numb from the cold.

"The screams started up again. Men hurried past, jostling me to one side. I yanked large, shapeless mittens over thick, fingerless work gloves, trying to save my fingers from the freezing air. I'd lost track of how many digits I'd had to amputate from other men due to frostbite or gangrene over the course of our failed voyage.

"I could see Captain Fitzjames in the darkness. He called out to Lt. Le Vesconte and Mr. Bridgens, both of whom clutched swinging oil lanterns. I pressed back against the wall, trying to give them plenty of room in the narrow wooden corridor.

"More screams echoed down the stairs, loud and full of terror. Captain Fitzjames and Lt. Le Vesconte clambered up as quickly as they could, boots slamming, their breath shooting out in great plumes of mist. Mr. Bridgens, however, stayed back, shivering next to me. He watched the higher ranked men disappear to the top deck, then turned to me with wide eyes.

'What do we do?'" I forced myself to stop reading aloud, resisting a shudder that the ominous passage brought forth.

"What are slops?" Dennis leaned against the crowbar. "Or a, what was it? Welsh wig?"

His brother paged through the index again, quickly researching with one eyebrow raised. "I guess the slops are waterproof layers of wool and canvas. And the wig looks like a wool hat. Covers the head, ears, and neck."

I nodded up at *Franklin, Found.* "See if it talks about a surgeon."

"No." Ryan shut the book. "We need to get into these cabinets."

"But this was locked down here, too. It's just as important."

"Maybe it's just someone's way of passing the time." Dennis shot a look at his brother.

Ignoring him, Ryan sighed and turned to the book's index. His fingers slid down the page, then he flipped to the front of the book. "Four medical professionals on the voyage. One doctor on each ship, both with an assistant surgeon."

Unable to get the filing cabinets open, he dropped the crowbar on the desk and peered over Ryan's shoulder.

I glanced back down at the journal. "Which ones were aboard the ship called *Erebus*?"

"Dr. Stephen Stanley," Dennis said, squinting at the book in his brother's hands. "And his assistant surgeon was Henry Duncan Spens Goodsir. There you go, Annie: H.D.S.G. He went by Harry. Ooh, cool, he was Scottish. Bet his accent kicked ass."

"Goodsir," I muttered to myself. Holding the journal closer, I flipped to the back. A small black-and-white photo slipped free from blank pages. I stared at the boyish face of a young man in a Naval jacket sitting in a relaxed pose, staring off camera without smiling. He looked pensive, curious, almost as if he was distracted by his own thoughts.

Ryan kept browsing *Franklin, Found*, reading aloud. "The ships *Erebus* and *Terror* set sail in 1845 to find something called the Northwest Passage and completely disappeared. For the most part it looks like they probably starved to death, but there's also mention of cannibalism."

I ran my thumb over the man in the photo. "He looks so young."

He flipped a few pages. "It says Goodsir was twenty-six when they set sail."

Dennis went back to the filing cabinets, grabbing the crowbar. "Damn. That's two years younger than us, Annie."

I touched the open page of Harry Goodsir's journal, thinking about what horrors he'd gone through. About what final, terrible thing happened that ended his life, that prevented him from returning home.

"Only a few bodies have been recovered." Ryan skimmed the pages before him, trailing his fingertips along the sides. "Some relics. Most of what was found was scattered around a nearby island. King William Island. Hmm. It says back then they didn't even know it was an island. The entire area up there was almost all uncharted."

Recalling scrawled green coordinates, I looked up, my jaw slack. "The maps. Is it where they found this Goodsir? This journal?"

A slam scattered my gathering thoughts. Dennis whooped, grinning at us from next to a dented drawer slowly expanding on metal tracks. Ryan strode forward, dropping *Franklin, Found* on the dusty top of a cabinet and reaching inside the open drawer.

"There you go again, taking control," Dennis growled.

"Seriously? I have to ask your permission? Fine, you do this." Ryan threw a file on the desk. It landed open to show a boy with black hair and ice-blue eyes with 'Subject One' stamped in red above his head. A name, Jaxon, was written beneath the photo.

I launched off the desk, glaring between the brothers. "For fuck's sake, will you two grow up and stop fighting? You're both right. Now knock it the fuck off and start going through this shit."

Dennis grinned, his eyes bright. "You swear way more when you're angry."

I flipped him off. "Come on. We each bust open a drawer."

"Can't we eat something first? It's been go, go, go since you guys got back. Aren't you hungry?"

Remembering the rotting canned food, I paused. "No."

"I think we should talk about the food tonight." Ryan pulled a few more files from the drawer.

"Well, I'm starving. If it can wait, I'll whip us up some dinner."

"No, this can't wait." I ignored the sensation of Ryan's eyes boring into my back. "We're running out of edible food."

"What?" His face paled. "I was just with the supplies, fixing the gennie. We still have enough left to get us through the next three months, just as planned."

"That's not what she means." Ryan snapped the file shut and shot me a quick glare. "Canned food is gonna go bad soon, gonna rot. We need to figure out what to do in the next few weeks. I'd thought we could brainstorm the issue later, though. Didn't anticipate getting the impossible door open."

I shrugged. "Dennis needed to know."

"Wait, the two of you didn't tell me? Why?"

Shaking my head, I ran a hand through my hair. "He just told me while we were outside."

"And I just realized this a day ago." Ryan tossed the files on top of the cabinet. "We would have discussed it after we tried the combos earlier, but the gennie died, Annie and I were nearly killed, my leg got messed up, and now we're digging around back here. There hasn't been much time to talk about the fact that we're going to be out of food in a few months' time, okay?"

"There were *plenty* of times to tell me this important little fact." Dennis began to pace, glaring at his brother.

Ryan sighed and leaned against the cabinets. "Gee, thanks, Annie."

"Me?" I shouted, incredulous. "You could have told us right off the bat and didn't. I'm with Dennis on this one."

"Fine," Ryan snapped. "So sorry I'm such a fuck up." He snatched a handful of files from the drawer and tossed them on top of a cabinet. They fell, slipping open, and the entire group fluttered to his feet. Instead of picking them up, he dug in for more, throwing folders, papers, and photos to the floor in anger.

A file fell open, revealing a photo of a grinning boy with shaggy brown hair. Red scribbles lined the sides of the top page titled Subject One. I knelt and grabbed it just as another file titled *Scott Fischer* joined the growing pile on the floor. A handful of loose papers followed.

Ryan stopped suddenly, silently staring into the half-empty drawer.

I scowled at his back. "This could be really important. It could help us. What the hell are you thinking?"

Ryan didn't answer. He slowly turned to face me, holding three plastic cassette tapes in a hand. In the other was a small handheld video recorder.

Six

Harry
1848

Echoes and booms sounded mere feet above my head as the battle raged along the top deck. I struggled to force my fear aside. Each man aboard the *Erebus* and *Terror* had understood our voyage would be ruthless, even possibly deadly, but nothing could have prepared us for what we continuously faced on the Arctic waters.

Huddled next to a petrified Mr. Bridgens, I stared after the retreating forms of Captain Fitzjames and Lt. Le Vesconte taking the bouncing lights of their oil lamps up the narrow wooden steps.

"What do we do?" Mr. Bridgens turned his unsteady gaze on me.

We stood there, anatomist and steward, only able to listen as men battled the demonic creatures that attacked our ship. Heavy thuds shook the walls. I steadied myself against one of the nearby partitions, its wood scraping against my heavy mitten. My breath lingered in the air in thick clouds of mist. If I went up top without the rest of my layers, I would quickly lose my nose and ears to the cold.

The entire ship shuddered.

"What the hell was that?" Mr. Bridgens backed away from me, mouth agape. Tiny sparkles of frost decorated his dark eyelashes and brows.

"It's all right," I said softly. "We're safe down here."

A deafening *crack* shot through the air, startling us both. It was followed by splintering and what sounded like chewing. A sudden pressure of unseen force accosted my chest and left me gasping for breath.

Not again.

Each time I felt the pain, people died. I clutched at my chest and hunched forward.

"Goodsir? Are you unwell?" In his fear, Mr. Bridgens was beginning to hyperventilate. His eyes told me everything I needed to know, and how quickly I had to act to avoid his panic.

I forced away my own dread.

"We must get down to sick bay," I said with finality. "My operatory will soon be full."

"What do I do?"

"You can assist me."

Mr. Bridgens didn't protest. He followed me through the narrow wooden halls without a word. Upon entering *Erebus's* tight medical quarters, I tore off my bulky slops and fastened my medical apron. Not more than five minutes after I explained the proper dosages of wine of coca and laudanum to Mr. Bridgens, two bleeding patients were brought in. One was Able Seaman Morfin, who was unconscious and bleeding freely from the scalp. The other, a Marine, I could not identify, as his face had been torn apart.

Thick blood pooled on the wooden floor beneath my boots. I slipped twice attempting to help lay the faceless Marine on the operating table. The men who'd brought me the injured hurried off without a word, back into the fray.

Blinking down at the gurgling man, I frantically tried to recall anything that could possibly help him. I dodged past Mr. Bridgens and first opened a large bottle of laudanum, tipping a full dose past what remained of the Marine's lips.

"Assist Mr. Morfin." I doused a clean rag with chloroform and quickly draped it over the dying Marine's face, burying my face in the crook of one arm.

Mr. Bridgens stood at the other end of the room. He inspected the scrape on Mr. Morfin's scalp, dabbing at it with a damp cloth and steady fingers.

Turning my focus back to the now unconscious Marine, I began to deftly stitch what I could of the faceless man's flesh. Sweat tickled the back of my neck. I snipped a bit of useless, dangling skin away from one ruined, leaking eye. Dropping my surgical scissors into a nearby tray, I used my forceps to clamp loose flesh together and went to work with a suture.

"Mr. Bridgens, please wipe the blood away."

"Sir, I'm not sure it's worth it."

Heart thudding in my throat, I kept my voice firm. "Every life is worth it. I must try."

"He has no face, Dr. Goodsir. Barely a nose left. Neither eye remains."

I stared down at the Marine, whose breathing had turned harsh. What flesh I could see through the blood and gore was deathly pale. Convulsions began to ripple through his body, and the back of his head banged against the wooden table.

I lunged forward and grabbed his shoulders with my blood-coated hands, holding him down. "Retrieve the bit. Place it between his teeth."

"Goodsir." Captain James Fitzjames stumbled into view, half his face streaked red. His eyes were wide but focused. Curls of tousled brown hair protruded from beneath his officer's cap. "We must abandon *Erebus*."

"Understood, sir." To hide my shock, I deftly cut open the Marine's uniform, looking for any other injury we may have missed, but found none.

Captain Fitzjames grabbed my arm. His voice, tinged with a lisp, stayed firm. "A fire has started below. It's spreading too quickly. Do you hear? We must go now."

I stubbornly held onto the Marine's shoulders; the seizure was abating. I felt for a pulse, my bloodied fingers slipping along his wrist. "Mr. Bridgens get my kits. Take what you can in thirty seconds, then make your way to *Terror*."

Mr. Bridgens nodded once and spun, strands of long hair falling loose from his ponytail. He began packing, bottles clinking together dangerously.

I was no longer able to find a pulse in the bloodied Marine. I clenched my teeth together and closed my eyes in grim defeat. After a whispered prayer and apology, I draped a small stained cloth over his face.

A shallow bowl of chilled water sat nearby. I dipped my bloodied hands, then wiped them dry on my apron before assisting Mr. Bridgens stow the remaining medications into two wooden kits. I ordered him out with one. He ran from the operatory, guiding an unsteady Mr. Morfin.

Turning from a still agitated Captain Fitzjames, I quickly wrapped my bloodied surgical tools I had just used into my portable kit. "Are there others injured?"

I jammed the bundle into my knapsack. Hurrying past the captain, I snatched up my slops and made my way to my cabin.

"I have instructed the men to carry them to *Terror* where you and Dr. Peddie can operate."

"They may not make the journey, sir."

Captain Fitzjames held himself steady against the wooden doorframe. "We can only pray they do."

Buttoning my naval jacket with cold fingers, I slipped into what had been my room for the past few years. I collected my hat, an extra set of clothes, and my diary, pushing the meager belongings into my sack with the wrapped medical instruments. I hesitantly passed over the drawings I'd done of sea creatures I'd found near Greenland but left them for the chance to gather my microscope, shutting the big wooden box.

"Doctor," barked Captain Fitzjames.

"Aye, yes, I apologize. Please carry this, sir." I hefted the packed microscope into his arms. He gave me a harsh look but said nothing.

I pulled my bulky, shapeless slops on once again, stuffing my extremities into the dirty white coverings. As I turned to leave my little room for the last time, a glint of metal caught my eye. The case of silver spoons and forks my brother John had given me in Edinburgh sat open. I shouldered my knapsack, reaching out to slam the case shut, and lifted it into my arms.

The floor beneath our feet jolted suddenly, sending me flying face first into the wooden wall. I turned in time to save my nose from a severe break, but my left cheek connected with a low shelf. Pain sliced through my upper teeth and up to my eye. Sparks overrode my vision. I barely felt Captain Fitzjames pull me out of the cabin.

I stumbled through the ship in a daze. Clarity finally hit me again at the very top of the narrow stairs. I clung to the thick rope handles and shook free of Captain Fitzjames.

In control of myself once more, I rushed up the last few steps and into the deathly Arctic cold. Glacial air stole the breath from my lungs. I pulled my scarf tighter. Still dazed from the blow to my head, I tripped, but Captain Fitzjames was once again there to steady me. We hurried to the starboard side of *Erebus* where three men stood waiting, bundled and unidentifiable in the night.

"They got 'em, sir," one of them said. "All four creatures are dead."

Captain Fitzjames nodded, glancing down the ship.

In the light of the moon, it was clear *Erebus* had suffered. The jagged splinters of two of her masts stretched toward the night sky. I could not see where the tops had fallen. Barely discernible smoke billowed from a cavernous clawed hole in the stern, the deck beams exposed and jagged.

"The fire below is too large. She's lost, men." Captain Fitzjames, his face now wrapped and hidden as well, led us over the side. We leapt onto the surrounding snow drifts, an endless stretch that was once the Arctic sea. I could make out more fleeing men in the distance, all heading for *Terror*, frozen in the ice about half a mile ahead of *Erebus*.

My legs carried me forward despite the pulsating dizziness and throbbing ache in my jaw. The nagging pressure in my chest that only occurred when the ice demons were near had faded, but I struggled to look around regardless, gripping my belongings tight.

"The demons have been slain," Captain Fitzjames shouted at me over the crunching of our feet in the ice and snow. "But there could be others. Focus on getting to *Terror*."

Easier said than done, of course. I spent the entire trek half sprinting, half falling over pressure ridges protruding from the ice. With each step I was prepared to feel the sharp slice of a demon's claws snag the back of my slops.

After less than twenty minutes of haphazard stumbling through snow and ice, we quickly climbed aboard *Terror.* I was already exhausted. Walking along *Erebus's* sister ship was hazardous; *Terror* had been pushed up by the force of compounding ice to nearly a forty-five-degree angle. White canvas stretched starboard to port to keep fresh snow from the deck. Pulling back one of the flaps and standing aside, Captain Fitzjames watched us duck beneath. He cast a final glance out into the clear night before following.

I trailed behind the other men as we made our way below in single file, again gripping the ropes for balance. I pulled my scarf free, finally able to breathe, and wiped sweat from my face before any moisture could freeze.

The other men we'd arrived with quickly scattered, looking for any way to assist the men on board *Terror.*

"With me, Goodsir." Captain Fitzjames roughly lowered my microscope to the wooden floor and tossed his slops behind the stairwell. I followed suit but paused, glancing back at Mr. Bridgens and the still-dazed Mr. Morfin.

Mr. Bridgens shook his head. "I'll get him down below to Dr. Peddie. You go ahead, sir."

Grateful, I nodded, handing over my knapsack and case of silverware. He gestured at a passing man and together, they led Mr. Morfin from my sight.

Following Captain Fitzjames through the narrow corridors of *Terror* took some getting used to. The short metal nubs under my boot coverings gripped the tilted wooden floor, but the angle at which the ship sat made walking a struggle. Its ceilings were just as low as those on *Erebus;* I could not help but feel claustrophobic.

We held ourselves upright with a hand against the walls and made our way toward the stern. I ran my tongue along the teeth in my upper jaw. It still ached terribly and throbbed with each step I took, but I did not feel any cracks or breaks.

Captain Fitzjames and I arrived at a closed door and Mr. Jopson, a short, bearded man from London. He smiled and raised a knuckle to his forehead in a salute, then pulled the door wide.

With all its personal effects removed, the painted captain's cabin on *Terror* seemed nearly identical to the one that had belonged to *Erebus's* late Sir John Franklin. Captain Francis Crozier sat at his table, which was held horizontally with thick ropes descending from the ceiling. Four of its six legs no longer rested on the floor. Someone, no doubt Mr. Jopson, had removed all the fragile items from the shelves so they did not fall and shatter. Nothing could be done about the chairs, which had been carefully placed to best combat the harsh tilt of the ice locked ship.

The expedition's remaining lieutenants, their expressions grim, watched us enter. Captain Francis Crozier glanced up with one eyebrow raised.

"Tea, Jopson," he said, his Irish voice firm yet very tired. He stood from a table covered in scattered paper maps.

His steward nodded once and immediately disappeared into the narrow wooden hallway.

Captain Fitzjames eyed his superior, lowering himself into an open chair nearby. I remained standing near the door, unsure as to why I was brought along. Flexing my fists for warmth reminded me of the Marine's blood still drying on my hands. It had mixed with sweat during our flight from *Erebus*, and now my skin felt as if it were dipped in marmalade. Deep red splashes dotted along my white sleeves.

"I won't waste any time." Captain Crozier regarded us all with a steady, cool gaze. "The demons out there have been attacking us since Beechey Island. They've terrorized us for nearly three years, yet once we became ice locked, their attacks nearly stopped. It's been nearly six months free of even a sighting, yet now they destroy *Erebus* in a single night. Somethin's changed. Whatever the beasts may be, they now clearly want us gone.

"Too many of our men have been slaughtered. I have decided the time for action on our part is now. Despite killing the creatures, more always follow. They chased us on open water, and now they pick us off as we're trapped in the ice. We have never been able to predict their attacks. Tonight, we were shown that using our ships as cover will work no longer. They will come aboard to kill us. We have no choice but to abandon both ships and walk out in search of safety."

I was not the only one who stared at him with a slack jaw.

"Walk out?" Captain Fitzjames asked incredulously.

"We'll be sitting ducks, sir," Lt. Le Vesconte cut in. "Those things out there. They'll slaughter us."

Captain Crozier pursed his lips. "Perhaps so, but here we are stationary. Out there we have a chance of escape. If we are lucky enough to escape their claws, we will at least be walking toward possible rescue. Demons or no, it is a plan we've been anticipatin'. There hasn't been a thaw in two years. We have more of a chance to be rescued if we head south and look for open water than we do sitting here waiting to die."

"But *Terror* gives us shelter," Captain Fitzjames said, clenching his jaw, his eyes narrowed. "Protection we can't find on the ice. To leave and walk through the Arctic cold in hopes of being found…it's suicide. We cannot just abandon *Terror*, too, Francis."

"But we can leave a skeleton crew aboard," Captain Crozier stated, "in case leads open up and she can be ridden south. But someone needs to get an updated message to the cairns, especially at Victory Point, and I'll be damned if I sit here and let those things kill off my men any longer. We only have one ship now, James, and barely enough provisions to keep our men alive this year. Even then, the food in the tins is rotting."

Captain Crozier paused, eyeing us each with a piercing gaze. "The creatures attack at random. We kill them and more come. Another night like this could find *Terror* destroyed next. Our safety is not guaranteed in staying aboard; I believe it is more dangerous to stay."

Silence echoed throughout the cabin.

"James," he continued. "We will lead our men southeast to the Victory Point cairn with a message from us both. We will let people who find it know of Sir John's death and update them on our planned route so they can follow our trails."

Captain Fitzjames merely nodded, weary, eyes on the floor and gloved fingers flexing.

"As it is April now, we can hope we see a warmer summer than the last two. Days are still short, but I know if we're to wait for the perfect time, we will starve aboard this ship.

"I will lead half of the men south down the shore of King William Land in search of rescue parties and open water.

You take the other half to the north cairns then cut across the land toward Back River and Fort Resolution. It is there we will meet again.

"There are only two remainin' doctors between a hundred and five men, so one group will take Peddie, and Goodsir will go with the other."

Swallowing, I stepped forward. "Sir, I am just an anatomist, no doctor."

"You're more a doctor than any other man on these ships. Your skills and quick thinking have saved many these past three years. You earned the title long ago in my eyes."

My face warmed and I shut my mouth.

"King William Land is long, hundreds of miles across. We will need to leave much behind, but we can pack essential provisions and weapons into the sledge boats and haul them with us." Captain Crozier began to roll the maps on his table. "I told the men to break down mess hall tables so as to fashion runners. It will make haulin' supplies easier. It will be hard going, but with the boats, we can sail to quick safety should water open.

"Gentlemen, we will constantly battle treacherous terrain and deadly temperatures. But south there is more chance at fresh game. Possible rescue. Not here. Here there is only death."

He paused and straightened, considering his next words. "And if the demons find us on the ice, so be it. We will at least go out fightin'."

Seven

Annie
2020

I inched toward Ryan. We all stared at the little camera in his hands. Thin cords dangled from the machine, their ends bumping against his thigh.

Ryan didn't speak. He fumbled with the handful of clear plastic cases, pulling a small tape out at random. He pushed it inside and slapped the little door shut, then stabbed at the camera's buttons. "It won't turn on."

"The batteries are probably dead." I gently took the other tapes from him, peering at the block lettering on each spine. One had a green dot and was titled "Trial 73: Test 9." The other, however, was only labeled with three question marks and sported a black mark, more a smudge than a circular dot.

"We can plug it directly into the monitors by the panel." Dennis jogged out of the study, calling over his shoulder. "I'll grab some batteries. I saw some in the supply room."

Ryan and I followed a few moments later. He stared down at the camera, his expression calm, yet determined.

Dennis reappeared and nabbed the camera, pulling it out of his brother's hands with a grunt. He quickly replaced the batteries, plugged the cords into the side of a monitor, and dropped into one of the rolling chairs.

The top monitor flickered and changed the moment he pressed the play button. A thin man with a teased brown mullet and a white jacket faced the camera, regarding us from behind thick glasses. I squinted, leaning closer to the screen. The man held up a pad of paper with precisely written words: "Trial 73, Test 7: Chris Thompson. 8/7/1980."

Ryan slowly lowered into the other chair, not taking his eyes from the video. "It looks like the other room. The one with the platform in it. See? Look how the concrete walls are painted white."

"Maybe." I picked up the empty tape case he'd discarded on the table and turned it over to check its spine. It read, "Trial 73, Test 7." A carefully centered red dot was at one end. The sight of it made me uneasy. I tore my gaze away from the little plastic case and turned back to the monitor.

The man in the video stepped to the right, out of view. We could see through the large windows that separated the room we were currently in and the one with the platform. A young man with a boyish face and carefully styled red hair stood on the raised platform.

"Told you," Ryan said softly. "Same room."

The man on the platform, who I presumed to be Chris Thompson, wore strange flared jeans and a bright buttoned shirt. A round, flat, white sticker was plastered to his chest just below the neck. A cord dangled from the middle of it and disappeared into the pocket of his shirt.

He grinned, flashing crooked teeth, but his apprehension was obvious. Giving the camera a thumbs up, he licked his lips and nodded.

"Activating," came a woman's light voice. We could hear switches being flipped.

Chris Thompson took a deep breath. He balled both fists, face suddenly full of agony, and completely vanished in a large plume of grey ash.

I dropped the cassette case. It clattered to the concrete floor. "The fuck just happened?"

We watched the video, waiting for something else to happen. Long minutes stretched by in silence. I knelt down to retrieve the cassette case but the female voice off camera spoke again, stopping me.

"Return sequence initiated."

Watching the screen, I held my breath. Chris Thompson reappeared. At least, what was left of him.

The only thing of him I recognized was his bright shirt, now soaked in blood and speckled with gore. His body was bent at a horrible angle, and his skin was half-liquified. Dark red blood quickly pooled along the platform.

No one in the video reacted right away. Dennis made a disgusted sound low in his throat. Ryan leaned closer, squinting at the screen. I covered my mouth with one hand, unable to look away from the goo that had once been a man.

"What the living hell…?" Dennis whispered. He swallowed hard, eyes following the man with the mullet from before who slowly walked up to the dead man and reached for the electrode pad still stuck to melted flesh.

Before he could touch the pad, the screen flickered and changed to static snow.

"What the hell did they do to him?" Ryan whispered.

I snatched the cassette case from the floor and stared at the red dot again. "Put another tape in."

Ryan obliged, opening the case labeled with two question marks and a black smudge. He swapped the little tapes and hit play.

The camera was in the same place, but the horrific mushy corpse had vanished. The platform had been scrubbed clean. Mullet Man was again facing the camera, wearing a different set of clothes but the same white coat. He held up the notepad: "Trial 73, Test 8: Kevin Saunders. 6/17/1933."

"I don't get it." Ryan rubbed one eye. He stood and began to pace despite his limp. "What was that?"

I shushed him, sat in his chair, and scooted closer.

Mullet Man backed away from the camera again, slipping off to the side and revealing a handsome, older man. Built like some sort of football player, he, too, had one of the flat, round pads stuck to his skin just above a plain white t-shirt. He lifted his hand and flashed a peace sign at the camera.

"Activating," the mysterious woman's voice said.

"Not again," Dennis groaned. He clasped his hands and leaned forward, elbows on his thighs.

Just as before, this new man – Kevin Saunders – vanished after hunching forward in obvious pain. Ash fluttered down silently. Nothing else moved.

Minutes ticked by. I twisted a lock of hair in my fingers, staring hard at the screen, blinking as the still image burned a temporary block of white in my vision.

After what seemed like a longer wait, the woman's voice came again. "Return sequence initiated."

Ryan, Dennis, and I moved closer, unable to look away. Just as quickly as Saunders had disappeared, a figure popped back into existence – only it wasn't the man from before.

A boy of maybe ten or eleven now stood on the platform, dark hair and eyes wild. He whirled on the spot, squinting around the bright room as if he'd just come out of a dark theater. He clutched the white, corded pad in one hand. Noticing the camera through the window, he took a startled step backward, tripped, and landed hard on the platform.

Shouts sounded this time:

"Oh, what the hell?"

"Who is that?"

"Grab him. *Grab him!*"

The boy had leapt off the platform. He bolted to the left. A split second later, three men in identical white coats sprinted across the screen, reaching for him and yelling. There were sounds of a struggle, and then the men returned, dragging the now-screaming boy by the arms.

The video changed abruptly. Now, the camera was set up in a different room entirely, one that looked like one of the bunker's bedrooms, only sans the meager furnishings and mattress. The young boy sat at a round table identical to the ones in our dining area. His eyes were glazed but now held defiance. His wrists were in tightly clamped handcuffs.

"Oh, God." I held my face with both hands, wanting to look away but not daring to.

"Day four," said the same female voice from before. "Tell us your name."

The boy turned his exhausted gaze away, staring to the right of the camera. "I'm hungry."

"Tell us where Kevin Saunders is. Then we can bring you some food."

"The hell?" Ryan spat. He watched over my shoulder.

"I want to go home," the little boy said, his voice wavering.

"What did you do to him?"

"Nothing! I swear!"

"Where is he? Tell us and we will let you go home."

"I don't know!" The boy slammed his fists down, the cuffs rattling along the plastic table.

"We've been nice," said the woman, "but you are in a lot of trouble, and my patience is wearing thin. Where is he?"

"I wanna go home!" The boy started to cry.

"For fuck's sake, Jerry, I've had enough of this."

Mullet Man appeared in the frame. He gripped the boy's bicep in one hand, pulling him to his feet.

The woman, still unseen, sighed heavily. "I didn't want to do this, but we're going to take him to Lab 14."

"What for?" Jerry asked, pushing his glasses up with one finger. The boy tried to pull out of his grasp, but Jerry only tightened his grip and shoved him down.

"We need the mind reader."

Jerry shot a nervous glance down at the boy. "The Synths are even younger than this kid. I'm not comfortable transporting an Evo. You saw what he can do."

"We'll continue to sedate him," the woman's voice replied harshly. "And if he tries anything, we know what scares the little shit."

The boy shuddered. He began to weep.

With a quick burst of static, the video ended, leaving us in shocked, horrified silence. Dennis was staring blankly at the monitor. Ryan began to pace again while blinking rapidly.

"Rewind it." I lunged forward, desperate for answers for what I'd just seen. We watched the entire video again, then again. After the third time, I fell back into one of the rolling chairs, bracing my feet on the hard concrete floor.

"What the hell is an Evo?" Ryan demanded. "Or a Synth?"

Numb, I pulled the final tape free of its case and swapped it with the one of the boy. I ran a thumb over the green dot on its spine as it began to play.

Mullet Man was back again, holding up a pad that read: "Trial 73, Test 9: William Pardee. 1/25/1908." He stepped aside and we saw a third man, balding despite his younger features. He was clearly nervous. Sweat shone on his forehead and he kept swallowing, his Adam's apple bobbing up and down, up and down.

I frowned at the written date; they kept going backwards. "This can't be the day the test was done," I pointed out. "It isn't possible."

"I'm not going to keep watching these fucks murder and torture people," Ryan growled. But he didn't turn away.

We watched the same string of events occur. The woman off screen announced the activation. William hunched over in pain and disappeared in a puff of ash. We waited a few minutes until the woman again informed us of the return sequence.

This time, the test subject returned whole, unharmed. No one on camera reacted at first, but then the speaker crackled, the whoops and cheers were so loud. Mullet Man ran up to William Pardee and hugged him, then began to pat him down as if he were TSA.

"I don't get it." Dennis paused the video. His face was very pale.

Something about the dates kept gnawing at the back of my mind. Standing quickly enough to make my head lurch, I stormed out of the control room, heading for the study.

The three of us dug out more tapes, stacking them in small piles on top of the filing cabinets. In all, we found thirty-five, including the three Ryan had initially dug out. Each label began with "Trial 73" and was followed with a number. Thirty-one bore green dots, three had red dots. There was only one with a black dot, the one we'd already watched.

"The greens must be successes," I murmured.

Ryan shot me a look over his shoulder as he dug into a drawer. "We won't know that until we watch them all."

Using the crowbar, Dennis busted open more filing cabinet drawers to reveal rows of files. I reached inside the closest drawer as he continued down the row. Flipping through the top manila envelope, I found my gaze falling on words like 'experiments,' 'children,' 'war,' and 'mind-wipes.'

One file held photos and stats on a shaggy-haired grinning boy that bore no resemblance to the one in the video. Similar to the one of Jaxon from before, this was labeled "Subject One" and below the photo was the name Shawn Thorton. A bright red "MISSING" was stamped over his first photo. The pages that followed described in detail different experiments that had been performed on him. Acidic bile rose hot in the back of my throat. The more I saw, the less I wanted to know.

"There's so much." Ryan's low voice cut through the quiet room, overpowering the shuffling of paper. He held up a thick black binder he was studying. "Listen to this: 'Since the mid-nineteenth century, people have been born with abilities. By 2016, the population was riddled with evolved humans.' And then there's an entire section on what they call Evos."

"Abilities?" Dennis asked. "Like superpowers?"

"I don't know. There's a whole list in here of confirmed Evos, but some names are blacked out. Some pages are torn clean out. Further back, there's something else, a description of 'synthetic humans.' That has a much shorter list."

"Synths," I breathed.

Ryan snapped the binder shut, his face a mask of revulsion. "They used Evo DNA to breed people with stronger powers that they could use in war."

"Subject One." I tried to keep my fingers from shredding the papers. "How could anyone do that? And to children?"

"What the hell was Mom even doing here?" Dennis sifted through a handful of large folders stuffed full of papers. He pulled out a thick, poorly bound book and dropped the rest on the desk nearby. "What is this place?"

"Holy hell." Ryan straightened, tightening his grip on the binder. "Guys…on this Evo list…it's Harry Goodsir."

I blinked. "Okay, so that at least explains why the books are down here. And his journal."

Ryan chewed on the inside of his cheek. "Maybe they found his remains, dug him up and took his DNA to make one of these Synths?"

"Look for more files," I said. My mouth had gone dry. "See if there's any that say which DNA was used for what."

"Never go to a time in which you already exist," Dennis interrupted, reading from the front page of a thick, poorly bound book with a missing back cover. "Not under any circumstances. The laws of time mean it will eliminate the duplicate. If you go back to yesterday, for instance, you, not your yesterday self, will experience the catastrophic effect of temporal juxtaposition. The physical form sent back will be profoundly incompatible with life and the duplicate will be eliminated. See Trial 73, Test 8: for video documentation. Use of the—"

He stopped, lips moving wordlessly. His eyes suddenly widened.

"What is it?" I demanded.

Dennis flipped back to the front cover and stared at it. After a moment of silence, he let out a high-pitched sound. "The Use and Control of E.M.S. 4500-AB. for Simple Timeline Navigation."

Ryan and I stared at him.

Dennis looked as if he was about to laugh. His eyes glittered and his cheeks flushed. He flipped the flimsy book around to show us a familiar rectangular metal box on the cover. "Personally, I think it should be titled 'Time Travel for Dummies.'"

Eight

Harry
1848

I ran along the loose, ice-covered stones that made up King William Land. My ankles threatened to twist beneath me as I fled.

Men shouted in all directions, but it was the horrific, high-pitched demon screams back near the cairn that spurred me forward. Others fleeing with me, also bundled in the same slops as I, sprinted into the night. One tripped and fell with a sharp grunt of pain.

I leapt to one side in time to avoid colliding with another running man. His frenzied panting added to my panic and I almost didn't stop to help my fallen comrade.

Snowflakes as hard as ice blew into my eyes, stinging what little skin was exposed of my face. There was no sign of the tall, demonic creature that had charged as soon as we'd been more than a hundred paces from *Terror*.

Heart in my throat, I quickly doubled back and fell to my knees beside the fallen man.

"Can you stand?" I asked, my voice choked with fear.

He rolled to one side, grunting and attempting to get his feet beneath him. I could just make out the deep-set eyes of Edward Little, *Terror*'s First Lieutenant, in the moonlight.

"Aye." Lt. Little tried to scramble up but kept losing purchase on the stones. I roughly yanked him to his feet, and we ran through the whipping snow. Large chunks of hail fell at random, cracking against stone and ice closer than I would have liked.

I shoved my damp scarf higher on my face, covering more of my nose. My constant heavy breaths barely kept the moisture from freezing to my skin. I shivered from the cold and fear.

A great pressure suddenly grew in the middle of my chest, taking my breath away. I stumbled, my heavy boots slipping on the shale stones. Lt. Little caught my arm right before I fell to the ground.

"Faster, doctor." He scanned the dark desolation behind us.

"Where do we go?" I managed to get out.

"As far away from the bloody creature as we can."

"There's only one demon attacking," Captain Fitzjames shouted somewhere on our right. "To the ice, men! Use the seracs as cover! Let the Marines fight first."

Another screech echoed. The demonic sound was followed by the report of a shotgun blast. I flinched and threw up my hands, covering my head.

Lt. Little gripped my arm, wheeling me around to the left. We changed course and sprinted behind other men toward high towers of ice barely discernible in the meager light of the moon. We ducked into a narrow opening between two seracs.

My quick breaths fogged the air, shimmering much like the stars above. I leaned against a serac to allow myself a moment's reprieve. The ice chilled my back despite my thick layers, but I stayed propped against it, one gloved hand clutching my pain-ridden chest.

I was no fool. No other stress brought the pain upon me, and as it had been consistent with the attacks for nearly three years, I had long ago ruled out a medical issue. It was clear the pain signaled when the demons were near; it did not signal an impending attack, and therefore I couldn't give the men an ample warning. I breathed deep, attempting to focus on the waves of crushing pressure in my sternum. I might not be able to fight the huge, barreling creatures, but perhaps I could at least direct the men to safety, using my pain to guide me.

Men's voices rose from the surrounding maze of tall seracs. Lt. Little straightened next to me.

"With me, sir," I gasped, taking a weak step further into our cover.

Before we could move, the familiar Irish voice of Captain Crozier boomed in the night.

"Silence!" he shouted.

I pushed off the ice, lifting my head to scan the black sky filled with perfect pinpricks of white stars. The pelting snow could not reach us any longer and I was finally able to see clearly.

The frozen towers surrounding us looked too much like the demons. Our sanctuary was their perfect camouflage.

"We must get further away, sir." I rubbed my pained chest with a gloved hand, wincing, still staring upward. Nothing moved.

"I told Francis we shouldn't have abandoned *Terror*," came a voice right behind me.

I jumped and craned my neck to see Captain Fitzjames crouched nearby, his scarf loose and dangling. Light frost glittered along his cheeks and furrowed brow. He squinted into the dark alley of ice. Lt. Little offered a weak salute, touching his gloved hand to his forehead.

I held my breath. The pressure on my chest pulsated, and I squeezed my eyes tight, wiping moisture from the corners. "Sir, the creature is coming."

"Follow me." Captain Fitzjames jerked his head and made his way deeper through the narrow corridors of ice. Lt. Little and I scrambled behind Captain Fitzjames in the now-silent night.

"Watch it," he said suddenly, bringing up a glinting musket. A group of three men had rounded the corner, startling us all.

"James." Captain Crozier lowered his large pistol. He put up a hand, signaling a halt to a panicked Mr. Jopson and Lt. Le Vesconte, whose gazes remained clear and calm.

"This is madness." Captain Fitzjames' whisper held anger. "We need to get back to *Terror*. To shelter."

Captain Crozier shook his bundled head. "It didn't follow us into the seracs. It's still out there, as if darin' us to show ourselves. The Marines are using the blizzard as cover to surround the creature and kill it."

Lt. Little gestured wildly at nothing. "We all need to fight. There's only one, and if we rush the beast—"

"Keep your voice low."

"Sir," I gasped, still holding my chest, silently praying for courage. "We could easily mistake the demon for a serac. They are too similar. We are no safer in here than out in the open."

Captain Fitzjames grunted. We all glanced nervously at our surroundings.

Captain Crozier nodded once. "Lt. Little, Lt. Le Vesconte, find stragglers in the seracs. Bring them together as one and keep them silent."

The pair vanished into the dark, leaving me with both captains and Mr. Jopson.

Captain Crozier's gaze bored into me. "You may be right, Goodsir, but I have faith in the Marines. They will kill the creature before it shows it's face in here." He took the lead, deftly navigating through the seracs.

Captain Fitzjames tugged up his scarf, wrapping his face again. He continuously glanced over a shoulder. I, however, turned my gaze skyward, still searching the ice towers.

We hadn't gone more than a few yards before coming by a felled man with another hunched over him.

"Goodsir," Captain Crozier hissed, standing aside.

I pushed forward, boots slipping slightly despite the small ice spikes on their soles.

"What happened?" I lowered myself clumsily to the ice.

The eyes and voice of *Erebus's* John Bridgens came from the bundled mass of slops and scarves. "It's Mr. Peglar, sir," he said, breathing heavily. "I can't wake him."

I pulled off my outer glove and shoved up the sleeve of Mr. Peglar's sleeves, searching for a pulse.

"He just sorta fell to his knees." Mr. Bridgens was watching my actions closely, pale eyes intense.

Mr. Peglar's wrist twitched weakly in my grasp. "He's been showing early signs of scurvy. A fever, reduced appetite, but no weakness as of yet."

Mr. Bridgens dropped his gaze and said nothing.

"Help me lift him." I stood. "He's breathing, but we must keep him off the ice."

We pulled Peglar up, his bundled head falling to one side. His eyes fluttered. Captain Crozier again took the lead while Mr. Bridgens and I struggled to carry our comrade through the seracs.

The muscles in my arms quickly began to tire, and I tripped more than once. Just as I was beginning to fear I would drop Peglar's top half, Captain Crozier halted. He held up a wide, gloved hand. We huddled behind him while he peered out into the stubborn darkness.

A shout sounded from ahead. Captain Crozier stepped out of the ice maze and quickly ordered silence. We followed, free of the pressing closeness of ice.

Mr. Bridgens and I lowered Mr. Peglar to the ground in order to rest a moment. The blizzard had waned; the storm now merely tossed fat snowflakes in large, lazy swirls.

The pain in my chest spiked, crashing through me with such a force that I was nearly driven to my knees.

A screech pierced my eardrums. I slapped my hands over both ears, hunching over Mr. Peglar. Men scattered. Just as I'd feared, the ice demon slipped away from the seracs where it had been hiding. It reared in the night, its shattering scream sounding again. The towering creature swiped a large, ta-loned hand that just barely missed a big group of fleeing officers.

I flung myself over Mr. Peglar. Men ran past on either side. No one stopped to help me.

Gunfire roared. The reports of muskets, rifles, and pistols shattered the night, drowning out the blood-chilling screams of the demon.

"Get back!" Sergeant Tozer of the Marines shot past me, planting his feet a yard away and lifting his rifle, aiming at the demon's cracked white skull. The creature roared. It ran toward him, its mouth a gaping, toothless chasm. The rest of the Marines stopped just behind Sergeant Tozer. Together, they aimed and fired as one.

The boom of their weapons was deafening. I could barely see through the snow and pressing darkness. The demon let out another howl, turning with a sound of bones snapping.

"Again!" shouted Sergeant Tozer. Officers from both ships joined their ranks, firing at will while the Marines fell back to reload.

The demon shuddered. It mewled like a trapped animal, stumbling twice. It fell.

The creature's long body collapsed against two seracs. A cheer rose through the men. Three Marines, encouraged by the victory, fired once more in unison. Sergeant Tozer let out a shout. He pulled his sword free and charged forward. Others followed suit, pulling boat knives from side sheaths. Together, they descended upon the fallen beast, stabbing until it moved no longer.

I rose on unsteady legs to watch the demon's demise. The other men, those who did not partake, stood huddled a ways off. Others sat on the shale stones on their own. I gathered my focus, turned, and quickly waved down the man who had taken over as *Erebus's* captain.

"Captain Fitzjames," I said in a soft voice. "Some men are injured, but I am unable to help without the medical kits."

"I'm aware, Goodsir." He watched his superior approach with quick strides.

"James." Captain Crozier's voice was raw and gruff. "The doctors and I will stay with the injured. Take your lieutenants and anyone unhurt and able to haul. We need the sledging boats we abandoned in the attack."

Captain Fitzjames gave a curt nod and left without a word.

I glanced over my shoulder at the felled demon. It lay unmoving, its cracked, icy skin blending in with the seracs. I fought a great urge to approach the corpse and examine it. Instead, I massaged the middle of my chest – the pain no longer surged – and held my position.

"What if they are unable to get the boats?" I asked our leader. "There could be other demons nearby."

"It isn't far," said Captain Crozier. "They will retrieve the boats, haul them here."

"Do we need to get them all, sir?" came Mr. Bridgens' quiet voice. He stood near the still unconscious Mr. Peglar.

"Aye." Captain Crozier nodded. "They're our only hope if we find open water."

He turned to me, shielding his face from a sudden gust of snow-filled wind with one gloved hand. "Do yer rounds, Dr. Goodsir. See to the injured men as best you can until Captain Fitzjames returns."

Recruiting two nearby men, I gestured down at Mr. Peglar. "Continue to attempt to wake him. If you are unable, pick him up and carry him a while, even if in circles. It will keep your circulation flowing and prevent him from lying on the ice."

They set to work. I trudged toward the closest injured man. With no supplies, I could not do much, but most merely had scrapes and bruises. The worst ailment I came across was that of *Terror's* caulker's mate, thin, pale Mr. Hickey, who sat perched on a hard mound of snow. His scalp had begun to bleed freely.

Using his kerchief, I wiped the slowly oozing blood away. "The scurvy is setting in worse now, Mr. Hickey. Are you able to walk?"

He nodded and spat; his saliva was tinged with red streaks. "Aye, sir. But I'm so tired."

"We will have our tents and supplies soon enough." I pulled his eyelids open one at a time, checking the pupils. "Captain Fitzjames will be back."

Mr. Hickey didn't reply. He stared at me, his pale, pocked face half-hidden in the moonlight. I gave his shoulder a hard squeeze and instructed him to keep moving to combat the relentless cold.

A loud cracking sound shot through the night. Instinctively crouching with my hands raised, I looked for the source. The noise came again, just like bones snapping under great force. Men gathered around the fallen demon. I slowly stood and inched forward to peer in between the shoulders of Lt. Little and Captain Crozier. The corpse of the creature shuddered, and another echoing crack sounded.

"No need to worry, men." Sergeant Tozer glanced around the crowd. "It's dead. Jus' watch."

I watched in grim fascination as the demon's corpse slowly began to crumble. Its body fell apart, the cracking sounds diminishing as it did, until there was little more than powder left that quickly flew off with the blowing snowflakes.

"What causes it?" I shouted over a sudden gust of wind.

"We 'ave no idea." Sergeant Tozer shouldered his rifle, gripping the strap tight. He put his back to where the demon had been moments ago and walked away, his hard gaze flickering around, watching for further danger. I flexed my hands against the cold and continued my duty, mind still awhirl.

Disease had taken too many of our men already on this voyage, and those who remained were only slowly getting worse. I checked each man as time stretched on with no signs of Captain Fitzjames or demons.

After checking on the still unconscious Mr. Peglar again I finally stopped and stood near a serac on my own. I pressed my lips together hard behind my scarf, sniffling, unable to wipe at my running nose. How could we possibly survive a frantic flight to safety that may not even be there?

A faint scraping brought me out of my miserable thoughts. As one, we turned toward the sounds, instantly on edge.

Captain Crozier squinted into the dark, his pistol's barrel aimed at the black sky. "Easy, men. It's not an attack."

Sure enough, Captain Fitzjames appeared in the darkness at the forefront of a small group, straining against a canvas harness strapped around his torso. Behind him, more men pushed forward against the weight of our six sledge boats, the makeshift skis beneath them pushing aside handfuls of loose shale stones in their wake.

A feeble cheer rose throughout the exhausted, half-frozen men. I ran forward, meeting Captain Fitzjames as he breathlessly struggled out of his harness. His blue scarf hung loose around his neck again, and his long coat was barely buttoned. He wiped sweat from his forehead with the back of a glove. I quickly attempted to check his pulse, but he just waved me off.

"I'm fine, doctor," he panted, mouth set in a grimace. He sniffed and removed his hat, releasing his wispy brown hair. "Just need to catch my breath."

Men swarmed the boats, pulling aside the canvas covers and digging out coveted weapons, food, or other supplies.

Unsure of where my medical kits had ended up, I hung back, letting the initial wave of men search the boats. I stood between the captains, wishing above all that any fresh game would wander across our path. My stomach churned at the thought of the rotted tins despite my ever-present, ripping hunger.

"We will part ways now, James." Captain Crozier turned his gaze away from the huddled men.

"Sir…" Captain Fitzjames looked at him, incredulous.

"We continue with the plan." He reached out and clasped Captain Fitzjames' shoulder. "We will see each other again, James. I know it."

Captain Fitzjames nodded, keeping his head held up high. "I'm sorry to report that Lt. Irving was killed in tonight's attack. We can bury him here, then you take Le Vesconte so as to have two officers."

The leaders of our voyage clasped gloved hands, pulling each other close and speaking low. I left and joined with the dwindling fray among the boats.

The snow had almost completely tapered off, but the wind picked up, cutting through our ranks. I found my medical kit in the third boat.

After a brief service that followed covering Lt. Irving in a pile of shale stones, we hurried on our way. Captain Crozier pulled on the lead canvas harness of the front sledge boat, straightening it along his torso. He hollered out instructions while keeping a wary eye on the night pressing around us. I quickly helped lift Mr. Peglar's limp form into the front boat, tucking him beneath my own bed furs.

"He's most likely been concussed," I said to the other six who were to pull the boat with our captain. "We can put him in one of the sledging boats. I will walk aside and keep watch over him."

"What if more demons attack?" Mr. Bridgens kept his voice low, nervously tugging on his harness.

"Tha's what we got guns for." Sergeant Tozer appeared, rifle resting on his shoulder.

I glanced around for Captain Fitzjames, but he had moved off. His lisped voice barely reached us, but it was clear from his hand gestures he was preparing his men to haul as well.

"Cap'in Crozier was right," Sergeant Tozer said. "Now we got visibility. On the ships we was confined and scramblin' through tight quarters. Out 'ere, those things could come at us in droves and we'd just shoot 'em down."

"Yet a single one of them managed to scatter us away from our supplies and kill Lt. Irving."

"That's what happens when men panic." His voice rose, and others glanced over. "If we woulda just stuck together, had each other's backs...if the men run like that, we can't protect 'em."

I knelt to inspect the contents of my medical kit. One of the glass bottles had shattered, spilling Dover's powder all along the bottom and lining it with jaggedly sharp edges. With no time to clean the mess, I administered a dose of laudanum to Mr. Hickey and wiped salve on the blistered knuckles of three other men.

Finally satisfied I had done all I could, I stored my kit next to Mr. Peglar and took my place near the lead boat.

"All together now, men, and *pull!*" Captain Crozier's voice boomed, strident. They threw their weight against the canvas at the same time, the harnesses wrapped tightly around their torsos. They heaved, groaned, and strained, trying to match each other's strides, feet digging into the ground. Wood scraped against stone and the boats finally lurched south.

I glanced over my shoulder one last time at the other half of our men, those being led away by Captain Fitzjames, then hurried away, trying not to think about how our rendezvous point was over eight hundred miles away.

Nine

Annie
2020

I stared at the large mass of cables haphazardly protruding from the metal rectangular box we'd found. No markings or brands lined its sides. Dual green lights glowed bright and steady, almost happily, as if urging us to give the contraption a whirl.

"It's so much smaller than I'd expect a time machine to be." Dennis lightly touched the side of the machine.

Ryan reached out and picked up a long cord from the lower shelf. A tiny metal rectangle dangled from one end, the other attached to a round, flat pad, reminding me of the ones used with an EKG.

"That's what the man had on in the video." I jerked my chin at the pad.

"This is a joke. It has to be."

"Did we watch different tapes?" I glanced over handwritten scrawls in the margins that consisted of shorthand I didn't understand.

"Time travel, people with powers…" He shook his head. "It shouldn't be possible."

"So those homicidal smoke demons flying around outside are just imaginary?"

"It seriously is a damn lot to take in," Dennis agreed. "But we saw it happen."

"It could be fake."

"Oh, okay." Dennis barked out a laugh. "Make fake videos and a fake instruction manual, then lock it all away to never be found. Sure, dude."

Ryan tossed his head, flipping loose hair away from his eyes. He twirled the thin cord between two fingers. "Even if it is real, it doesn't mean we're going to use this thing."

Dennis balked at him. "What? Why not?"

"You seriously want to mess with time? This reeks of *The Butterfly Effect* or some shit. You can't go back and change anything, because you'll ultimately change the future, which is currently our present. You know that."

Dennis grumbled something incoherent and stepped back from the strange machine with a wary eye.

"Say we went back and accidentally got someone in the past killed. That person's entire family line is now wiped out, which then prevents someone of great importance from being born. Or hell, one of us. Come on, so many time travel movies cover this. And it doesn't matter anyway, because there is absolutely no reason to use it. You read what happens when you go back to a time in which you already exist: you die. So we can't stop the end of the world, we can't save our loved ones. What else would be the point?"

"We could go back to the seventies." Dennis grinned. "Get out of here and live in the past, see our favorite bands live. Can you imagine?"

"Oh yeah?" His brother tossed a hand in the air. "Who'd be here to work the machine? You said the manual says somebody has to work the controls, so we can't all go running off in the past."

An idea suddenly formed in my mind, one so ridiculous I barely wanted to say it out loud, but the words were past my lips before I could stop myself. "The ice demons."

"What?"

"Goodsir and John Franklin's men. They were chased by some kind of huge demons in the Arctic."

Ryan laughed, a short, loud bark. "People can hallucinate from starvation and disease. You can't possibly know if that isn't just the beginning of his crazed ravings."

"Maybe. Or maybe it's real. If it is, this Goodsir could help us somehow. What if there's a link between the ice demons and the wraiths?"

Ryan scoffed. "Come on, Annie. We can't go back to the eighteen hundreds."

"Why, yes," Dennis cut in, "we can."

His brother pinched the bridge of his nose. "Even if we could, what the hell good would this Evo be to us? He's from almost two hundred years ago. Our world is dead. And do you really think going back in time into a place that legit killed all of these men is a smart move?"

"I don't know, it was just an idea." I shrugged. "We could save his life at least. Bring him here. All of Franklin's men."

Ryan nearly dropped the electrode. His jaw fell open and he stared at me, horrified. "Are you out of your damn mind? Taking even one person out of history—"

"But they all vanished," I said, cutting him off. "They died in the Arctic. They didn't get to come home, didn't get to start new families. If we took this Goodsir from the past for any reason, nothing should change because he's already disappeared in history."

Ryan studied me, slowly realizing I was right. He let out a low whistle and stood. "Okay…I'll give you that. But no. It's not happening. You saw that Thompson guy come back as a pile of organs and melted flesh."

"True, but that tape had a red dot. A fail. Over thirty were green. And that was just the seventy-third trial, which we can assume means more were before and probably after. We can watch all of them, study everything. We have to at least *try* something, Ryan." I waved the instruction manual, its pages crinkling. "We can't leave the bunker. The food is rotting. We are totally fucked. So, we either try to figure out if this machine can help us or sit here and starve to death. I know damn well which I'm going to choose."

Dennis rubbed his jaw, brown eyes boring into me. "I think Annie's right."

"When don't you?" Ryan muttered. He tossed the cord on the shelf with a sigh.

"We saw it work." Dennis's face softened. "In the video. And all those tapes with green dots have to be successes. We can watch them first to be sure, but dude, it's been done before."

"It's too dangerous. Too much is at risk." Ryan dropped to one knee. He pulled up his left pant leg, revealing a black cast boot, and adjusted the top strap.

Dennis sidled up beside me. "Annie and I vote that we try the machine. Two against one."

Silence fell. The three of us stared at each other.

"No" Ryan said at last. "We have to study everything they left first."

"And *then* try it."

Ryan snorted. "There's no way I'm hooking one of us up to this thing. You saw what it did in the first two tapes."

"Maybe that was before they knew the rules of time travel," Dennis offered.

I tossed the instructions aside. "Then we can test it on an inanimate object. Like a can of beans or something."

"I second this," Dennis said. "We can at least see if the machine works first. I guess I'd rather not turn inside out, like that pig lizard alien thing in *Galaxy Quest*."

"We'll go through the rest of the files." Ryan leaned against the shelving unit and crossed his arms. "Sure, Goodsir might be an Evo, but unless he has an ability that can prevent the end of the world, he stays in the past. Does he talk about any special ability or power in his diary?"

I shook my head. "His chest hurts each time the demons are near. Other than that, no. But I haven't finished reading it."

"All right. Then the only thing I'm willing to agree on is using the machine to find a way out of here before our food runs out. Or at least to find fresh food. I don't know how yet, but we have time to form a plan. Before anything, though, we carefully research every single thing in that study. You keep going with the books and the Goodsir journal, Annie. I will look through the stuff in the filing cabinets, and Dennis, you watch the tapes and work on figuring out how this machine works."

"Already on it." Dennis held the manual open. "We need coordinates, a date, and a time, which already poses a problem. Even if we have the who and the when, we definitely don't have the exact where, especially without access to the Internet."

Ryan stared at the small machine. "No coordinates, no time travel."

Something tugged at the back of my mind. "Wait…"

Both brothers looked at me with curiosity.

"Holy crap." I jogged away, through the back rooms and into the study. Stopping at the tall bookshelves, I stood on my toes again and yanked down the maps, then spread them open on the nearby desk.

"Look." I pointed at the green X and string of handwritten coordinates.

Ryan eyed the green scribbles, then he turned and stared at the nearby closet door. "I'll be damned. That's gotta be why the parkas are here. They were gonna go back to the Arctic. Or maybe they already did."

"Pretty sure there's no fresh food up there." I twisted a thin strand of hair between my fingers, still eyeing the markings on the map. "And I for sure don't want to go visit somewhere that cold."

"Okay, look." Dennis rubbed his hands together. "I have to say this: we have freaking time travel. If we figure out specific coordinates, we could go anywhere as long as we don't already exist. How is that not freaking awesome? How are you not as excited as I am?"

The enormousness of our situation dropped on me like a weight. "Pig lizard, Dennis. Don't forget the inside-out pig lizard."

Ten

Harry
1848

Once we abandoned *Terror*, the rest of our numbers dropped quickly. The walk that should have taken a month or so, even pulling such weight, dragged on much longer. I tried to keep track of the passing days but eventually gave up.

We were only able to make a few miles a day hauling the sledge boats. I needed to remove extremities of my friends on a regular basis. Men died nearly every week from starvation and exposure. Others succumbed to illness, be it scurvy, frostbite, or pneumonia.

Mr. Hickey was too weak to haul but refused to be placed in one of the sledging boats. Instead, he kept pace with me near the front, talking on an endless loop of his childhood home in Limerick.

Any fat I'd sported before that hadn't trimmed down during my time on *Erebus* had now vanished. My ribs were more prominent than they ever had been. Blood slowly started to seep from the sockets of my teeth until it was a constant metallic flavor. I continued to brush my teeth, but to little effect. Soon, bruises appeared along my arms and legs for no reason.

My scurvy was in its early stages, but in that desolate land of nothingness, it was only a matter of time before I was too weak to do anything besides lie down and die.

Still, I forced myself onward, caring for the remaining men, pitching our large tents every night, and trudging through countless, bone-aching storms.

We stumbled through the scenery of relentless monotony. Nearly all of us spat blood, hacked, coughed, and shivered in our constantly damp slops. Some days my own body heat became unbearable, and I tugged off the canvas layers to continue with only my naval long coat shielding me from the elements.

A few men were further along in their scurvy than others. Many woke with blood staining their makeshift pillows, or wore caps permanently tinged deep maroon. Some came to me to dress old wounds that had healed years ago but now began to open and fester.

I despised the need for the boats. Many often complained, stating we should leave them behind so as to reach our destination quicker, but our stalwart captain remained firm in his orders. Because of this, something much worse began to consume the men of our group. Something more sinister.

Recalcitrance.

Constant whispers began to spread through the night as the men huddled in tents. Talk of taking over, of splitting off. Even worse, a few of the men had begun to eye the weak and injured the way a fox looks at a chicken.

Captain Crozier remained at the front of the boat sledge party each day. While not sledging, I trailed alongside the lead boat struggling to catch my breath as we traipsed over countless miles. Ropes creaked and boots crunched in an endless flow of harsh noise. It grated in my ears and added to the constant throbbing in my temples.

The sun, a full white orb that just barely hung above the horizon, tried and failed to pierce the constant layers of thin fog surrounding our group. Its faded, pale luminescence still reflected bright off the surrounding monochromatic white of snow and ice. I squinted at the harsh glare, wishing for a pair of the tinted snow goggles some of the other men wore, and pulled off my scarf.

My breath faded before me. The endless miles of walking hadn't gotten us out of the icy grips of the Arctic, but it was already quite a few degrees warmer. I ran a hand through my thick, dark beard and tried to decipher the best way to voice my unease.

"How do you fare today, Dr. Goodsir?" Captain Crozier panted steadily. His own beard had grown, reddish brown and sparkling from frozen sweat. "Are you well?"

"Aye, sir." I hefted my canvas sack of belongings on one shoulder and tried to ignore the constant ache and spasms of my muscles.

"Yer voice betrays you. We'll stop soon, set up camp."

I shuffled closer to him. "But sir, we've barely made a mile today."

"It's been four days since we finished the last of the polar bear the Marines shot. If no game is found today, we are back to the rotten tins. And no," he held up a thick gloved hand as I opened my mouth to protest, "there is no other option. We must eat."

I was desperate to argue but held my tongue.

"Halt!" Captain Crozier's voice boomed and echoed. "We rest here until the mornin'. Prepare the tents, set up a perimeter. Marines, choose some o' the strongest for yer hunting parties."

"Captain?"

"What is it, Dr. Goodsir?" He lifted his looking glass to one eye, careful to keep the metal from touching any skin, and peered along the horizon, turning in a slow circle.

"A word in private, if you will? Away from the men?"

He dropped his arms and shrugged free from the canvas straps. "Lt. Le Vesconte, do Goodsir's rounds for now. Make sure the men are all right and accounted for."

The lieutenant wiped sweat from his brow. He dipped his head, shifted his hat, and obeyed.

Captain Crozier led me a few yards away from the men. "What is it, doctor?"

I fought the urge to wring my hands. Instead, I removed my knit cap and let my hair, damp with sweat, tumble free. "It's some of the men, sir. I've seen certain looks and heard whispers. Without some sort of intervention, I fear this will not end well."

Crozier ran a thick-fingered hand through his light reddish hair. "We've already discussed this."

"I no longer speak of food, sir."

He stared off into the distance, his pale eyes narrowed. He slowly spun the looking glass in one gloved hand. "And what do ya propose?"

I risked a glance over a shoulder, eyeing the men pitching tents and unstocking our supplies. "Somehow show there's still hope, even if there is none."

Crozier met my gaze and nodded. "We have to be getting close to the river that will lead us out of here. A day or two at most."

"We might not last that long, sir."

"I know."

"Captain, I worry that there may be—"

"I understand what you are saying, doctor. Go to the men and do yer rounds. Take note of those who may be a threat. We can separate the worst of them and spread them out." He put a heavy hand on my thin, stooped shoulder. "This is why I wanted you with."

My helpless gaze met his determined eyes. "Sir?"

"You see things others overlook. Dr. Peddie is a fine man and doctor but was better suited to go with James."

I didn't ask for more clarity. Now that our procession had stopped, my toes had begun to tingle. I stamped my feet to little effect, then turned and went back to the group.

"Doctor." Lt. Le Vesconte strode over, concern in his eyes. "Mr. Hickey is no longer able to haul, and three other men report the beginnings of painful stabbing in their knees."

Ignoring the aching in my own limbs, I hurried after the *Erebus* lieutenant.

Too many men stared at me with already dead eyes. Their skin was clammy, bloodless, whiter than the endless snow. While inspecting the worst cases of exposure and illness, I caught shifting eyes, glares at our leader, huddled whisperings that stopped the moment that I approached. My fear of a possible mutiny heightened.

I kept my face impassive and knelt down next to thin Mr. Hickey, rummaging through my medical kit. He had always been a thin young man, but now he was nearly skeletal. He smiled at me, flashing teeth stained red.

I examined a widening black spot of frostbite along one cheek, then lifted a small glass bottle between us. "This will help ease your pain."

"I'm sorry, sir." Mr. Hickey's fingers trembled in time with his voice. "I want to keep pullin'."

Tipping a bottle of medication to his chapped lips, I smiled back at him. "You've done a fine job. You deserve a rest, now. Let the others set up camp this time, all right?"

"Too many of us are droppin', Dr. Goodsir." He swallowed the bitter mediation without a flinch, watching me with black eyes clouded by pain. "We ain't gonna make it, are we?"

I paused, choosing my words carefully. "Mr. Hickey, you should feel better soon. Once it's accessible, we'll get you in the medical tent proper. Now let's get you off the rocks."

"Thank you, sir."

Before I could help Mr. Hickey to his feet, a sharp wail cut through the Arctic air. I spun, glancing wildly about.

One of the men near the perimeter was backpedaling, dropping his side of a tent and staring out into a coiling, billowing fog that surrounded toward our little camp.

The man who raised the alarm stumbled, pointing into the shifting heavy mist. Everyone turned, looking into the bleak nothingness.

I stood, still gripping the bottle tight in one hand. We held our breath collectively as the thick mist enveloped us closer along all sides. No creatures stalked within.

Captain Crozier hollered at our group to stay calm, to stand still. He stalked back toward the man who had raised alarm.

"It's the demons," Mr. Hickey hissed. He twisted this way and that on the cold, uneven ground. "They've finally come for us."

I shook my head. "They left us alone for weeks. Ever since we parted with Captain Fitzjames. Why attack now?"

"A'course it's them. What else could cause this sudden disturbance?"

Smiling gently, I slipped the medication back into my kit. I was not gripped by the same terror as the others; the pain in my chest did not arise. "There is nothing to—"

A lone silhouette stalked toward us from the depths of the dense fog.

"*Demon!*" Mr. Hickey screamed. He scrambled back on all fours across the slippery ground.

Delirious, weakened men dropped supplies and tents all around. A few bolted out into the thick mist, away from the still advancing figure. Others took up arms, aiming rifles and double-barreled shotguns.

"That is no demon!" I shouted, squinting at the large figure. "It is not big enough. Please, stop!"

Nobody listened. Twice I was jostled aside by frightened men who ignored all common sense.

"Hold yer damned fire!" Captain Crozier's voice joined my pleading.

A rifle boomed despite his order. I slipped and went down hard. My teeth slammed together. Sharp pain shot through my upper jaw, bringing tears to my eyes.

Heart hammering, I scrambled after Mr. Hickey. He stared behind me, his mouth opening and closing.

I looked over one shoulder, but the thing in the fog had vanished.

"Where did it go?" Mr. Hickey's thin, long hair hung along his face in greasy strands.

Lt. Le Vesconte ran to Captain Crozier, his deep-set eyes wide and glassy. "Sir. We're exposed. It'll pick us off."

"Flip the boats."

"Sir?"

"Flip the damn boats and get the men underneath. *Now*."

Without waiting to hear more, Lt. Le Vesconte hurried to the closest boat. He tore the canvas cover free, shouting at the throng of panicked men to keep calm and follow suit. I chased after him, pulling Mr. Hickey with me.

The three of us slammed against the wooden port side of the sledge boat. It creaked and shifted on the makeshift skis but did not tip.

Shouts shifted around us, growing louder, more full of fear and panic. A group of officers bolted past.

"Help us!" Lt. Le Vesconte shouted at them. Two broke off, changing course and adding their weight. Seconds later, a grunting Captain Crozier was on my left, straining with us, and finally, the boat tipped.

I ran around the stern. Our supplies lay strewn across the shale stones in haphazard piles. My boots sent a handful of cutlery scattering.

"Over here!" I shouted. "Underneath the boat!"

Men slammed into each other. Captain Crozier vanished but I could still hear him shouting, his booming voice slicing through the dense fog.

"Stop yer damn running, all of you!" he ordered. No one listened; the men were now fueled on panic alone.

Glancing around, I still could not see the lone figure in the mist. There was no crushing pressure in my chest. I took a tentative step toward the fog where the figure had been but was pulled backward by Lt. Little.

Bodies crammed together underneath our boat, leaving little space. We reached up and pulled. The side of the boat slammed against the rocks, encapsulating us all.

The surrounding shouts and cries of the men still outside became muffled. I could hear others around me in the darkness, feel them pressed close. My back was shoved against the hard side of the boat, and something bulky dug painfully into my knee. I could see nothing but a dim line of light between the boat's lip and the uneven ground of hard rocks. The men's scared voices were deadened, flat, in the enclosed space.

Lt. Le Vesconte shouted for silence, his voice a loud rasp above the others' panicked murmurings.

Booted feet ran past. More muffled shouts emitted from beyond our wooden sanctuary. We did not move.

Captain Crozier's loud voice echoed again, yelling something unintelligible. The sound of his voice chilled my blood. I'd never heard him afraid before.

The boat shuddered above us. I clamped one gloved hand over my mouth to keep from shouting. A rifle discharged very close by.

I closed my eyes and forced myself to focus on my uneven breathing instead of the whispers from the men nearby. More men ran past us. Captain Crozier's shouting became more frenzied.

And then, all at once, the yelling stopped.

In the distance, a strangled cry arose. I'd heard enough cries from men in my years as a ship's surgeon to distinguish fear from pain. This was one of deep grief.

I lurched forward in the darkness. "Help me lift the boat."

Someone next to me, quite close, pulled my shoulder in the darkness. "Not yet, Goodsir."

"I have to tend to the wounded."

"We can't be sure the demon is gone."

"There was no demon, damnit." I snapped back.

Before we could say more, the side of our boat lifted clear off the rocks.

Able Seaman John Morfin stared down at us. With him was Sergeant Tozer and a man I only knew as Walker. All three men were covered in thick blood spatters. Behind them sat Mr. Hickey, watching us with glazed eyes.

Morfin and Tozer tipped our now empty boat backwards. It fell with a loud slam, then rocked to one side.

"What happened?" I croaked, squinting at the streaked red blood on Morfin's weathered face.

He lunged at me. He grabbed my arm and painfully yanked me to my feet.

Walker lunged forward. "Not him. He's needed."

I shook free of Morfin's grasp, massaging my wrist. I tried to step around him to go to Mr. Hickey, but he pushed me back.

"Morfin." Lt. Le Vesconte strode forward, one hand on the butt of his pistol. "Let him pass."

"What's happened?" I tried to keep my voice steady but failed. Glancing behind them at Mr. Hickey, I tried to go to the small man, intent on helping him stand.

"The demon." Sergeant Tozer blocked my path, hefting his rifle in both hands. "Di'n't you see it?"

"Dear God." Lt. Le Vesconte was staring at something to my left, beyond a glowering Morfin blocking my view. I took a step aside and followed his gaze. I stared for a long moment, then let my eyes fall shut.

Fresh blood coated the icy rocks beneath a scattering of dead men. Blank, glossy eyes stared. Gore trickled from a cracked head, and intestines glistened. Captain Crozier lay off to one side, multiple slices opening his torso, his neck nearly severed.

His steward, the quiet Mr. Jopson, crouched by the corpse of our leader, howling out another one of the ragged cries I'd heard while beneath the boat.

My knees weakened. Morfin reached out and caught me before I stumbled, his grip strong and painful. I turned my gaze away from the dead and caught a glint at his hip. His knife, hastily slipped through a belt loop, was slick with red.

"It's all right, men." Morfin stepped back. His grin was riddled with holes from missing teeth that scurvy had claimed. "The demon is gone."

"There was no demon!" The suffocating fog deadened my harsh shout. I could not tear my eyes away from the stained blade.

"What have you done?" Lt. Le Vesconte pulled his pistol free. Tozer whipped his long rifle around and pushed the barrel against the lieutenant's face.

Sudden movement flashed on my left. Lt. Little let out a shout, but his warning came too late. Morfin slammed the butt of his own weapon against Lt. Le Vesconte's temple, sending him flying to the limestone rocks with a clatter.

Walker came forward. His light ashen hair was stained crimson in the front. He slowly knelt beside the unconscious Lt. Le Vesconte. With rough, thin hands also stained with blood, he plucked the dropped pistol from the ground. He turned his pale green eyes on me.

"They killed 'em." Mr. Hickey's voice pitched higher than normal. "They killed 'em, I saw it all. Oh, God up in Heaven, they killed 'em all."

Walker stalked toward Sergeant Tozer. "I told you to take care of him."

Tozer shrugged. "He's no threat. Could help us haul after a few fresh meals once his scurvy's gone."

Grabbing the stock of the sergeant's rifle, Walker tugged it away, took aim, and blew a gaping hole in one side of Mr. Hickey's head.

Blood, chunks of skull, and long strands of hair flew. The report drowned out my cry of shock and despair. Mr. Jopson did not flinch but continued to sit with his fists clenched and head hung low over Captain Crozier's corpse.

"There." Walker hefted the rifle back toward Tozer. "One less mouth to feed."

I quickly surged forward, blind with rage. Morfin snatched my wrist, this time bending my arm and pulling me up short with a sharp, shooting pain. Cold metal pressed into the soft flesh of my neck; Morfin cocked the pistol he held, the loud *click* a plain suggestion of what would come next should I continue to fight.

"Now there's only thirteen o' us." Walker ignored me. "We only need one boat, and we 'ave plenty of food to go around thrice over every day."

I stared open-mouthed in stark horror at Sergeant Tozer. He wouldn't meet my eye. Walker moved past, patting down the men who had been beneath the boat with me and relieving them of all weapons.

"Tonight, we eat." Walker's words were tinged with mania only just hidden beneath confidence. A near-perfect line of blood droplets dotted along one cheek. "And tomorrow, you seven will haul."

"You dare murder our friends? Our *captain*?" My trembles took over, wracking my legs. I fought against Morfin despite the nose of the pistol digging into my throat.

"Quit strugglin' or I'll knock your teeth in." His sour breath shot across my face. "You don't need 'em."

"They resisted," Tozer quietly pleaded. His hat was askew, and tufts of red hair poked out from underneath. "Attacked us."

"That's a lie," Lt. Little growled. He tensed, eyes narrowed, clearly weighing the odds between compliance and a fight. "You'll hang for this. Right out here."

Walker barked out a laugh.

Mr. Bridgens strode toward Walker, ignoring Tozer, who turned the rifle on him. "And what the hell do you think will happen when we're rescued? You'll all rot in a cell."

Walker stepped back. He looked Bridgens up and down and grinned. "You'll all be thankin' us soon enough, when yer bellies are full. You'll see we was right in what we did. What we had to do for at least some of us to survive."

Morfin released my arm but kept the nose of his pistol stuck to my neck. The frozen metal had adhered to my skin. I could not quell the trembles of my fingers. All the hope I had felt at Captain Crozier's mention of success was quickly snuffed out.

"Men." Walker held up both hands. Sergeant Tozer and the rest of the mutineers trained their weapons on us. "Bury the dead as best you can, then finish the tents. Make sure to place the medical tent in the middle, where we can see Goodsir. Once we've settled, we prep the cap'n."

A burst of frigid air swirled the surrounding mist, settling a deep chill into my bones. I shivered violently and pulled my long coat tight with slow movements. Letting my eyes fall shut, I murmured a quiet prayer, realizing what Walker had just said.

Morfin grunted. He lowered the pistol, bringing a thin layer of my skin with it. I winced and slapped a hand over the little superficial wound. With an angry but wary glance at a glowering Morfin, I knelt next to Lt. Le Vesconte, feeling for his pulse with one hand and pulling back his eyelids with the other.

The lieutenant's chest rose and fell in a shallow but steady motion. I rolled him onto his back. "He needs my help."

"You can help him here," Morfin snapped.

I stood and strode toward him. "You monster."

He shoved me back with one hand.

"Morfin." Sergeant Tozer hefted his long rifle. "Leave him be. We need him whole."

Everyone turned to stare at me. I was shaking in my fury. Lt. Little closed his eyes and lowered to the cold ground, gripping fistfuls of his salt and peppered hair in both fists. He let out a moan I would not soon forget.

"All is well, men." Walker paced before us all, his eyes half desperate, half mad. "We will camp here until the scurvy in us all gone, and then continue on our way. Goodsir will tend to us until we've healed."

"I won't," I said firmly, pressing my lips together.

"You will. You'll see," he said, his smile manic. "This is what had to be done for us to survive."

"It was not your choice." I felt faint. My vision flickered. I didn't know what to do. Hot bile surged through the pit of my stomach. When I tried to turn away, Morfin shoved me again. I threw my fist into his jaw.

Sharp pain laced through my hand and wrist, splitting open the consistent frozen numbness. I gasped, cradling my right hand. Morfin stumbled back, arms whirling.

A haggard cheer surged through the scared group of men. As one, they leapt forward, uncaring of Tozer's loaded rifle.

The deafening roar of a musket ended our short-lived retribution. I flinched backward just as Mr. Bridgens spun to one side in a spray of blood and gore.

Something hard struck the back of my head, and all focus slipped from my mind. I went down to one knee next to Lt. Le Vesconte's prone frame. I stammered, my tongue heavy, barely able to comprehend as bitter darkness wrapped me in oblivion.

Eleven

Annie
2020

I pulled open the door to the platform room. Ryan stood at the E.M.S. 4500-AB, still slightly favoring his injured leg. He held *Franklin, Found* open in one hand. A string of bright red numbers glowed from the machine's digital display.

Dennis knelt by the platform, carefully adhering the round adhesive pad of the corded electrode to a large can of Del Monte green beans.

"Any luck on your end?" he asked.

I shrugged, trying not to let my disappointment show. "Not really. I read some of the Franklin books, looked over those maps again. No mention in any of those about some kind of ability, except in Goodsir's journal."

"Oh?"

"He feels a pain in his chest when the demons are near. I'm almost through it, though; I can't tell if it means he has a power or if it's just, like, fear."

"The files didn't help, either." Ryan shifted his weight and deleted the string of numbers from the machine's display. He poked the buttons while carefully studying the machine's manual nearby.

"Do you think they're a dead end?"

"Hard to say. I mean, I found plenty of information about the machine and a long, boring list of each trial. There's ninety-three in total which took all week to get through. But never a mention of what power this Goodsir had or if they went back and took his DNA." He glanced up at me. "Why'd you save the diary for last?"

"Because it's fucking horrific. I just got through the mutiny. They kept Goodsir alive, but then some of the men started eating each other to stay alive."

"Holy hell." Dennis tugged at the cord of the electrode to ensure it didn't budge. "That's horrible."

"I can't imagine how scared he was." I stretched, reaching my hands up high and brushing my palms along the low concrete ceiling. "And those ice demons that chased them are terrifying."

"I'm having second thoughts about this." Ryan didn't seem to hear me. "The back page of the manual is missing. I don't like it."

Dennis took the paper booklet and flipped it over. "For all we know there nothing was on it."

Ryan finished inputting the numbers and took a step back. "I think that's it."

Staring at the lone can of beans on the platform, I twisted a lock of hair between my fingers. "This is unreal."

"I think it's badass." Dennis dropped an arm around my shoulders. "Let's see what this baby can do."

"And we will. From the safety of the control room." Ryan limped away.

Dennis graced me with an exaggerated eye roll. We filed past the platform, out of the back room, and toward the table with the monitors. Each screen shone brightly, showing us empty rooms and the dead world surrounding our bunker door outside.

He went to the control panel and studied the instructions in silence, running the pad of his thumb over a small scab on his forearm.

I stood next to Ryan and stared through the tall windows. The big can sat in its place with the cord draped from the electrode pad and the attached rectangular box laying on the raised platform.

"Let's do this thing." Dennis reached forward, flipped two switches, and slapped his palm onto the large red button. We leaned forward together, staring through the thick glass.

In a puff of ash, the can vanished exactly like the men had on the tapes. It was gone, electrode and all. I slapped a hand over my mouth. There'd been no sound, no flickering of the lights. The can was just there one minute and gone the next.

Together, we jogged back into the platform room. I knelt where the can had been and trailed my fingers lightly over the platform's surface, but they came away clean.

"Holy shit," Dennis breathed. His wild gaze met mine, and his cheeks were flushed. "It just…zapped away."

Ryan gaped at the spot where the can had been, then turned and stared over at the time machine.

"Hey," Dennis said. "You okay, dude?"

Ryan nodded. His face blanched, causing the persistent stubble along his jaw to be darker than ever. "That could have been one of us."

"Good thing we used the beans."

"Wait." I slowly stood. "Did it work?"

"No idea."

"Can't we bring it back?"

Dennis nodded. "The instructions say we just alter the time on the machine then push the button again. I say we give it thirty minutes. Let it get cold enough."

"You sent it to the Arctic." I started for the door. "It can't take long."

"Right, but the coordinates and date we used are in late spring. Believe it or not, outside of winter, it can actually get a bit warm up there." Dennis jogged over to the machine and deleted the time his brother had entered. He stabbed the buttons, entering the same hour but thirty minutes later. Without a word, the three of us hurried back to the control panel to huddle around the big red button.

I stared through the windows at the empty platform, unable to get the sudden image of one of us vanishing in a puff of ash out of my head.

"All right." Dennis leaned over the controls again. "Let's see what happens."

He flipped a longer series of switches, pressed two small black buttons at once, then slapped the big red one again.

The three of us stared in at the empty platform, trying not to blink. Nothing happened for a few long seconds. Then, in a large puff of white mist, the can silently returned.

Gaping, I struggled to accept that we'd sent something back in time. I'd seen it, but even that just wasn't fully getting my brain to admit what we'd just done.

Dennis let out a whoop. He jogged through the metal doors with his brother close behind. I followed in a half-trance.

The brothers knelt next to the can of beans, pointing but not quite touching the surface, which was now coated in a light frost. Loose snow slipped from the electrode pad.

"It worked." A grin spread across Ryan's face. His cheeks were flushed red, and his eyes sparkled. It was as if life was finally returning to him; I hadn't seen him this excited since the first time we played a show for more than ten people. He and Dennis chuckled and high-fived.

"What in the hell is so funny?" I demanded. A low nausea wiggled at the pit of my stomach. "How do we know that it actually worked?"

This only made the Breckners laugh louder.

Dennis wiped at his eyes, still grinning. "Annie, look at the thing. It's half-frozen. There's *snow* on it. When's the last time you've seen snow?"

"I hate snow." I chewed my lower lip for a moment. "And that could just be the effect of the machine."

"None of the people in the videos we watched came back covered in snow."

"But it's been sitting here for God knows how long."

The two fell silent.

Ryan stared at the can. "Crap. She's right."

"We aren't scientists. It could be this cold for a number of reasons that we can't even begin to comprehend." I backed away from the platform, from the machine, shaking my head. "You were right, Ryan. We can't mess with this."

"Annie." Dennis grabbed my hand. "This thing is here for a reason. So are we. You said it before: there's a connection. We'll find it."

"And if we don't?"

"Then we don't use it again. Easy peasy."

I stared at the cold vapor rising from the can of beans. "I don't know…"

"I watched all of the tapes. The greens show nothing but success after success. We just happened to grab the shitty ones." Dennis gestured at the can. "Once they realized you can't go back to a time they already existed, they had zero casualties. I say we try it. The world is dead, guys, and our food is rotting. With this, we can go anywhere. At the very least, it's something to do."

"And you're willing to risk our lives based on what we've seen and read?" My heart thudded, hard and steady. "I don't know if I can. You saw what could happen if we fuck up."

"We can do it again," Dennis suggested. "Send something else back to see if we have different results at different coordinates."

"But we can't truly know that it went back in time. There's no proof. What if it just teleported instead?"

"Okay, fair enough." Dennis smiled. "No amount of testing on inanimate objects will prove that this machine is zapping things into the past."

I groaned, knowing exactly what he was going to say next.

Dennis hopped onto the platform next to the can of beans. "Send me back. I'm ready to get the hell out of this bunker. Stretch my legs. See some sights."

"No." Ryan's smile vanished. He turned to stare at me with eyebrows raised.

"I'm not touching that thing," I said, hands raised.

He scoffed and bent, pulling the electrode off the can of beans. "Dennis, get down from there. You're not going."

"The can came back fine. We watched the videos, studied the manual. Tons of others have done it without a problem. They perfected it. You saw the files, dude. Send me back." He bounced up and down on the balls of his feet and tugged down the sleeves of his hoodie.

Ryan stared hard at his brother, mouth turned down, brow furrowed.

"Guys. Seriously." Dennis hopped off the platform. "I'm going back in time. If this works, all we have to do is find coordinates for a tropical island in the nineteen hundreds and zap ourselves away from this God forsaken shit hole."

He sprinted out of the room.

I sighed, turning toward his brother. "He's not wrong."

"The danger outweighs the risk. I'm not sending him back, but I'll consider it if you take his place."

I grew very still and stared up at him. "Excuse me?"

"He's my little brother, Annie. I'm not losing the only family I have left." Ryan crossed his arms but wouldn't meet my angry gaze.

"So, I'm dispensable yet again." My anger heightened. I wanted to slap him, but my guilt flared; I totally understood his fear.

"Okay, I'm ready." Dennis reappeared wearing a dark grey parka and pulling on thick mittens. "Zap me to the Arctic."

I got another heated glare from Ryan. Swallowing my fear and ignoring my screaming inner voice, I lifted my chin. "I'll go."

Dennis slapped the electrode pad against his chest, below his neck. "Too late."

Ryan let out a low sound that was nearly a growl. I tried to think of what else I could do, but other than taking Dennis's place, there wasn't much.

"Dennis." I held out my hand. "Give me the coat. And the electrode."

"To quote my brother: 'absolutely not.' Guys, please." His eyes grew desperate. "I want to do this. I need to. I'm sick of sitting on my ass when I could be doing something that could save our lives. Come on."

I didn't look at Ryan but could sense his deep despair. I still wanted to help in some way, but all I could think of were the Franklin books, Goodsir's diary, the rolled maps back in the study.

An idea began to form. "Ryan," I said, "I think I know how to test this thing for real."

He looked up from the instruction manual with troubled, distracted eyes. I strode over to him and picked up *Franklin, Found*. The desolate frozen hell where Goodsir and the other men died was depicted in icy shades of blue and white on the cover. No life, animal or otherwise, roamed the snow-covered land. The sky, a toil of angry, dark clouds, gave the Arctic a menacing ambience.

"Dennis…" My heart increased its thudding rampage. Was I about to lose my best friend?

He zipped the parka, which was slightly too big on him, and pulled the hood up. "One of us has to step up. No more sitting around hoping things will get better. Ryan can't go because he's the doctor. Just let me do this. Please. For me. I'll be all right."

"We can't know that until it's too late."

"I want to do this, Annie. Sitting underground waiting to run out of food is not an option. We've found a way to fight this, so let's start fighting."

"Then let me go instead."

"Hell no." Dennis groaned. "I've already psyched myself up for this. Do you think I'm gonna give up the chance to time travel now that it's within my grasp? You're not going, and neither is Ryan, especially not with that leg of his."

I stared at him a beat, then sighed. "Ryan, I have different coordinates. As a test." I held up the Franklin book.

He stalked away. I followed him back to the E.M.S. 4500-AB.

Turning to the index, I scanned the page until I found the chapter I'd dog-eared. "Three men died long before the ships were lost." I kept my voice a low whisper so Dennis couldn't hear. "They were buried on a place called Beechey Island."

"And?"

"That was in 1846. Then in 1854 someone else died and was buried next to the three graves of Franklin's men."

"You want me to put Dennis back when there are only three graves."

I nodded. "To this day, there are still four graves. If we send him back to a specific time, before the fourth guy is buried, he'll only see three graves there, and we'll know the machine works."

Ryan leaned forward, propping himself up with his hands on either side of the machine. He stared at it in fury, his jaw clenching and moving back and forth. None of us spoke.

Eventually, he straightened and turned to look at me. He actually smiled "That's a damn good idea."

He took the book I held and spun it around so he could see the pages. After a few moments, he slowly entered the new coordinates and date.

"You okay?" I asked gently.

"I know we have to try this. I get it. We can't defeat the wraiths. I know this is our only choice right now."

"We don't *have* to. We could still try your idea, the indoor garden."

He shook his head. "I just…don't know if I can watch him do this."

"I know. I'm scared to death."

We both stared at Dennis in his oversized parka, white fur lining his face from the upturned hood. He struck a pose. "Now or never, guys."

Ryan strode forward and pulled his brother into a tight hug.

"What is this, a Midwest goodbye?" Dennis managed to choke out. "I'll be *fine*. Just don't leave me there in the cold. I have sensitive skin."

"The instructions say there's a mild discomfort at first." Ryan flipped a page of the instruction manual. "But it says it's only for a few seconds."

Dennis bounced on his feet. "Mild discomfort. Got it."

"Try to remember whatever you see, okay?" I hugged him as tightly as I could, trying hard not to let my fear show in my smile. He kissed my forehead and gave me a wink.

Ryan lingered by the platform. "Five minutes at the most."

"Go." Dennis leaned forward and shoved him away. "See you in five."

Ryan trudged out of the room. I trailed close behind, still gripping the Franklin book and glancing over my shoulder at a flushed but eager Dennis.

"This is all happening too fast." Ryan hesitated in front of the control panel. "What if he doesn't come back?" he asked quietly.

We stared at Dennis through the large window, comical in his oversized parka.

Ryan flipped the two starter switches.

"Guys?" Dennis called. "Do it. I'm starting to get some nasty back sweat."

Ryan's fingers hovered over the red button.

"Seriously, it's going down my ass."

Neither of us moved or spoke.

Dennis took a step forward. "If you don't send me back to the Arctic right now, I'm gonna come in there and—"

Ryan slapped the button.

Horrified, we watched Dennis shudder, blink twice, then hunch over. His mouth fell open. He gripped the front of the parka, fingers clawed and rigid.

In a burst of ash, he disappeared.

"Oh, God." I covered my mouth with both hands.

Ryan let out a guttural sound. He started to flip switches in the return order series, his movements frantic, but I lunged forward and stopped his hand from hitting the big red button again.

"Move, Annie," he snarled.

I pushed him back. "You have to go change the time on the machine, remember? If you bring him back now, you're just taking him from the second he arrived. We have to go in and change the time to five minutes later."

"Fuck you." He lunged for the controls again, but I blocked him.

"Dammit, you could seriously fuck this up if you don't follow the instructions!"

"He could be dead!" he yelled in my face. "You saw his face. He was in agony."

My confidence was quickly beginning to wane. I licked my lips. "The ash is normal. The pain is normal. What we saw looked just like it did in all those videos."

"And two of those trials ended with dead people!" Ryan shoved me aside and sprinted into the platform room. He ignored the spot where his brother had just vanished and ran to the machine.

Seconds later he was back at the control panel, breathing heavily. He flipped the final switch and slammed his palm down on the red button.

We stared through the window at the platform. Nothing happened for a few very long seconds. My heart skipped. I reached down and gripped Ryan's hand tightly. Then, just like the can of beans, Dennis was there again, returning in silence and white smoke.

Standing on the platform, his eyes distant and large, he clutched the front of his parka with tight fists. The hood had fallen off, and snowflakes slowly fell from his blond, wind-whipped hair. He let out a sudden breath and crumpled to the platform, shivering.

Ryan ran to his brother without a word, barely limping on his injured left leg. Through the windows, I watched them hug. I stood frozen and silent by the controls.

It worked. Dennis had gone to the Arctic and back in the span of mere seconds. But had he gone back in time?

I watched Ryan check his brother's vitals, his pupils, and pull him into another, fiercer hug. Dennis pulled free with mock irritation and discarded the coat, wiping melted snow from his neck. He left the platform room on shaky legs, assisted by a very shaken Ryan.

"It worked," Dennis breathed when he saw me in front of the bank of monitors. "I saw the Arctic. It's freaking huge."

Snapping out of my shock, I grabbed *Franklin, Found*, turning again to the Beechey Island page. "Tell me exactly what you saw, Dennis."

He shook his head in wonder. "It was beautiful. Terrifying. So big and open and *cold*."

"I'm taking you to the medical room." Ryan tugged on his brother, urging him forward. "I want to hear everything. It looked painful."

"Oh, hell yes, it was painful. 'Mild discomfort,' my ass. It felt like I was being shredded. Those damn instructions lie."

"Wait." I followed them with the open book in hand. "Did you see anything else?"

"Yeah." He briefly sagged against his brother. "Graves."

Ryan stopped moving and checked Dennis's pulse again. "How many graves?" he asked quietly.

"Three. The ground was covered in these loose stones. It was hard to walk but I tried to get closer so I could read the headstones."

"What did they say?" My hands shook so violently I nearly dropped the book.

"Hartnell. John Hartnell was the easy one to remember. Somebody named William. But I got zapped back before I could read the rest."

I flipped the book around to show the brothers an image of three small, narrow headstones, a faded name on each. "John Hartnell, John Torrington, and William Braine. They died while Franklin and his men were waiting out the winter at Beechey Island before the rest of the men vanished."

"Damn," Dennis breathed, eyeing the photo.

"Guys, I…don't think my brain accepted any of this until just now." I barked out a short laugh.

Dennis chuckled, shaking his head in amazement. "I can't believe it. The E.M.S Forty Hundred, er, I mean thousand." He shook his head. "Fuck it, I'm calling it the Zapper, and I can't believe it works."

He swayed and promptly passed out.

Twelve

Harry
1848

They ate Captain Crozier.

Almost all of him, right down to his very bones, which they sucked dry of marrow. He lasted them nearly a week. The cold kept his flesh frozen; Walker cooked it on one of our stoves each night before supper. After they finished with our captain, they dragged another dead man into a small tent for butchering.

Some of the other men and I survived off the rotting tins alone. Each time they brought me a plate of a friend, I refused to even look at it. At first, they found it comical, but when they realized I would rather die than eat it, things took a turn.

Walker and Morfin took turns threatening me, my family's safety should we ever return home again. I had no wife or children, but the inevitable horrific fates of my siblings and father were explained in great detail.

When they grew bored of verbal threats, they beat me. It did not matter. The weaker I became from starvation, the less pain bothered me. I could not fight back. I wanted to, but I was simply too weak.

Although my physical strength had begun to fade in the long weeks at the mutineers' camp, I was still able to keep my mind fresh. I recited cell theory notes from memory that

I'd made with my brother. I reiterated the basics of anatomy while trying to ignore the men being cut apart merely three tents away. I repeated lesser-known treatments for common ailments on the hour and counted my dwindling inventory of medications.

My refusal to comply enraged them, especially Morfin. He threatened to cut into my flesh, insinuating I didn't need all my fingers, my ears, my privates.

I was polishing my surgical instruments the night Morfin and Walker pushed into my medical tent. Both of their faces had regained color and they had begun to fill out again. They, along with the others partaking in cannibalism, no longer showed any signs of scurvy.

"Stand up," Morfin spat.

I slowly lowered my Liston knife and cloth and complied. He aimed a pistol at my right knee.

"Stop." Lt. Le Vesconte threw open my tent flap. "We can't survive without a doctor. The pair of you have lost any trace of humanity."

Walker didn't listen to him. He tilted his head to one side. "Which is why he needs to eat."

Morfin grinned. All his teeth had now fallen out. "He don't need both his legs, now do he?"

"I do." My voice somehow stayed steady, but my bladder nearly released at the sound of the pistol's hammer being cocked. "Any bullet wound would no doubt be fatal. I could try to operate on myself, but as I'd be quickly losing blood, there is no certainty I would survive."

To my great relief, Morfin lowered his weapon.

Lt. Le Vesconte threw his half-starved body forward. He collided into Morfin, who in turn fell into Walker. The three fell against my table. Freshly cleaned instruments scattered to the floor next to the men, who were struggling in a heap of swinging fists.

Morfin's right arm swung up in a tight arc. The blade of my Liston knife flashed; its tip was wet with crimson. Lt. Le Vesconte rolled away with a hand pressed against his belly.

"Enough." Walker took the knife and tossed it aside. It slid along the canvas floor of the medical tent and disappeared underneath the wooden instrument table.

Bleary-eyed, I went to Lt. Le Vesconte with a fresh cloth and gently dabbed a wound that was blessedly shallow.

Walker glared at me, shaking his head slowly for some time. "You're one lucky son of a bitch. I hope you know that. If you weren't th' only doctor here, I'd love nothin' more than to shoot you in th' face."

I didn't break eye contact. "If you let Morfin hurt or kill anyone else, you won't have enough men to haul."

He stepped out of the tent, but turned back, holding a flap aside and smiling. "We might need 'em all, but we don't need 'em entirely whole. Men can still haul minus their teeth and fingers. And that'll be on you, Goodsir."

Walker's footsteps crunched away. Morfin pulled Lt. Le Vesconte out of the tent shortly after I bandaged the knife wound. I was left alone with my bleary thoughts of despair and hopelessness. Weak with hunger, I returned to my own, smaller tent to lay fully dressed on my bed pad, huddled and shivering.

Drifting, I dreamt of the stringy seagull meat that had been brought to me three days prior. Even those few bites of fresh meat had slightly reversed my own scurvy.

I didn't even hear the shots that felled a small white bear cub. It wasn't until Sergeant Tozer, now looking healthier than ever, shoved quickly cooked meat under my nose that I roused enough to eat.

The moment food touched my tongue, I devoured all bites offered despite my clenching stomach.

"I snuck you this food." He watched me eat. "They said they'd only give you the stomach contents, but I snatched some meat away and cooked it after they all turned in fer th' night."

The meat he' brought was fatty and chewy, more delicious than anything I'd ever tasted. Life sprung back through me and roused my senses.

"Thank you, Dr. Goodsir," Tozer said to me as I ravenously chewed the last few bites. "For the medicine you gave me last week."

I said nothing.

"My cough is all but gone now. An' I stopped bleedin' from the gums."

"That's largely due to your diet. Not me." I glared at him above my final bite of bear.

He didn't reply, only smiled, stood, and walked out of my tent, his dirt-smeared red uniform still bright in the fading light of dusk.

After finishing the first fresh meal I'd eaten in many long months, I licked the flat, metal plate clean and lay back on my sleeping pad, pulling the blankets up to my neck. I tried to block out the bulges of rock beneath the furs, tried to ignore the steady, constantly throbbing ache in my upper jaw.

Hours passed. Sleep would not come, but I didn't mind. I rested a hand on my stomach, which gurgled softly as it digested. Twice, cramps of nausea threatened to bring the meat back up but I fought them by tightly curling into the fetal position and clenching my fists.

A tugging settled in my chest. I rubbed my breastbone. It took a few long seconds for me to recognize the pain for what it was.

A demon was near.

"Mr. Goodsir?"

The voice startled me. "What is it?"

My tent flap opened to reveal a calm Sargant Tozer. The metal of his rifle glinted in the meager light of his lantern. "I need your thoughts on somethin', if you will."

I shoved off my blankets, wary. The ache in my joints had gone, and I no longer tasted blood, but what I truly needed was rest. I needed to stop living in fear. I needed warmth.

I needed to go home.

Darkness had fallen long ago. It shrouded the camp and pressed all around us. I said nothing as Sergeant Tozer led me to the edge of our camp.

This was it. I was to be executed and carved up as the men's next meal. My eyes would barely stay open; I was too tired to care. Let them kill me, then.

The pain in my chest surged again, harder. I tipped forward, nearly falling.

"I didn't raise th' alarm," Tozer whispered. "It's just been standin' there. Watchin' us."

Suddenly alert, I froze, glancing in the direction he pointed. There, barely visible in the distance, stood a demon.

My first instinct was to run, but Tozer held me back. The Sergeant was right; it was just standing motionless.

I gasped weakly, clutching the front of my long coat where my pain pulsated again.

"It could attack at any moment." I took another step back. "We need to wake the men."

"And do what?"

"What do you mean, 'do what?' We must kill it!"

Tozer shifted his rifle, balancing it back on his shoulder, the barrel pointed to the black sky. He watched the demon thoughtfully. "I think it's just watching us."

"Watching us? Have they done that before?"

"No. Maybe they were protectin' somethin' back by the ships. That could be why they didn't follow once we left."

"Yet here one is." I frowned. Curiosity joined my fear. We both stood watching the demon, and it watched us. Another surge of pain shot through my chest.

Without knowing what I was doing, I mentally reached down inside myself and pushed. Something flared, a new sensation. The pain lessened the more I focused.

I pushed more forcefully, hoping to rid myself of the pressure entirely. This time, the demon shuddered, turned, and left.

Chills rippled along my arms and the back of my neck.

"Interestin'." Tozer sighed. He truly did look healthier, but his eyes still reflected how his constant struggle to live had nearly defeated him. He, like nearly all the other men, had given up on everything other than pure survival. "Well, it either kills us or we all kill each other. Don't think it matters no more, do ya?"

I stared out into the darkness where the demon had stood moments ago. All remained dark and quiet.

"What do you think they are, doctor? The demons?"

I thought for a moment. "Do you remember when we took a wrong turn on our voyage attempting to reach Disko Bay?"

"Aye. The men was haulin' supplies all from mornin' til dinnertime, but you and Lt. Fairholme ended up at that Inuit camp."

"I was able to speak to the natives at length. I started a dictionary of sorts."

Tozer gestured for me to follow him, his fingertips dotted black with frostbite. "I remember the lieutenant talkin' about that. Said you were beside yourself with wonder."

I pushed both hands beneath my armpits for warmth and glanced over my shoulder, but the demon hadn't returned. "They taught me many words of their language. I remember one I could not understand, a word that they were unable to describe. Perhaps they spoke of the demons. Perhaps they tried to warn us."

Tozer was silent for a moment as we picked our way back to my tent. We walked in silence, our boots crunching and slipping on the icy shale stones beneath.

"It's makin' sure we leave, then," he said finally. "A scout, like. Only thing that makes sense, why it didn't attack jus' now."

I thought of how I'd mentally fought the pain in my chest. Moments later, the demon had left. Too weary to even start to put all the pieces together, I simply continued to stare out at the night.

"How could you eat the flesh of our friends?" I asked quietly. "Of our captain?"

"Only way to survive," was all the Marine said.

"You have all lost your morals."

"Or our minds." The dead stare he fixed me with chilled me worse than the frigid air around us, worse than the sight of any demon.

I took a small step away from him.

"We tried to only take the weakest," he said. "We subdued them, but the captain, he was havin' none of it. Even though he knew the sick were jus' dead weight, that we'd have made safety by now without them, but he still fought like hell. Left us no choice in th' end. We're all jus' tryin' to live, Goodsir. To see our families. Don't you want to go home?"

The pain in my chest was gone, as was the strange new sensation I'd felt before the demon had left. I blinked, eyes heavy with exhaustion, my vision clouding.

"Goodnight, Mr. Tozer." I turned away.

It wasn't until I was inside my tent when he spoke again in a whisper. "Maybe it's them demons what's bringing the crazy to our minds."

I curled up on my little bed pad with a heavy sigh, crying out softly when cold air touched my still painful upper tooth. Clamping my mouth shut, I curled on my side, putting my back to the tent flap. My eyes and mind were heavier than they had ever been. Tozer's last words echoed through my mind on an endless loop.

What on earth could I possibly do? The mutinous men in the camp outweighed those who refused to cannibalize. We could not flee for fear of being shot down. Only one small glimmer of hope stayed alight in my mind: that our camp lay in Captain Fitzjames's southward path to Fort Resolution, where he and Captain Crozier had planned to rejoin. Even then, they would approach as comrades, with their guards lowered. I asked myself once again: what could I do?

Fatigue finally took me. I drifted quickly despite the bone-aching cold. I dreamt of nothing.

A crushing pressure in my chest tore me from my sleep. Moaning softly, I clenched my fists. My tent flap rustled and was pulled aside.

"Mr. Tozer, please," I mumbled. "I'm exhausted."

A loud snapping sounded behind me, like a bone breaking. My breath tightened. I tried to look back toward my tent's entrance but was unable to move.

A quick series of cracks and pops sounded, right behind me. Something shifted along the tent's floor. More popping, then a thud. The pain in my chest was pulsating, flaring quicker than ever before, leaving me breathless.

These were my final moments. I knew now how I was to die, knew what would end me. Not illness. Not mutinous, murderous men.

A demon was in my tent.

I scrambled off my pad, flinging blankets and furs. I lunged, reaching for my medical kit, mind focused on the bone saw or knife or any other sharp item I could get my cold fingers around. Before I could touch the case, something grabbed my shoulder and pushed me to the ground.

One of the ice demons towered above me, hunched over on all fours to fit in the small space. My shoulder burned deathly cold where it had touched me, despite the layers of clothing I wore.

The demon's skin – if that's what it was – truly was made of ice. Steam twirled lazily from its shoulders and long, narrow head, vanishing in the frigid air above. I stared at its face, or where I assumed its face to be, as it had no true unique definition. There were no eyes, just vertical grooves all along its head and body. It looked for all the world like a mobile tree made of ice.

It did, however, have a gaping maw full of jagged teeth.

My heart skipped, then slammed into my chest. Gasping, I attempted to call for help, but nothing came out. I tried to scramble back up only to fall again.

The creature reached out a long-fingered hand toward me. I shook my head, pushing myself backward, although there was nowhere in the tent for me to hide, no other exit for me to flee through.

In desperation, I reached inward once more. I didn't know why or how, but I again felt the calm, spreading sensation flood my core. Frantic, I tried harder.

The pain in my chest disappeared, but the pressure grew tighter. My body relaxed fully; I lost any control I had. My head tipped, and my eyes rolled skyward. My back arched. Frigid cold wind flew past me and seemingly through me, *into* me. It stretched on for an eternity of what may have only been seconds, and then I fell forward, collapsing onto my hands and knees, panting heavily.

Pushing myself up, I looked wildly around, but the demon was gone. I was alone in the tent.

My insides were frozen. It was the strangest feeling, quite like swallowing a piece of ice that wouldn't melt. Yet I did not shiver. For the first time in three long years, I was not cold.

Something moved inside my core.

I cried out in shock, my voice broken and harsh. I felt all along my torso, my neck, and my face, but I found nothing, no protrusion or open wound.

My vision, too, was strange. Everything I looked at held a harsh, bluish tint. Scrambling over to my wooden chest, I dug through my belongings, grazing the side of my wrist on a broken chunk of glass in the process.

I felt no pain from the shallow wound. A small crimson drop formed. It trickled down my palm to drip onto the canvas floor. I reached back into my case and fished out my small mirror.

My normally green eyes now shone an icy pale blue.

I dropped the mirror and fell heavily onto my backside. Sitting on the floor of my tent, my mind continuously refused to accept the only logical explanation: that the demon had somehow gotten inside my body. Or that I had absorbed it.

Horrified and confused, I tentatively reached inward again. My stomach lurched as the sensation of something moving inside my core came again, stronger this time, as if trying to claw its way out of me. I lurched upward on shaking knees and stumbled out of my tent.

Sergeant Tozer glanced in my direction. I weakly gestured at my trousers, indicating the need to urinate. He turned his back on me, staring out into the night once more.

Nearly vomiting, I stumbled around my tent. Once hidden from the three men on watch duty, I collapsed forward. The ice didn't freeze the bare skin of my hands. Sweat beaded on my forehead and trickled down my face without freezing.

The thing inside me lurched. My vision swam, and I began to tremble.

Reaching inside myself, I tried to push out instead. The thing in me cowered and shrank. I rose to my knees and mentally shoved the fullness in my core out as hard as I could.

The frigid air blew past me again, but this time, it shot out, away from me. Something drained from my body, from my chest, in a gust of wind so cold I nearly passed out.

Moments later, I was myself again. I opened my eyes. The ice demon loomed above me.

I lay flat on my back and just stared at it.

The demon took a step closer. It reached a clawed hand toward me, so I reached inside and shoved outward once more.

It stared at me with its featureless face. It took three slow steps backward, then turned and fled into the night with loud strides, moving much faster than I could comprehend.

I wrapped my violently shaking arms around myself and gasped for breath, wincing again as the frozen air took its toll. Clad only in two layers and my naval coat, I was wildly exposed. I tried to stand but fell repeatedly. I tried to shout but it felt as if my throat had closed.

My consciousness quickly began to fade just as footsteps sounded. Rough hands grabbed me. A loud voice shouted for help, and then all went dark.

Thirteen

Annie
2020

I sprinted barefoot out of my little bedroom in the bunker, passing the tally-marked wall before turning into the dining room. Mind racing, I ordered my heart to chill out. It had begun to pound the moment I had finished reading the last entry in Goodsir's diary.

I knew what we were supposed to do now. The puzzle pieces all fit. The open, not-so-impossible door loomed tall before me, but I didn't hear Ryan and Dennis's argument until I pulled open the study's door to the control room.

"I don't care," Ryan shouted, waving his yellow-handled screwdriver. "I want it taken apart."

Dennis stood before the door to the platform room. His arms were crossed tightly across his chest and he stared up into his brother's face with a calm stubbornness. "No. We need it."

"You were out for almost a full day. We have no way of sending all three of us somewhere, so using the machine to get out of here won't work. There's gotta be another way to survive. Some way to fight the wraiths and move outside undetected. Anything other than this terrifying machine that might just kill us in the blink of an eye."

Dennis didn't move.

"If you won't disassemble it," Ryan nearly shouted, "then you're forcing me to break it. I don't want to go that route, but I will."

"You wouldn't dare. It wasn't that bad. I was exhausted, yeah, but that's it. I didn't turn inside out, and I didn't die."

"Hey." I strode over and stood behind Ryan, clutching the journal. They ignored me.

"It doesn't matter." Ryan tried to shoulder past his brother. "One wrong move or flip of a switch…"

Dennis stood his ground. "This is the only way. Hell, what if Mom used it? Maybe that's why she wasn't here when we arrived. What if she's trapped somewhere?"

"This isn't a damned movie!"

Before Ryan could shove Dennis again, I quickly jumped in. "I found something."

Ryan shot me an irritated look over one shoulder. "What?" he growled.

I handed the book over, open to the page detailing what I'd discovered. Dennis grabbed the journal and began to read but didn't move away from the door. His lips moved while he skimmed through Goodsir's careful handwriting. Ryan tilted his head to one side, reading upside down. It was clear when they got to the end, as both of their faces went slack.

"Wait…what the hell?" Dennis closed the journal and turned it over in his hands, inspecting both the front and back covers.

"This is proof he's an Evo, and a damned powerful one."

Dennis pulled the copy of Goodsir's photo, which I'd been using as a bookmark, from between two back pages. He peered at the slightly blurred image.

Ryan scratched the side of his jaw. I could see the gears in his brain turning; his eyes stared into the distance and flicked back and forth.

I eagerly voiced what had formed in my mind earlier. "What if he can do the same thing to the wraiths?"

"Could. He's long dead."

I shot him an exasperated look.

"No." Ryan shook his head. "Absolutely not. One hundred percent no."

Dennis chuckled. "You want to bring him here. I love it."

"All the more reason to destroy the damn machine now." Ryan pushed past Dennis, still brandishing the screwdriver.

"Stop." I grabbed his shoulder and pulled him back. "Just hear me out. You were considering it yourself just now, I saw it in your eyes."

Defiance flickered over Ryan's face. "Sure. Doesn't mean anything."

"He could use his power on the wraiths."

Ryan stared at me. "I'm not bringing him here. I've thought about what you said, how we could save his life. But Annie, his remains were still discovered, right?"

"Yeah."

"If we brought him or any of the other men here, then their bodies aren't ever found, and that *is* messing with history. If we went through with this insane plan, he'd have to go back. He'd have to still die in the Arctic."

"But…" Shit, I hadn't thought of that. "Couldn't it be any of the men they found?"

He raised his eyebrows. "So now we either bring a man here to help us, then send him back to die, or we keep him one hundred and seventy-two years in the future and what? Plant a different guy's dead body in his place?"

"No." I shook my head. "I say keep him here. I found no evidence that his remains did anything other than help shed some light on how he may have died. Other bodies have been found, too, and they've found the ships. Ryan, this is our only chance. He could help us."

"How? He trapped a single demon. All of this could also be hallucination, you realize. This Goodsir of yours could have just been batshit crazy."

"He isn't," I said fiercely.

"Why are you so adamant to save his life, Annie? What if he wants to save the rest of the men, like you mentioned when we found the thing? We have weak-ass medicine and barely enough to keep us going for much longer before it's not safe to use. And there were, what, over a hundred men that died on that expedition. Sure, I agree, he might be able to help us if his demon absorbing is real. But can he even control it? And what do we do with him after? That is, if we all survive."

I inhaled slowly. "We have no other options. We're trapped in a dead world. To go outside means we'll be slaughtered. To stay here means we starve to death. You fuckin' pick. What fate do you want for all of us?"

Dennis's lips twitched. "Oh, my God."

His brother glared down at me with nothing short of fury. The three of us stood in a close-knit triangle, not speaking. Dennis flipped slowly through the journal. I refused to break eye-contact with Ryan.

"We just go back with two of those little electrode things," Dennis said quietly. "Slap one on him before time's up, and bam! 1848 to 2020 in a super excruciating instant."

Ryan's eyes widened. I made a sharp kill gesture across my throat with one finger.

"Not sorry, Annie." Dennis shrugged. "It hurt like hell, and I won't lie about it."

"Despite the split second of pain," I said, "yes, we bring Goodsir here."

"You're insane." Ryan stalked away, throwing the screwdriver to the concrete ground.

Dennis blinked, looking up at me with hesitation. "He's right, though. I mean, even if this worked, what would he do once he saved the world as we know it? If we put him back somewhere safe in the eighteen hundreds, he'd know way too much. He could, like, invent something someone else was supposed to, and mess up the timeline that way."

Ryan nodded, rubbing the back of his neck. "And that is why he'd have to go back to the Arctic after saving us. To die an excruciating death. I couldn't do that to anyone, and I know you couldn't either, Annie."

"Agreed. We keep him here."

"We are not bringing Harry Goodsir out of the past to live in our time. We have no clue what we're doing as it is, and you want to bring a half-starved, disease-riddled, possibly crazy person into our home? Forget it."

"You know." I scowled at him. "I'm getting really sick of this. We've seen the machine work. We've come up with a plan that might stop the wraiths and maybe even get rid of them. And here you are, telling us no yet again."

"How can you not understand the raw power we have at our hands? This thing could kill us or wipe our existence from time itself. How does that not terrify you?"

"What the hell is the difference between going out or going back to survive, Ryan? We die either way, and I for one am not fucking staying down here to starve to death!" I tossed the diary onto the table and got in his face.

He took a step back. "Things may seem black and white now, but there has to be another way. Something else we haven't thought of yet."

Dennis picked up Goodsir's journal. "Look, I get that you're concerned, but she's right. We die regardless. Why can't you ever take a chance? This can work."

"Of course. My fault again." Ryan rounded on his brother. "Will you back off? I'm trying to remain sensible and keep us alive."

"No, we just proved that your option to not do this will end in our slow deaths. I don't want to starve to death either. Or go get carved up for wraith dinner."

"All three options mean we could die!"

I dug my fingers into my hair and squeezed my eyes tight. "Both of you just shut the fuck *up!*"

They fell silent and stared at me.

"You said it yourself." I jabbed a finger into Ryan's chest. "More supply runs won't matter because the canned food will be rotten. We can't build a garden outside because the wraiths suck the life out of everything."

"We have seeds. Grow lamps." Ryan held his hands out toward me in a placating gesture.

"Yet we still need dirt, usable dirt, not the crap outside. Fertilizer, tools – all of which are heavy and would require going outside many times to lug these things for miles. And *if* that actually works, *if* we're not slaughtered in the process, the seeds actually have to take."

"Yep," Dennis muttered, hands in his pockets.

"Want me to keep going?" My voice rose higher, louder, echoing through the control room. "Soon, we're going to run out of propane. Yes, we can loot the tanks from houses that kept a couple on hand for their grills, but when those are gone? Then what?"

"And those tanks are heavy." Dennis chewed a thumb nail. "Forty, fifty pounds each at least. With only two of us out on runs, it'll be impossible to get more than a couple back here safely. *If* we get them back here; carrying those is super slow going. Add a few more pounds each of other things in your packs and…well, we'll get our asses killed out there."

His brother dropped into one of the rolling chairs, silent. Desperation and fear slowly replaced the anger that had shone in his eyes.

I reached out and lightly touched his arm, forcing myself to speak quieter. "No fuel, no power. We can't cook, and the air will stop recycling. Come on. Think about this."

"I know." Ryan dropped his head into his hands. "This is the only safe place. It's the only control we have, that *I* have. We've been able to maintain this sanctuary longer than I had ever hoped, and now it's all crashing down around us. It's happening too fast."

"Look, you've done an amazing job protecting us all down here, but this part of our lives is over. No one is coming to save us. At least, not from the world out there."

I knelt down next to his chair. "If we could figure out a way to contain or kill the wraiths, Goodsir could use his power to help us trap them for good, and then could safely go outside again. Find a new place to live. We could build acres of gardens."

"He's only fought one demon. There are *tons* of wraiths out there. Even if he was able to get a good chunk of them, just what the hell are we supposed to do then, exactly?"

I hesitated. "What if we seal them all in the platform room? We know they can't go through walls; otherwise they would have gotten down here long ago, and these metal doors are airtight. I vote Goodsir draws the wraiths in and releases them behind the impossible door, and we lock the fucks in."

The brothers shared a hopeful look.

"It's a shaky plan, I know." I ran a thumb over the diary's cover. "But we have to decide."

Ryan sighed and crossed his arms. "Even if this works, if we're able to bring this Goodsir here, how are we supposed to convince him to help us? He's going to freak out. With all that he's been through already, his mind could be so far gone that this pushes him over the edge. Even if it doesn't, he could just tell us to fuck off."

"He won't. He's a good person."

Dennis chuckled. "So, he's a good sir…is that what you're saying?"

"Cute." Tension fled from my shoulders. "So, are we going to go save him or what?"

Fourteen

Harry
1848

A shapeshifting man with a mutilated face vividly haunted my dreams. His black, soulless eyes watched me wherever I went, and no matter how many times I cowered away, he was there in front of me. His smile split his face in two and bared teeth that ended in clawed hands. They reached for me, stretching, twisting. I stumbled back just as the many fingers brushed my shoulder.

"Dr. Goodsir?" A strange, soft voice, sudden in the Arctic silence, tore me from sleep in an instant. I inhaled sharply and rolled away, bringing my hands up to defend my face.

In the flickering light of the oil lamp, I locked my gaze with wide green eyes set in a face surrounded by a fur hood. At once, I knew I must still be dreaming, as I was staring at a woman.

Her soft features bore none of the signs of a hard life in the Arctic. Light from my oil lamp glinted off her copper red hair. I sighed and massaged my forehead.

"Dr. Goodsir, please. I need you to come with me." She knelt next to my bed pad, not taking her eyes from mine.

I chuckled. She reached toward me again. The moment her fingers touched my arm, doubt began to trail through my thoughts. Studying the woman's terrified face, sensing her warmth, hearing the quick breaths she inhaled, all told me I was very much awake.

"Who—" I began, but she shushed me, putting her hand close to my mouth.

"Shh. Please, not so loud." She turned a frantic glance at the entrance still darkened by the night.

I brought my blankets up to my chin. My thick beard tickled the backs of my fingers. I glanced behind her, but she was alone.

"Who are you?" I whispered as loudly as I dared. "How did you get into this camp?"

"Please," she said again. "I'm here to help you."

I stared at her, fighting the urge to shout. I lowered my hands. She sank further to the ground and sat.

My body went slack. I looked down at my hands, clad in my old fingerless work gloves. "I've died, haven't I?"

"I…no. No." Her cheeks were beginning to flush from the cold. She leaned closer to me, keeping her gaze direct and her voice soft. "Dr. Goodsir, I want to help you."

"Help me?"

"Yes." She pushed back her hood. Light freckles dotted her pale skin.

I let out a sigh and rubbed my eyes, sitting up. "I thought of doing it myself, you ken. I've thought about it just tonight, even. Where are we to go? Heaven, I pray."

"I'm so, so sorry," she whispered. "For everything you've gone through. But you're very much alive, and we're getting you out of here."

Frowning, I considered her words, the truth of them. If I had been dead, my tooth would not still be aching. Hunger would not be currently pulling my insides apart.

Her coat was of strange material and design, its color a deep purple, with an odd metal strip slicing down the front in place of buttons. The woman inside had begun to shiver in the flickering light, her lower lip trembling, further proof this was all real: angels would not feel the cold.

More clarity came to my sleep-addled mind. "Your accent. It's American."

She tipped backward as I stood. I hadn't meant to startle her, but her face filled with fear, and what color in her cheeks quickly drained. She scrambled away and stood. I took a step back, my boots flattening the furs I'd used as a pillow.

"Who are you? I whispered, confused yet still on full alert. "Help me understand. I will not shout. Most men in this camp are my enemies."

"I...I was sent here to take you out of this place. To take you somewhere safe."

Shaking my head, I flexed my half-numb fingers. "What for? Why me? What about the other men?"

Her face took on a pained expression. "They did horrible things."

I felt my face twitch. "They are good men hindered by the desperation."

She glanced again at the flap of my tent. Circling around, she took in the meager bottles of medication and my surgical tools. She did not answer.

"Where would we go?" I pressed. "How are we to even leave without being apprehended?"

She lightly touched her chest. There was slight panic in her eyes. "We must hurry. There isn't much time left. I'll get you out of here and then can explain everything. Is that all right?"

I sighed heavily. "Either I am dead, or about to be. I have no way of returning home. The men will turn on each other again soon, of that I am sure. I have nothing to lose at the moment, so I see no reason to refuse."

She smiled then and lifted her chin slightly. "I promise you will be safe with me, Dr. Goodsir."

I ran a hand through my hair. "Give me a moment to gather my things."

I picked up my long coat, fingers grazing the cold golden buttons along the front, and slipped my arms inside. My cold weather slops followed; I pulled the bulky things on with increasing speed.

The woman touched my arm just as I fetched my scarf and knit cap. My movements stilled.

"You won't need anything else. Please, trust me."

I stared deep into her eyes. She gazed back up at me with what looked like slight wonder or awe, as if she looked upon something large and immaculate instead of a nearly starved Scottish man on the brink of death.

She offered her hand. After a moment's hesitation, I took it. I didn't resist when she pulled me a few steps closer, or when she placed a small, round pad from her pocket to the side of my neck. I fingered the strange cord that ran down from its center, trying to discern its material.

"Just hold still, Dr. Goodsir." She smiled up at me in relief. "We'll be out of here any minute now."

I gave up trying to understand. She was not making sense, but I stood still regardless. We waited.

Footsteps sounded outside my tent.

The sound grew louder, crunching along the stones and ice. I could just barely make out the low sound of a man's mutterings.

The woman pushed me behind her, standing between me and the tent opening. Her body went rigid. "Come on, come on."

I shut my eyes, accepting whatever fate would follow.

The footsteps grew closer still. A hand pulled aside the flap of my tent. Sergeant Tozer stared in at us. "What the bloody hell…?"

My entire body began to burn, an agony greater than any I'd felt before. I tried to scream but no longer had a voice. I could not move, could only endure the great waves of pain. And then, nothing.

Fifteen

Harry
2020

I came back to consciousness with a sudden stab of pain. It spread until I burned alive, my entire body consumed with raging flames I could not see. My stomach lurched. The muscles in my tightly clenched shoulders began to spasm, and still, I could not scream. No breath would pass my lips.

Despite my efforts of being a good man in my short years, a demon, or perhaps the devil himself, had tricked me. Now, I was being dragged down to Hell, to be trapped beneath all creation, to suffer for eternity.

A dull ache in my face brought a brief moment of clarity to my pain-riddled mind. I hesitated, then flexed my jaw. My fingers twitched. The horrific fire in my body died in a single and sudden breath.

I gasped deep, finally filling my lungs with air that didn't chill my lungs. Warmth graced my skin. I blinked until my vision cleared and looked about a narrow, dimly lit room.

Instead of the treacherous stones beneath my boots, I now stood on a flat, small, wooden platform. Walls painted white surrounded me in light that shone steadily from a few round points in a grey ceiling nearly as low as those of *Erebus* and *Terror*.

I stepped away on weak legs and nearly stumbled off the platform. The floor beneath it held an unnatural shine.

"Where?" I looked up, focusing on the woman who stood nearby, blinking against the glare.

"It's all right." Her eyes were glazed and unfocused. She gripped the sleeve of my slops with trembling hands.

"Where are we?" The thud of my heart shook my words. I pulled out of her grasp, wanting to flee, but was too shaken and confused to do so.

"You're safe." She shrugged out of her large coat, tossing it to the grey floor that stretched throughout the room. "It's warm here. And we have food."

"Food?" I eyed her. "What trickery is this?"

She shook her head and stared at me with pleading eyes. "No, please. I want to help you."

I touched the side of my face, flexed my hands, swallowed and licked my dry lips. Was this Hell or was this real? "How did we leave the camp?"

She made no further attempt to approach me. "I know you're scared, but I had very little time to explain before we left. Please know we're here to help you, all right?"

"We?" I looked up, peering into the dimness surrounding us. My appendages tingled as they began to warm. I took off both layers of gloves, massaging my fingers and gently breathing on them. Peering past the red-haired woman, I stared at a short stack of odd shelves along the far wall with blinking lights at its center. The light from above reflected off large windows set into a wall to my left, creating a glare my gaze could not penetrate.

"My friends and I." She looked at me as if I were a caged animal that had just escaped. "My name's Annie Ross."

My eyes narrowed. "Friends?"

At my tone she took a step back and held up her now bare hands. "Dr. Goodsir. It's okay."

I could feel how wide my eyes were. I stepped off the little platform. The only exit I could see was a tall door on the far left. Sweat trickled down the back of my neck. I yanked off my Welsh wig and threw it aside. My breaths were quick and irregular. I felt trapped, cornered.

"Ryan?" The woman kept her eyes on me. "A little help?"

The door opened. I flinched downward and threw my hands high.

A tall man with mussed brown hair and a square jaw stood in the open frame. He smiled, but his lips were pursed tight, and his body was clearly tensed, as if poised to run. After a moment he awkwardly clasped his hands before him.

"Where am I?" Panic cracked my words.

"It's all right." The man stayed by the door. "I'm a medical professional. I hear you are as well."

I straightened reluctantly, swallowing and nodding. "How do you know me?"

"We've heard of your work, Dr. Goodsir. You've had quite the impressive career."

I said nothing. I desperately wanted to pull off my slops.

"My name is Ryan Breckner. My colleagues and I, we've discovered a way to…" He gestured in the air. "Move to and from a place quickly."

"We learned of Franklin's lost voyage," the woman cut in. "Of what you went through. We wanted to help you."

I licked my chapped lips. "So, I am not dead?"

Mr. Breckner let out a soft chuckle. "No. Not in the least."

I didn't know whether to be relieved or full of despair.

"Like Annie was saying, we have food. And medications to make you feel better. Will you let us help you?"

I glanced back at Annie, who was unashamedly shedding layers of clothing. I tried not to stare at her strange attire. Her wrinkled white shirt revealed more than anything I'd seen a woman wear in public; its neckline cut downward at a harsh angle to show a large circular white pad adhered to her skin. She wore loose men's trousers, much like what Mr. Breckner had on, but of a design I had never seen. My face flushed hot and I turned away from her attire, but not before she smiled at me, a graceful upturn of her pink lips. I stared down at the strange sheen of the floor beneath my black, scuffed boots.

"We can answer your questions soon, Dr. Goodsir." Mr. Breckner casually stepped into the room. He scratched the dark stubble along his jaw and looked me over. "But if you'll excuse my language, you look like shit, and I'd really like to get you some medicine."

My mind flew through half-thoughts and grappled with the urge to run. There was nowhere to go, however; that much was clear.

I gave in. My shoulders slumped. I let my hands hang slack and limp. I nodded and made no move to fight or flee as the two strangers carefully helped me out of my slops.

Annie peeled off the strange, flat object from my neck. I instinctively reached for it, curiosity outweighing all else, but Mr. Breckner gently turned me toward the door.

"Let's get to the medical room."

"I'll be right in." Annie stepped over her discarded coat and hurried over to the blinking lights, peeling off her own white pad from her skin.

Mr. Breckner kept talking, trying to solidify eye contact with me, but I just stared at my boots. We emerged into a larger room with a conspicuous mound of sharp angles hidden beneath large blankets. Too tired to care what it was, I just trudged along.

When we entered a small study, Mr. Breckner hurried me past things I would have normally stopped to inspect. I tried to mentally keep track of directions but as fatigued as I was I could not track even the simplest route. My eyes burned with exhaustion, my jaw ached, and my muscles twitched on their own.

I let Mr. Breckner weave me through a strange kitchen, a large room with round tables, and into a long hallway. My gaze traveled over many foreign objects, but the only thing that gave me pause was a wall covered in tally marks.

He cleared his throat, guiding me away to the left and into a stark white room. It was full of the most advanced tools I had ever seen, and I yearned to go to them, to pick them up. Instead, I was led to a long, metal table stretched to the left. I let Mr. Breckner pull off my long coat and shirt, and then lowered myself onto the metal surface.

After pulling on light blue skin-tight gloves, Mr. Breckner examined my chest using a stethoscope with a long, thin tube I hadn't seen before. I watched his motions through bleary eyes. I attempted to breathe deeply and let out a weak cough.

"Your heart is strong." Mr. Breckner's accent matched Annie's, full of flat vowels and with barely a cadence. He moved the head of the stethoscope around to my back, slipping his hand beneath my wool layers, apologizing for the cold metal against my bare skin.

"Where…?" My voice came out croaked and shattered. I swallowed and tried again. "Where am I?"

Mr. Breckner's brown eyes were kind, his smile gentle. "You're in Nevada. In the United States."

I stared at him. "How is that possible?"

"We'll explain everything soon. I'm sorry, Mr. Goodsir, but you very nearly died. You look like you're about to pass out. Let me get meds in you first, okay? The healthier you are, the easier it will be for us to hold conversation, especially one so important."

The always present ache of hunger nearly doubled me over. "Do you have anything to eat, doctor?"

Mr. Breckner nodded. "We do. Canned vegetables and meats, mostly. My brother's bringing you some. And I'm not a doctor, just a nurse."

I almost laughed; I often uttered a nearly identical phrase during the time after our ships were ice locked. Men had resorted to calling me doctor after our chief surgeon, Steven Stanley, had met a brutal end.

A surge of nausea low in my belly came at the thought of tinned food. "Do you happen to have anything to combat scurvy? Some fresh game, perhaps, or lemon juice?"

"Sadly, that's much too hard to come by at the moment." Mr. Breckner straightened. He gathered some of the skin on my arm between his thumb and forefinger. "Right now, though, you need fluids, a small meal, and some rest."

Sleep sounded like a heavenly dream. My eyes drooped and I swayed on the cold exam table.

Mr. Breckner steadied me. He felt my biceps, then lifted my arms. "Your muscles are only slightly atrophied. How long were you without food?"

I stared at his gloves. "We'd survived mostly on stale ship's biscuits in the last few weeks. When those ran out…we tried to find fresh game, but it was few and far between."

"Anything else?"

"We ate from the Goldner tins. Half were rotten. Inedible. We survived on those alone for many months after the salt pork was gone."

Mr. Breckner took a step away, halting his examination of my finger joints. "When was the last full meal you've eaten?"

Just the talk of food made my stomach snarl. My mouth watered and I swayed again. "The men shot a bear a while ago, but…I am not even sure what day it is."

Mr. Breckner nodded and resumed his examination. His fingers prodded down along my spine. "Don't worry. We'll get you something to eat soon."

"I'm very tired."

"I know. I have plenty of medication to give you. It should help, but I need to check your vitals first."

"I feel like I have not slept for months."

"I can imagine. Open wide." Mr. Breckner peered into my mouth and down my throat with a curious metal object that shone bright at one end.

"What is that, sir?"

"Please stay open. Do you have a wound? Bite yourself, perhaps? There's blood along your gums."

Closing my mouth again, I shook my head. "I could not bring myself to eat the…fresh meat in the camp. Only a bit of seagull and bear cub. Not enough to reverse the scurvy in me."

"The vitamins I'm going to give you contain Vitamin C. That should clear up your symptoms pretty quickly."

"Vitamin C? What is that?"

"It's this." Mr. Breckner handed me a small white tablet. "You just pop it in your mouth and use a little water to get it down. I have something for the pain but can't give it to you on an empty stomach, so we'll have to wait for Dennis."

I held it in my upturned hand but made no move to comply. "Why won't you answer my questions?"

His confident motions slowed. He regarded me with a steady stare much like the woman had. "Because it is a lot more complicated than just stating where we are. I know you have no clue who we are, but please believe we just want to help."

I was more curious than afraid now. Looking down at the small white pill he'd handed me, I did as he instructed. Mr. Breckner offered me a small paper cup of water, which I gratefully swallowed. I tried not to make a face of disgust at the bitter taste leftover. I scratched my beard and winced, inhaling sharply at the stab of pain in my upper left jaw.

"You all right?" Mr. Breckner watched me carefully.

"Just a toothache."

"No such thing as 'just' a toothache. Open back up. Show me where."

Too tired to care, I did as I was told.

"How long has it been hurting?"

"A few days. I hit my face fleeing *Erebus* a while ago, but only recently did it flare."

Mr. Breckner backed up and started rummaging through small orange tubes with white caps. I leaned forward on the table in curiosity and nearly toppled off from fatigue alone.

"Whoa, whoa." Steadying me with one hand, Mr. Breckner showed me the tube he'd selected.

"What is this material?" I picked up the tube, fascination momentarily dominating my weak state of mind and body.

Mr. Breckner smiled again. "Like I said, later. Please, Mr. Goodsir. We need to get you well first. Will you let me do that?"

I nodded, relinquishing the small tube.

"We need to start you on these antibiotics. When you hit your face, you could have cracked a tooth. I'm not a dentist, but I know that's an easy way to get an infection. Did you, uh, keep your teeth clean in any way? Brush them daily?"

I nodded. "Aye."

"Does anything make the pain worse?"

I gulped down the small mouthful of water he'd offered in the little paper cup, swallowing the new tablet easier than I had the first time.

"Cold," I gasped. "Cold makes it worse. And biting. What are antibiotics?"

Mr. Breckner took the cup from my still trembling fingers. "The medication will help, okay? A couple of days, a week at most."

I didn't bother asking more questions; he would merely continue to avoid them. I rubbed at my unfocused eyes with one hand and sniffled.

A soft knock sounded at the door. I lifted my head, hoping to see the woman called Annie, but it was a stranger. A man stood in the open door frame, smiling and pushing shaggy blond hair from his eyes. He held a small tray in one hand upon which was a small bowl and fork. I began to salivate even before the smell of food hit me.

"Mr. Goodsir, this is my brother, Dennis."

Tearing my gaze from the tray, I gave the newcomer a small smile and dipped my head. "It is a pleasure to meet you, Mr. Breckner."

The man held the food out to me. He was a bit shorter and thinner than his brother but with similar cheekbones, wide nose, and kind brown eyes. "Just Dennis, please."

I eagerly accepted the tray from Dennis; it was all I could do to not tip the contents of the bowl down my throat in one swallow.

Ryan seemed to read my mind. "Take it slow, Mr. Goodsir. A few bites at a time. Too fast and you might vomit."

I obliged. What looked like green beans that tasted much different than the ones I was used to half brought me out of my tired stupor from the first bite. I spooned more into my mouth and chewed, careful to keep the food away from my aching tooth.

"How are things going in here?" Dennis was watching me with that damned fascination that seemed a bit much. I did not care; I had not a clue how I had arrived here, but I at least was finally eating unspoiled food. I closed my eyes and let myself savor every small bite.

"Fine," Ryan answered. "Where's Annie?"

Dennis glanced at me. "I made her eat something first, but she seems fine. She didn't, uh, have the same complication as me."

"Good." Ryan nodded. "I'll check on her in a moment, once I'm finished with Mr. Goodsir here."

Dennis nodded and left after gently taking my empty bowl, gracing me with another wide smile before shutting the door behind him.

"Let's go next door and get you a bit more comfortable, shall we?" Ryan led me to the sink and had me rub a sweet-smelling bar of soap between both hands. Again, I stared curiously at everything: the sink's fixtures, the line of orange bottles nearby, the steady points of glowing light right above our heads.

I washed off the dirt, grime, and flecks of dried blood that had been a constant part of my skin for months. I scrubbed my hands, wrists, and forearms until they tingled.

When rinsed away, the soap did not leave any residue, only a brief memory of its smell. The cleanliness brought a greater relief than I could have imagined.

"Here, dry your hands on this." Ryan handed me the softest towel I'd ever felt. I smiled and refrained myself from rubbing it against my cheek.

Next, he handed me a clean white shirt with long sleeves. I pulled it on gratefully, covering my pale, thin upper frame. I followed Ryan out of the door, sliding the fabric of my new shirt between two fingers.

We took a few steps down the hallway to the next room, a small living quarters with something I hadn't seen in too long: an actual bed.

Just as it had done when Dennis brought me food, my body reacted without my permission. My eyes grew heavy and my knees weak. I ached to lie down so fiercely that I bumped against the nearby wall.

Ryan gestured to a thin, tall, metal stand behind the bed. "I need to do one more thing, Mr. Goodsir. Did you have IVs in your…" Ryan caught himself, stopping mid-sentence and frowning. "Do you know what IVs are?"

I examined the contraption. "I ken what an IV is, aye."

"Ken? What?"

I nodded. "Ken. I ken."

"Uh, well, this will speed up your healing process. I can administer fluids and medication while you sleep."

I barely heard Ryan. I had stopped caring about everything around me aside from the bed.

Without waiting for permission, I sank fully clothed onto the mattress. It was bigger than what I was used to, softer, the pillow plumper. I pulled the blankets high, the bone-aching cold of the Arctic already a distant memory.

"Thank you," I whispered, my eyelids fluttering.

Ryan fished my left arm from beneath the covers. "You're gonna feel a bit of a pinch, Mr. Goodsir. It's just me getting the IV in."

I could hear his voice, but it seemed to float around from side to side. The room began to fade. He slid my sleeve up and swiped a soft white ball along the crook of my elbow. It left a cold, wet trail along my skin.

"It's important you don't remove the IV," he said softly. "All right?"

I think I nodded. The pinch in my arm he spoke of barely registered.

Unable to hold off the layers of fatigue, eager to finally be at peace, I let my eyes fall shut. I had no understanding of what was happening or how it came to be, but for now, I finally was able to welcome sleep.

Sixteen

Annie
2020

My heavy plastic spork clattered against the bowl Dennis had pushed in front of me. Steaming hot green beans lay limp within, but despite my hunger, my stomach churned. The food only made me think of the can we'd sent back to the Arctic, which then reminded me of the volunteers in the videos. And then Dennis. I'd watched them all puff right out of existence, leaving nothing but fluttering grey ash.

That had happened to me. I could have been ripped apart, or turned inside out, or stuck in the past, or…

I closed my eyes, shutting out the dining area; the nausea still refused to relent. I could still feel the frigid cold ripping through me.

The panic had set in when I'd nearly been spotted by a patrolling Marine. It only worsened as the clock ticked down and I could do nothing but try to calmly convince a freaked-out Goodsir to trust me.

I pushed away from my food. With a lurching head and a pounding heart, I trudged out of the chilled dining area on weak legs, twisting the hem of my hoodie. The boots I'd taken from the coat closet left short, dull echoes behind.

I braced myself against the wall, the concrete rough and pocked beneath my palm. Dennis had told us about his side effects before, but I didn't remember him having waves of sickness or weakened legs. Then again, he had passed out soon after returning. So why hadn't I?

The etched tally marks stretched along the wall; some old, others fresh. I had stopped counting long ago but for some reason, Ryan refused to stop gouging one into the concrete each day.

"Holy crap, I can't believe he's actually freaking here." Dennis whisked past me, holding Goodsir's empty bowl in one hand, tray swinging in the other. His steps and grin both faltered when our eyes met.

I hadn't told him how I truly felt. That I'd barely had time to react when I popped into existence between a canvas tent and the back of the Marine with a very real gun. I tried to smile and repress the horror that I felt each time I realized I could have been shot and killed in seconds.

"It gets better." Dennis put an arm around my shoulders. "I promise. The shivers are the first to go, then the nausea. After that, you'll just want a good week of sleep."

I nodded and rubbed my eyes. "Is he okay?"

"Yeah." His face softened. "Thanks to you."

"We all had a part to play in it."

"But you had the balls to risk your life for him once Ryan got overprotective of me."

I rested my head on his shoulder and didn't respond. We stared at the marked wall together in silence.

"Three years," I said softly.

"And we've still yet to play a full D&D campaign. Which is totally unacceptable."

"If you can convince Ryan to try again, I'm down."

Dennis let out a snort and let go of me. "Naw, he was too butt hurt when he couldn't figure out the mechanics. And don't you remember his aggressive table flip when he died before hitting level two? Maybe if we could feed him some Xanax first."

He started for the dining area, only stopping to pick up my untouched bowl of beans.

Once in the kitchen, I slowly pushed myself up to sit on a counter. I flexed my fists; Dennis was right, the shaking had nearly stopped.

"He's shorter than I expected," he went on. "Goodsir, of course. And I was right about his accent."

My mind flew back to what we'd done, to the man who was just feet away in another room of our home. Had we picked the right thing to do?

Dennis tossed Goodsir's plastic bowl into the kitchen sink. "This just blows my mind. I mean…shit, he's from 1848. And he's here getting an IV in 2020. How cool *is* that?"

I wiped my suddenly clammy forehead, frowning.

"Hey, Annie. What's wrong?"

"Nothing. Just felt a bit too nauseous for a minute."

He glanced over at my untouched food. "Eating helps. Trust me."

"I know. I do." I flicked a few crumbs off the counter. It was my day to clean the kitchen, but I couldn't bring myself to go grab a rag. "What's he like?"

"Wonderous. I only saw him a few minutes, but…hell, I still can't believe he's real, that he's here. I think I'm still in shock." He let out a short, loud laugh and tossed his hair to one side.

I managed a weak chuckle. "You're acting like a little kid on Christmas."

"And you're not. How is this not blowing your mind?"

"Oh, it is. I think that's the problem." I grimaced. "Well, that and the sheer panic I felt when I appeared next to an armed stranger."

Dennis paused, his eyes searching mine. "Come on. Ryan's finishing up with Goodsir. We'll get you checked out and feeling better. When I went back, he gave me something for the nausea. With that and a good, long sleep, I was back to normal."

We left the kitchen, but not before he grabbed a small can of pork and pressed it into my hands. Leaving the cooling green beans behind, I forced my legs to work and followed him back through the bunker.

Dennis stopped just outside the open door to the first bedroom, which had been Ryan's before Goodsir's arrival. He glanced back at me over one shoulder with a wide grin. I slipped the can of meat into the pocket of my sweats and casually leaned against the door jamb.

My heart stuttered when I saw Harry Goodsir again. He was asleep, eyes twitching back and forth beneath closed lids. His dirty, bearded face was serene, showing none of the panic and confusion and suspicion I'd seen in the Arctic. His chest slowly rose, paused, and fell, repeating in a peaceful monotony.

Ryan was crouched next to the bed, listening to Goodsir's heart with a stethoscope.

"Is he going to be okay?" I asked the moment he rose.

"Yeah. I think so." Ryan pulled the plugs from both ears. He stared down at Goodsir in awe. "This is insane, Annie," he said quietly.

I slowly shook my head. "I can't believe it worked."

Ryan rubbed his neck. "Do you know what 'ken' means?"

"Huh?"

"His accent is thick. Hard to understand at times. When I asked if he knew what an IV was, he said 'I ken.'"

"That was in some of the books I read." I smiled down at the sleeping man. "It's how Scots say, 'I understand.'"

"He's pretty sick, but I think it's all curable. With medication not as potent as it used to be, it could take a bit longer, but it can still help him. From my initial observation, all we need to do is reverse his scurvy. A few doses of Vitamin C and some fresh food will help with that. He also might have a broken tooth that's infected." He peeled off his latex gloves and wiped both hands on a towel. "I'll have to keep a close eye on him these first few days, but I think he'll be feeling better really soon, maybe even tomorrow."

I moved a bit closer. A few loose curls of dark brown hair lay scattered across Goodsir's forehead. Something about his absolute helplessness, the amount of suffering he'd endured, pricked a surge of sudden protectiveness in me. I bit down on a thumbnail, worry blossoming. "How long do you think he'll be out?"

Ryan shrugged and bent to check the IV tape in Goodsir's left arm. "Could be a few hours or a few days. I really haven't done something like this before. We'll take watches just as we discussed, keep an eye on him around the clock. With what he's already been through, I'd be shocked if he didn't at least sleep through the night."

He straightened and checked the IV bag hanging next to the bed. "This'll get some antibiotics and vitamins in his system. He's going to be okay."

"I hope so," I said softly.

Satisfied, Ryan turned to me. "Are you all right? Did you keep food down?"

I risked a glance at Dennis, but he was staring at Goodsir, not listening. "Fine. The shakes are gone, but still a bit sick to my stomach."

He lifted one hand and felt my forehead. "What was it like? What happened?"

An image of the Marine bursting into Goodsir's tent flashed in my mind, renewing the terror and absolute helplessness that had shot through me.

I tried not to recoil from my friend. "Why don't you zap back and see for yourself?"

He scoffed. "Come on. How cold was it?"

"Fucking frigid. I'd never felt anything like it. It was like my bones were freezing inside of me."

"Wow." Ryan let out a breath. "And the camp? Did you, I dunno, materialize in the right place?"

I gathered the bed's discarded blanket and draped it over Goodsir. Dennis jumped in to help, unlacing the heavy boots on the surgeon's feet and pulling them off slowly.

"This is like something out of a movie," he murmured.

"Out. All of us." Ryan turned off the overhead light. Only the illumination from the nightstand's small lamp remained. He pulled the door shut and locked it one handed.

"Do you still think he could be dangerous?" Dennis asked.

His brother sighed. "No. I don't know. Either way, it's for the best that he doesn't wander quite yet."

We walked slowly down the hallway to my room. Dennis plopped into the small chair by the bed and I lowered onto the mattress, which let out a soft squeak.

"Lie back. You need rest." Ryan took my left arm in both hands and slipped his blood pressure cuff over my bicep.

"Annie, come on." Dennis watched us carefully. "Spill. Tell us everything."

I took a deep breath. "I actually ended up next to Goodsir's tent. Which sucked, because two men were nearby. One was in a red Marine uniform. He had a long rifle. I couldn't really see the other because they had their backs to me and were leaning over…over a dead guy."

"Oh, shit." Ryan looked up at me, face slack. "You're sure he was dead?"

"Parts were missing." I briefly shut my eyes, but that only brought the image of blood-coated rocks back. I turned my head on the thin pillow and watched the cuff tighten as Ryan squeezed the bulb. "It was dark, so I couldn't see the body real well, but I could hear what they were talking about."

"What were they saying?" Dennis stared at me.

The cuff slackened and Ryan sat back on his heels, eyes hard.

"It was so quiet," I went on, "and cold as all hell. The tents were bigger than I'd expected. Warmer. They were burning something in lamps, but I didn't see what. All I know was that it smelled. Hell, everything smelled."

"I can't imagine." Dennis rubbed his neck. "That camp had to have been rank."

"What was it like?" Ryan asked. "Using the Zapper?"

I rubbed my bleary eyes. "Painful. It hurts. Like you're on fire, but on the inside."

"It looked like you'd been totally vaporized." Ryan chewed his cheek. "Same as Dennis."

I shuddered.

"It was horrible." Dennis looked away.

Touched, I smiled. "Aw. You guys care."

Ryan graced me with a warm smile, something he rarely did lately.

"But if you didn't come back," Dennis said with a grin, "we were just gonna have to chalk it up to a horrible malfunction and continue on with our lives."

I let out a laugh. "Thanks."

The brothers both chuckled, but Dennis reached out and squeezed my hand. "Seriously, though. I can't tell you how terrified I was." He glanced at his brother. "Now I kinda get why Ryan was so freaked out."

Yawning wide, I tried to keep my eyes from drifting shut. My stomach had calmed considerably, replaced with a deep hunger, but nothing was more prominent than the sudden weariness dragging me down. "Can I get some sleep? I'm so tired."

Dennis smiled down at me. "You deserve it. All I had to do was see a few graves and a crap ton of snow."

I let my head fall back onto my pillow. A cold sensation blossomed on my chest as Ryan listened to my heart. I heard shuffling feet and the low voices of both brothers, but my eyes had already fallen shut.

Sleep took over, dropping me into a dreamless state from which I could not escape. It was suffocating. I tried to thrash myself awake; my limbs wouldn't cooperate. Giving up, I drifted, losing track of time.

—

Both brothers were gone when I finally bolted straight up on the mattress. I had no clue how much time had passed. I got out of the bed and made my way to our bathroom, squinting against the bright glare of light in the hallway.

The thin film of sweat covering my skin began to cool while I relieved myself. A few handfuls of warm water from the tap chased away most of the grogginess. I dried my hands on the towel and squeezed the excess from my wet sweatshirt cuffs.

Someone knocked softly. I pulled open the door and smiled up at Dennis.

"How do you feel?" he asked.

"Like I've been hit by a train. Run over and dragged behind one." I attempted to flatten my mass of tangled hair. "Was I out long?"

"Almost twelve hours."

I gawked at him. "Are you serious?"

Ryan appeared, striding towards us down the hall, a glass of water clutched in one hand. "I was just coming to check on you."

"She's fine." Dennis gave me a playful punch on the arm. "Aren't you fine?"

"Always am," I lied.

"I'm going back to the control room," Dennis said as I gulped down mouthfuls of water. He glanced at his brother.

"I've been going through the files again, rewatching the videos we found. Trying to find any clues I can that might explain what happened to our mom."

He jogged away before I could speak. Passing the empty glass to his brother, I rubbed my face with both hands. "Now what do we do?"

"Well, for starters," Ryan raised his eyebrows, "Goodsir's awake."

That woke me right up. "Is he okay?"

"I don't know. Saw him stirring on the monitor just now. I wanted to make sure you hydrated first since I saw you were up."

"Well, what are we waiting for?"

We approached the bedroom together. Ryan pulled a key from his pants pocket and unlocked the door.

Harry Goodsir's eyes were dark green and full of unasked questions. He sat rigid on the little bed, legs swung over its side, watching us enter.

"Do you feel all right?" Ryan asked slowly.

"Aye." Goodsir frowned slightly, his thick beard shifting. The red patches on his face had already begun to clear up, and his lips weren't as chapped. "What have ya given me?"

"Just those vitamins and antibiotics that we discussed earlier."

"Antibiotics, sir?"

"Just Ryan. No need for formalities here." He stuck out his hand. "It's a pleasure to see you up and about, and properly make your acquaintance."

The surgeon hesitated a moment but took the offered hand, shaking it. "Henry Goodsir of Her Majesty's Ship *Erebus*."

His voice was light and quite pleasant, with a thick Scottish accent that shaped his words into what was almost like a song.

"The ship's doctor." Ryan was smiling.

Goodsir shook his head. "Just the assistant surgeon. I'm an anatomist. Where am I?"

I opened my mouth, but Ryan spoke before I could. "We're going to brief you shortly. I'd appreciate it if you'd let me take your vitals first, though."

"Tell me, what is that material?" He was watching Ryan unwrap his blood pressure cuff. Ryan paused, then held it out. Goodsir took it in his hands. He held it close to his face and turned it over and over.

"I can use this to take your blood pressure." Ryan held up one end of his stethoscope. "And this to listen to your heart."

Goodsir glanced over at the blue stethoscope but seemed disinterested, looking back to the cuff a moment later. "I've no' seen an instrument such as this before."

"I can show you how it works." Ryan held his hand out for the cuff, which Goodsir reluctantly gave back. "Is that all right?"

Goodsir nodded. Ryan gently took the surgeon's arm and wrapped the cuff around his bicep. He made sure to use slow, slightly exaggerated movements.

It was the first time I'd seen Goodsir up close without danger or one of us panicking. The shirt Ryan had lent him hung on his thin frame. His skin was extremely pale. As he watched Ryan's slow demonstration with wonder, some locks of his dark brown curls fell forward. Goodsir brushed them away, and I noticed his knuckles were bruised.

Ryan explained as much detail as he could at every step. Goodsir was alight with childlike curiosity, smiling slightly and watching with enthusiasm. When Ryan squeezed the ball and the cuff began to tighten, Goodsir stared at his arm, blinking rapidly.

I watched in quiet fascination from the door frame. Once Ryan had finished and recorded Goodsir's blood pressure, he removed the cuff and set it aside. Next, he showed him the digital thermometer.

"I've heard of a thermometer," Goodsir mused, "but nae have I seen one like this. How do the numbers change?"

"Later. I promise we'll explain as much as we can. But you still have a fever." Ryan popped the stick's slip into the trash. "I have to give you more antibiotics."

Goodsir didn't respond.

"We want to help you get better."

Instead of answering Ryan, Goodsir suddenly looked at me. "And you, miss. Who are you?"

I glanced over at Ryan, but he was busy sterilizing the thermometer near the sink. Stepping forward, I held my hand out. "I'm Annie."

"Aye, that much I recall." Goodsir took my hand, held it between both of his, and dipped his head. He seemed unsure of what to do next. "What is yer part in all this? Why did you rescue me?"

"Because you didn't deserve to suffer the way you did." I'd said it before realizing my mistake. Ryan shot me a look.

"But why just me? Why not the rest o' the men?"

"We'll get to that," Ryan cut in. "Everything. But I'd really like to get more meds in you, and some more food. You need rest right now. We have plenty of time to talk."

Goodsir looked down at his stockinged feet. "Until then, could I trouble you for a bath?"

Ryan handed him two small white pills. He glanced at me. "Have Dennis show him to the bathroom."

I stalled, to giving Goodsir a quick, reassuring smile then backed out of the door and jogged back through the bunker.

Dennis sat backwards on one of the rolling chairs in the control room. His back was to me, his focus completely on one of the monitors where he watched the tape of one of the Zapper's trials.

"Hey, are you ready to bathe our new friend?" I asked as I approached.

He didn't answer.

"Dennis?" I poked him in the shoulder, but his eyes didn't pull away from the screen.

The video that had been labeled with a black dot played before us. Dennis lifted a hand and paused it on an image of the scared little boy the people in the lab had tortured. The child's eyes were wide and horrified, his dark hair mussed.

"Dennis?" I repeated, softer this time.

"We're doing the right thing, aren't we, Annie?"

I grabbed the other rolling chair and sat next to him.

"I mean," he said, gesturing to the video. "Look at this. The people who tested the Zapper, the ones in this video, only cared about their work. They abused this poor kid with zero regret. It's like the power went to their heads."

His shift in confidence shook me. I touched the back of his hand. "That won't happen with us. We're all going to keep Goodsir safe."

"Until we throw him to the wraiths." Dennis turned troubled eyes on me. "It all sounded like a good plan until just now. Until I saw this little boy again."

"We won't let anything happen to him," I said with hard determination.

He gave me an exasperated look but said nothing.

On a different screen, a small black and white Ryan was letting Goodsir listen to his heart with the stethoscope.

"He barely knows what anything is," Dennis said. "How the hell can we convince him to risk his life now? It's too much to ask. There's no way he—"

"Stop it." I kicked Dennis's shoe. "We haven't even talked to him about this. It's his choice; if he refuses, then we come up with a new plan."

He looked at me with tired eyes. "I know. I'm sorry, I just don't know what's going to happen."

"None of us do. But this...Dennis, it's the only chance we have left."

"We're not gonna get anyone back. We aren't gonna save anyone." Dennis ran a hand through his blond hair.

The thought of my parents brought forth a dull ache of grief. "But we'd be making a difference for those still here."

Dennis said nothing. We both looked back at the monitor and watched Ryan and Goodsir share a laugh.

I smiled. "We need to make sure he's healthy, first. Clean and fed and well before we talk to him about the rest."

Dennis nodded and stood. "I'm worried about that. Telling him. Won't it like, break his brain?"

I shook my head slowly. "I have a feeling it won't. He's different than what I expected. Stronger. Unique."

"What does that mean?"

Clearing my throat, I finally looked away from the monitor. "He sees things in ways we can't."

Dennis stared at the monitor screen. "I just can't shake this awful feeling that we've made a horrible mistake."

Seventeen

Harry
2020

Warm, gentle water cascaded down over my fingers from a dull metal faucet. I hadn't been able to properly wash my hands since the men had abandoned *Erebus,* and even then, it wasn't quite as wonderful or thorough as this. Dirt and grime I'd missed the previous day swirled lazily around the white sink. I wielded a small, slippery bar of soap, swiping it over my palms, wrists, and arms with a desperate savagery I hadn't realized was in me.

"What is this odd scent?" I wrinkled my nose.

Dennis stood next to me, working a shaving cream into a lather. He sniffed. "I think it's supposed to be vanilla."

"Not any I've smelled before." I kept scrubbing, my skin quickly turning pink.

"Did you have soap in your…uh, on your boat?"

"Oh, aye." Satisfied with the fresh, tingling sensation of my hands, I dried them on an exquisitely soft blue towel. "All us of men were required to keep ourselves neat and clean, even after we became ice locked. If one lacked, they were considered duty owing. Holystoning the deck, for instance. Or an extra shift on watch. Losing their evening grog."

Dennis spread the shaving cream over his stubble. His gaze caught mine in the mirror. "Holystoning?"

I nodded. "Scrubbing the ship's deck."

"With stones?"

"A type of sandstone. It helps keep the wood smooth and clear."

"Oh. Like sandpaper."

I didn't bother to ask for clarification. Instead, I nodded at the strange, tall bottle beside him. "May I shave as well?"

He smiled. "Sure, but you should shower first. No offense, but this transformation of yours will go smoother with clean hair."

Dennis pointed behind us at a tall rectangular area divided with what looked to be a glass window. He reached out, jaw still smeared with white cream, and pulled on the window's handle. It swung open to reveal a drain in the floor and large nozzle secured the wall.

"Just turn the handle for water," he said. "Don't get in first, though. The water heater takes a minute to warm up."

I did what I was told, making a mental note to inquire of this heater of water later. To my absolute delight, water shot out of the nozzle in a cluster of streams, ice cold that hit my still-pink hands. A memory of the ice demon's touch rose to the surface of my mind, and I drew my hand away.

Dennis turned his back to me, reaching into a cabinet and pulling out a small blue object. He began to slowly bring its flat edge along his face. It was clearly a type of razor.

Swirling steam drew my attention back to the falling water. I breathlessly shed my dirty clothing, anticipation growing. Once my trousers, undergarments, and borrowed shirt lay in a tidy pile on the grey floor, I closed my eyes and stepped into the most luxurious sensation I'd ever experienced.

Layers of filth trickled off my skin. Using the same bar of soap from the sink, I scrubbed myself raw, smiling in bliss despite the too-sweet smell of vanilla. I breathed deeply and let my body relax for the first time in years.

Tears of relief fell from my eyes, mixing with the hot water. I found myself gritting my teeth, face in my hands, trying not to sob aloud. Thoughts of Captain Crozier, Mr. Bridgens, Lt. Le Vesconte, all the men on both ships, whirled through my mind. I thought of my brothers, my father. Images of the beauty of the Arctic came next, but they were replaced with ones of blood-splattered stones and ice. Trembles accosted my limbs. I struggled to combat the grief and pain.

The hot water helped. I stood in the small downpour with my hair plastered along my temples and against my eyelids. Deep breaths finally filled my lungs. The shakes abated. I pushed the painful memories aside and was left wondering what type of culture I had been brought into. With strange, advanced tools and casual way of life, it was not anything I had heard spoken of or read about. Mind flying with unanswered questions and curiosities, I stood in the hot water until it was no longer tinged with grit.

"See those bottles on the floor?" Dennis was no longer visible through the waves of steam coating the glass door.

I glanced down, eyeing two tall bottles emblazoned with images of large peaches near my feet. "Aye."

"That's called shampoo. Squirt a little in your hand. Not too much."

My fingers slipped on the bottle. I struggled to open it until upon closer inspection, I noticed the word "push" near the rim. When I obliged, the top quickly popped open. I upended the bottle and a strange, thick substance slowly oozed out onto my palm.

"Did it work?"

"Aye. Is this liquid soap?"

"You got it. Rub it into your hair and beard."

The lather that worked up moments after massaging the shampoo into my hair was nothing short of miraculous.

"I suppose it sort of does have a slight peach scent," I said to myself.

Dennis chuckled. "Don't use too much. Annie loves that stuff."

I allowed myself a second shampoo regardless, grinning like a complete fool when I finally stepped out of the water. Dennis, eyes averted, held out a towel for me. He turned off the faucet while I dried. Tying the damp towel around my waist, I wiped fog and condensation from the mirror.

Dennis's use of the word 'transformation' had been quite accurate. Even with my beard, I still looked years younger. My skin, scrubbed clean, shone beneath what Dennis told me were light bulbs. My grown-out hair, normally flat and thin while short, curled lazily beside my face in a dark mess. It was as soft as silk to the touch, even wet.

"You ready for the shave of a lifetime?" Dennis wiggled a strange, narrow, black device. Its top was jagged with what looked like teeth.

I nodded, longing to rid myself of the persistently itchy mass of hair that had grown wild along my jaw, untouched by a blade since the night Captain Crozier had ordered us to abandon *Terror*. I stared curiously at the device that Dennis wielded with clear experience. He shifted his thumb and the long object suddenly let out a tinny buzz. Watching with fascination and apprehension, I let him draw the apparatus near.

A shave that would have normally required an hour took mere seconds. Thick patches of my hair succumbed to the bee-like drone of the strange razor, clogging the sink. Still more fell to the counter and floor. It covered my bare feet and caught on the towel wrapped around my waist. I watched in awe, nervously running a thumb over the red skin on my elbow where the IV had been.

It was nearly impossible to recognize the man underneath. I stared at my oval face, astonished at the sunken cheeks, the dull, dark circles beneath my eyes, the cracked lips. Was this truly me?

Dennis's voice broke my uneasy contemplation. "You look good. Younger."

I glanced away from my strange reflection.

"Here." Dennis handed over the other razor, the little blue one he'd used earlier. "Get it nice and smooth."

He picked up the bottle, spraying shaving cream into my palm. I stared at it, fascinated. "How did that come out?"

"No idea." Dennis smiled. "Just does."

Unable to even begin to place the scent, I lathered my face and dragged the small razor along my jaw as he had done. The shave was nowhere near as smooth as I was used to. The blade dragged along the stubble and caught painfully more than once. I winced but did not complain.

"So, like, what was your voyage like? Your ship?"

I continued to shave, slow and steady. "We set sail from England on two war ships. *H.M.S. Erebus* and *Terror*. I was stationed on the former."

"War ships?"

"Aye. Repurposed for exploratory service once peace reigned. Both fitted with a steam engine as well as thicker hulls reinforced with iron plating. To break through the ice."

Dennis shook his head, staring at me in wonder. "I don't know if I'd ever have the guts to sign up for something like that. To go into uncharted, barely hospitable lands."

"Oh, I was quite excited to be accepted. Captain Fitzjames chose the crew almost entirely. I'd known Drs. Peddie and McDonald from previous encounters, but the fourth was a stranger, Dr. Stephen Stanley. A cold, unfriendly man, but a brilliant surgeon...when he could be bothered to work."

"But all of you went knowing the dangers. That you might not return."

With the right side of my face shaved, I switched to the left. "Of course. But anything can kill you. One could be trampled in the street or die of disease. At least this way, I had a chance of seeing wonders few had laid eyes upon. I could study new creatures, such as the great white bear or the Arctic fox. I found many new things, even sent home a few notes and drawings to my brothers. Before we got trapped, that is."

"What happened?"

"From what was explained, many little things occurred in succession that contributed to our misfortune. We left later than we should have. A wrong turn was made and went uncorrected. We had to overwinter the first year and lost time and men. We were able to continue, but soon after that, things worsened."

Dennis watched me with fascination.

I cleared the flimsy razor beneath running water from the faucet. "Despite the seasoned Arctic experts on board, we became ice locked. We'd been prepared, of course. The ships were provisioned for up to three years, maybe even five if we were careful. Sir John, he wasn't worried, so none of us were. At least, not at first."

"Sir John Franklin?" Dennis didn't tear his gaze away.

I nodded and wiped the remaining trails of watery shaving cream from my face. "When he died, however, Commander Fitzjames took his place as captain of *Erebus*."

"What happened to Sir John?"

"He was killed quite viciously."

"Who killed him?"

We locked eyes in the mirror. "You might not believe me if I told you."

"You'd be surprised what I'd believe." Dennis blinked, silent and thoughtful a moment, then smiled at me. "You're like a whole new man, Dr. Goodsir. Do you want me to cut your hair, too? Buzz it down a bit?"

I sidestepped away, eyeing the razor. "I rather like the look of the curls."

He withdrew and gestured to a pile of folded clothing, stepping out of the bathroom. "I hope these all fit. You're a bit shorter than Ryan and me, but it'll at least be better than what you had. I'll wait out in the hall while you change."

The door swung shut behind him. I let the towel fall to the hair-covered floor. The clean clothes were a bit baggy but otherwise fine. I glanced over at my dirty pile of ragged attire but was distracted again by my intense reflection in the mirror.

The man minutes away from death a day ago was gone. There was a color in my cheeks that had been lost for many months. My green eyes had a shine to them, and my quickly drying hair shone. With the ghost of a smile, I looked away and considered the midden I had left behind.

Shaved hair littered the counter, sink, and floor, and I'd left puddles of water behind. I wiped the room down, ensuring I even cleaned all crevasses on the hard grey floor. The towel became soggy, but I was able to wipe up all stray hair and leave the room clear and clean.

A soft knock came as I stood, the wet towel bundled with a pile of loose hair inside. I pulled open the door.

Dennis gave me a quizzical look. "You doing all right in here?"

"Aye. Is there a place I can throw this away?" I held up the tightly wrapped towel.

He hesitantly took it from me, eyeing up my handiwork. "Hey, man, thanks. That wasn't necessary."

I wasn't sure what to say.

"Come on." Dennis put his arm around my shoulders and led me down the hallway. "Let's go have a chat."

The bunker's narrow hallway turned right at the tallied wall and the space opened up to the large area populated with chairs and round tables. Dennis led me to one and we sat.

The woman who'd rescued me from the Arctic, Annie, entered the room. The glare of the steady light above shone along her copper hair. I could not help but stare at her. I had seen only unwashed men and the claustrophobic insides of a Navy ship for nearly three years, and after that, only desperate comrades and friends-turned-murderers. She was the most beautiful sight my eyes had fallen upon, and the last I had expected.

Forcing myself to sit still in an uncomfortable, flimsy chair, I folded my hands on the table's surface. Like the shampoo and medication bottles, it was smooth, but of a material I could not place. A quick inspection when I'd first sat down had shown the entire piece of furniture was light enough to lift with a single hand.

I shifted back in the chair. Dennis smiled from across the table. Annie lowered a steaming mug to the table and slid it over to me, then sat as well.

"Do you remember how we got here?" she asked, tucking a stray lock of hair behind one ear.

I rubbed my jaw, pleased to feel smooth skin instead of my scratchy beard. I then realized the ever-present ache in my tooth had waned considerably.

"Aye," I said, nodding. "You appeared in my tent and told me you were to take me somewhere safe. I at first thought I had died, and then I burned up on the inside. But that is all I remember."

She smiled. "Yes. And I'm sorry that there have been more questions than answers. We really needed to get your health somewhat stable before we chatted about anything else."

"Which I greatly appreciate. The medication that Mr. Breckner provided, the vitamins…they are so small. I have never seen the like."

Her gentle eyes held the same fascination I felt inside.

"Do you know where you are?" Dennis's deeper voice was soft, calming.

"Your brother told me I was somehow in Nevada, in North America, but that is not possible. I can only speculate." I paused a moment. "Do you ken that the Inuit people believe that all things have a spirit? I spent a bit of time learning from them while our ships were being stocked, well before we got trapped in the ice. Before certain horrors surfaced."

Both watched me, not speaking.

I reached for the cup before me. A white string draped off one side, a little paper tag at its tail. Pulling the cup toward me, I caught a whiff of what smelled like a very weak lemon tea.

"According to them," I continued, "when a spirit passes on, it lives in an entirely different world."

Annie leaned over the table, her wide, penetrating green eyes boring directly into mine. The small cup warmed my hands, a pleasant contrast to the stubborn chill of the rooms I'd been in. I slowly lifted the tea, inhaled, and took a sip. I swallowed what tasted like hot water with a splash of lemon with a grimace; I couldn't even call it tea.

"They believe that a person consists of a name, body, and spirit. Their soul." I lowered the cup. "And when they die, it is only the body that perishes. That the soul itself and even the name can continue living elsewhere."

Dennis shifted, also sitting forward and clasping his hands on the table's surface.

I took a deep breath. "That is what this feels like. That I've died and gone elsewhere, somewhere new, but my body is still back in the Arctic, frozen on my cot, and my spirit is now here. Somewhere strange and new."

"I know it all must be very shocking, very confusing, but I guarantee you're alive." Annie produced a writing device and began to scribble on a small pad of paper.

"What...how...where does the ink come from?" I leaned toward her, eyes rapt on the letters she wrote, not caring what they said. I reached forward. "May I?"

She glanced at Dennis, who shrugged.

The odd pen she handed to me was captivating. Without knowing what it was made out of, the design was at least simplistic. Once I pressed a small button at its base, what looked like a fat nib popped out the other end. Close inspection showed me the ink was trapped in a barely visible tube.

"Fascinating," I breathed.

Dennis coughed. "Mr. Goodsir? Sorry, Dr. Goodsir."

I shook my head, brushing a few loose locks of hair out of my eyes. "I appreciate the respectful formality, sir, but as assistant surgeon, I have yet to earn the title of doctor."

"Here, a surgeon is sometimes held in higher esteem than doctors." Annie was watching me inspect her writing device.

"How did we physically leave the camp? Ryan told me you were capable of moving great distances in seconds, but I still struggle to understand." I lowered the pen, placing it gently on the table close to the steaming cup.

"There's a lot to talk about. Dennis knows most about the traveling. Ryan can help you with medication, and I…well, I'm not of much use right now."

"You saved my life."

"No, we all did our parts to help." Her mouth twitched and she looked away, pulling her chair forward. Its legs scraped across the floor in a vicious squeal and we all flinched.

I closed my eyes briefly, suddenly recalling the cries of the ice demons and the sharp, bone-snapping sounds that accompanied their movements. The dead, hopeless looks in the eyes of my friends. Blinking rapidly, I leaned back, trying to keep my breathing steady.

Annie regarded me with eyes full of sorrow. "I'm sorry."

I swallowed. "Why am I here? What is this place?"

Dennis spoke next. "Okay, I know this is going to be a great shock to you…"

"More than everything that's already come to pass?"

"We've brought you to our home," he continued, "to our time, to show you the fate of the human race."

His words could not be true despite the things I had seen. "Your…time?"

"The year is 2020," Annie said in her soft voice. "Earth is dying and most of the human race has been wiped out."

I stared at her. "Two thousand…twenty…? You're saying that I've moved forward in time one hundred and seventy-two years in the blink of an eye?"

The pair nodded.

I glanced back at Annie's pen, at the table and chair made from odd material similar to the razors Dennis had used to help shear my wild beard. I recalled the medications Ryan had used. With my vision beginning to swim, I dropped my head, rubbing both eyes.

"Mr. Goodsir?" Concern flooded Dennis's voice.

I held up a hand. "I will be all right. Please, just allow me a moment."

The silence that followed was crushingly loud. I settled myself forward, taking a few deep breaths. "There are no windows here."

Annie shook her head. The lock of hair she'd tucked away tumbled free once more. "We're underground."

"People live underground now?"

"What's left of us. Honestly, we haven't encountered any survivors in over three years."

The tallied wall came to mind. "You're trapped here."

"We are." Her face grew sad. "Three years ago, the world was attacked. Someone had control of these creatures. They created them or brought them here. Nobody really seemed sure. But someone released them, and they slaughtered everyone all over the world, from what we can tell. We can't go outside. They're still out there, ready to flay us alive if they catch us. We've had to live in this bunker ever since those things showed up."

My insides quivered. *Creatures,* I thought. *Not again.*

"They suck the life out of everything, even plants. The three of us got lucky. We made it to this bunker and have been here ever since." He paused, glanced at Annie, and cleared his throat. "It's basically impossible to start over. But we found a machine that was capable of going back in time. We also found some files, and videos of people testing the machine. But there's also, uh, books. About, well, Franklin's voyage. And you."

"Videos? What do you speak of? Books about me?" My breaths became shallow and my eyes very dry. I found it difficult to catch a full breath; I felt as if I was being slowly suffocated. It was all too much to process.

"It would be easier to show you." Dennis finally sat back in his chair, his face drawn and tired.

I knew they told the truth. Deep in the back of my mind, what they explained made a horrifying sort of sense. But I needed to be sure. I stood, drawing myself up to my full height. "There are two things I require right now."

Annie nodded.

"First, I'd like to see outside."

"We can show you on cameras," Dennis replied.

She shot him a harsh glance and stood, both paper and pen forgotten. "Mr. Goodsir, why don't you get a bit of rest?"

"I have rested plenty. If the world truly is as destroyed as you say, I will see it before I agree to listen to anything more. That is final."

Dennis stood as well. "And your second condition?"

I paused, weighing my next words carefully. "If what you say is true, that you have power to go back in time, I refuse to ignore the perils of my friends. I want you to rescue the rest of Franklin's men."

Eighteen

Annie
2020

I watched Ryan stalk back and forth in the control room.

"Absolutely not." He shot a glare at the nearby monitor that showed Goodsir back in his room. "Not a chance."

"To be fair," Dennis cut in, "I probably wouldn't believe the world outside is a desolate crap hole filled with monsters unless I saw it for myself, too."

"I'm talking about his other demand. To bring back, what, a hundred men who died in the eighteen hundreds? What the hell are they going to do here? Goodsir has taken all of this better than I'd anticipated, but you can't guarantee they all would. And we just don't have enough medication, weak as it is now, to go around. There aren't people out there making vaccines anymore. We'd just be giving many of them a different death. Speaking of, we could have done the same to ourselves."

"What are you talking about?"

Ryan stopped pacing to stare at me. "I don't suppose you had a TB vaccination, huh? I never even thought about that before we brought him here."

"No." Dennis snorted loudly. "Why would we have? And what does it matter? You said Goodsir seemed fine aside from the scurvy and tooth infection."

"TB symptoms can take months to show. He could have it and I wouldn't even know right away. You said he had chest pains, Annie, in his diary. That's one of the first signs. Along with a fever and weight loss."

"Oh, so you don't believe the demons are the cause. Or, hell, stress from everything he went through." My words were tough, but his fear began to bleed into me.

"He has to go back. I'm not risking us all getting infected, if we aren't already. Even if we don't, he's wildly susceptible to deadly viruses here without modern vaccinations that we don't have. There's nothing we can do, Annie."

"We are *not* putting that man back to die," I snarled.

"Whoa, whoa." Dennis held up a hand. "Let's keep our cool here, all of us. Ryan, what's done is done. This has to work, because if it doesn't, well, fuck, we all starve to death. But we can't back out now."

"Just let him look out of the door," I shouted. "We can all be there, supervising. Bring him right back in."

"Yeah," Dennis agreed. "We can show him we're at least willing to cooperate."

Ryan swiped a hand over his gruff face. "Are you two stupid? That man is an explorer. If you think he'll be content simply sticking his head out of the door and going, 'Oh, okay, yep, it's pretty dead out here', you're very wrong. He's been here barely two days. He needs more time to heal, to acclimate. We haven't even told him everything. He could very well snap and try to kill us."

Dennis groaned. "God, why do you always have to be so dramatic?"

"It's kept us afloat this long, hasn't it? It's kept us safe since the world went to shit."

"Look." I got to my feet, pushing the rolling chair aside. "We have the cameras. We can make sure the coast is clear before going out there. We'll give him exactly two minutes to take it all in, then get him back inside. One of us can stay here and monitor for danger."

Dennis perked up. "We can use those walkies I looted last year."

"They didn't work through the ground." Ryan sighed.

"Because the door was shut. It'll be open this time."

I stared at Goodsir on the monitor. "Nothing will go wrong, Ryan. Okay? Because we have to give a little. To show him he can trust us."

His laugh was bitter. "I'm sorry, what? Give a little? How about the fact that we risked our lives to save his ass? How can he not already be grateful? He should be thanking us."

"Dude, calm down." Dennis tipped back in his chair and used his feet to push off the console desk. The wheels of his chair scraped along the concrete floor as he rolled past. "Give the guy a break. You're acting like a psycho ass."

Ryan's shoulders fell. He rubbed the back of his neck, a guilty look flitting over his face. "Yeah. I know. I'm sorry. I'm just…I'm just exhausted."

"Get some sleep," I offered. "Dennis is on watch, and I want to finish my notes. Go lie down, make it an early night, and tomorrow we'll solidify our plan. Okay?"

"Yeah." Ryan nodded, his eyes, his entire face, suddenly drawn and heavy. "I'm sorry. Both of you."

"We get it, man." Dennis rolled back the way he'd come, his face serious.

I stepped in front of Ryan and looked up into his troubled eyes. "Look, this could fall apart at any moment. Yeah, we could have just been exposed to a horrible disease, but we all knew we were getting into some serious shit when we agreed to do this. Whether we cough up our lungs, get torn apart by wraiths, or we get annihilated by the Zapper, we're at least trying to survive now. We can't sit here and do nothing, and we have to all work together."

Dennis nodded, turning hopeful eyes to his brother.

"I get it. I know." Ryan smiled and squeezed my shoulder. "I…gotta lie down."

I dropped back into the chair, a heavy weight lifting off my chest and rested my head on the top of the chair. "Holy shit."

"Dude needs some Xanax," Dennis grumbled.

"Careful, he'll hear you. Ten bucks he comes back in here and starts a fight."

"Nah. Dude's gone soft since he started school. I, on the other hand, continue my workouts." He flexed his biceps.

Rolling my eyes, I glanced over at Goodsir again. He lay on his back, hands on his stomach, eyes closed. I watched him curiously, wishing I knew what was going through his mind.

"Mmhmm," I said, distracted.

"What? Is he doing anything?" Dennis rolled his chair toward mine as hard as he could. When he collided with me, I went flying.

"*Dick!*" I laughed and held onto the chair underneath my legs. My momentum slowed enough so that I barely tapped the far wall before coming to a rest.

Dennis watched the monitor. "I'd be flipping the fuck out if I were in his shoes. This guy is hardcore."

I walked my chair toward him. "He's processing. He had a lot dumped on him in a very short amount of time."

He went limp and slid down into his chair, then wriggled back up.

"I think he's kind." I ignored his fidgeting. "Humble. But most of all, curious. Haven't you noticed his face when he looks at stuff? All these things we're used to, that we take for granted. Tables, chairs, cameras. Everything is new to him. Hell, he tried to take apart the bed in his room just to inspect the frame. Ryan had to remove the lamp so he didn't pull that apart, too."

"Well, yeah, everything is pretty different from what he's used to. All the more reason for a freak out, I say."

"Good thing he's not a spaz like you, Dennis."

"And now, you pay." He spun around, putting the back of his chair to me. He shoved against the floor and shot toward me again.

I easily scooted out of the way. "Fail."

"I'm bored. Annie, I'm so bored right now."

"Clearly."

"There's never anything to do. It sucks. I miss television."

"I miss my guitar." I mimed strumming a few chords.

A grin lit up his face. "We were damn good."

"What else do you miss?"

Dennis sighed, turning his gaze to the low ceiling. "Video games."

"Omelets," I countered.

"Skateboarding."

I threw him a look. "I thought you were a biker. What are you, twelve?"

Cackling, Dennis flipped me off. "I had actually just started learning before the world ended, thank you *very* much for your close, loving friendship."

"You never told me." I made my voice a grumble.

"Just like you never told me you tried and failed to learn the banjo."

I threw a pen at him, laughing when it bounced off his left shoulder. "It's hard!"

Dennis snorted and swung back and forth in his chair, eyes distant. "I miss sex."

"Gross."

His mouth fell open. "What? I'm human. How do you not miss it, too?"

"Who said I didn't? I just don't want to picture you of all people doing it."

"Weren't you seeing that one dude?"

"That ended a year before I started my master's. He was a dick."

"Jerry?"

"Uh, no."

"James?"

"Shut it."

"It was something with a J."

Eager to change the subject, I started to mess around on the console. "I miss Cheetos. Crunchy and puffy."

"Beer."

"Yeah, beer, too."

"I also miss those tiny tables you got in pizza boxes. Well, and pizza."

A small sting sprung up at the corners of my eyes. "I miss my parents."

We fell silent. Dennis dropped his gaze and nodded. "Those graves outside…"

"We don't know what's buried there. Or if they're even graves at all."

"Come on, Annie." Dennis's light brown eyes glistened. He cleared his throat and straightened in his chair. "I miss my killer drum solos."

I tried to smile through my somber waves of grief. "I miss music in general."

"You can't miss something you have constant access to."

"I meant playing it live. The thrill of seeing a crowd surge toward us as we started off our set. Trying to throw off Ryan by bashing into him during his one bass solo."

Dennis cackled. "He'd get so pissed."

"Yeah, well, he acts tough, but he's a big softie." Longing for the normal, safe world we'd lost brought me down another notch, and my smile faded. "But now I have to listen with my earbuds, or he'll bitch."

"Maybe it brings back the same memories. Ryan isn't huge on emotions. You know that. He's probably just trying to cut out as much sadness as he can. Like that time after our epic mess at the battle of the bands."

"That was in high school. Of course, we were terrible."

"Yeah, but that was the worst series of fails of our lives. Remember how my shitty cymbal cracked in half and fell apart just as we started? And then Ryan's strap broke and his bass broke two of his toes?"

I cackled. "Yeah, okay, that was awful."

"Ryan shut himself in his room for almost a week. Skipped school, pretended to be sick. He's a sensitive dude."

"I know, I know. I just miss singing. Especially some old school AC/DC or some Joan Jett."

Dennis grinned. "Give me your iPod. I've got this control panel figured out pretty well."

"Oh, no. I'm not going to be the one to blame for whatever idea your brain is concocting."

He held out his hand. "Just trust me."

I narrowed my eyes at him but relented, digging into the pocket of my sweats and passing over my small iPod. He deftly hooked the device up to the control panel's side.

"Not only did my brother switch bedrooms to the one with a broken speaker," he said with a grin, "but this part of the bunker is soundproof."

Realizing what he was about to do, I sat up straight, mouth falling open. "You fucking genius."

"Just because Ryan's a crank ass it doesn't mean *we* can't have fun." He squinted at the board, flipping switches and fiddling with a group of knobs.

"Like the time you made us play that copy of Monopoly you found in storage? The one with half the pieces missing?"

Dennis sighed in mock sadness. "Using crackers as pieces would have worked fine if you hadn't given up and eaten mine." He paused. "Great. Now I miss carbs."

I let out a laugh just as loud drums started to echo through the console room. I tapped my hand against a thigh in time as Toto's "Rosanna" kicked in. "You opened my yacht rock folder. You hate yacht rock."

"Yeah, but it's your favorite." Dennis licked his lips and his face grew serious. "Wow. Been a while since I heard this."

"Who could forget Toto?"

"Gotta bless them rains."

"You put *Africa* on at every bar we went to."

He snorted. "That was my go-to jam!"

"And that's is why we stopped going anywhere that had a TouchTunes. You ruined it even for me."

Dennis was laughing openly now. I reached out, twisting the volume until I could feel the bass tremble in my chest.

"Fuck yes." Dennis jumped up, slamming down with invisible drumsticks just in time to two of the song's epic beats.

Letting the flow of the song pulse through me, I got to my feet, still nodding in time. I joined Dennis's air band, long hair flying loose around my shoulders. Mimicking the slams right before the chorus, I grinned and sang along.

He continued on the fake drums, gently biting the tip of his tongue in concentration. His cheeks were flushed with the exhilaration of finally being able to cut loose a little.

I switched to air guitar, stumbling through the lyrics since I couldn't stop laughing. Soon, the quieter pre-chorus began. I spun and the stacked screens behind us caught my eye.

Harry Goodsir was sitting straight up in his bed, head tilted, eyes wide. He was listening to something.

I dropped my arms. "Can he hear this?"

Dennis, now lost in air keyboard motions, didn't hear me over the music. I bent over the control panel.

The next chorus kicked in. I reached out for the iPod, intent on turning it off, but stopped when I saw Goodsir's face.

He was nodding in time to the song. And he was smiling. Broadly. Incredulously.

The catchy keyboard interlude started up. I peered at the switches that were flipped up: one labeled 'speaker on/off' and, further down the panel, another labeled with the number one.

Oh, shit.

"Uh…" I looked back at the screen.

Goodsir's smile grew. He swung his legs over the side of his bed and slowly stood, looking around for the source of the music.

"What is it?" Dennis had finally noticed. He paled, staring at the monitor. Sweat glistened on his forehead. He shoved loose hair from his eyes. "Can he…?"

The keyboard solo kicked in, and all I could do was watch as Goodsir raised a hand to his chest, his smile growing wider still. In came the guitar. Both instruments wailed with the drums, then all slowly started to fade out until Dennis and I stood in dumbfounded silence.

"Uh…" Dennis blinked. "I think he liked it."

We watched Goodsir. He stared at the small speaker in his wall, still wearing the ghost of a smile. I tried to scold myself, saying over and over how irresponsible that had been. Surely someone from over two hundred years ago who'd never heard rock music would have been mortified.

His smile told me different.

"You can never. Ever. *Ever* tell my brother about that." Dennis flopped into a chair with a heavy sigh.

I pushed the second switch back down to cut off the speaker to Goodsir's room. "If Ryan hadn't switched bedrooms, that would have been him in there."

We looked at each other. A grin stretched across my face. Soon, we were both laughing. Dennis grabbed my hand and spun me around to the opening chords of Little River Band's "Reminiscing." He was a terrible dancer but fully embraced it, swaying the wrong way or bumping into me on purpose, trying to make me laugh even harder.

Movement to my left caught my eye. Goodsir had climbed up on the little chair in his room and was now attempting to disassemble the speaker.

"Dammit!" I let go of Dennis and ran for the door, pulling it open. We bolted out of the control room without stopping the music. "Could he like, electrocute himself?"

"Not likely." Dennis careened through the bunker with me. "But possible."

Arriving at Goodsir's locked door, Dennis fumbled with the key. "God, we suck at this job." He finally slipped the key into the lock, twisted, and yanked the door open.

Harry Goodsir paused in his exploration of the speaker, turning to us with a curious look. Dark curls obscured one eye.

"That's dangerous." I squinted at the wires poking out of the wall.

He instantly lowered his hands and hopped to the floor. "That music. Can I hear it again?"

"I..."

"Sure." Dennis reached toward Goodsir, putting an arm around his shoulder. "But it's louder in the other room."

He turned and led Goodsir out of the room before I could protest. When I jogged after them, Dennis caught my eye, pointed at his ears then down the hall toward Ryan's room.

I fell into step next to Goodsir. He was smiling again. "How are you feeling?" I asked.

He tilted his head. "Physically I feel wonderful. Even better than I have since before *Erebus* set sail."

Swallowing, I tucked a strand of hair behind my ear. "Mr. Goodsir, I'm really sorry we didn't tell you everything right away."

He turned his direct, searching gaze over to me. Normally such intense eye contact made me uncomfortable, but with Goodsir, it was warm, friendly, even welcoming, despite all we'd dumped on him. Guilt pricked within me again. We still hadn't told him everything.

"I just...I know all of this is a huge shock to you. I mean, of course it is. I can't imagine what's going through your head right now, and I'm sorry to be the cause of it."

Goodsir smiled. "It is nae fault of yours. If this is to be mah path, I will follow it."

My breath caught. "You will?"

He raised his eyebrows. "Do I have any other choice?"

"Well…yes. We can always send you back."

"To die in the Arctic? I would rather stay here, underground and still utterly confused." His face was serious, but his eyes danced.

"I'm still sorry." I didn't meet Dennis's quick gaze. "You wouldn't be in this predicament if it weren't for me. For us."

"You're correct." He stood and faced me. "I would be in the last hours of mah life, struggling to breathe without great pain. I would nae doubt be hallucinating before quite an agonizingly slow death. Unless I were to be murdered, first."

I looked at Dennis, unsure of how to respond.

"Regardless of where I am now, you still saved mah life. And I am grateful to you three for it."

Dennis stepped forward, keeping his voice soft. "We can't save your friends. We want to, of course we do, but to bring them here just wouldn't work."

"Because of the creatures, you mean?"

I chewed my lower lip. "This is the only place we know to be safe, and it's small. With those things out there, it's too much of a risk trying to find another place to live. Plus, we don't have adequate medication for everyone. But we can go back at any time, you know. If things change, if we stop the wraiths, we can return for them later."

Harry was silent, a thoughtful expression on his face.

"Do you want to have a look around?" Dennis jerked a thumb down the hallway, toward the dining area.

Goodsir's green eyes lit with excitement. "Oh, I would very much like to."

We led him through the different rooms, stopping for a bit in the storage area. His fascination grew with every new thing he saw, from the big water heater, to the laundry units, and even the bottles of shampoo and rolls of toilet paper stacked high.

Goodsir stood in awed silence while Dennis explained the generator. After a moment of contemplation, he stepped forward and lightly ran a hand along its warm, smooth side. He seemed to understand the extremely basic explanation we gave for how the bunker's cameras worked, but when I tried to explain electricity, he just shook his head, blinking rapidly and not speaking.

He acted uninterested in our food supply, but I caught his eye roaming over our small pile of canned food in a lingering fashion.

"Are you hungry?" I asked.

He let out a soft laugh. "I never thought I'd say this again, but nae, not right now."

Wandering through the kitchen was simple; nothing was there that hadn't been used in the nineteenth century aside from the stove and refrigerator. I couldn't help but smile as Goodsir ran his hands over every surface he passed or as he put his face very close to each thing he inspected.

Next, we hurried him past the books and files in the study, unsure of how he'd handle what they held, and stepped into the control room. No part of me told me to stop, and the grin on Dennis's face encouraged me to try and find as much as we could to show Goodsir.

When his eyes landed on the monitors, he audibly gasped. He bent over, staring at the various images on the screens, his face close. The glow turned his face even more pale.

"How is this possible?" he asked, reaching out to touch the closest screen. He jumped and laughed at the buzz of a static shock.

We sat him in one of the rolling chairs. His eyes crinkled at the corners from his wide smile. He pushed himself back gently, chuckling as the chair's back bumped into the desk.

"These are wonderful," he said in his light, melodic tones.

I still wanted to show him more, to see what really held his interest. He marveled at metal fixtures, wired devices, and anything plastic. He spent ten minutes scribbling with my pen without saying anything, clearly able to understand how it worked. The keyboard by the monitors, however, baffled him.

"Why have the letters out of order?" he wanted to know. "What if the user speaks a different language, what then?"

Dennis looked just as overwhelmed as I was beginning to feel. He sat on the desk and gently took the keyboard. "All in good time, my man. Honestly, there's way too much we can't explain."

"I wish I could see things the way you do." I leaned back in my chair and stretched.

"Could…" He was looking at me with a half-smile. "Do you think I could hear that music again?"

Dennis picked up my iPod. "Absolutely."

Leaning over the console, I glanced at another monitor that showed both hallways on a split screen. There was no sign of Ryan; his door was firmly shut.

"So," I said. "'Rosanna' is one of the greatest songs ever made."

Dennis tapped on the small screen of my iPod, holding it so Goodsir could see what he was doing.

The surgeon watched carefully, not speaking, his eyes following every movement. "I must admit, it was atrocious at first. Your music, it is quite loud. Fast and distractin'."

I laughed. The familiar drum beat kicked in. Goodsir's face twitched in a wince, but the moment the keyboard started up, his smile came back. He sat forward, his back straight, arms resting on his knees, staring at nothing with unfocused eyes as he listened to the music.

I closed my eyes and just listened. My head gently bobbed to the beat, and once the chorus kicked in, I started to sing along, keeping my voice soft.

Halfway through the song, I realized Dennis and Goodsir were both watching me. I stopped and looked away, shifting in the chair.

He didn't ask me how the recording was made, or about the instruments we were listening to, or how the iPod worked. Instead, he tilted his head and said, "You have an exquisite voice."

I closed my mouth, feeling my cheeks warm. "Thanks. I, uh, used to perform. We all did."

"Dinnae let mah presence hinder you."

Suddenly uncomfortable, I reached out and cranked up the volume just as the keyboard kicked in for the outro. The song faded out slowly and, after a pause, was replaced by *Walk of Life*.

Goodsir's eyes lit up. "Och, this is wonderful."

After a moment of listening, his head began to bob along, too. I nearly snorted with laughter at the sight of a man from the mid-nineteenth century bopping along to Dire Straits.

I sang the chorus, unable to help myself. I shot a glance at Goodsir, whose smile broadened when he heard my voice join the music again.

Ryan stalked into the control room as the song faded, face shocked and livid. "Turn it off. Now."

Twitching and nearly dropping my iPod, Dennis tapped the screen, cutting Kenny Loggins short just as he started to tell us how hard he'd been working.

"Ryan…" I began.

He cut me off with a sharp hand gesture and stalked toward Goodsir, who'd already risen to his feet.

"What the hell were you two thinking?"

"Everything's fine." Dennis rose from the desk, stepping in between the two men.

Barely contained anger shone in Ryan's eyes. A vein pulsed in the side of his neck. I'd never seen him so angry. To Goodsir, he said, "I'm sorry, but you need to go back to your room. We just can't risk anything happening to you."

"Is there somethin' you're no' tellin' me?"

Ryan's jaw worked back and forth. He crossed his arms, staring at Goodsir, who stared right back.

"Stop. I'm serious." I strode forward, getting in Ryan's face. "He's not a prisoner."

"And he's not a fucking *pet*."

"What the fuck?" I sputtered.

Goodsir shook his head. He stepped past Ryan, heading out of the control room.

I glared at Ryan a second longer. "God, you're a dick."

He shot me a disappointed glance then followed Goodsir, leaving Dennis and me in the control room.

"We are in serious deep shit." Dennis groaned and hustled out of the control room, following his brother. Fuming, my fists clenched, I bent over a monitor and watched Ryan lead Goodsir back to his room and lock him in.

I dropped into the nearby chair, fuming, not taking my eyes off Goodsir. He stood still a moment, staring at the closed door, then he shuffled to the bed. He laid back on the mattress, crossing his feet at the ankles and clasping his hands over his stomach. He grew very still.

Ryan and Dennis argued in the dining area on a different screen. Chin in my palm, I scrolled through my iPod, which was still plugged into the console, and tapped on "Listen to the Music." I sighed heavily as the Doobie Brothers started to sing.

I fought the urge to join the brothers' argument. Instead, I reached out and flipped the switch for the hanging speaker in Goodsir's room, sending the Doobie Brothers inside. His head shifted on his pillow. He turned and stared into the eye of the camera that watched him, right at me, and smiled.

Nineteen

Annie
2020

"Will you just *listen* for once?" I glared up at Ryan, watching him pace around the dining area.

"Let him sputter out." Dennis, seated at one of the round tables, shoveled a spoonful of reconstituted mashed potatoes into his mouth. "He's been pissy since the whole musical fiasco yesterday. He'll chill sooner or later."

Ryan sucked his teeth, watching his feet as he paced. "What the hell are we supposed to do here? We have a guy from 1848 learning our technology, our medications, our way of life. If we keep him here, he could very likely die. If we send him back, he absolutely will. Jesus, why didn't we think this *through*?" He kicked an empty chair, sending it scattering.

"We did." I flinched and watched the plastic chair clatter against the far wall. "What else were we going to do? Just sit down here and starve? Remember our dwindling food and fuel? We're doing the best we can with the cards we've been dealt!"

"We have to test his power on the wraiths, but he's still not a hundred percent. He needs more rest and has to get rid of that damned tooth infection." Ryan scratched the side of his face, leaving faint red marks in his skin.

I'd never seen my friend like this; he'd been yelling at us since he found us playing music for Goodsir the day before.

While Ryan had always been stubborn, he'd never went on rampages. He was someone else entirely. Someone about to snap.

Hoping to placate him before that happened, I pushed my bowl away. "Ryan, everything is fine right now. For the time being, we still have enough food. We have the propane. You said yourself the meds are still potent enough to work if you monitor the dosage correctly. We just need to take this one thing at a time. All right?"

He stopped pacing and stared at me. "Say this all works. What do we do with him if we even survive the wraith battle? Keeping him here, in our time, unvaccinated and without any access to updated modern medicine, means he could die here instead."

I shrugged and sat back, lifting my chin in defiance. "We could put him back in his time in the path of a rescue party. More than one went looking for the missing men. We have exact coordinates for each of them, in those Franklin books."

I glanced up at Dennis, but he was shaking his head sadly.

Ryan snorted. "Thanks to you two, he knows way, way too much. Rigging the past so he gets rescued means we risk the fact that he might try to replicate what he's seen here, which is now a lot."

Dennis chewed on a small piece of canned meat, watching his brother. "How could he possibly recreate anything here without the technology to do so?"

"He can't." Ryan rubbed his face slowly. "But say someone later in his family line kills the guy who, I dunno, invented antibiotics, and that carries down the timeline and changes everything. Goodsir's survival in the past could really mess things up."

"Or it could better things," his brother shot back. "But, and I hate saying this, Ryan's right. We can't know until it's too late."

"So, we keep him here, as we originally planned." I threw a hand in the air, frustration boiling.

"Not without proper medications, plus vaccinations, and—" Ryan stopped pacing, staring at the far wall with unfocused eyes. "Wait a minute…"

"Uh, so I know we were going to handle one thing at a time, but I might as well tell you both now." Dennis inhaled the last bites of his food and straightened. "We're running out of propane."

The last bite of bland, mushy pasta wedged itself in the back of my throat. I coughed, spitting it out into my creased cloth napkin. "You said before we had enough for weeks."

"We do. But with Goodsir here, we're running it longer."

"Shit."

"That's what I said." He swiped his own napkin across the table, clearing a few big drips of gravy he'd spilled. "I didn't realize until we were in there showing him the gennie. The fuel tank is lower than normal already. It's three days ahead of schedule."

"How soon until we have to do another supply run?" The vivid memory of nearly being disemboweled by the wraiths the last time flashed clear.

"Now." Ryan faced us. "Today."

Dennis sipped from his glass of water. "Now? I mean, it's not that dire yet."

"We need propane, yes, but I need something else." Ryan let out a deep, long sigh. "I need to examine a dead body."

That threw me off. I squinted up at him. "What for?"

"I think I figured out why none of them are decomposing properly." He crossed his arms, tapping a finger on his bicep. "What if the wraiths are doing way more damage than we thought?"

"Whoa." I ran my fingers through my hair, gut sinking.

"We can't plant anything out there because the next time wraiths come by, they suck the life out of everything. Right? So, what if it isn't just humans and animals and plants?" He dropped his head back, staring at the ceiling. "What about viruses? Bacteria?"

"Well, if that's true, Goodsir can stay here no problem," Dennis said bitterly, turning his chair around and sitting on it backwards.

Ryan gazed at his brother. "It means none of us can. If I'm right, the entire ecosystem out there is changing and might even become uninhabitable, even without the threat of the wraiths. If it isn't already."

We fell silent. Our generator hummed in the distance, a constant reminder of our quickly depleting life support.

I gently placed my palms flat on the table, fingers tingling with the sudden burst of adrenaline Ryan's revelation had brought. "Are you saying that even with the wraiths gone we might not be able to survive out there?"

He fell into a chair. "I don't know, but it's possible."

"Fucking awesome." Dennis threw his empty bowl across the room. It clattered along the concrete floor, leaving gravy and bits of food in its wake, and joined Ryan's discarded chair by the wall.

"Hey," I said sharply. "We have a time machine. I thought we discussed using it to go live somewhere else. If Dennis could keep learning the Zapper's workings, couldn't that still be on the table?"

"He's right." Ryan sighed. "But one thing at a time. We deal with the most pressing issue at hand: we need to tell Goodsir everything. The sooner we stop the wraiths, the less damage they'll continue to do outside. But then we instantly go out for more propane, because we need enough fuel to power the impossible door long enough to ensure it seals with those things locked inside. So yes, we do this now."

I stood, fearful but eager to break the cycle of speculation and finally move into action. "Are we going to the gas station or looting houses?"

"Annie, no offense, but you stay here this time." Ryan said with an apologetic smile. "I appreciate it, but I need Dennis's speed and strength if we're gonna haul a few tanks back and forth."

"And your leg?"

He lifted it and spun his ankle in a few circles. "No break, no sprain. I just twisted it, and I'm all healed up."

"Fine. But Goodsir needs to see the outside first."

"We don't have time for that."

"Five minutes, tops."

"He'll demand more."

"And we'll tell him no," I cut in, raising my voice. "One of us can monitor the cameras, someone will go with Goodsir, and we keep someone on the bunker stairs to help pull him back inside if anything happens. With the door open, we can use the walkies."

"And if he runs?" Ryan was clearly stalling.

"He won't run. Where would he go? And if Goodsir gets hurt, you'll fix him."

Dennis snorted. "Hell, I wouldn't be shocked if the guy operated on himself. Dude's a badass."

"Five minutes." Ryan pushed away from the table, stood, and stalked away. "Let's go."

Relieved, I grinned at Dennis over my shoulder. He gave me a discreet thumbs up and jogged over to the supply room door, and for a moment, all we could hear was him rummaging for something.

"Here we go." He reappeared, holding three walkie talkies and ignoring Ryan's skeptical look. "Better than nothing."

Ryan clipped one to his waist and gave us a slightly pained smile. "Let's do this, then."

We strode to Goodsir's door. Ryan quickly unlocked it but paused and stepped away from the door.

"Annie, why don't you talk to him instead?" he whispered.

"Why me?"

"He responds to you better."

I shrugged and pulled the door open. Illuminated in the room's pale light, I smiled in at Harry Goodsir. "You ready to see the gorgeous landscapes of 2020?"

He rose from the little chair by the bed, lowering a pad of paper and pen. Detailed inked sketches of a massive ship decorated the top page.

Goodsir smiled at me, face relaxing, then dipped his head. "Good to see you again, Miss Ross. Mr. Breckner."

Dennis grinned and shook Goodsir's hand. "Up for a quick stroll outside?"

"If that's all right with everyone, yes." The surgeon cast a sideways glance at Ryan, who looked sheepish but held his gaze.

Ryan nodded. "Sorry about earlier."

"You're under enormous strain, I ken. This is difficult on us all." Goodsir laid a hand on Ryan's shoulder. His reaction threw me off, but I could only smile.

Ryan cleared his throat. He led us down the narrow concrete hallway toward the entrance. Goodsir fell into step next to me, with Dennis bringing up the rear.

We quickly passed the medical room, then the tallied wall, reaching the concrete steps that led up to the bunker's large metal entrance. I stared up at the only barrier that kept the wraiths out and us in, and a shudder of fear tickled between my shoulder blades.

After a moment's hesitation, Ryan climbed the steps.

"Are you sure it should be you going?" Dennis had one foot on the bottom stair. He watched his brother with caution. "You're the only healer in our group."

I bit my tongue, trying not to make another D&D reference.

Goodsir blinked. "Not anymore. Mah knowledge may be much different than yours, but I'm fully capable of assisting in an emergency."

"I'll be fine." Ryan jerked his chin at us. "Dennis, keep the doors propped open. Annie, you go check the monitors and make sure the coast is clear. I'm on channel three. Tell us if it's all clear."

I gave him a half-hearted salute and shot an encouraging smile at Goodsir, twisting the little knob on my small walkie. It flared to life in a burst of static. I wound my way through the bunker and into the control room, switching to channel three as I jogged. "You there, Ryan?"

"Yes." His voice was tinny over the speaker in my hand. "See anything?"

"Hold on." I released the side button and leaned toward the monitors, close enough to feel the slight tingle of the screens. Nothing moved. I scanned the skies and surrounding trees carefully, squinting into the ruined building nearby and even checking the cameras that were hung further in the woods. I took my time, staring hard at the dead world outside. No movement caught my eye on any of the cameras.

Finally satisfied, I activated my walkie. "All clear. Keep an ear out, though."

"Ten-four," came Dennis's voice. "Opening up now."

On the left screen, I saw the flat metal door of our bunker shudder the moment the airtight seal released, then it rose up. A little black and white Ryan poked his head outside. He looked up and around nearly as long as I had studied the screens.

"Anything?" I whispered into the walkie.

Ryan's image lifted a hand to his face. "Nothing. No sound, no movement. I think we're good." He climbed up and out of the bunker. Goodsir appeared, stopping halfway up the stairs, his hair shifting in a slight breeze.

The screen didn't show the best detail, and both men's features were grainy. I watched the screens close.

Ryan continued to look around, mostly staring up into the sky. Finally, he shuffled aside and waved to Goodsir, who fully exited the bunker and followed him a few paces away. The two stood in the desolate surroundings. It looked like a scene in a movie.

Ryan started pointing this way and that, waving a hand. He was talking animatedly. They both looked up and squinted at the sky. Goodsir pointed at something and my stomach did a flip. I half rose, but when Ryan turned to look at whatever was in the distance, he just nodded and kept talking.

I lowered into the chair. My heartbeat didn't slow. I forced myself to release my death grip on the walkie and instead watched the image of Goodsir. His hands were down at his sides, his expression unreadable on the screen.

Goodsir brought a hand up to cover his mouth. I had no idea what Ryan was saying to him. The surgeon then knelt, picking up rocks and rolling them between his fingers. Dressed in his borrowed clothes, he looked nothing like the man we'd rescued from the Arctic days ago, even through the screen.

A sudden chill shot through me. They had been out there about five minutes now, but Ryan showed no sign of coming back in. It was making me more nervous by the second; his fear and concerns from earlier seeped into my confidence. I wished the cameras had sound.

"Hey."

I jumped so hard I nearly fell from the chair. Turning, I saw Dennis walking up, hands in his pockets.

"Shit, you scared me," I breathed. "What are you doing in here?"

His eyes were more haunted than I'd ever seen them. "I needed to tell you something. In private, before Ryan and I go out for more propane."

I focused on the monitors again. "What's that?"

"I found mold in three cans of food when I was making our breakfast this morning."

My stomach sank. "Shit."

"We need more food, too, but with just Ryan and I, we can't carry more than one, maybe two propane tanks at a time. The houses are two hours away. That gas station we found once is even further."

My blood chilled. I risked a glance up at him. "Why don't you want Ryan to know this?"

He watched his brother and Harry Goodsir on the screen. He didn't respond for a long time. Finally, he turned back to me.

"We have no way to test Goodsir's power. Before we throw him to the wraiths."

I shook my head, refusing to even consider what he'd said. "We've been over this. This was the reason the lab had the Franklin books, the information on Goodsir's whereabouts. No other men were listed or documented in such detail. Harry is important."

Dennis finally met my gaze. "But we keep pushing aside the fact that they might have just had all that info so they could go back for his DNA. They were frozen, preserved in the ice. They could have gone and taken a sample from him at any point to help make that creepy kid with the ice blue eyes. Subject Zero."

"Jaxon?" I muttered, remembering the files we'd all poured over at some point. "All of the other Evo DNA was taken from live donors. Subject One, for example. Shawn, the kid with superhuman strength, remember? They took it from an Evo called Scott Fischer, gave him a shit ton of money in return and just sent him on his way. The donors no doubt didn't even know what their DNA was being used for."

Dennis looked unconvinced and quite freaked out.

"Either way," I said, "our plan is still going to work, okay? Goodsir stops the wraiths, we finally get to leave this damn bunker, and then we figure out a way to restart. Hopefully, we run across more survivors on our way, and the world is still hospitable."

He didn't reply.

On the monitor, Ryan stopped Goodsir from going over to a dead bush nearby. He made an apologetic gesture. Seconds later, the pair of them returned to the compound's entrance.

I counted to five once Ryan shut the door behind them to make sure it was completely sealed, then fell back against the chair in relief.

"It was just a thought," Dennis murmured.

Swallowing, I sat in silence a moment. "I get what you're saying, but if they only needed to go to the Arctic to get a sample from a dead guy's body, they wouldn't need all of the Franklin books, or Harry's diary. Or especially the ones about life in the eighteen hundreds."

"True." Dennis's eyes slipped out of focus. He chewed a thumbnail, watching his brother lead Goodsir back through the bunker via different camera angles.

I rose from the chair, head held high, making sure I didn't show any ounce of the raging doubt our conversation had instilled.

We jogged back to rejoin Ryan and Goodsir, whose pale face was drawn and thoughtful. His cheeks, however, still held their color, and he broke into a soft smile when he saw us approach.

Ryan was talking animatedly. "We were playing a show when it happened. There was no warning."

"The three of you were the only ones to survive?" Goodsir ran a hand through his curled hair.

"Yeah. Well, that we know of. We made our way here hoping our mom was hiding down here. But she was, uh, she was gone."

Goodsir stopped and gave Ryan a sympathetic look. "I am deeply sorry to hear that. Losing a loved one is a most difficult and heartbreakin' thing."

Ryan didn't meet his gaze. "Yeah, well, we made it work here, the three of us. We only wanted to kill each other a few times here and there, but we've made it so far, which I consider a success." He grinned widely, something I hadn't seen in days.

The four of us walked back down the hallway toward his room, but upon arriving at the first bedroom door, Goodsir paused.

"Must I go back in?" he asked politely.

Ryan hesitated.

"I mean no offense but staying in this room is quite boring despite the wonderful books you were so kind to provide. But I'd much rather spend mah time here learnin' more from the three of you."

"Well, I suppose we could." Ryan let the door swing shut.

"Or a game of cards, perhaps? That is, if you have some."

"Uh. I'm pretty sure that's all right."

Goodsir's eyes lit up. "I'd very much like to play."

I smiled, trying to ignore the swell in the center of my chest.

"I'll get the cards." Dennis jogged away. "Maybe a few of the board games."

"Not Monopoly," Ryan called after him.

"Can't play it anyway," his brother shouted back. "We're out of crackers."

We made our way to the dining area and awkwardly settled around one of the tables. Dennis appeared from the supply closet, shuffling an old white and blue deck of cards. He casually flipped the top card into the middle without stopping the rhythm.

I let out a low whistle.

"Got bored last year and tried to teach myself a few tricks," Dennis said with a sheepish glance at me.

"Were you successful?" Goodsir asked, leaning forward.

"Eh. Not particularly." Dennis shuffled the deck again, this time tossing in a different flourish. "But my shuffle game is on point."

"On point...?" Goodsir asked, raising an eyebrow.

"It's, uh, slang. For..." Dennis shrugged. "Really good?"

I snickered.

"I see." Goodsir nodded knowingly. "So, mah anatomist knowledge is on point? I use it that way, correct?"

I laughed and waved a hand at the deck. "Sounds right to me."

—

We taught Goodsir a few different games, from Blackjack to Euchre. After a few rounds of the latter, he showed us a game he called Maw, something he played with his family and friends. It consisted of winning tricks, much like Euchre, and playing both brought back memories of family reunions I loved as a child. I remembered my grandparents, mother, and father all sitting around a rickety card table in the garage on a hot summer day, tossing cards into a pile and laughing at rules I never understood as a child. I could almost smell the smoke of my grandpa's cigarettes.

Dennis changed things up by suggesting we play a couple hands of Texas Hold 'Em, but Goodsir had such a bad poker face that we all broke down into gales of laughter too often to play seriously.

"Remember game nights at home?" Ryan tossed his hand of cards face down on the table and leaned back in his chair.

"You hated those," Dennis said.

"Not really. I just couldn't keep up with the games you'd make us try." Ryan chuckled. "You were never content with a round of cards like this. It always had to be something new and obscure."

"Yeah, well, that's why Mom and I always let you win in the first few rounds. To ease you in."

Ryan interlaced his fingers and propped up the back of his head with his palms. His face softened, and he didn't reply.

"Mom loved the campaigns I came up with," Dennis said softly.

His brother's smile was warm yet strained. "We both did, in our different ways."

I threw my crappy stack of cards on top of Ryan's and let their memories linger, propping my chin in one hand.

Goodsir looked between the three of us, his eyes twinkling and cheeks pink. "Mah younger brother often invented new games for us tae play when we were lads. He used tae love creating treasure hunts. He'd have us runnin' all over the house just to see who'd find his hidden trinkets first."

Dennis grinned. "I can't believe I never thought of that."

Now Goodsir looked lost in his own memories. He glanced up at us, cleared his throat, and lowered his cards. "What were in the files you discovered doon 'ere?"

The room grew quiet, still.

Ryan tossed his own cards face down onto the table. "We might as well show you. Come on."

The four of us rose from our chairs, leaving the card game unfinished and old laughter hanging in the air.

In the control room, Goodsir's eyes widened the second he spotted the handheld camera Dennis picked up.

"How does this work?" he asked quietly.

"Uh, well. I can explain it later." Dennis watched Goodsir reach out and tentatively touch the camera.

"May I?"

Dennis shrugged. "Fine by me."

Goodsir pushed buttons and fiddled with the strap, his face a transparent mask of fascination. "This is wonderful. What is this material it is made out of? How does something so small work with a simple touch?"

I couldn't help but grin at the barrage of endless questions. I snuck a glance at Ryan, who watched with worried eyes, cables gripped tight in one hand. He caught my gaze and his mouth flickered into a slight frown.

"Here." Dennis gingerly took the camera from Goodsir and the cables from Ryan, hooking the device up to one of the monitors. He hesitated, then jabbed the play button.

After a burst of static, and the man with a mullet wearing a lab coat appeared again. Instead of the first tapes we'd found, we showed Goodsir a recording of a successful time travel.

He gasped and leaned closer to the square monitor. "Can these people also see us?"

I shook my head and lightly touched his arm. "This is a recording from a long time ago. It was here when we arrived at the bunker. It's...it's like a photograph, but it moves and speaks."

Goodsir blinked. "A moving photograph..."

"A recorded image."

"A daguerreotype that moves and speaks?"

I nodded dumbly.

Ryan cut us off with a sharp gesture as the recording continued. Goodsir backed away from the monitor, mouth slack.
He became very still, eyes focused on the screen, listening
and watching.

Instead of watching the recording as I had so many times
already, I watched Goodsir. His eyes were wide. When the
video got to the point where the test subject returned on the
platform, he clamped a hand over his mouth but didn't look
away.

"We know this is a lot to take in," Dennis said quietly, now
also watching Goodsir.

"Aye. It truly is." The surgeon's voice was soft. He looked
like he was going to puke.

Ryan sighed. "This is how we knew we could come get
you." He unplugged the camera and the monitor snapped
back to the live feed of the back hallway.

"But..." Goodsir frowned, his eyes intent on him. "None of
this has ana'thin' to do with me. Why come for me?"

The Breckner brothers and I all shared a look. Clearing my
throat, I stepped forward. "If we tried to change anything in
the past, we would be changing the future. Which means
possibly erasing something crucial, even stopping our own
timelines. Or the time machine itself."

"Then why risk using this machine at all? Are things truly
that desperate?"

Ryan ran a hand through his hair. Goodsir blinked rapidly,
gaze moving back and forth but not focusing on anything.

"Along with the tapes, we, uh, found extensive information
on, uh, on the Franklin Expedition," I continued nervously.
"Coordinates, names, locations, but your...your diary in particular."

Goodsir was breathing quicker than normal. "Mah diary?"

I let my eyes fall shut and took a deep breath. I knew this
was inevitable, but we had to be honest. My heart began to
pound. I hurried into the study and retrieved the journal.

When I returned with the book, Ryan shot me a look full of
apprehension.

"Mr. Goodsir," I said softly, holding up his diary.

He stared at it, unblinking. I couldn't even imagine what was going through his mind. The confusion, the fear. It tore at my heart to see him this shaken.

"I left that in mah tent," he said quietly. "I didnae bring that with. You told me to leave everythin' behind."

"You did." I held it out to him. "Archeologists found this during a rare thaw, according to the notes we found."

"I died there." He wouldn't look up, didn't take the book. "I never made it home."

"You—"

"I knew I was going to die." Goodsir's lower lip trembled a moment. He swallowed and ran the back of a hand across his mouth.

"I'm so sorry." I could barely get the words out.

"But you're here now." Dennis's voice was just above a whisper. "You're okay."

Goodsir blinked at me, paler than before. "That means I've been dead for over a century. Nearly two."

I suppressed a shudder, unable to even begin to how such information must be making him feel. "No, you're here now. Alive. You haven't died at all."

"I never saw mah family again." Goodsir's eyes unfocused, his gaze slipping down to the concrete floor.

Torn between comforting him and giving the man space to grieve, I licked my lips and clasped both hands before me. "You didn't deserve to die. To suffer. I…we wanted to save you."

Goodsir brought his eyes around to settle on his diary. He lightly touched the center of his chest. "The creatures you spoke of, the ones tormenting the world now. You want me to try and trap them."

I shared another look with the brothers, then nodded.

He took a step back. "I dinnae ken how to even do that."

"If what you said in this diary is true," Ryan said, "then you have a power no one else does. You did something with the ice demon in the Arctic, and now we'd like you to try with the wraiths outside."

The fear on Goodsir's face grew clearer.

"We're running out of food. We can't go outside without being attacked, and there's only three of us. The chance of us surviving once our food is gone…" Ryan gestured at the surgeon's chest. "If you can, I don't know, somehow suck the wraiths into yourself, you can release them in the back room. It's sealed. They'd be trapped inside, and the world would be safe again."

"You weren't saving mah life at all," Goodsir said, still staring at me. "You merely needed to use me. What on earth were you to do with me once I accomplished this? That is, if I am able?"

Dennis sighed and ran a hand over his face, clearly uncomfortable. "Well, you'd stay here. In our time."

Goodsir's eyes narrowed slightly. "No' put me back?"

An immense wave of guilt flooded through me, and I still couldn't make words form.

"You could put me back in Scotland. I could continue mah work." Goodsir looked at the diary I held. "In cell theory. Perhaps I can…can change the course o' study somehow. Stop the experiments that led up to this. I could go home."

Dennis sat in one of the chairs, dropping his head into both hands. All trace of wonder and excitement I'd felt at the progress we'd made came crashing to a halt.

Twenty

Harry
2020

The Breckners, Miss Ross, and I had nothing to discuss once the cat was entirely out of the bag. Of course, there was much to go over, but my mind and very soul could no longer bear any more shocks.

"I appreciate your disclosure," I said wearily. "But I think it would do me good to get a wee bit of rest. Have some time to think."

Annie looked miserable. It was clear that she wanted to say more but didn't. She looked away, breaking the intense connection I'd felt moments before.

I was touched at her determination, her passion. Although I'd only been among the three for a mere few days, I felt a sort of bond developing with Miss Ross. Neither she nor Dennis didn't find my questioning to be an annoyance, but she also didn't try to beat around the bush about anything. If I wasn't mistaken, despite the strangeness of my current situation, I believed I was developing a fondness for her.

All of that was shoved aside the moment I realized exactly what these people were asking of me.

"I would like to lie down." I started toward the front of the control room, heading back toward the dining area, intent on crawling into the little bed they'd given me. I glanced at Annie as I passed, noting the sadness in her gaze.

"Mr. Goodsir." Ryan's voice was firm. I stopped to face the taller man.

He reached out, offering his hand. "I understand how difficult this may be for you. It's been hell on us, too, but we can do this together. We can survive, all of us."

I looked at him a moment, watching his face for any slight shift of expression, but his gaze held. I nodded and shook his hand. "It is a lot, aye. There's much to think about."

Ryan's mouth twitched. "I get it."

A clap on my back caused me to jump. Dennis was smiling at me. "You're a good dude. We want to help you, too."

I glanced at Annie again. She watched us but stayed quiet, standing off to one side, holding my journal.

I left the room. The scattered blue and white cards were still atop the table where we'd shared our games. The joy of the new experience was now bitter in the back of my throat. I quickened my pace, my boots thudding dully along the grey floor. I passed the tallied wall and hurried into my room.

Shutting the door behind me, my body finally reacted. It wracked itself with uncontrollable trembles. The constant coolness of what Dennis referred to as our "concrete home" now seemed frigid, and I picked up my long coat from its place over the chair back. I slipped my arms inside and buttoned the front, then lowered down onto the side of the thin mattress.

I tried to unlace my boots, but my hands shook so badly that I could not get a grip. Instead, I lay back and stared up at the ceiling, trying to steady my racing, cluttered thoughts.

Coming to terms with the fact I had traveled forward in time had been simple. I had seen it happen. One moment I lay on my bed pads in my tent, then I was underground in a dead, empty world full of strange objects and materials. I had yet to see these creatures the three spoke of, but all else had been true, so I allowed myself to believe in their existence. I had seen what they called videos and the machine that played strange music, windows that responded to a mere touch of a finger.

And I had seen my diary. The one I had lamented over for leaving it behind. A copy of my daguerreotype lay within its pages, something I had not taken with on the journey. Then there were the books I had glimpsed, but not been allowed to read. The ones written about Franklin's journey. Yes, it was clear I had, in fact, time traveled, as there was no other logical explanation. But that mattered not.

I was no hero. I was a quiet soul who had been ripped from one fate only to be thrown into one as equally dangerous. I preferred my books and my research and the occasional trip to collect samples. Chaos unnerved me.

Could I even do what these people were asking of me?

Staring at the rough, pocked ceiling above me, I let myself simply sit and breathe for many long minutes. My breathing began to steady, as did my heart.

Annie had risked her life to rescue me from the mutinous, cannibalistic camp. The three strangers had the utmost confidence that I was the answer to their issue, but I could not bring myself to agree.

After a few contemplative moments, I promptly fell into a strange half-sleep. My mind attempted to show me strange images that could have soon developed into dreams, but I stubbornly shied back, trying to wake myself. All I could hear in the muddied haze was what Ryan had told me with utmost sincerity: "You have a power no one else does."

A pressure in the middle of my chest tore me back to consciousness. I gasped deeply, sitting up.

Nothing had changed. My door remained shut. The sharp white light from the ceiling beat down upon me, unwavering. I rubbed my face with both hands, hoping to clear the cobwebs that had weaved through my still-racing mind.

I thought of the constant struggles I'd endured in the Arctic. Sir John Franklin and my comrades may have been killed, my family just as unreachable as before, but perhaps if I could help those who'd helped me, they would fulfill my other request in exchange. I could save Franklin and his lost men. I could even try to persuade the three to let me go home somehow. First, however, I needed to learn how to control this power of mine.

Closing my eyes, I relaxed until I could slowly unclench my fists. I took three deep breaths and massaged the sharp divots my nails had made in both palms. Reaching down with my mind as I had in the Arctic, I found I could feel the part of my core that resided behind my breastbone. It was calming. It felt right. I pushed slightly harder. A sharp, quick pain sliced through my breastbone, then was gone.

The door to my room slammed open. Annie stood before me, her cheeks flushed and red hair disheveled. Thin white strings similar to what Dennis had used trailed down from near her face to the small device in her hand – her iPod. She clutched my diary in the other hand, and her breathing was uneven, full of panic. "Harry, we need to get outside. Now."

I rose from the mattress. "What's happened?"

"The gennie's shooting steam, and it's flooding the bunker. It's too hot to even breathe. We have to get out of here."

We wasted no time. Coat tails flailing, I bolted out of my room close behind Annie. She held one hand up to her face, covering her nose and mouth and gesturing at me to do the same. My eyes burned hot the moment we ran down the hallway. The sensation reached my lungs no matter how hard I buried my face in the crook of an arm.

Intense heat shrouded us both. The loud hissing of steam echoed through the hallway like a giant, furious snake.

"Where are the brothers?" I shouted against the fabric of my sleeve. "We need to get them out of here as well."

She pocketed her iPod, white strings and all, shoving the small bundle into a trouser pocket. "They aren't here. They went above for more propane tanks."

We sprinted past the tallied wall. Annie bent at the waist the moment we reached the bunker's stairs, reaching down for a peculiar knapsack.

"Hurry." She still held one hand over her mouth, and her eyes watered just as badly as mine.

We quickly ascended the stairs. Annie twirled the large, spinning lock on the door. I began to choke. The noise of the door's suction was drowned by the generator's hissing. The moment the large door shuddered upward, we both threw our weight forward, shoulders colliding with the slick metal.

Bright light accosted my eyes. I paused halfway out of the bunker, swallowing large mouthfuls of outside air. A quick glance around showed nothing had moved since Ryan and I had stood in the same place.

The heavy door slipped from my fingers and fell fully open. Its resulting clang was deafening; we both flinched away.

"My apologies," I said. Dirt and gravel crunched beneath my boots, shooting my mind back to a memory of the shale stones I'd trudged over on King William Land.

"Oh, God." Annie inhaled deeply, wiping her forehead with the back of one hand. She still held my journal. "What do we do?"

I blinked at her, perplexed. "I have not the faintest. If your generator is broken, we need to devise a way to fix it."

"We can't even get near it." She knelt and gingerly slipped my journal into a front pouch on her pack. Still breathing heavily, she shouldered it, stood, and turned in a slow circle. Her gaze traveled over our barren surroundings. "And what if we can't? The generator keeps our air recycled, gives us electricity and heat."

A dull pressure began in the center of my chest. I lifted a hand and absentmindedly pressed three fingertips against my breastbone. "Do you ken which way they went?"

Unshed tears stood in her green eyes. She shook her head. "I've only been outside once since the end."

"All right. We wait here until they return."

"In the open?" She looked up at the clear blue sky.

I considered the nearby ruins that could potentially offer shelter. Without its roof, however, it would not be much.

The pressure in my chest spiked, shattering my focus. I doubled over, clutching at the front of my shirt through my open coat.

"Mr. Goodsir? Harry?" Annie grabbed my shoulder.

I let out a shuddering breath. My mind flashed and for a moment, I didn't know where I was. All I could feel was the pressure that signified an ice demon was near. My voice was harsh and my cry wordless. Slowly, the pain subsided, and I was able to see the dead world of the Nevada woods once more.

I had yet to know what type of beasts tortured the world now, but the sensation I'd just experienced had been identical. With my blood chilling despite the heat surrounding us, I gasped, "It's coming."

She took a step back then, eyes widening. "You can feel the wraiths? Like you felt the demons?"

Hunching over further, I nodded. "If that is what this is, then aye. But this is much, much worse."

"Oh, no. Oh, no."

"We must hide." My back shuddered. "In the bunker."

Annie dug a hand into her red hair. "We can't even breathe down there!"

"Then in the woods. Or this building. Anywhere."

She knelt, tearing off her pack and pulling my diary free. With a sorrowful apology, she ripped a page from the back and began to scribble on it with one of her pens.

I bent forward, wiping my sweat-slicked brow and glancing at her scribbled words: "Gennie broken, could not breathe, wraiths coming."

Annie glanced up at me. "Which way is North?"

"Oh…" I peered at the sky, turning in a quick half-circle before pointing.

She hunched, scribbled something more, then placed the paper in the dirt next to the door. I lifted a nearby stone and handed it over, which she used to weigh down her note.

We quickly pulled the metal door shut. Without hesitation, Annie leapt onto its surface. The door lowered further with a soft sucking sound followed by a series of clunks.

"How are they to get back inside?" I asked.

"Ryan found keys down there when we first arrived. He always keeps a set."

"Seems a wee bit dangerous if being chased."

"We always had someone stay behind, just in case. But if we leave it open now, the wraiths might get inside and then we'd truly be fucked."

I steeled myself against another sudden surge of intense pressure. Tearing my eyes away from the sky, I searched the ground. The dirt was displaced all around, with faded footprints leading every which way. I knelt and touched the ones I had just left myself.

"Can you tell which way they went?" Annie continued to stare at the sky, turning slowly in place.

I continued my inspection, trying to ignore the pain in my chest. Using shoe size and shape, I ruled out my footprints as well as Annie's. Identifying what could only be Ryan and Dennis's, I could see there were multiple trails, some prints deeper than others.

"How often did they leave for supplies?"

Annie didn't take her eyes from the sky. Her body was less tense than it had been, perhaps from seeing there was no immediate danger.

The increasing pain in my chest told me otherwise.

"Not often at first, but now, every few months." Her words came out in short bursts.

I put a hand on her arm, trying to keep my voice steady as yet another surge of pain shot through me. "We will find them," I said, gritting my teeth to avoid gasping again. "But we need to go, right now."

Annie covered my hand with hers and glanced back at the paper note she'd left. "I remember Ryan said he'd spotted a gas station when they were scouting north of the bunker. I wrote that we'd go there. If they were going for fuel, that's one of two places they could have gotten it."

"Then we will go north."

"We have nothing to defend ourselves with," she said in a thin voice.

I smiled at her despite my pain. "But you have me."

She stared at me, hard, and nodded once.

I had no idea if I could even control this alleged power of mine. I did know, however, that I didn't want to die. Undeterred by the clashing feelings I had for the trio, I also did not want Annie to meet any type of horrific fate.

A screeching wail sounded far in the distance to our right, stopping the breath in my throat. It sounded like no beast or creature I'd ever encountered before, not even the Arctic's ice demons.

The sound spurred Annie into action. She turned and ran the way I'd pointed before. I kept pace behind her, watching the still clear sky for any movement.

New fear kept pulling panic to the surface of my mind as we plowed through the lifeless trees and surrounding brush, high-stepping and dodging often.

Regardless of how fast we fled, however, without shelter, Annie and I were both in very real and quickly approaching danger.

Twenty-One

Annie
2020

Harry Goodsir and I charged through the dead woods, casting quick glances up and around as often as we dared. The go bag I'd grabbed bounced against the small of my back, the weight of the metal bottles of day-old water and cans of food weighing me down. My lungs were alight. Dead leaves and brush crunched beneath our boots. My eyes watered from the kicked up dirt, and we both had begun to choke on our gasps.

After what felt like hours, I was accosted by an endless hacking that forced me to slow and lean against a nearby tree trunk, its bark sharp against the bare skin of my arm. My tank was soaked through, but I wiped my hands on the front regardless, then rubbed both burning eyes.

Goodsir stared back the way we'd come, one palm flat against the middle of his chest. He didn't gasp for breath as I did, but his cheeks were flushed red and sweat dripped from a few of his curls. "The pain has abated."

"But the wraiths never came." My still-pounding heart flew against my chest. "Are you sure?"

His troubled gaze searched past the bare branches above. "In the Arctic, it was much different. The pain only came once a demon was already near. Yet we hae been outside for over an hour and remain unassaulted."

"That doesn't mean we're safe."

"Quite the contrary." He finally met my gaze. "We should keep movin'. If the brothers are at this station you speak of, we will intercept them and devise a plan going forward."

Dread worked its way into my mind. "And if they're not? If they went somewhere else for the propane?"

"If we find the station empty, we can double back toward the bunker, as long as no creatures attack."

"What if they're…" I couldn't finish the thought. Mouth dry, I wiped the trickling sweat from my forehead and tried again. "What if the wraiths didn't come after us because they were…they were attacking…"

"Miss Ross." Goodsir's tone softened. "They will be all right."

I slid down the trunk of the tree. My breath was slowly returning. "Either Ryan and Dennis are dead, or they won't be able to get back inside the bunker because of the steam. They're just as stuck out here as we are. We should have just stayed by the bunker's door."

"Had we done that, any approaching creatures would hae seen us." He tilted his head to one side. "Mah pain is gone. Fleeing ensured our safety."

"But not theirs." I swallowed, glancing behind him, unease still growing. "And now that your alarm isn't going off, do we continue or go back? I don't know the right thing to do."

"Sometimes the right thing is no' the easiest to choose." His smile was kind, his eyes soft. Still sweating, he knelt, closely inspecting the dirt beneath our feet. "Does anything around look familiar to you?"

"No." I kicked out at a nearby fallen branch, vision blurring from unshed tears. "Ryan was too damn stubborn to use the walkies as their range was pathetic, and now look. We could have had them. Now we're going to die out here."

"We will no' die out here, Miss Ross." He stood swiftly, his coattails flapping against his thighs, and offered his hand. I let him pull me to my feet. "I will fight with everything I have if the creatures show. We will get back to your friends."

"Don't make promises you can't keep, Mr. Goodsir." I couldn't keep the anger out of my voice. Instantly regretting my harsh tone, I looked up at him to apologize, but his gaze was focused on something behind me.

"There's somethin' there," Goodsir said quietly. He was looking over my left shoulder into the surrounding branches.

I turned to peer through the dead trees for dark clouds of mist or clawed hands reaching for us. Instead, my eyes found something I hadn't seen in years. "It's just a pickup truck."

"It's marvelous." His breathing had returned to normal. He stepped forward, his gaze fixated on the vehicle.

We picked our way over to it. Brown spots of advanced rust had taken over the truck's forest green paint. The truck sat at a slight angle, with its nose pointing upward and left side drooping to the ground.

I searched for movement but nothing stirred. "Maybe we can find something useful in it."

"Can we use it? I assume it is for transportation. I would very much like to try."

"The tires are flat. And the windshield is busted. I bet no one's driven this thing in a long time. I doubt it even starts."

Goodsir's disappointment was plain. He stared at the truck wide-eyed as we drew closer. Tentatively reaching out, he lightly touched the scratched metal grille.

I left him to his wonderment and quickly stepped around to the other side, peering in through its dusty windows. The hot Nevada air had already begun to cool, and it dried my damp tank top, but I longed for a shower, or at least to get out of my no doubt disgusting sneakers.

The seats and floor were all littered with empty water bottles and crumpled fast food wrappings. I opened the passenger door as quietly as I could.

Goodsir opened the driver's door. He leaned inside and ran a hand over the steering wheel, the knobs on the radio, then bent to inspect the pedals at the floor.

Nothing but loose, yellowing paper filled the glove box. I nearly gave up but when I stuck my hand beneath the seats, I felt something familiar that sent my heart soaring.

"This could come in handy." I held up the heavy, dusty, black-handled revolver I'd found. Sunlight shone along its dull metal barrel.

Goodsir's eyes widened when he saw the weapon. He had picked up one of the bottles and to inspect the cap, rubbing a thumb across its loosening label.

"In handy?" he repeated.

"Useful. Could be useful." I leaned forward and brushed the other bottles aside. My forgotten iPod pressed lightly against my thigh in the shallow pocket of my jeans.

"Would this, too, be useful to hae at hand, perhaps if we came across any fresh water?"

Eyeing the crinkled plastic bottle, I debated. "Honestly, we don't know how clean it is. What was in it last. I wouldn't risk it. Besides, we have water." I patted the shoulder strap of my backpack.

Goodsir dropped the bottle into the pile with the rest of its comrades with a slight disappointment. His attachment to things I took for granted every day, especially before the end, made him strangely endearing.

Turning my attention back to the revolver, I opened the chamber with care, keeping the barrel pointed to the ground and my finger off the trigger. I barely knew anything about guns, but my dad had often taken his collection out shooting with me in tow. The chamber was full. Another, more careful inspection of the truck didn't turn up extra ammunition.

"Miss Ross." Goodsir was again looking at something he'd discovered nearby. I stepped away from the truck, revolver in hand, and followed his gaze to see the truck's tire marks leading away, further into the dead woods.

I slipped the gun into the waist of my pants. "Nice eye, Goodsir. That could lead us to shelter."

"Aye." He pulled his coat off, draped it over one arm, and smiled at me. "And please, call me Harry."

"All right." I chuckled. "But only if you stop calling me Miss Ross."

We followed the path, sticking to the tree line instead of walking along the tire marks. Goodsir's foot snagged over a thick bundle of dead brush. Catching him with both hands, I grunted, struggling to right him. He was breathing heavily. With one hand, he shoved back his plastered hair.

The path finally opened up to reveal a small and very worn building next to a single gas pump. Both were surrounded with brown weeds and a flat area of gravel. We stood at the edge of the dead trees, staring at the building's windows that glinted sunlight back at us. Nothing moved in or around the building. Without living creatures to fill the air with sound, the woods remained deathly silent.

"Is this the station you spoke of?" Harry asked.

I nodded, heart sinking. There was no sign of anyone. "I think so, but I don't see signs of Ryan or Dennis. We need to go back."

"It doesnae hurt to check. Perhaps they're inside."

His optimism was beginning to grow on me. I steeled myself and stepped out into the open. We took slow, steady steps forward, and I led him around the back of the building.

"Hold your hands up and out." I showed him what I meant. "In case there really are other people inside. We don't want to look threatening."

When we reached the back door, Harry politely knocked. I resisted the urge to facepalm and tried the handle. It was locked. Glancing up at the deep blue sky, I motioned for him to follow and carefully made my way around to the front.

The gas pump nozzle lay discarded on the gravel ground, as if someone had actually been about to use it when the wraiths came, but instead drove off in a hurry. It was an eerie sight with zero cars around.

After checking in the large storefront windows for any movement or signs of life, I felt comfortable enough to pull open the front door and slip inside.

"Oh." Harry stared at everything. He tried to go to the closest shelf, but I held him back with one hand on his arm.

"We have to make sure that we're alone," I said in a whisper.

A few long minutes later, we'd scouted the entire building, even in the back employee area and small storage room. Our footprints stood out in the thick layer of dust along the floor. They were the only fresh ones. All of the counters, shelves, and equipment were equally coated. The lack of cobwebs everywhere unnerved me.

"No one's been here in a while." I nabbed a tub of Clorox wipes and popped the top open. The solution inside had dried up long ago, but I dipped a splash of water onto a sheet and used it to wipe down the front counter. Soon it was relatively clean and lemony fresh. I tossed the blackened wipe aside and hopped up, ignoring how my pants stuck to the still-wet surface. I shrugged out of the heavy backpack. My tired body thanked me, singing in relief. I slapped at the loose legs of my jeans and watched puffs of dirt float into the air.

Harry was engrossed with investigating literally anything he could get his hands on, exclaiming here and there, eyes full of questions. Weary from our sudden flight from the bunker and the heat of the day, I rubbed my face and fought the urge to close my eyes.

"We should see if there's anything here we could take back to the bunker and head out." I slid off the counter.

Harry didn't reply. He was busy trying to figure out how to work a flashlight.

I smiled at the determined look on his face, guileless and full of wonder. "You need batteries."

Scanning the shelves, I found the right size and attempted to explain how they worked. I showed him how to unscrew the bottom, how to know which way to drop them into the flashlight. His questions were endless. Although I couldn't properly describe everything, I did my best, and it seemed to at least satiate his curiosity for the time being.

Harry exclaimed in surprise when he pressed the little button and the beam of light illuminated the other side of the store. He gleefully waved it around.

Leaving him to his new discovery, I made my way back through the store toward the silent, darkened refrigerated section. With the unit off, its frozen food had either melted or rotted.

Stacks of rotten microwavable food filled some of the darkened shelves. Colorful ice cream pints lined another unit, a few streaked with trails of the melted dessert. Dried puddles stained the bottom of the freezer. Dead flies and bigger insects littered the floor, and a whiff of a horrendous smell leaked through the glass doors.

Ignoring the rotten food, I moved a few doors down and stared in at rows of bottled water, soda, and energy drinks. The sight of water reminded me of how thirsty I was.

I made my way back toward the front of the store and grabbed my backpack. The noise of the zipper brought Harry out of his current marvel: an unsteady display of various sunglasses.

Pulling one of the metal water bottles free, I twisted off the top and offered it to him first. He accepted with a smile. He tipped his head back, hair falling away, and chugged a few mouthfuls with eyes closed. I watched him, still in awe that he stood here with me now.

"Thank you," he said, and handed back the bottle.

I wanted to drain it dry but relented, downing only two gulps and wiping my mouth with a sleeve.

"We should eat, too." I dropped the bottle in my backpack, then drew out two cans of food. "Before going back. Keep our energy up and all that."

"Must we eat from the tins?" He was staring at the food in my hands as if it would jump up and bite him.

"We've got nothing else." I straightened and handed one over. "Ryan and I had thought of starting a small garden underground, in the bunker, but didn't have time to get it started. Or all the materials. Once all of this is finished, we'll work on that and have fresh food soon. Promise."

Harry nodded, taking the can of yellow corn. I thought of how his journal had detailed Franklin's men, who had been slowly starving, with nothing but rotted tinned food to eat. I hated that he was now dealing with the same thing in our time.

The weight of what we'd done, of the pure terror of the last few hours, all hit at once. This was my fault. All of it. Disagreeing with Ryan had led us to this moment, separated and on the run from monsters. Our home was gone, and I had no idea how to fix it without Ryan and Dennis, who I couldn't help but fear were dead. I looked away from Harry's kind smile and sank to the floor, dropping my face.

All emotion from the day, from the weeks, poured out. My shoulders shook, and my sobs echoed in the dead room. I pulled my knees to my chest and just kept crying. For Dennis and Ryan who we couldn't even help. For Harry, the man we'd ripped out of time itself just to endanger him again. For my parents I'd never see again.

Harry's fingers brushed my arm. "I know this is difficult. Overwhelming, frustrating."

I sniffled loudly. "Sorry. I'm…sorry."

"Please, no." He smiled. "I, too, often felt panic set in while in the Arctic. I'm no' ashamed that I broke down as well. Many times."

I blinked at him through my tears. I was being comforted by someone who had been starving for years and nearly cannibalized. He'd lived through horrors he couldn't forget, lost loved ones, just like me. I felt a growing closeness to him in our shared traumas, different though they were.

"Thank you." I awkwardly reached up and laid my hand on his.

Harry squeezed my shoulder again, his grip strong, and let go. He sat on the ground and rested his back up against the counter. The flashlight he'd found sat in his lap.

Too aware of my gross face, I turned away and scavenged a box of plastic cutlery from the shelves before sitting next to him. I leaned back against the counter like him and pried open his can, the cut of its tab sharp against my finger. "Ryan told us that most canned veggies stay good for up to four or five years."

He watched closely. "We had thousands of tins aboard the *Erebus* alone."

Pulling the tab on my own can, I dug a fork into the watery yellow depths of corn. "So, uh, I read about that. That some were rotted."

"Aye." Harry stared at the top of his can. "Aye. Apparently when purchasing provisions for the expedition, those in charge of stocking our stores went with the lowest bidder. We got what we paid for."

He grimaced, looking up at me with haunted eyes.

I paused, first bite halfway to my lips. "That's terrible."

He dropped his gaze back to his can and stared at the peeled lid. His expression flitted back to that awed stare he always got when he'd discovered something new. "This is wonderful. How did they make its little tab lay so flat?"

I handed him a spoon, which he promptly rubbed between finger and thumb.

"What is this material?" he asked.

"Uh, plastic." The first bite of food awoke my hunger. I spooned more into my mouth quickly, careful not to spill. "And the cans are made out of steel. Or aluminum. I think."

"I have nae idea what that is." Harry started to eat just as quickly as me.

We ate in silence until both of our little utensils scraped the bottom of the cans. My last spoonful of food got stuck in the back of my throat. I coughed weakly, swallowing hard and clearing my throat.

"We should go back." I lowered my empty can to the floor, suddenly aware of how late it was. "How long will it take to get back?"

"I'm sure we will be fine for the night."

I nearly dropped my can. "Are you kidding me? We can't stay here."

"We can accomplish nothing if we—"

"They'll find us. The creatures."

"They won't. We hae shelter here, and I will know if they draw near." He lightly tapped the center of his chest.

Infuriated, I chewed on the plastic spoon. "We have to find our way home. If Ryan and Dennis got back, they're freaked out and pissed enough to come looking for us. They could get killed."

"And if they did, in fact, return to the bunker, they would hae already found your note. They'll either find a way to fix your generator or they will come find us here. It is better for us to stay put so they are able to track us down. If they do no' arrive by mornin', we will head back to the bunker then." He paused. "I can take first watch, if you would like me to."

"First watch?" I snorted. "Oh, like I'll be able to sleep. This is stupid, Harry. We're going back. We can be careful."

He shook his head. "The creatures described to me are dark, just like the sky is aboot to be. We should exercise caution and go back at first light."

"For fuck's sake."

He winced and looked out the window, silent.

I paced up and down the three aisles of the station. I glared at the shelves, not seeing much of anything. The last thing I wanted was to stay overnight in a filthy gas station instead of looking for my friends, but Harry was, of course, right.

Stumbling around in the woods in the dark could bring the damn wraiths right up on our trail and we wouldn't even notice.

I refused to panic. Ryan and Dennis were smart, and they were together. But unless I wanted to cry and worry all night long, I needed to keep my mind busy. The dusty magazines at the front of the store provided nothing of interest, but with little else to do, I took three.

Carefully emptying the contents of my backpack onto the counter, I squished it into a lumpy, makeshift pillow and pulled Harry's navy-blue overcoat on as a blanket, settling down on the hard, dirty floor next to him. A tear threatened to roll down my cheek, but I angrily wiped it away and held up a 2017 issue of *Sports, Illustrated.*

Less than five minutes later, I tossed the magazine aside. Seeing the bright pictures of celebrities and various types of ugly sports memorabilia only made me realize how much I missed the world before it had ended. The somber emotion mixed with my frustration and fear for Ryan and Dennis, so instead, I stared at the ceiling and tried to talk more sense into myself.

Harry remained silent and watchful by my side. He rolled a button of his borrowed shirt between two fingers.

"There's no way I can sleep," I said finally. "Maybe you should try first instead."

"Nonsense. You'll be asleep within moments. Then we will switch. At first light, we can carry this fuel you need, in case we are able to fix your generator upon our return."

I didn't respond. We were all so royally fucked.

After a few quiet moments in the gathering darkness, Harry spoke again. "These creatures you speak of…can they smell us?"

I shifted my head on the backpack. "No, I don't think so. Otherwise they'd have been swarming the entrance to the bunker after each supply run."

He nodded slowly. "Hear us, then?"

"I assume so. Or they're triggered by movement. Honestly, I've been hiding underground so long, I have no idea."

Harry scooted closer and smiled down at me. "Get some rest. We'll move again the moment day breaks."

"How are you not terrified?"

"Oh, I am. But you forget that I've already been through somethin' similar. I still can be an asset even though I'm a hundred and seventy-two years behind the times."

My eyes had grown heavy. "I'm beginning to believe that."

Harry lightly placed a hand on my arm. "I'm so very sorry we couldnae locate Ryan and Dennis."

"Maybe they already got back."

"I hope so."

"They're gonna flip."

"They're both canny lads. If they fixed that generator of yours, they'll know not to leave at night. Or they will have found shelter of their own. We will hopefully be back before they venture out again to look for us."

I gave him a weak smile. His presence was starting to bring a calming sense of comfort. "How are you always so positive?"

"We may be trapped in a perilous situation, aye, but we are here regardless. The only thing we can do now is figure out how tae survive. Everything else comes after."

Twenty-Two

Harry
2020

I had not meant to startle Annie awake, but could not risk a sound. I pressed a palm over her mouth and brought a finger to my lips. Her green eyes flew wide open and she began to squirm.

"Annie," I said in the lowest whisper, quickly pulling away. "Annie, I'm so sorry, but there's something out there."

She looked toward the tall windows through which weak dawn light filtered. Bare tree branches waved sullenly in a slight wind. She pushed herself into a sitting position, my coat falling from her torso.

"I'd fallen asleep," I admitted. "I hadn't meant to, but I drifted, and woke to the sound you described."

"Oh. Oh, no." Annie reached up, wiping at her tired eyes. "Harry…are you sure?"

I nodded, helping her to her feet. "Aye. I'm sure. The pain in my chest came back. It's what woke me."

"We need to hide." Annie picked up her pack and replaced the bottles of water and canned food she'd brought. "Now."

I snatched my coat from the floor, its long coattails flinging patches of dust into the air. Annie secured her pack and slipped her arms into its straps. A distant howl sounded outside. The fierce, sharp pang that hit me in the middle of my chest nearly drove me to my knees.

I backed away from the windows, quickly stepping over the small pile of items I'd been inspecting in an attempt to stay awake. Things I'd never before seen, objects that would not work no matter how much I attempted to understand their function. With a surge of dismay, I left them all behind.

"We could hide in these." Annie reached the tall glass doors at the back of the shop and flung open the nearest one. No sooner did she throw a handful of strange little boxes to the floor than an awful, heavy stench hit us both. Gagging, eyes blurring, I turned just as another shot of pain laced through my core.

"They're near," I gasped through clenched teeth.

She let out a curse I had not heard from a lady's lips and pushed the door shut. We sprinted away while covering our noses.

In the small back room, Annie began to scour the shelves. I attempted to be of assistance but found myself at a loss.

The wailing came again, louder, closer. I wrestled with the idea of running but knew we might not get as lucky as we did the day before.

But perhaps my ability could save us.

Leaving Annie to her scavenging, I let my eyes fall shut. There came a gentle yet firm tug at the center of my torso the moment I forced myself to focus inward. As I did in the Arctic, I reached further, searching for any kind of answer but feeling nothing. I hesitated, then reversed it, pushing out with my mind.

A spreading sensation poured through my torso that now reminded me of the flashlight's beam shooting out from the device. What I could only describe as another awareness lit up. Invisible eyes turned in my direction. I opened my eyes with a gasp and released the hold with a horrified realization dawning.

I was a beacon.

That brief moment had connected me to something, and I had been able to know what it knew for the merest second. These things, like the ice demons, could feel my presence. They were being drawn to me, and when I pushed my power outward, that beacon flared.

It made every sort of sense. It's why the ice demons continued to follow in the Arctic. It's why these creatures in this time arrived hours after Ryan and I had gone outside. I had been a lure and I had just unknowingly called them right to the little station in which we hid. And I had no idea how to stop it. How to turn them away. How to save us, save Annie.

I also realized that they could not find me based on my beacon alone. We needed to hide, right now.

The night I'd faced the ice demon seemed so long ago; I could barely understand how I had stopped that demon back then. Now, we were faced with dozens, possibly hundreds all at once, without the protection of the bunker.

"If they're made of smoke as you say, of mist," I said, noting the slight tremor in my voice, "can they not simply pass through these walls?"

Annie was pulling large brown boxes from a small closet, shoving them behind her. She slid them along the dirty floor, leaving long trails in the dust.

"No," she wheezed. "At least parts of them are solid, like their claws. I really don't understand. If they could, though, I'd assume they would have been in the bunker years ago."

"Your revolver, will it nae work against them?" I fell to one knee and helped her start to stack the boxes.

"I doubt it." Her eyes were hard and determined.

"What are we to do?"

"Stack 'em higher. Make just enough room for us to hide behind."

I raised my eyebrows, staring down at the flimsy boxes in doubt. "This will work?"

Annie cursed when she nearly slipped on a dirty rag on the floor. "I have no idea. But we have to try something. I'm not dying in a damned gas station."

Together we began to build the most pathetic attempt at a sanctuary I had ever seen. The wailing outside grew louder. The tugging in my chest grew to new heights. I clutched the front of my shirt, gasping and holding myself up against the nearby wall.

Annie was at my side in an instant, her mouth set in a thin, determined line. She tugged my arm and pulled me behind the boxes. We fell to our knees. Having a good foot of height on her, I was able to pull the boxes above us back against the wall, closing us off from the storefront entirely and wrapping us in meager darkness.

Light seeped through between the boxes. I was reminded of how I'd cowered beneath the sledging boat as men were slaughtered mere yards away. I shut my eyes. If I could just grow my courage and attempt to understand my ability, I might save us, eliminate the creatures, and in turn be able to go back and help the rest of Franklin's men.

Or I might get us killed.

Uncertainty and fear stopped me from taking action. The howling grew closer still. I found myself wondering what Captain Crozier would have done in my place. Surely, he, a much braver man, deserved to have control over the ability instead of me.

Our little hiding place quickly grew warm, claustrophobic. The pain deep in my chest blossomed again. The horrific sound outside echoed through the station.

Annie let out a small whimper of fear. Something in my heart twitched. I reached out and felt along her arm until I clasped her hand in my own. Her terrified breaths matched my own.

"We'll be all right," I said in the barest of whispers. "They won't find us."

The lie weighed heavily on my tongue. I clutched at my chest again, unable to ignore the tugging sensation that raged through my core.

What if the only thing I could do was draw them to me? Had I truly trapped the ice demon or did exhaustion and starvation merely make me think I did? It felt so long ago that it was difficult to even remember that night. Regardless, the one thing I knew for certain was that if I accessed my ability again, even just to learn, it would call the creatures right to us.

"Oh, Harry." Annie's voice was just next to my right ear. She was going to perish because of my presence. Because I could not control these things from sensing me, and as I was too afraid to face the creatures.

I wrapped my arms around Annie's shoulders, pulling her against me as best I could. Her closeness did nothing to quell the pain in my torso, but it steadied my uneven breaths. I rested my forehead against hers.

"Dinnae be afraid." My words sounded hollow. She clung to me, her fingers digging into my arms. I attempted a deep, shuddering breath, trying to steady my heart, my hands, my mind. I focused on her. "I will try to draw them away."

"Harry, no." Her grip on me tightened.

"I must try."

Something slammed to our left, a sharp echo that startled us both.

Something was inside.

My body tensed and I prepared myself to leap out of hiding. There came a shuffling nearby, somewhere in the building, quite close to where we cowered. Annie whimpered again. I held my hand to her lips just as something hit the boxes.

I bit down on my tongue to prevent my own cry from escaping. The confidence I felt seconds earlier quickly drained. The top boxes shifted and fell, exposing us, drenching us in light.

"You wanna live, get the fuck up and run."

A stranger, wild-eyed and blond, pulled more boxes out of the way. Dirt streaked the white shirt he wore; it was almost identical to my borrowed one. A long rip stretched across one side of his thin brown overshirt.

I acted without allowing myself time to think. Throwing my weight forward, I all but fell out onto the floor. The man yanked me to my feet. Turning back, I grabbed Annie's hand and we bolted out of the back room, our footsteps inaudible compared to the loud screams of beasts I had yet to see.

Annie and I fled.

We followed the stranger closely. He dropped his shoulder and slammed into the door separating the back room and the narrow store. We ran past the shelves as quickly as our legs would take us. The wailing was incessant, horrific, piercing.

"They're not quite on us!" the man shouted, his words half-drowned. He reached the front door and burst outside, the tall glass windows rattling in their frames. A pack similar to Annie's bounced up and down on his back as he ran toward the dead woods.

Annie stopped in the open door, but I tugged her out into the open, my eyes on the dawn light that was slowly being blotted out. I focused on the man running ahead, the sides of his open shirt flailing.

I urged my legs to run even faster.

"*Come on!*" the stranger cried. I had no clue where he was taking us, but anywhere had to be better than where we'd been.

Sweat trickled down my back. My throat was on fire, and I could not tell if I was screaming. We flew into the woods, back down the path we'd found yesterday. Our feet thudded in the dirt as we flew past the inoperable pickup truck. The wails didn't lessen.

Deep into the trees Annie and I raced, leaping over fallen branches and knotted tree roots sticking out of the ground. My sole focus became not falling on my face. My legs and lungs burned, and still, we ran.

The stranger fled faster than us, now kicking up dirt a few yards ahead. The pressure in my chest snapped into a full-fledged, searing pain. I choked and struggled to stay upright.

Moments later, we burst into a small clearing. The stranger stopped a few paces away next to a mound of dirt. He began waving his arms in frantic half circles, staring up at something in the trees behind us that I could not see. With a dull clunk, the ground before the man trembled, then opened to one side on its own.

It was another bunker.

Annie let out a relieved cry, gripping my hand tight. The stranger turned his face upward, watching back the way we'd come, urging us to close the short distance between us with hurried hand gestures. "Let's go, let's go, let's *go!*"

Annie and I nearly crashed full force into him. He pushed me along, using my momentum to shove me down a set of hidden stairs much like the ones at Annie's underground haven. I tripped and fell forward only to be caught up in a large man's arms.

I pushed away and spun, running back to the stairs. Annie tumbled inside and I caught her in my arms with a grunt. I in turn bashed into the large man who had caught me.

"*Fuck!*" The blond stranger leapt inside. "*Now!*"

Rough hands shoved us to the ground. A sudden burst of frigid air flooded over me.

"Y'all keep yer asses down!" shouted a gruff voice. "Don't move!"

I glanced up from the floor in time to see a very large man wielding some sort of weapon: a hose attached to a cylindrical metal tank strapped to his back. Air that reminded me of the deathly chill in the Arctic shot out of the hose.

The outer door slammed above us and the tall blond man who'd saved us tumbled headfirst inside with a cry, and I finally beheld the wraiths that had destroyed Annie's world.

Two horrific, ghost-like creatures had flown in behind him. The screeching wail deafened us all. I scrambled back, pushing Annie behind me and away from clawed hands.

Gaping eye sockets seemed to search the brightly lit hallway we'd fallen into. Smoke pooled and twisted around skeletal bodies ending not in legs, but in a dark, strange, whirling mist.

Both wraiths dropped open their mouths impossibly wide. They looked nothing like the ice demon but were just as horrific, if not more.

They were inside.

With a loud curse, the large man with the tank whirled in time to blast at the beasts once again. This time the closer monster howled and spun, raking its jagged claws down the man's back. Three vicious, bright red wounds opened in his flesh before the wraith was consumed by the blast of frigid, white air.

The man cried out in pain and anger but continued to smother the beast in frozen air. It quickly slowed, its entire body hardening into tiny droplets of pure ice. They fell to the hard bunker floor, shattering. Its counterpart, now exposed, quickly met the same fate.

"Good fuckin' Christ, that hurts." The big man dropped to one knee, pulling off the container and letting it clang to the floor.

Blood flowed freely from the man's wounds and splattered around his feet. The blond stranger looked on in shock. He did not move away from the wall. His huge stomach heaved and shuddered.

My surgeon's instincts took over, dulling my fear. I let go of Annie, who stared at the dropped canister, and fell to the ground next to the big man, my boots slipping in the growing pool of blood.

Annie jumped into action. "Show us where to take him."

The man who'd saved us jumped, startled out of his shock. His fair hair was wild, just like his eyes. He surged forward to help, his boots trailing crimson. Together, the three of us struggled to get the big man to his feet. He, too, was in shock, muttering, but still able to half-walk, half-stumble.

We were quickly led down a short hallway and into a side room. Our surroundings continued to remind me of Annie's bunker until we passed where their tallied wall would have been – the one here was smooth and clear of any markings – and hurried into a large medical quarters twice the size.

The moment my eyes fell on a metal table, I directed the big man to lie on his stomach. "I need to clean his wounds, close them."

I threw off my coat and wiped my palms along the front of my borrowed shirt. Annie was already yanking open drawers and cabinets, hands flying through supplies. I recognized many although their designs were much more modern. She returned with gauze and a plastic bottle labeled "saline."

I had no time to marvel at anything. She next handed me a pair of scissors and I quickly cut open the big man's shirt, only slowing to unstick the fabric from the claw wounds. The cuts sliced deep through the man's flesh, from shoulder to the bottom of his scapula, stopping just before his spine. The stark white contrast of his bone stood out in the pooling blood.

"Do you have sutures?" Annie snapped at the blond man who just stared at his friend bleeding out on the table.

He didn't answer, didn't move.

"What's your name?" I asked gently, glancing briefly up at him.

"I, uh. I'm Tristan."

I glanced at the door and saw strangers gathering, watching with horrified faces. Ignoring them, I focused on my patient.

"Tristan, I need you to do what Annie says. All right?" I fumbled momentarily with the bottle until realizing I simply needed to squeeze it.

Focus. Focus.

A cool, clear liquid shot out onto the big man's back. He flinched and grunted.

"And what is your friend's name, Tristan?"

"His name is Eli. He's our…he's in charge here." His eyes narrowed and he turned toward the onlookers. "Go get Dr. Stephens!"

I deftly dabbed at Eli's wounds with the gauze Annie had handed me. My eyes met hers over the big man's back.

The big man groaned.

"Eli." I spoke in a calm tone, desperately hoping the tremors in my throat didn't come out in my words. "This is going to sting, but I will get you through this."

The big man let out a grunt, either in agreement or out of pain, I was not sure. I quickly cleaned his open wounds.

Tristan arrived at my side, holding out a curved needle and very thin black suture. I swiped the back of one hand across my forehead. The needle, smaller than what I was used to, slipped in my bloodied fingers.

"Get me two more of those."

Tristan nodded and busied himself by rummaging through a drawer.

With Annie and the crowd of strangers watching, I began to stitch Eli's jagged wounds. He clenched his fists but did not cry out. His flesh was not sliced in perfect lines, and it was difficult work, but I ensured the stitches were deft and tight. Once the first claw wound was closed, I snipped the suture and held out my hand.

Tristan handed me a new curved needle and I went to work stitching the second of three slices. I was halfway done with the third claw wound when a tall, lanky man with mussed black hair pushed through the crowd and into the room. I nearly cried out; the man before me was almost the face of Dr. Stanley, my superior on *HMS Erebus*. He gaped at me in mute outrage.

I nearly dropped the needle. Blinking rapidly, I took a step back, but quickly realized that the new arrival was, in fact, a stranger. He was much thinner, more gaunt, with a different set to his eyes and a longer jawline.

"What in the hell are you doing?" His incredulous, angry tone gave me pause.

Annie wiped seeping blood from Eli's back with a clean white rag. "He's a doctor. Your friend is hurt."

He didn't look at her. He glared at me with brown eyes so dark they were nearly black. "Where's the anesthetic? Did you medicate him?"

"His wounds have been cleaned." I turned to my patient, irritated at the interruption.

"You're stitching him up with your fingers? Why aren't you wearing *gloves?*"

Some of the people in the doorway murmured.

I lowered my hands to Eli's back. "There is no time for—"

The angry man grabbed my arm and pulled me away. I dropped the suture, stumbling back.

Annie was on him in seconds, shouting into the tall man's face. "Harry just saved his life. What the hell's wrong with you?"

"Eli's diabetic! A fucking infection could kill him!" the man shouted back. "Tristan, get them the hell out of here."

Tristan looked confused but was also staring at my bloodied hands. "He was just—"

"*Now!*" roared the other man, his deep voice reverberating in my ears. He was already pulling on skintight blue gloves. I watched, confused and furious.

Annie and I were hustled out of the medical room. The onlookers moved aside, watching us.

"I'm sorry," Tristan said in a soft, tense voice. "That's Dr. Stephens. He's kind of a dick."

I blinked and snuck a glance at Annie, who watched the floor as we were hurried away. A tantalizing scent of something sweet wafted through the corridor. My stomach grumbled.

Tristan was watching me. "Are you guys hungry? We have some muffins left from breakfast if you are."

"That would be amazing," Annie replied softly.

He nodded and sped up slightly. "I didn't even think about getting you gloves," he continued. "I'm such an idiot. I'm so sorry."

I shook my head. "I dinnae understand…why do—"

She grabbed my hand, fingers sticking to the drying blood, and quickly changed the subject. "What were those metal backpacks, Tristan? The ones that killed the wraiths?"

"Liquid nitrogen. It's the only defense we've found. It took a while to make those things, but they work really well." He led us down a dimly lit hallway, away from the clamor of the medical room. The smell of freshly baked food grew even more defined.

We came to a four-way junction where Tristan politely told us to wait. He disappeared for no less than thirty seconds before returning with a small sort of cake in each hand. Both were shaped oddly and smelled quite good.

"Hope you like these." He handed them over. "The box mix is old, of course, but with a bit of applesauce mixed in, you can barely tell."

Annie took hers and instantly bit into it with a smile. Her expression transformed into that of bliss. "This is delicious."

I followed her lead. What Tristan had called a muffin was too sweet for my palate, but I nibbled at it while he led us down the right hallway.

We took multiple turns as we went. It was impossible to know which direction we faced. I continued eating the muffin, swallowing it in small bites until all that was left were a handful of crumbs.

There weren't any landmarks, any ways to distinguish one monotonous corridor from the next. As my adrenaline wore off, my legs began to feel numb, rubbery. I suddenly wanted nothing more than to sleep.

"You can get cleaned up. We've got an open room left at the end of the hall here. The bathroom is a bit small, but it should do."

"The bedrooms have bathrooms?" Annie's voice held quiet wonder. "How big *is* this place?"

Tristan smiled, although he still struggled to catch his breath. "Big. Clean up and get some rest. Once Eli's stable, I'll come back for you, okay? We'll get to know each other, show you around. Until then, let's just have you stay back here, away from the commotion. Good?"

Annie and I both nodded, stopping when he did.

"You can take the room here, on the left." He gestured at a half-open door and gave us a quick smile, rubbing his clean shaven, square jaw. He had a gruff but young face and kind eyes.

I held out one of my crimson-covered hands. "Thank you, Tristan. For everything. We would have died without you."

"I wasn't about to leave you guys." He eyed my bloodied hand but did not take it. Instead, he leaned to the side and bumped his elbow on mine. "I have a good feeling that you'd have done the same."

I let my hand fall and turned to the room that Annie had already entered. I couldn't help but smile in relief at the sight of a mattress. The room also had a large, plush armchair and a little table with a bright lamp that was similar to the ones in Annie's bunker. "Thank you. This is heaven."

"Of course. Oh, and if you need anything, just bop this big button on the wall." Tristan pointed to a small white box near the door. It had three bright buttons along its bottom and a lit screen in its middle. It seemed quite reminiscent of the impossible door and its controls that Dennis and Annie had shown me.

"There's always someone up," Tristan was saying. "Just let 'em know you're in the south hallway and explain what you need. Okay?"

I nodded and fully stepped inside.

"I need to go clean up, too." Tristan gestured at his muddy pants and dirt-streaked shirt. "I'll be back so I can check on you in a little bit. I hope you understand I have to lock you in, though. Security measures, and all. Oh, speaking of…"

Tristan's blue-grey eyes dropped to stare at Annie's waist. She frowned and took a step back, shaking her head. "I keep the gun."

He lifted both hands, palms out toward us. "I get it. But like I said, we don't know you. I have our people's safety to think about."

Letting out a sigh, I licked my lips. "Annie. He's right."

She frowned, hesitating but not protesting. She pulled the weapon from the waist of her trousers and handed it over, eyeing Tristan with cold frustration.

"Thank you. Really. Your trust means a lot." He smiled and backed out of the room, shutting the door quietly behind him. We listened to the lock being turned.

More weary than ever, I stepped into the small bathroom. My boots left sticky outlines of bloody footprints along the concrete floor. Twisting the knobs by the sink, I stuck both hands underneath the cascade of water without testing the temperature. I scrubbed my skin, desperate to rid it of Eli's blood. Some had splattered the white hem of my shirt.

I could not stop my mind from recalling the torn and bloodied face of the Marine I'd tried to save back on *Erebus*. Of the specks of his blood that had stained my sleeves and the way I hadn't been able to prevent his death. I scrubbed my hands until they tingled in pain.

"Harry."

I turned, startled, and collided with Annie. Standing close behind me, she wrapped her arms around my waist before I could speak. I held my dripping wet hands aside for a brief moment before gently returning her affection. When I shut my eyes and dropped my face to the top of her head, my heartbeat finally began to slow. My breaths steadied. Her cheek was warm where it pressed against my shoulder. I don't know how long we stood there, tightly embraced, holding onto each other, trying desperately to rid our minds of the horror we'd just narrowly escaped. We clutched each other close until our trembling subsided.

With a bit of reluctance, I pulled away and smiled down at her. "Are you all right?"

She nodded and stepped back. "Are you?"

I was not sure how to answer. Instead, I dipped my head and turned back to the sink's running water.

Once fully scrubbed clean, I stepped back into the large bedroom that we'd been granted. There were many things I wanted to discuss, but I only had eyes for the bed.

Annie dropped her pack to the floor and pulled the small music device from her trouser pocket. She slipped it into the pocket of my naval coat.

"We won't be here long," she mumbled.

I sat quietly in the chair near the bed as she quietly closed herself in the bathroom for a shower. When it was my turn, the heat and soap that scrubbed my body clean of grime was nowhere near the euphoria I'd felt at the other bunker.

Annie was pulling back the comforter when I opened the door. Small drops of water fell from her still-wet red hair to darken the sheets. I wiped at a rivulet trickling down my own neck as I approached. We simultaneously realized the lack of space on the single bed.

"Get some rest." I averted my eyes and tugged off my coat, its tails brushing the cold, grey floor, and stepped up to the strange box near the door. "I can call Tristan back, see if Dr. Stephens will take my assistance with Eli."

"Wait." I felt Annie's hand on my back. Her voice was soft but desperate.

We stared at each other in embarrassment. Surely, we could not share the bed. Although there was room to easily fit us both, where I came from, one did not simply sleep next to a woman he'd met a week ago.

Something in her eyes begged me to stay, and I could not deny that I wanted to as well. I stepped away from the door and instead lowered myself into the chair.

"You don't have to stay." She openly blushed. "I just…you make me feel safe."

I smiled despite my sudden battling urges – the need for sleep viciously fighting curiosity for Annie, what it would be like to in fact lie next to her. Perhaps with an arm around her waist. I dismissed the thoughts. "I ken all about fear, how it taints the body, exhausts the mind. And safe rest is what you need right now."

"But so do you."

"I've slept in much worse conditions." I chuckled, but it was a hollow sound.

Annie settled back on the mattress with a smile. "*Erebus* and *Terror*… can you tell me about them?"

I scooted the chair closer to the bed. "Aye, of course. Despite the horrors that soon befell us, the voyage was still an extraordinary experience. I had never been to sea before. The opportunity to advance my studies was too great to pass up.

I learned much, and quickly. We had the typical cases of illness and the occasional but expected injury.

"The Arctic itself was exquisitely beautiful, even as things quickly took a turn for the worse. It was utterly breathtaking. I loved how the waves that rolled beneath us rocked the ships, large as they were.

"I had a private cabin, but often, I'd sleep in a chair in sickbay for patients who needed a wee bit of extra care. Dr. Stanley didn't approve, but he wasn't much of a, should you say, kind man. He was a good doctor, you ken. He had quite an impressive reputation, but while on board, he often made me do all the work. It is unsettling how much the doctor here resembles him. It's almost as if…"

I fell silent; Annie was already asleep. I watched her a moment, then brushed a strand of her hair off her cheek. There was something about her that made me stare at her a moment longer than what was appropriate. Something that brought a flush to my face and more than curiosity to my heart. I gently pulled the blanket up, bringing it over her shoulders.

Settling back in the chair, I stretched out my legs and stared at our locked door, trying not to panic.

Twenty-Three

Annie
2020

I tossed off the covers and got up from the strange bed, trying to chase the heaviness of sleep from my mind.

Harry had passed out in the chair, his head tilted to one side, his chest rising and falling. There was no clock in the room; I was not sure how long we'd been asleep, locked in the little room.

I quietly made my way to the bathroom and relieved myself. The toilet's flush was strangely silent. The sink's water was cool and didn't warm up regardless of how long I let it run. I eventually gave up and splashed a handful on my face, then went to Harry's side and touched his shoulder.

He bolted upright. "Annie. Are you all right?"

"Yeah." My voice was hoarse and weak. I sat back down on the mattress. "Just woke up. I'm starving."

Harry rose, rolling one shoulder and massaging his neck. He pointed to the intercom Tristan had told us to use. "We could try that. See if they could bring us some food."

"Hold on." I smoothed the front of my shirt, which was still streaked with dirt, and yawned wide. "We need to talk before going back out there. And about those canisters that they used to kill the wraiths."

"I was thinkin' aboot that after you fell asleep."

"That's how we win. We have you trap the wraiths, release them into the platform room, then shoot 'em dead with the liquid nitrogen. This can really work."

"What is the temperature of this liquid nitrogen?"

I blinked. "I have no idea. We could ask them."

Harry brushed a stray curl from his eyes. "I've seen fog and mist turn to ice midair while we were aboard *Erebus*. Some nights got so frigid that even mah breath turned to little ice droplets."

"Damn," I breathed.

Harry raised his eyebrows. "What if we could use that?"

"Use what?"

"Those weapons only froze the wraiths when they flew into its stream. The creatures are fast, though, and there is great room for error. What if we instead brought the wraiths to the cold? To the Arctic?"

"Oh." I covered my mouth with a hand. "They'd have nowhere to go, no means of escape."

He lowered back into the chair. "I believe so."

"Holy hell." I stared at him. "And then we would pull you back, get you out of the Arctic once and for all. Genius."

He didn't smile. "Would my survival in the past truly erase your family line? Or your machine?"

I breathed in slowly. "We have absolutely no way to know until we do it, and then there's possibly no changing what's happened. I promise you, that is the truth."

Harry considered me a long moment. "I return here, then, and we decide what to do once I'm back."

"I'm sorry we can't do more for you."

He took my hand in his. "You saved mah life. You've done plenty for me, and I can do this for you. We just need to get back home, first."

"These people are going to ask questions. They of course can't know about the Zapper."

"You're afraid they'd take it for themselves."

"Of course. If that power fell into another's hands...if they used it for themselves, who knows things they'd mess up."

Harry regarded me with his kind, soft gaze. "So, what is our story, then?"

Reclining on the mattress again, I propped my head up with one arm, facing Harry. "How about we're two no-nonsense cops fighting against the supernatural in desperate search of the truth."

Harry looked perplexed. "Supernatural? Do you mean the wraiths?"

"Sorry." I giggled. "Scratch that."

"I can act no-nonsense if I must."

I laughed, long and loud, falling back against the mattress. My reaction deepened Harry's confusion. Sitting up again, I wiped both eyes. "No. Ignore that. I'm making things worse. Okay, so I already blurted out you're a doctor, which is fine, but that Stephens guy is going to catch on pretty quick that your knowledge isn't modern."

"I can learn. Study his books if need be. I'm eager to learn the ways of your time."

"We won't be here long enough to have to resort to that." I sighed. "We're just Harry and Annie. Surgeon and student. We are who we say we are. You're gonna have to try to catch on from what Dr. Stephens talks about. It's just, well, we need to solidify a story about where we *came* from. There's no way we'd have been out in the open for three years."

Harry sat forward in the chair, leaning his elbows on his thighs. "Would it be feasible to simply stick as close to the truth as possible so as to have little room for error? Say that we were in a wee compound with others but were attacked, separated. Turned around and lost. If we stick together, you can prevent me from soundin' like a fool about things I have nae knowledge of."

"Yeah. Just don't go telling everyone where you're really from and that should work."

"Shall we call for them? I'm quite hungry, and anxious to meet our saviors properly."

I pushed off the bed and went over to the intercom. Harry excused himself, stepping into the bathroom and shutting the door. I pressed the left button.

"Yes?" came a tinny female voice.

"Hi, um, we're the people that came in with Tristan. Is there any way we could get something to eat? We're in the south hall."

There was a long pause in which I slipped my feet into my worn sneakers, then the woman was back. "Someone will be there shortly."

The bathroom door opened. Harry, his hands and face still wet, stepped out. "I cannae get enough of warm water," he said with a soft smile.

I changed places with him but stopped and brushed my fingers against his hand. We regarded each other, not speaking, for a few long seconds.

His deeply green eyes held confidence and strength I hadn't seen there before. I looked away, then shut the door behind me.

Splashing warm water on my face was a godsend, waking me fully and rinsing the remaining sleep away. I dried off while relieving myself, eager to return to the bedroom before someone arrived. I was washing my hands, staring at my limp, knotted, red hair in disdain, when I heard a sharp knock on the bedroom door.

I wiped my hands on a towel and hurried back into the bedroom just in time to hear the door's lock turning.

Dr. Stephens stood in the hallway with his arms crossed.

"Oh, goodie," I said before I could stop myself.

"Yep, me again." His voice was slow and deep. "Dinner already started, but Eli wants to see you both first."

"Dinner? We were out all day?"

"Mm." He nodded.

"How is that possible?" My heart fell. We'd been out for hours. Night was falling again, if it hadn't already. Ryan and Dennis would have gone from full panic to action already, possibly getting themselves killed in the process. Unless they hadn't made it back to the bunker at all. We'd never know until we got outside, and now it would be too dark once more to safely find our way back.

I tried to stifle a sob of despair, turning away from Harry and Dr. Stephens. My hands tingled and tears sprang out of my eyes. I wiped a hand across my face. Harry was right: Ryan and Dennis were smart. They were alive. They had to be. I wouldn't allow myself to think otherwise. We'd leave at first light to find them. Steeling myself, I turned back.

Harry had stepped into the corridor and held out one hand. "Doctor. Thank you for comin' when you did. How does Eli fare?"

Dr. Stephens blinked down at him. "Where are you from?"

Unfazed, Harry dropped his hand. "Edinburgh. And you?"

"Montana," came the dry response. The other doctor's eyes narrowed but he stepped aside. "Follow me."

We followed behind Dr. Stephens, not speaking. It took great effort to resist the urge to sneer childishly at the tall man's back. I instead focused on our surroundings and tried to keep track of which way was which.

Dr. Stephens led us back down multiple hallways. He only stopped at an identical entrance to a bedroom even larger than ours. Eli, shirtless torso bandaged, looked up from a tattered paperback copy of *Watership Down*. He scratched at his salt-and-pepper goatee and grinned at us. He tossed the book and rose from the armchair near his bed.

"You shouldn't be up and aboot already, sir." Harry's light voice held concern.

"Doc's given me pain pills, cleaned me up plenty." Eli ran a hand over his grey buzzed hair. His deep Southern twang rumbled through the room. He nodded at Dr. Stephens, who leaned against the open doorframe with vague disinterest.

The big man watched Harry with curiosity and folded his hands over his considerable stomach. "The name's Eli Fink. I hear you were the one that stitched me up."

Harry dropped his head in a single nod.

"Nearly," I interjected. "But your doctor interrupted him. Pulled him away."

"I heard. For the record, mister, I'm damn thankful for what you did before Stephens got to me. Gloves or no gloves, I thank you."

"Och, just doin' my job."

"Yer a doctor, too, then, I take it?"

"Oh, no. Anatomist."

Eli frowned. I let out a forced laugh and fought the urge to nudge Harry. "He's actually studying to be a surgeon. Well, was, before the end."

"I didnae mean to tread on your doctor's work," Harry said. "Only to help until he arrived."

Eli snorted. "You did what you had to do in an emergency. Ignore Stephens. He's an ass."

"Thanks." Dr. Stephens pushed away from the door frame. "Feel free to change your own bandages."

Harry watched the other doctor disappear down the hall, his eyes helpless.

Eli grunted and sat on his bed. Harry stepped forward in an instant, silently placing a hand on the big man's bare shoulder. He plucked the flat pillow from behind Eli and moved it away from Eli's wounds. He then turned, his eyes darting over things he'd never seen before, trying to be of some use.

"I'm good, I'm good." Eli sighed. "Although this really puts a halt to jamming."

"Jamming, sir?" Harry stepped back, settling next to me, hands clasped.

"Haven't met anyone from another country." Eli grinned. "Tristan doesn't count; he's Canadian. And yeah, we'd been plannin' a little shindig in a few days. Somethin' we do down here to combat the crushing monotony of life. I was s'posed to play drums this time."

My heart skipped a beat, and I completely missed Harry's reaction in lieu of my own. "Drums?"

A slow grin spread over Eli's face. "Ah, I know that tone. A fellow musician, I presume?"

I nodded. "Guitar."

"What kind?"

"Les Paul electric. Gorgeous dark red finish. I miss it every day."

He chuckled and scratched the grey stubble along his jaw. "Bet she sang like a beaut. I'd kill to hear it."

I glanced at Harry, who was watching the exchange in silence.

"Anywho, don't let Stephens bug ya." Eli reached out with his good arm and clasped Harry's hand in his own. "He's a podiatrist, and I always joke he's just cranky he chose to stare at people's tootsies all day."

Eli guffawed, slapping his thigh with a hand, then wincing. "Hell, I'd have bled out for sure if you weren't here."

Harry's cheeks turned a slight shade of pink and his jaw clenched. "Podiatrist? A...doctor of feet? Not a surgeon?"

Eli laughed and shook his head. "Nope. Although I admit, he's been invaluable down here regardless."

Harry's mouth was open in shock. Again, I cut in before he could speak.

"We are, in turn, grateful to you as well," I said, stepping forward and shaking Eli's hand, too.

"It sure was a close one. But the more the better. In this case, quite literally, since we now have a surgeon of sorts." His smile faded. "Now that you two are up and about, we should talk about your parts here. Harry, you can work with Dr. Stephens, but we'd need a job for you, miss."

Harry tensed next to me. Mind still lamenting over Ryan and Dennis, over failing our plans so miserably, I struggled to keep a straight face.

"We'd like to head out in the morning, actually." I kept my tone light.

Eli grunted. "I trust the room Tristan got you situated in is suitable?"

"It was perfect. Thank you again."

"He nearly died getting you two here. Same with me. The least you can do is tell me how the fuck you ended up in that gas station. It's full of rotten food, and we'd looted it for meds long ago. It's been empty ever since. So, tell me, where exactly did you come from and why were you there?"

I forced a smile despite the sudden coldness of his tone. "There's a compound out past the state line to the east. We'd love to tell you all about it."

"How did Tristan find us if there was no reason for him to be at the station?" Harry asked quietly.

Eli put on a wide smile. "He'd been sent out on a run that took him past that useless little shack. Said he noticed foot-prints in the dust when he went by. And a pile of stuff on the floor. He took a chance and found your little cardboard fort."

"You send people out regularly?"

The big man shifted on the low bed. "We send Tristan out, mostly for more medication and liquid nitrogen."

"Nae food?"

"Sometimes. That canned crap can help, but we have a nice garden down here."

At this, Harry's eyes lit up. "Could I see it?"

Eli's pale eyes sparkled. "I suppose. Just ask Gloria. She's in charge of the plants. Speaking of food, help me up, here. I'm starvin'.."

"I'd much rather you rest, sir. Allow me to bring the food to you."

"What you can do is get my ass out of this room, down the hall, and settled a'fore I miss chili night." Eli pushed himself up off the bed with his good arm.

Harry shot forward. "You and your arse need to slow down, I'm afraid." He reached out to stabilize the big man as he fell back onto the mattress.

The big man barked out an incredulous laugh. He pointed to a shirt draped over the foot of his bed. Harry graced me with one of his slight smiles while he pulled Eli's shirt over his head with careful movements, then helped him stand.

"I'm good. Not like I can't walk." Eli waved a large hand, insinuating we get out of his damn way, and quick.

Hands up in mock defeat, Harry backed out of the room with me following close behind. Eli led us down two different hallways until we reached a huge, bustling common area full of about two dozen people.

A mouth-watering aroma of chili wafted over us as we entered. My stomach snarled with a low ache, reminding me we hadn't eaten since the muffin Tristan had brought us.

"Everyone listen up." Eli's deep voice boomed over the din of the room. People quieted, turning in their seats. Tristan stood near the back, holding an empty tray. To his left, Dr. Stephens sat at a nearby table on his own, watching us with a scowl and twirling a spoon in one hand.

Once the room was vaguely silent, Eli spoke. "This here's our latest addition. Harry here, he's a surgeon with a badass accent. I'm sure most of y'all watched him save my life this morning."

A round of applause and whoops echoed through the common room. Dr. Stephens didn't join in.

"His girlfriend here is Annie," Eli continued over the loud clapping. "She assisted him like no other until Dr. Stephens was found. I owe them both a hell of a lot."

The applause continued. I felt my face grow warm, cheeks prickling, but said nothing. Catching Dr. Stephens's hard gaze, I forced a smile and stared right back at him.

"We in turn owe you our lives," Harry said quietly to Eli.

"I need to sit." The big man clapped Harry on the shoulder. He grinned around the room at people who looked up at him with admiration. "Eat up, eat up. Don't be weird."

With that, he shuffled up to the closest table. Three people scrambled out of his way while scooping their bowls away. They wandered off to a different table. Harry fussed over Eli, seemingly unaware of the strange behavior. He pulled out a chair first for the big man, then for me.

"What were you, Annie? Before, I mean." Eli inclined his head at Tristan, who held a steaming bowl in one hand. He squeezed past a trio of women eyeing up Harry.

My stomach grumbled again, loud enough to be heard over the chatter in the room. "Just a college student. Played a few gigs every month or so for a little income."

"Student of what?"

"I was just finishing up my master's in history when the end happened."

"The end. I like that." Eli nodded, watching Tristan place the bowl of chili before him. He pulled it close, snatching a small spoon out of its depths and lifting a heaping mouthful to his lips. He blew on the food, its steam disappearing momentarily.

"And you, sir?" Harry asked.

Eli squinted at him. "Mechanic. Nothin' too crazy. And quit callin' me 'sir.'"

"Apologies." He didn't seem phased.

"More food is on its way, don't you worry." Eli stuffed the spoonful of chili in his mouth, grinning. "It may be canned, but damn, is it tasty."

I wasn't listening. At the far end of the room, something had caught my eye. My heart fluttered at the sight of a small purple-rimmed drum set.

Eli's eyes lit up when he noticed what I was staring at. "Hell yeah. It's not the best kit, but it works. Tristan tried learning, but mostly sticks to the keys. If you're up for it sometime, we've got a pretty decent Epiphone electric. It probably not as good as your Les Paul, but it does the job."

At the mention of the guitar, something buried inside for many years tugged free. The mere thought of playing music again brought a lightness to my frantic thoughts and a sense of calm to my raging anxiety.

Harry was silent, watching me with curiosity.

"I'd be thrilled," I managed to say.

"Well, here they are." An elegant Latina woman with a wide smile appeared at our table, holding a tray of four large steaming bowls. Her caramel eyes roamed over Harry.

Tristan followed behind her, bearing a fistful of napkins and silverware. "Hope you're hungry."

"Starved." I smiled my appreciation, nabbing a utensil and stirring the bowl of hot food.

"I'm Gloria." The woman lowered into one of the chairs, eyes never leaving Harry. She fussed with her perfect dark waves pinned at the back of her head. "I was in the garden this morning, but I heard of Eli's close call. We can't thank you enough for what you did."

Harry beamed.

Careful to blow on my first spoonful, I inhaled a mouthful of the best chili I'd ever tasted. Harry followed suit. My eyes watered at the temperature of the beans and meat, but I swallowed anyway. The food burned a slow trail down my throat.

"They're gonna stick around a while." Eli was nearly done with his dinner, hastily spooning the food with his good arm.

I opened my mouth to protest, but something in my gut told me to do otherwise. A deep unease was beginning to work its way through me for reasons I couldn't pinpoint yet. I ate another bite of chili and said nothing.

Gloria's eyes danced. "Oh, you two will be so happy here. And we'll be happy to have you. A surgeon and, oh, Annie, what were you, other than a student? Before the end?"

"A musician," Eli cut in, his eyes suddenly hard.

She turned her unfaltering, bright, perfect smile on me. My heart skipped a beat. I clutched my spoon tight and tried to remember if she'd been near when I'd told Eli about my past.

Harry shot me a subtle glance. "We're happy to help where needed."

"Oh, will you listen to that voice!" Gloria squeezed Harry's arm. "Your accent is gorgeous."

Harry looked baffled and settled for spooning chili into his mouth.

Eli drained his cup in two loud swallows. Tristan instantly stood, refilling the big man's water. He then excused himself with the nearly empty pitcher.

Harry watched him leave, a curious look in his eye. "Has he always been your steward? Or just down here?"

Eli rumbled with laughter. "Steward? God, where are you from, son?"

I stared down at my bowl of food. Something was way off. I swallowed another bite of hot chili and looked up to see Dr. Stephens watching us, staring in particular at Harry.

Gloria waved a hand. "I want to hear everything about you two. Where did you even come from? How long have you been together?"

"Nae long enough," he said. He blinked quickly.

I tried to stifle a grunt and nearly choked on my dinner. A quick sideways glance at Harry showed he was keeping his composure just fine.

Gloria's eyes lit up and she let out a squeal just as Tristan returned with a fresh pitcher of water.

"Oh, no," he said. "I know that sound."

"They're newly in love." Gloria clapped her hands twice. "This has got to be an even better story. Tell us how you fell for each other amid all of this *muerte y destrucción*."

Harry broke eye contact with Gloria. He took another huge bite of chili and shot a glance in my direction.

"I didn't know Harry for a long time," I said carefully. "I mean, I knew *of* him, but it wasn't until a few weeks ago that we officially got to know each other."

Gloria raised her eyebrows.

"I'd hurt myself doing something dumb. Harry patched me up. We hit it off quickly, and the rest is history."

Harry covered a laugh with his napkin.

"And just where exactly did y'all come from, if I may ask?" Eli finished off his chili, smacking his lips.

Harry sat back. "Quite far, actually. There is a compound across the state line. Somewhere we thought to be safe. We were attacked many weeks ago and fled."

"On foot?"

"Aye."

"Just you two?"

Harry shook his head, not breaking eye contact. His face stayed relaxed, and there was a ghost of a smile on his lips. "There were more, at first. Now it's just us."

"On the run, outside for that long…you'd surely have been attacked."

"We had plenty of encounters with the creatures, and with other survivors. Hiding in vacant buildings helped. A truck, once, too. But the wraiths, they dinnae stay around long, as I'm sure you're aware. Since you run for supplies so often."

Although I'd slept through the day, my eyes grew heavy. Eli stared at Harry for long, long seconds, who casually finished his bowl of chili.

He looked away and addressed Gloria. "Could I please see your garden?"

She turned her smile on Eli. "Well, I don't see why not."

They shared a look. "Soon," he said. "We'll give you the grand tour and all."

My eyes drooped. How was I so tired again?

Tristan cleared away our empty bowls without a word. Seconds later, Dr. Stephens appeared behind us out of nowhere. Eli gave him a nod and stood.

"I need to rest." The big man gestured at his injured back. "No offense meant, but for now, for the safety of our people here, I would like it if y'all could stay in your room."

I stood without complaint; I wanted nothing more than to get away from the strange people so we could talk about our next course of action. Harry rose when I did, stifling a yawn.

The podiatrist poked Eli on his good shoulder and held out a hand. "The key?"

Eli turned his piercing eyes up to him, chewing the inside of his cheek. He dug into the front pocket of his jeans and tossed a small keyring to Dr. Stephens. "You understand, of course. I need to protect my people, and we ain't quite there yet. Holler if you need anything in the night."

Harry and I followed Dr. Stephens out of the dining room. The podiatrist's layered black hair shone beneath the glare of the lights we passed beneath. Every eye turned to watch as we left.

A shudder threatened its presence at the base of my spine as we stepped into the deserted hallway. "I thought you said we slept all day," I hissed.

"And you did." The podiatrist didn't look back at me.

"Then why am I already tired?"

"The near-death experience yesterday? Sleeping in a new place amongst strangers? How the hell should I know?"

He was right, no doubt. Still, something nagged at the back of my mind. I glanced at Harry who was paying attention to each turn we took.

Halfway back to the south corridor, Dr. Stephens slowed so quickly, Harry and I nearly collided with him. He continued walking but spoke over one shoulder in a whisper. "The less you say, the better."

I reached out and touched Dr. Stephens's shoulder. "Are we in danger of some sort? Did we do something wrong?"

"Eli has little cameras. Everywhere. The hallways are the only place safe to speak because they're so spread out, but don't. And for your own sake, quit asking to leave. He won't let you."

"What? Why?"

He didn't reply. When we reached the door to our room at the end of the next hallway, he stopped but refused to meet my angry glare.

"In you go." His voice was slightly louder.

"Are you serious right now?"

He fixed me with a level gaze so cold, I briefly thought he might hit me. Thankfully, Harry pulled me backward into the room before I could say more.

Dr. Stephens's flat expression didn't change. "I'm on watch most nights, so if you need anything, say it now. I don't like to be bothered."

"We're good, thanks," I said with as much sarcasm I could muster.

He shut the door in our faces without another word.

Twenty-Four

Annie
2020

A harsh pressure on my bladder tore me from deep sleep. I sat up, groggy, my fear and suspicion returning in a flash. I glanced around the room, looking for the little cameras Dr. Stephens had warned us about – if he'd been telling the truth – but found nothing in the corners or cracks I could see. I tossed the blanket aside and hurried to the bathroom.

Despite not seeing anything out of the ordinary, I fought the urge to cover myself while I used the toilet. On one hand, Dr. Stephens might just be fucking with us. The strange behavior of the colonists, though, made me wonder otherwise. Of course, if he'd been honest and Eli was watching, covering myself would show I knew his disturbing secret; in case the podiatrist's warnings were true, I had to act nonchalant. I couldn't risk doing anything that might prevent Harry and me from getting out.

Regardless, I lowered my pants with disgust, clamping my legs together and trying like hell to block as much as I could from view.

Quietly passing a still-sleeping Harry propped up in the chair, I returned to bed to lay in the soft lamplight, unable to focus. No matter how hard I tried to look apathetic, I again glanced along the ceiling, into the corners, even at the lamp for some sign of a camera or microphone.

Nothing.

I rolled onto my side and squeezed my eyes shut.

That, however, only brought visions of Ryan and Dennis's possible fates flashing past my closed lids. Getting caught by the wraiths. The gennie exploding when they tried to fix it. Leaving to find us and starving to death outside.

If I had been able to fix the damn generator, none of this would have happened. Now, we weren't just stuck in a new bunker with ominous strangers, but we were being prevented from leaving.

We hadn't really tried, though, had we? What would happen if I just went to the front door?

Tossing the covers aside, careful not to disturb Harry, I rose from the bed and approached the door. Trying the handle, I was startled when the door swung open on silent hinges. Dr. Stephens must have forgotten to lock us in. But he didn't seem the kind to make such a mistake.

The hallway lights had been dimmed. Nobody was at either end. Curiosity won over logic and I stepped out of our room, leaving Harry to hopefully dream of things other than monsters.

My socks did nothing to stop the chill of the concrete from seeping into my feet. I hurried forward, listening intently for any signs of a cranky podiatrist or large mechanic coming for me. Or maybe they would send the friendly Canadian. Or the beautiful woman with the frozen smile and eyes hungry for any attention. I kept trying and failing to understand the strangeness of Eli's people; they almost reminded me of a cast in some campy horror movie.

Voices and soft laughter drifted softly down the hall.

"No, no, what about the Eileen song?" That was Eli's deep drawl. "Used to be huge."

"Ah, yeah," came Tristan's light voice. "I'll add that to the list."

I paused next to the closed dining area door to listen. My heart thudded steadily in my ears, and I held my breath.

"You must really want to play that guitar," came a whisper from right behind me.

I spun and threw a fist, which collided with Dr. Stephens's stomach. He grunted, his face twitching, and stumbled back a step.

"Why the hell do you keep appearing out of nowhere?" I demanded in a low voice.

His narrowed eyes glared at me. He rubbed his stomach with one long-fingered hand, keeping his voice at a whisper. "All the better to catch duplicitous behavior."

I drew myself up, though my five-foot-seven stance clearly did nothing to intimidate the six-foot-tall podiatrist.

"I'm not being duplicitous," I shot back. "I can't sleep."

"You missed breakfast, so it sounds like you slept just fine."

I scowled at him. "If it's morning, where is everyone?"

"Doing their chores. Plenty of those here."

My suspicion deepened. "There's no way this place is that big. What, do you lock everyone in their rooms?"

"Who's out there?" Eli's voice boomed suddenly.

Dr. Stephens's eyes widened, fear blanching his already pale face. He swallowed hard, staring down at me with his dark, almond-shaped eyes. "You needed peppermint."

"Huh?"

He stepped around me and shoved open the door, a half-smile, half-grimace on his lips.

Eli rose from behind the drum kit. He glared over at Dr. Stephens with eyes that held such anger I stopped walking.

"What the hell are you doin' away from your..." The big man noticed me. "Annie? What the hell is goin' on?"

Gloria sat in a folding chair near the big man with a pad of paper on her lap and pen in hand. Her still glued-on smile gave me chills. Blond, soft-eyed Tristan occupied a chair at the table closest to them, plucking leaves from a small herb plant and crushing them with a ceramic mortar and pestle. His hands stilled when he saw us.

Dr. Stephens jerked a thumb at me. "She needed something for a headache, so I provided her with some peppermint. She kept yammering about music, so I figured I'd see if she could keep up with you."

Eli laughed, rage quickly fading. "Well, I can't argue with another adding to the mix, I guess. You're good, Martin, you can go."

Dr. Stephens didn't move. "I can't tell you harshly enough how much I advise against playing drums with that wound."

"Ah, I'm usin' brushes. I'm fine." Eli stretched his neck to one side with a wince.

"Clearly." Dr. Stephens shot me an uncomfortable look, hesitating, then quickly turned and left in silence. I watched him go, unsure what to think about him.

Gloria let out a light, theatrical sigh. Her big smile finally faded. "Why do we keep him around again?"

"Hush." Eli squirmed on the stool behind the drums a moment. "He's saved my ass more than once. We needed a doctor, and he's stuck by us. He's more than earned his place despite his, oh, let's call it grouchiness."

I sat in a chair near Tristan, uncomfortable and on edge. Dr. Stephens's behavior was so back and forth I wanted to slap him. Eli clearly had a temper problem and the others were weird as hell, but did that mean they were a threat? If I didn't believe Dr. Stephens's warning, the behavior of the colonists in the big bunker could merely be chalked up to being stuck underground for years. Besides, even if there were cameras in this bunker, well, ours had them, too.

Now I was just going in circles. Ultimately, something was still off. I didn't want to stick around long enough to find out what, and I didn't want to waste time investigating when we could be looking for Ryan and Dennis instead.

Without physical proof in front of me, I couldn't possibly assume anything, I could only be wary and cautious. Harry and I needed to get out, and get out today, so I decided to play along to try and earn some trust.

I smiled at Tristan and watched him grind some of the plant leaves for a few seconds, then directed my attention at Eli.

"Thought you weren't going to try playing." I nodded at the drum kit.

He scowled up at me. "You already sound like Martin. That damned doctor complains about everythin' under the sun if you let him. I ain't playin' tomorrow. Just messin' around."

"We're figuring out a theme for the monthly social." Gloria stood and brought her pad over. "I used to play the organ at my church, but music isn't really my *traje fuerte*."

My eyes trailed over her swooping letters, ever aware of Eli's piercing gaze.

"Hip hop? Country?" I shook my head. "Yacht rock's key. Add some classic rock and you're golden."

Eli shuffled his brushes around on the snare drum. "What the hell is yacht rock?'

"Picture a rich old guy sipping champagne on his yacht." I mimed what I described. "What kind of music do you picture him listening to?"

"Michael McDonald," Eli said instantly. "Mellow shit with a sax or two."

A snort came from Tristan. He glanced up from the small plant's leaves. "We haven't done that before."

Gloria giggled. "No, no, we need something with *energy*."

Eager to look like I wanted to bond, I gestured at the pen in Gloria's hand. She handed it over along with the pad, and I read out loud as I scribbled: "'Celebrate,' 'Rock This City,' 'Zoot Suit Riot,' 'Dancing in the Dark,' 'You Shook Me All Night Long.'"

Writing the songs brought on an intense wave of déjà vu, reminding of the set lists Ryan would always hastily scratch out before a show. I pushed it aside and sat back. "There. Some of the seventies, a bit of the eighties…and all of these have plenty of energy. If people here aren't dancing to 'em, they're dead inside."

Gloria nodded while peering at my hasty chicken scratch. Her wide smile returned. "Hey, maybe she knows."

I glanced between them. "Knows what?"

"We were tryin' to remember this song." Eli scratched his dark, greying goatee. "Problem is, only thing we recall are a coupla words. If you grab the guit, we can mess around, see if it comes to us."

My heart leapt. "Sure. Love to."

Eli gestured behind him without turning from the drum kit. Behind the big man was a little alcove full of instruments. I picked my way past a dusty Ibanez bass and hefted a black Epiphone guitar. Its neck was smooth, like glass. I slipped the strap over my head and the guitar's weight settled on my left shoulder.

Memories of Dennis and Ryan distracted me and made me feel like an ass. I was desperate to get back to them yet here I was, about to play music with strangers instead. The knot at the center of my chest tightened.

Eli was watching me. He tossed over a bright orange pick. "I think Martin tuned it yesterday but might want to check."

I cleared my throat and forced a smile almost as wide as Gloria's. The tuning pegs were slick and cool. I fingered the fretboard, smiling at the familiar bite of the metal strings. My callouses had faded.

I pressed down hard, recalling chords of songs I'd played hundreds of times. "All right, what's this elusive song?"

Gloria rolled her eyes. "It sounds terrible. If we don't figure it out, I won't be upset."

"Nonsense." Eli wielded a drum brush in each big hand. "We only remember a few words. Something about fishing."

"Fishing?" I frowned.

"No." Tristan laughed from the table, still grinding herbs. "It rhymed with fishing. I think."

I strummed a few more chords, dropping my head to hear the notes above their chatter.

"It's an acoustic electric." He nodded behind him at what turned out to be a small guitar amp in the shadows. Plug in."

The amp was heavy but had wheels so I could roll it next to the drums. After a few seconds of scrounging for a cable, I plugged the guitar in. A loud *thump* shot through the room the moment I flipped the power switch. I twisted the volume knob and let a C chord ring out. The sound was nothing compared to my Les Paul, but it still brought a lightness to the center of my core.

"Okay," I said. "Fishing."

Gloria rested a keyboard along her lap and flicked it on. She pressed down hard on random keys, singing off key. *"Fishinnnng. I've been missing fishinnnng."*

We all laughed, a warm, hearty sound that did nothing to dispel my disquiet.

Tristan watched the older man with disapproval. "You're going to pull out your stitches."

"Nah." Eli tapped the crash cymbal lightly. "I'll be careful. Slow. I know my own limits."

"Yeah, well, don't look at me when you start bleeding."

It was a very un-Tristan thing to say.

Eli glowered at him. "I said I'll be fine. Martin can fix me if need be."

"Or Harry could," I cut in.

"See? We're all workin' together already."

Tristan's face spasmed almost imperceivably. He smiled at Eli. "You're right. Sorry. I wasn't thinking." He went back to mashing the leaves.

I squinted at the small plant in front of Tristan. "What is that? Is it for cooking?"

"Medicine." He sat back with a sigh, flexing the hand that had been using the pestle. "We've got one heck of a holistic setup down here."

"Now that modern medicine has lost some of its potency," Eli added, "we've been relyin' on the plants. And as for that song, 'feeding a line' is ringin' a bell..."

"Oh, God." I sniggered. "Blues Traveler?"

I positioned my hand into a G chord and hit the first note. After a steadying breath I began to strum through the first chords of "Run Around."

"That's it! Ah, fuck, I forgot about that damned song!" Eli's brushes gently tapped out a rhythm on the drums. He was careful not to raise the arm on his injured side too high.

Every minute we spent in the bunker was one we weren't out looking for Ryan and Dennis. But despite the unsettled feeling in the pit of my stomach, playing music again set my soul soaring.

Gloria laughed, bright teeth flashing as she tried to follow along on the keyboard. The song unfolded. Tristan watched, his eyes bright.

Without thinking, I began to belt out the lyrics. The words came easily, tumbling past my lips without a second thought, and I briefly lost myself in the music. Eli continued to keep the tapping beat, holding back as much as he could. Gloria used the keyboard to lay a backing bass line as I sang.

I glanced back at Eli and briefly saw Dennis at the drum kit instead. My enjoyment faltered. The thought of him tore out a piece of my soul, and a wave of misery hit hard. I stopped moving around and I forced my thoughts to focus on how Harry and I were going to get out.

Unaware of my conflicting mind, Eli did an impressive and quite unnecessary one-handed drum fill as we came into the first chorus. That's when I saw Harry Goodsir. He stood in the half open door, holding his long coat and watching. His mouth hung open.

At the sight of him, my grief shifted into a soothing relief. I stumbled the last line of the chorus but smiled around the words.

Harry stepped into the room and let the door fall shut behind him. Fascination was etched all over his face. His eyes took in every possible thing they could, from the guitar I held to Eli's drum set to the laughing Gloria pounding away on the keys. Tristan noticed Harry enter and waved him over. Harry sat at the table, still watching me. I sang louder and he beamed.

Looking away before he could notice my blush, I grinned at Eli as the moment I'd been waiting for arrived. The lyrics they'd been thinking of made me laugh and I again missed a note. Eli guffawed and missed a few beats. The entire song fell apart. We laughed, making fun of the lyrics.

Harry simply smiled at me. I held his gaze for a moment until I felt my face beginning to flush again.

I turned away and looked over at Eli. "What else you got?"

The old man snorted. "Everything. Just start it off and I'll hop in."

"Oh, no you don't," Gloria said. "Really. No more drums until you've healed."

"She's right," Tristan said. "If you don't rest soon, Martin will have our heads."

Eli grumbled something crude about podiatrists, but he still dropped the sticks on top of the bass drum.

"Another time," he told me with a wink. "You play damn well."

"That you do," Harry chimed in. "I've no' seen the like."

Gloria raised an eyebrow at him but said nothing.

Lowering the guitar back onto the stand, I made my way over to Harry. "Did we wake you?"

He smiled, still looking at me with those eyes on fire with a new discovery. "Nae. My jaw woke me. You were gone, and I worried."

I tried to hide my smile. "Are you all right?"

Harry's head dipped in a nod. "I went out in an attempt to locate Dr. Stephens for more medication, but I heard your music first. I couldnae believe what I saw."

Nervous that Tristan or the others would hear, I gently took Harry by the elbow and led him away from the little group. He stopped talking, solemn, already understanding. I gazed up at him, quiet for a moment, just taking in his steady gaze, his kind eyes, his easy closeness.

"You're something else, you know that?" I murmured, my face still hot.

Harry merely nodded as if he totally knew how wild and strange it was to be in his company.

"If it's all right with you," he said softly. "I would like to see how those particular instruments work. And to see you play once more."

I smiled and turned back. "Eli, could I borrow the guitar?"

The big man frowned. "No, but we can get you a speaker if you want to listen to music. Tristan, take her to that supply room in the second wing. Make sure to sign it out," he added.

"Sign it out?" My laugh was cut short at Eli's stare. "Oh. You're serious."

"A'course I am. We keep track of things down here. Gotta maintain control somehow."

Twenty-Five

Harry
2020

The fear that had coursed through me when I woke to find Annie gone barely abated when I found her in the common room. Surrounded by Eli's people, the music she played with the strangers was marvelous, but it did very little to still my thumping heart.

When Tristan split us up again, I nearly followed after them out of pure anxiety. Something about this place was wrong, but I knew Annie could fend for herself. That did not calm my fears, however. I lifted my head and instead headed out, turning down the south hall. Until we were forced back into our room, I found it wise to have a look around.

I slipped my hand into the pockets of my coat. My fingers brushed the sleek metal of Annie's little iPod. I fished the device out and placed the strange buds into my ears as I'd seen Annie do, the long white strings dangling down along my chest. I tapped on the front of the machine, mimicking Annie and Dennis's actions. Its top half lit up to show me a list. I recognized one, "Rosanna", but wanted to hear more.

Fascinated, I took my time, reading through the options. Trailing my thumb along the lower half of the iPod caused me to inadvertently press a button flush with the frame. The screen changed, showing me pale orange squares instead of the song titles I'd seen before. Each was labeled with large black letters. I poked at the words "New Favorites," delighted when soft music began in my ears.

Wandering the narrow hallways of the bunker brought on the same claustrophobia I'd often felt aboard the *Erebus*. The ceilings were nearly as low as the ship's, where I'd often had to push aside my comrades to reach a patient or get to and from the medical quarters, but in these corridors, two to three people could pass comfortably.

The song in my ears switched just as I turned a corner to see two sentries posted at the end of the hall. A short, balding man and a large woman with long, grey-streaked, mousey brown hair pulled back tight.

The pair stood before the entrance to the bunker. Neither seemed to have weapons, but their aggressive stances and unblinking eyes unnerved me. I briefly considered leaving, but decided I'd been cowardly enough on this new journey of mine. I stopped before the pair blocking my way and took the little buds from my ears.

"Good morning," I said with a smile and a quick dip of my head.

The man and woman before me did not smile back. In fact, neither looked over at me or gave any indication that they'd heard my greeting.

I stepped a little closer. "May I pass?"

Their heads snapped toward me in unison and both locked eyes with me. They clenched their fists. Both tensed as if to leap forward.

Startled, I withdrew, holding up a hand. The moment I was back to where I'd rounded the corner, the pair relaxed and their gazes unfocused once more. I stood still, blinking at them and considering my next move.

A dull ache suddenly twinged in my upper jaw, pushing my thoughts of escape aside. I touched my tongue to the tooth that had given me such issues. With an inward sigh, I turned back, recalling the route to the one person I least wanted to see.

The lights in the hall were dimmed. Shadows chased each other from corner to corner as I made my way toward Dr. Stephens's medical quarters. A husky female voice sang in my ears when I replaced the little buds. She crooned about something called the wild west. She told me that I could get everything I'd lost back again. I smiled, knowing it would be true if we could find our way out of here.

The door to the medical facility sat ajar. Steady white light filtered out into the hall.

I approached with caution, pulling a bud from my ear. "Dr. Stephens?"

The empty room was clear of any clutter and so clean each surface shone. Before I could inspect anything, my eyes fell on the most beautiful thing I'd seen since Annie huddled in my tent in 1848.

A microscope like no other I'd seen sat on one long counter. It loomed large and robust. The room's light gleamed along its black finish and sharp edges. It was reminiscent enough of the one I'd brought along on *Erebus*, but wildly different in so many other ways. With wonder overriding my senses, I gently placed the iPod next to the great machine, one bud still in my ear, and bent for a further look.

A tiny, unmoving, white worm was held between two thin slides. I hunched over and peered through the eyepiece. I squinted against a bright light, but my vision quickly cleared.

My gasp was louder than the music in my ear. The sight of the worm magnified shocked me, its skin now papery and dotted with wrinkles and bumps. Tufts of white hair stuck out on either side of the round head where I also saw small pink openings.

"Pretty cool, huh?" a voice said behind me.

I whirled. Annie's iPod was yanked from the tall counter. To my dismay, it clattered along the floor and came to rest at the shoes of Dr. Stephens. He regarded me with irritation from the door.

I flattened against the counter. "My apologies, doctor. I was just curious."

He stepped inside and pulled the door shut behind him. I dropped to one knee to retrieve the fallen iPod and inspecting it for damage but finding none.

"What are you listening to?" Dr. Stephens pulled a round rolling chair much like the ones in Annie's bunker up to the microscope. He sat, his melancholic face relaxing.

"I'm not sure," I admitted. "Something new."

He leaned forward and took the iPod from my hand before I could protest. He scrolled through the songs with a frown, tapping and poking the device while I watched.

"You did not lock us in," I said in a soft voice.

Dr. Stephens tensed but he did not look up. "I don't consider you a threat."

My boldness grew. "Are you watching us somehow? In our room?"

His laugh was incredulous. "Am I watching you? Of course not. Why the hell would you ask *me* that?"

I noted his level eye contact, the way he held himself with pride but very little confidence. I'd already taken note of the man's strange behavior but could find no reason to fear the podiatrist. I followed my instinct.

"I'm not from here," I said.

Dr. Stephens snorted. "Shocking."

"Why won't Eli let us leave? Why does he insist on locking us in? We're not enemies, so why are we being treated as such?"

"Ah, this is a good one." Dr. Stephens spun in his chair and plucked a cord from a nearby drawer. He plugged Annie's iPod into a speaker hidden behind the large microscope. Music filled the room, louder than I'd anticipated.

"It is not my wish to be rude, Dr. Stephens," I shouted over the noise, "but we simply prefer to take our chances outside, on our own."

He waved a dismissive, long-fingered hand. "You can call me Martin. We're both doctors living in tight quarters. I don't mind."

Frustrated, I just nodded.

"What did you want?" Martin pulled a pad from the drawer. He flipped through and I caught glances of sketches of birds and insects. The naturalist in me yearned to join the doctor in his studies, but I stuck to why I'd come.

"I have had a tooth that has been aching for some time. In our last home, I was on a round of antibiotics." The word felt strange on my tongue. "I was hoping I could obtain another dosage."

He began to sketch one side of the strange worm. "With meds weakening, I'd recommend pulling the tooth, but we don't have a dentist, so I suppose I can dispense some. Which one were you taking?"

I hesitated. Ryan had never told me the name, and I hadn't thought to inquire. The only thing I could remember was a strange name for one of the small, odd capsules he had offered once I'd eaten a full meal.

"Aspirin?" I tried.

"No, the antibiotic."

"I'm…unsure."

Martin stared at me. "A doctor who doesn't remember what antibiotic he was on?"

I quickly realized my mistake, but squared my shoulders, mind recalling Ryan's words as accurately as possible. "Dr. Breckner had me on a continuous cycle of an antibiotic as well as aspirin and vitamins. I'm unsure as to what type, as I've been through quite a harrowing ordeal and am having difficulty recalling its name."

"A 'harrowing ordeal,' huh?" Martin pulled a small silver key from his pocket and unlocked a cabinet. He rummaged inside, withdrawing a small orange bottle nearly identical to the ones Ryan had stocked in his medical quarters.

"I'll give you some Amoxicillin." Martin twisted the top off a little white bottle. "It's the one we have most of here. Unless you're allergic?"

Not knowing what else to do, I simply shook my head.

Nodding, he dropped a tab into my hand and gestured at the sink opposite the microscope. "Just stick your head in the faucet, but make sure to eat something soon, if you haven't already. You can take this bottle. Make sure you take one every twelve hours and do a saltwater rinse after each meal. Peppermint might help, so I'll chat with Gloria to obtain that. I'll also grab you some aspirin."

I leaned down and swallowed water from the faucet, swiping the back of one hand across my mouth and grimacing, still not used to the bitter taste of the tablets. I turned back, attempting to seem casual.

"What made you want to study feet, doctor?"

Martin snorted. "After I graduated, I wanted to open my own practice, but life decided that I'd go down a different path." He tossed me another, smaller bottle. It rattled when I caught it. "Take that for pain."

I twisted the top in one palm the way I'd seen him do, but the cap didn't budge. "But what drew you to feet in particular?"

He flipped his pristinely placed dark hair and peered into the microscope's eyepiece. "My father and I were close. He had Erythromelalgia, among other many ailments over the last decade."

I listened, pocketing the bottle of aspirin and leaning back against the counter to his right.

"It's a rare disease, as you know. He had a lot of joint and bone issues, but that never stopped him. He lived in daily pain, smiling, going to work as if he didn't want to curl into the fetal position and die." His voice softened. "A hero I have yet to live up to."

"He must have been extremely proud of you."

Martin looked up as if seeing me there startled him. "He died of a heart attack two years before the creatures came. After living life in daily agony, he died of something totally unrelated."

"I'm sorry, Martin," I said quietly.

He chewed a fingernail in silence for a moment, lost in his thoughts. "When he developed Erythromelalgia, it was the only time I'd seen him crippled from pain. I couldn't do a thing to help him. It seemed no one could for a while."

"How old were you?"

"Let's see." He scratched the back of his head, fingertips moving underneath his jet-black hair. "That was right at the end of AZPod."

I frowned. "Is that a…"

"Arizona. It's in Arizona."

Without a clue of which he spoke, I simply nodded.

Martin let out a long sigh and reached for the pad of paper. "What about you? You're on the run with that firecracker out there. Annie. Your girlfriend? Wife?"

I shook my head. "Neither."

Martin looked up at me from his chair with a pleased smile. "Finally. Some truth."

I was yet again reminded of the callous, cold Dr. Stanley aboard *Erebus*, whom I'd grown to detest. Telling myself this was not that man, no matter how uncanny the likeness, I forced a smile.

"Where did you study?" was his next question.

Clearing my throat, I glanced at the closed door. "Oh, back home. In Edinburgh."

"Haven't been to Scotland." He fixed me with a level stare. "I hear it's cold and rainy."

I chuckled. "It can be dreich, aye."

"Hmm. What college?"

"The Royal College of Surgeons. I also studied cell theory with my older brother, but my other true passion outside of medicine is nature." I glanced down at the microscope. "I learned anatomy as well, but when I was offered a position at Surgeons' Hall as Conservator…"

Martin was staring at me again. His gaze traveled along my naval long coat. "How old are you, anyway?"

"I'll be thirty November third."

"Huh."

Realizing I'd havered on too long, I pushed off the counter and reached for Annie's iPod. "Thank you, Martin, for the medication. I should get some rest now."

Pulling the cord and cutting off the music, I attempted to turn the device off. I turned the iPod over and poked a few buttons to no avail.

"Out of curiosity," Martin said, watching me struggle. "Are you a Proclaimers fan?"

"I am unsure of what you're asking."

"They're from Edinburgh, too." He tilted his head. "I didn't think any Scots existed that didn't know them."

"Well." I attempted a smile. "Quite engrossed in my studies and research."

He fished a similar iPod from his pocket and connected it to the speaker. "Stay here a second. Let me educate you on the melodies of Craig and Charlie. I guarantee you've at least heard that five hundred miles song."

I hesitated, slipping the iPod into the pocket of my coat.

Martin suddenly seemed quite eager to continue our tense conversation. "Want to see a butterfly through the scope? It got trapped down here before the end. It's dead, of course, like the worm, but still fascinating to look at."

"Oh, aye. Absolutely."

"Sweet." Martin checked his watch, then quickly tapped his own iPod. Moments later, music started up again; I was delighted to hear my accent reflected in the singers' voices.

I took his place on the stool and watched him slide open a drawer. He retrieved another slide and stood close, twisting a part of the microscope at random.

"Don't speak of anything incriminating in your room," he said suddenly, his voice low, and again hard to hear over the music.

I shifted my head slightly toward him but otherwise gave no indication I'd heard. "Why can't we leave this place?"

He changed the slides out and dropped the one holding the worm into the drawer. He shut it with his hip. "Trust me. It's safer for you in there."

"Can't you let us out? We just want to go home."

"No. Eli's always watching. But I at least wanted to tell you to—"

A loud rap on the door startled us both. It opened without hesitation and Gloria smiled in. "Well, lookie here. What are you two doing?"

Martin leaned back against the counter, crossing his arms. He stared her down, eyes unblinking. "Science stuff. What do you want?"

"Eli needs you, Martin."

Fear flickered across the podiatrist's face. "Why?"

Gloria only tilted her head, smiling wide, then disappeared down the hallway.

Cursing, Martin ushered me out of the medical room. He would not make eye contact with me. He slammed the door behind us, locked it, and hurried away.

Twenty-Six

Annie
2020

My heart soared when our door opened to reveal a flustered Harry Goodsir.

"Are you okay?" I surged off the bed where I'd been staring at the wall and nervously picking the tiny grey clumps of lint from my socks. "I thought you'd be here when I got back."

Harry smiled and pulled me into a tight hug.

"I was with Martin," he whispered. "As we both feared, this place is dangerous."

I stilled in his arms. "What do we do?"

Harry pulled back and spoke louder. "I'm so sorry to have frightened you, but dinnae fash yourself. I merely needed medication for mah tooth." He pulled a bottle of pills out and shook it for good measure. With it came my iPod.

Whatever Harry had learned, it had clearly shaken him.

"Did they give us a speaker?" Harry slipped off his coat, folding it neatly and placing it on the chair.

I swallowed my rage and frustration and horror. "Uh, yeah. It's on the bed."

He stepped around me and picked up the small, rectangular, grey Bose speaker. He handed it over to me. "I'd love to hear more music."

"Now?"

He merely lifted his hand higher.

I took the speaker and hooked it up to my iPod. I tapped its screen and Christopher Cross' "Sailing" started.

"We need to leave." Harry sat on the bed, pulling me down with him, keeping his voice under the volume of the song. "There's something wrong with the people here."

"Tell me about it. What happened?"

"There are two guards at the entrance. A man and a woman. Unarmed but…dangerous. Eerie. Something was no' right with them."

"Holy shit," I breathed.

"Martin confirmed that Eli is watching us. He warned me that the safest place for us is here in this room. He greatly fears their leader." Harry dropped his head, his face pained but thoughtful.

I resisted the urge to scan the low ceiling. "Harry, if they're listening to us, they're going to catch onto this quick."

"What do you propose?"

I stood and pulled Harry up, placing his hand on my waist. "The only thing that's natural with music. Dance."

I'd never seen anyone more afraid of the notion of swaying back and forth before.

"It's not hard." I chuckled. "I'll show you the basics."

"Are there no' steps to learn? Courtesies and etiquette to memorize?"

"Uh, not really, no. Not even close. Trust me."

Harry smiled then, his deep green eyes staring into mine. "I do."

Those two little words shook me. Nearly two weeks ago, he had shied away from me, terrified and near death. Now, he stood quite close, smiling and pulling off some covert shit using yacht rock as cover.

I showed him how to move back and forth, leading him in slow circles until he caught on. Once we found a nice, easy rhythm, I rested my cheek on his shoulder.

"I have no idea how to get back home," I whispered.

"Martin may be of great use," he replied, just as softly, "but it's clear he's been scared into obedience. To convince him to help us, to fight back, would take much longer than we dare wait."

"God, I hope Ryan and Dennis are okay."

"I believe they are. They have each other. Just like us." He pulled back and looked at me with such kindness, my face flushed.

The song changed to "Old Time Rock and Roll", and the different tempo threw Harry off. His boot grazed my foot. He gasped and let me go.

"Loosen up a little." I pulled him back into place. "Don't sway too much, you'll fall over. No, no, careful. That's it."

Harry laughed in between songs, face alight. He raked his fingers slowly through his loose, dark curls. "This is utterly ridiculous. I feel like some sort of bird or creature, bouncing up and down in a mating ritual."

I flushed.

"Does all your music sound so angry?"

"This is nothing. Remind me to show you some deathcore later."

His deep frown only made me laugh harder. I stepped close to him again, smiling as he carefully placed his hand back on my waist.

The harp-like guitar intro to "Here Comes the Sun" sprang to our ears next.

"I think we keep finding ways to earn their trust," I said, back to business. "Get them to drop their guard. You should keep assisting Dr. Stephens with Eli's care. I guarantee that will help. God, I don't want to stay here that long, though."

Harry wasn't listening. In fact, he wasn't even moving to the music. Eyes unfocused, he stared past me at nothing in particular.

"This is quite bonnie," he said.

Something flickered over Harry's face as the lyrics started. His features relaxed, and his eyes grew more distant.

"Oh…" Harry still held me, but he was far away. The drums played along with the guitar and bass. George Harrison's voice was soft and encouraging, telling us that everything would be all right.

And just like that, Harry Goodsir began to weep.

I watched two tears streak down his cheeks and drip off his chin. More followed. He cried silently, listening to The Beatles, and I nearly lost it myself. I didn't speak, just rested my head back on his shoulder and let him feel everything he needed to feel. Of his loss of friends, of family. The constant danger and threat of death.

Of escaping his inevitable fate. Of being rescued in a way he'd never dreamed.

Of hearing music again.

Music had been my lifeline, from childhood and on. It had kept me sane when everything else crumbled around me. Although our times were wildly different, I fully understood what he was feeling in that moment.

A lump grew in my throat. Pulling him closer, I embraced him. I held him tight the way he'd held me in the gas station. Harry clung to me, his soft sobs drowned out by the second verse.

I held him until the music faded.

"I'm sorry." Harry cleared his throat and pulled back, not meeting my eyes. Red blotches dotted his cheeks. He looked away. "I dinnae ken what came over me."

"Just music," I said quietly. "That's what it's supposed to do."

He nodded but still wouldn't meet my gaze.

I reluctantly let him go, reaching out for my iPod. The screen glowed softly, displaying one of my most treasured folders. "My parents…they got my name from this song."

Boston's *More Than a Feeling* faded in. We didn't dance. Instead, we sat on the bed and stared down at the floor as the music took over.

"Mary Anne?" he asked after a while, above the guitar and lyrics.

I nodded, grimacing. "I hate it."

Memories of my parents jumping and twirling together in our living room years ago played over and over. I could almost hear their voices mingle within the music.

I shut my eyes. Harry's hand slipped over mine just as Boston's song swelled. We sat close, both lost in the music, in our pasts.

Eventually, the song faded out, the words of the final line transforming into a ghost-like echo. Harry and I stared at each other, not moving.

"I'd very much like to keep learning," he said finally. "If it's all right with you."

I nodded and cleared my throat. We had gotten distracted and needed to get back on track. If Eli was truly watching, though, I hoped we were boring him to tears.

"Of course."

"Thank you, Annie. For this. For everything. Rescuing me. Saving mah life."

"Harry, I…"

He stood swiftly, pulling me off the mattress. Huey Lewis began to sing about the power of love. I pulled Harry closer than was necessary, my smile returning and face heating.

I showed him how to twirl me, a basic in and out spin.

"It would be smart to see how heavy those canisters are," I said quietly as I returned into his arms. "To make sure we could carry more than one when we do get out of here."

I let him twirl me again, but my feet caught, and I stumbled. Harry steadied me, then gently pulled me against his chest, dropping his hands back to my waist. I looked up into those damned soulful eyes of his. My cheeks were so hot, too hot, and not from embarrassment or exertion.

"Harry…" I couldn't focus on our plans. On the danger we were in. All I could think about was him. "I really care about you."

"And I you." He reached up and ran his fingertips along my cheek.

We lowered to the side of the bed, listening to the shuffling songs that continuously flowed. He slipped one arm around my lower back, but he never presumed, never let his hands wander. We sat close, pressed against each other, with my head resting on his shoulder.

Eventually, we lay down together. We talked in whispers of ourselves, our pasts, our fears, and our longings. We chatted about music and books. At one point I tried explaining CGI to him, which was a total failure. We laughed, lying together on the twin bed, finally able to fully open ourselves to someone else, someone who cared unequivocally.

My mind began to drift. I traced slow figure eight patterns across his chest.

"I'm sick of sleeping," I said as the last song faded, and our room fell silent.

Harry trailed his fingertips along my arm. "Tomorrow we can confront Eli," he whispered in my ear. "More forcefully. I grow weary of being a prisoner. It's time to fight back."

Twenty-Seven

Annie
2020

I lay awake next to Harry long after he'd fallen asleep. My restless tossing and turning did nothing to stir him from what seemed the first solid sleep he'd gotten in years. I'd tried keeping my eyes shut, hoping they'd grow heavy, hoping I could sleep away the hours we would be trapped again in the little room, but nothing slowed my mind.

Martin hadn't used the key before, and this time, Harry had come back on his own. We weren't locked in. Pondering thoughts of a possible ally, albeit a douchebag one, I rolled over.

Harry's eyes were open. Face impassive, he was clearly lost in thought. I watched him a moment before slipping my arm across his chest. He looked over at me, his troubled expression shifting to bring forth a radiant smile.

"Good mornin'." His voice was soft, the barest whisper.

Twice I opened my mouth, and twice I closed it, wanting to tell him of my clashing, confusing thoughts but knowing others were listening. The silence stretched.

"I had a peculiar dream." Harry stared up at the ceiling. "Of mist that turned mah eyes to glass. I was terrified to blink and tried so very hard not to. When I finally did, mah eyes shattered."

I sat up, shifting my bra so the underwire stopped cutting into my side, and stared down into his expressive green eyes. It made my heart skip too many beats.

"That sounds awful, Harry," I said.

He sat up and settled his back against the wall. "Back when I joined the expedition, I wanted to explore. I had so hoped to gather new specimens, bring them home. Show them to mah family. See them again."

I stayed silent as he struggled to find the right words.

"While the adventure was much more horrific than I'd ever imagined, I had come to a sort of peace that I would die in the north, surrounded by the most breathtakin' scenery. But all that changed in unimaginable ways when you arrived."

We made eye contact, and something in his gaze slowly began to break my heart.

"I thought I'd been hallucinatin'. Or that I had died. How could I not? And then I thought that maybe I'd been thrown into some sort of purgatory to make up for my sins."

I took his hand. The thought that he of all people believed he was a sinner hurt to hear.

"Yet this is real," he continued. "So real. And I could die here instead. As could you, if I dinnae at least attempt what I was brought here to do. But Annie, we must come to terms with what will happen after if we do survive."

He pulled me to him. His closeness was exhilarating but did nothing about the mounting misery in my heart.

"Annie." He said my name so gently, so soft. "I understand why Ryan doesnae want me to return but I cannae stay here in your time. I cannae leave my family to mourn mah death while I hide in the future."

I didn't want to hear what he was saying. I knew the danger in Eli's bunker, of the world should we find a way out. A part of me had continuously refused to believe that Harry could die trying to stop the wraiths. Now, hearing him speak so softly of his potential demise – and his determination to return to the past – I realized I might lose him just as quickly as we'd met.

A sudden thud shook the door of our room, making us both jump. I sat up fast, ready and on guard, but no one entered. Harry and I shared a look and rose from the bed.

Muffled shouts blasted past the door. Cautiously, Harry opened the door. A group of people hurried down the hall. I ducked beneath Harry's arm and peeked out but couldn't discern what had everyone so worked up.

Harry pulled me back inside. After a quick shared look of determination, we discreetly merged into the crowd just as Martin Stephens bolted past with the rest. The gangly, dark-haired man didn't seem to notice us join the fray.

"What's going on?" I shouted.

He didn't turn but replied in a loud voice. "There's people outside. Tristan went to meet them."

My body went numb. Harry and I picked up speed, trying to get further up in the crowd. Bodies of strangers pressed tight all around, sleeves and skin brushing against my arms. We rounded the corner just behind Martin, nearly colliding with him as he skidded to a halt. Before us stood a glowering Eli, who blocked the hallway with his big frame.

"Interestin' week we're having." He stared me down. "First you two show up after we haven't seen a new soul for three years, and now there's more out there. Anything you need to tell us?"

"With all due respect," Martin cut in, "the last time new people arrived, you and Tristan nearly died. How about we save the interrogation for later?"

Eli pursed his lips but didn't argue. "You're responsible for these two. Lock 'em back up, then get your ass back here and be of some use."

Martin just shrugged.

The big man turned and led the group of people the rest of the way through the common room. They approached a side door that I hadn't noticed before. He glanced over his injured shoulder at Harry and me.

"Take 'em outta here," he snapped.

Martin touched his fingers to my arm, a surprisingly gentle gesture. "Come on."

Eli hunched over a lit keypad, punching in numbers while shielding it from the gathering crowd's view. The back of his shirt was dotted with blood seeping through his bandages. I glowered at him but followed the podiatrist away.

"Move it." Martin pushed Harry into the hallway.

I stepped between them, glaring at the lanky douche. "You wanna back off?"

Harry lifted his chin at the podiatrist. "You either stand for something or you live in the background. Are you going to fight back or no?"

The two men stared each other down. A door opened back in the common room and spurred Martin out of his scowl.

"This way." He roughly pushed past Harry, their shoulders colliding.

Neither Harry nor I moved.

Martin grunted, casting a worried glance behind us. "Let's go. Now."

"Fuck off," I snarled, grabbing Harry's hand. "We're out of here."

"Annie." Martin's face showed clear frustration, but he put his hands out in my direction, palms up. "Don't look back."

I blinked. "Huh?"

Harry glanced over his shoulder, but the hallway remained clear.

"There's a new day breaking." Martin didn't take his eyes from mine. "It's been much too long since I've felt this way."

After a pause, he began to back down the hallway with a flash of his dark eyes. Was he helping us after all? Could we risk running to the bunker door if the guards Harry had discovered were still there, or was it smarter to listen to the strange code Martin was suddenly spewing?

Fuck it. I stared forward, Harry's hand in mine, and we jogged after Martin. After a few turns into new halls, Martin shoved a hand in his pocket and pulled out a key ring.

"Today's the day," he said firmly.

Could he really be trying to quote Boston right now? I didn't want to doubt myself. I didn't want it to be coincidence, but we had too much to lose if I was reading the moment wrong.

I took the bait. "Do you see yourself in a brand-new way?".

Martin finally, genuinely smiled. It transformed his face, brightening his brown eyes and actually made him look quite handsome, even friendly. His nod was slight but was the only thing I needed to see to solidify my decision. He changed direction, cutting through a small oncoming crowd of stragglers, and I chased after him.

Harry followed without question. The three of us sprinted along the corridors, turning left, then right, then left again. We at last stopped before a door directly across from Eli's bedroom.

Martin unlocked the door, not looking back at us. He kept his voice quiet and low. "Shift to the left, until you can see the door inside. Don't move or speak for any reason."

He swung the door wide and stepped into a large room. Despite being able to only see a third of the room from where we stood, I still noticed an odd assortment of things.

A lone lamp on a desk looked as if it belonged back in the forties. Strange, abstract paintings of red, green, and gold littered the armchair and concrete floor beneath it. I caught a whiff of a strong chemical smell I couldn't place. The desk held stacks of mason jars full of a brownish red opaque liquid next to the inner door Martin had mentioned. He ignored it all and quickly approached the door by the desk, fumbling with the keys again.

A small grunt came from Harry, barely audible. I followed his gaze above the desk to see large, hand-drawn diagrams of humans taped along the wall. Each anatomical figure was cross sectioned to show what lay inside in great detail. Scribbled notes in different handwriting decorated them all. The diagrams were all labeled with a person's first name.

The most yellowed diagram, its sides curled with age, had 'Tristan' scrawled on top. A fresher one was titled 'Gloria.' A carefully sketched smile stretched eerily across the face in black ink.

My heart began to pound. The freshest diagrams, identical to the others minus the notes in the margins, were labeled "Harry" and "Annie." Harry's sketched head was severed at the neck and a handful of thin lines pointing out arteries and parts of the exposed spinal cord. I clapped a hand over my mouth, silencing a gasp.

Martin unlocked a side door and pulled it wide. Stepping into a bright glow, he shifted aside and finally looked back at us. I tore my gaze from the drawings to see stacked rows of monitors quite like the ones we'd had back home.

The screens showed countless views throughout Eli's bunker. Martin leaned on the table with both hands, still off to a side so we could see the left-most column of screens. Ones that showed the outside world.

Two figures stood squinting in the bright sun and arguing with a third. Martin fiddled with a keyboard and the camera zoomed in close enough to see their faces.

It was Ryan and Dennis.

My heart soared. I let out a choked moan and exchanged a quick glance with Harry, who was grinning broadly.

"They need to run," Martin muttered. He twisted a knob, leaning closer to the monitor. "What the hell're they doing?"

The three on the screen turned as one and gaped up at the sky. Tristan suddenly bolted, leaving both brothers behind. Ryan grabbed Dennis by the arm, and they chased after Eli's weird butler.

Martin pulled the door shut and hurried past us out into the hallway. "They're running this way."

Harry grabbed the podiatrist, gripping his biceps tight and drawing close.

"Take us to the entrance," he said in a steady, low voice. "Let me outside. I have a weapon against the wraiths, a way to fight them that can complement the liquid nitrogen. I can help."

Martin stared down at him, his mouth twisting in flurried contemplation. He turned his hard gaze on me. "She stays behind. Collateral."

I nodded furiously. "Go, Harry. Now!"

We careened down the hall, following close behind Martin. My lungs burned by the time we reached the entrance, a place we hadn't been near since arriving. The guards Harry had said he'd encountered were nowhere to be seen.

Martin leapt up the steps. He reached above his head and quickly twisted a series of dials. The large metal door above clunked and hissed. It rose on its own, lifting free of the ground over our heads. Bright sunlight trickled in, bringing with it a distant chorus of wraith wails.

Without a word, Harry launched up the steps. I instinctively reached for him, horrified this might be the last moment I'd ever see him. Martin grabbed my arm and pulled me back into the depths of the bunker.

I fought against him. "*Harry!*"

Martin held me in an oddly strong grasp. I kept shouting, no longer caring about Eli or the creepy bunker or anything other than the three people I had left in this world, who were all outside and at the mercy of a power Harry didn't even know how to use. I knew he had to try at some point, but in the moment of terror, emotion battled logic.

"Stop fighting me," Martin grunted.

I backhanded him. He let go of me in his shock, one hand going up to clutch his jaw. An incredulous laugh shot out of his throat.

I ran back down the concrete hallway just as Eli and Gloria appeared, the latter hauling two of the metal liquid nitrogen backpacks.

"The hell is Annie doin' up here?" the big man demanded. His gaze shot to the open bunker door. He stormed up to Martin, grabbing the front of his shirt. "You let the Scot go?"

I grabbed his wrist and roughly shoved him away from Martin. "Dammit, Harry's trying to save them!"

"With what, his fuckin' charm?"

I didn't respond. I snatched one of the discarded canisters. Taking the concrete steps two at a time, I burst outside, both feet scrambling in the dirt. I gasped at the bright light that accosted my vision, but piercing howls of the wraiths that surged all around spurred me forward. I pulled the canister's straps over my shoulders and sprinted after Harry.

He was just up ahead, running toward Dennis and Ryan, with Tristan just ahead. Behind them all, a dark, undulating mass of outstretched arms and dangling jaws was quickly gaining.

Harry was almost to them, but it was too late. If he wasn't able to use his power on the wraiths, he, Ryan and Dennis weren't going to make it.

I risked a look down. My grip on the long metal nozzle's rubber handle was deathly tight, but I couldn't see a safety of any sort, just a trigger. Up ahead, Harry changed course. He ducked out of the way and passed the others, coming to a full stop right behind them.

Dennis and Ryan, shocked, glanced back at him but kept running. Behind them, the wraiths swarmed over Harry.

I cried out in raw despair. Tristan passed me, shouting that they wouldn't keep the bunker door open. Dennis slowed when he saw me, but I kept running toward Harry and the mass of wraiths tearing at him with teeth and claws.

"Go!" I screamed. Dennis spun but stumbled. He fell to the dirt on his hands and knees.

A few stray wraiths had broken from the mass that had swarmed over Harry and now flew toward us. I skidded to a stop, hair flinging into my eyes and mouth.

"Fuck you." I planted my feet, standing in front of Dennis, and pulled the trigger. The nozzle let loose a long burst of frozen liquid air. The creatures howled. Instant pearls of ice fell all around my feet and covered Dennis, who lay on one side, an arm flung high above his head.

The wraiths I'd missed twisted around, escaping the frigid death that had claimed a handful of their ranks. More broke loose from the cloud that smothered Harry and shot toward me. I let the long nozzle lead, shooting more bursts of liquid nitrogen sprays high above. When those wraiths fell prey to the frozen fate, I reached down for Dennis. He ignored me. His face was slick with sweat, and he stared behind me in mute horror.

The rest of the wraiths sped toward us in a giant cluster.

There were too many. I couldn't see where Harry had been, couldn't see anything but their empty eye sockets trained on me. They were going to swarm us, just as they had done to Harry.

I lifted the nozzle, but before I could pull the trigger, the creatures howled as one and froze mid-air.

I stumbled backward and fell in the dirt next to Dennis. He grabbed me, trying to pull me back toward the open bunker door. Claws stretched toward us, just unable to scrape my skin. Unhinged jaws hung low, swinging as if in a breeze. I urged my trigger finger to spray the fuckers, but fear had locked me in place.

"*Holy shit*," Dennis gasped from behind me.

The wraiths began to fly backward.

No, they didn't fly. They were pulled.

Harry stood behind them. Unscathed, arms tense at his side, he had his feet planted and palms turned upward. His fingers twitched, scratching the air. Wind whipped his loose curls around his face. His normally green eyes were pure white.

I watched in awe as his Evo power was finally released. Sweet, loving, childlike Harry Goodsir stood not twenty feet away, his body acting like some kind of magnet to the wraiths. They flailed, livid but helpless in his invisible grasp. Forming a small tornado, its apex at Harry's core, they squirmed and fought but couldn't break free. The entire mass of wraiths was quickly and viciously sucked into Harry in a whirl of wind, vanishing into his chest.

The world fell silent.

Harry stumbled. He clutched a hand to his chest and looked up. His eyes were still white, his skin as pale as a corpse.

I dropped the canister and ran to him. He pitched forward into my arms just as I reached out. His hands shook, and he gasped in deep, shuddering breaths.

"Harry," I breathed. "Harry, holy shit."

"…Annie…?"

"It's me. How…where did…how do you have them…?" I couldn't form a single solid question.

Dennis ran up and took some of Harry's weight.

"Nae." He pushed against Dennis, twisting out of his grasp and falling to the ground. "I cannae hold them."

Harry began to writhe on the ground. His hands clawed at the front of his dirt-smeared, sweat-soaked shirt. I backed up and grabbed the discarded canister, lifting its nozzle and aiming at Harry.

He cried out in pain and anguish. Sweat shone along his forehead and cheeks. He wheezed through teeth clamped together. With a desperate, hoarse cry, his back arched, and the captured wraiths poured back out of him. They flew toward the sky. I let the tip of the nozzle follow the fucks up and away from Harry, then unleashed frigid hell.

Wraiths froze and shattered. The constant wails pierced my ears. I held the trigger down as far as it would go. There were too many, but I wasn't going to give up. Harry needed me.

A second burst of icy air joined mine. Martin stood a few feet away, mouth set in a scowl, sweeping the air with his own nozzle. The monsters froze in clusters before the pair of us, their howls cut short. Whether they were confused or weakened by Harry's power, they were slower than before.

Martin and I sprayed a continuous stream until the last of the wraiths shattered around our feet. I kept squeezing the trigger, shooting at nothing. I couldn't stop firing.

"Annie!" Dennis scrambled over and put a hand over mine.

My nozzle sputtered and died. I only stopped firing when Harry went limp in the dirt. I squirmed out of the harness. Eyes on Harry's unmoving form, I fell to my knees amongst crystal debris of the dead wraiths.

"Please," I whispered, and pressed my ear to his lips. The faintest tickle of breath washed over my face. Closing my eyes, I rested my forehead on his and let relief wash over me.

Dennis was by my side in a second. "Help me get him up."

Before we could try, Harry's eyes opened. They were back to his normal green. He gasped and clutched at his chest.

"Harry." I lightly touched his cheek. "Oh, Harry, are you okay?"

He gasped and sat up. Frozen bits of wraith fell from his hair and tinkled to the dry ground. More screeching howls reached our ears from the distance, just barely audible.

"Let's go!" Martin shouted. He helped Dennis pull Harry to his feet. "Back inside. Now."

We had nowhere else to go. Dennis and I started to run back to Eli's bunker with a dazed Harry clinging to us. Martin grabbed my empty nitrogen container in one hand and followed, his chest heaving. Harry's knees buckled and I nearly toppled over.

"Annie," he sighed. "I cannae move."

"I've got you." My back muscles spasmed, and my legs wobbled under his weight. I risked a glance upward, but the sky remained clear. The wailing, however, drew closer.

Harry tripped and we nearly went down again. He let out a pained moan. "I'm trying. I'm so sorry."

Seconds later, we reached the bunker door. Dennis ducked out from under Harry's arm so he and I could fit down the stairs. Martin roughly shoved Dennis in behind us, then leapt below. He slammed the door shut, slipping its locks in place.

Eli and company stood a little way off. They stared open-mouthed as we stumbled down the main hall. Harry's head fell to one side. My muscles burned and I nearly tripped.

All weight suddenly lifted from me. I gasped in relief; Ryan had arrived to help.

"Stephens," Eli growled.

Martin dropped my empty container, then struggled out of his own. He left a panting Tristan behind and followed us.

Eli waved Martin off when he tried to assist the brothers. When we got to the medical room, Ryan and Dennis hefted Harry up onto the exam table with ease.

Martin took over, pulling Harry's eyelids back to check his pupils. Ryan stood on the other side of the table and felt for Harry's pulse. Eli, his shirt now streaked with bright blood along the back, came toward me, eyes shooting daggers.

Dennis stepped between us. Eli sneered at him. He turned and slammed the door on a large group of onlookers that had gathered, so hard the frame rattled.

"Stephens, step the fuck back."

Martin ignored the order. He slipped a blood pressure cuff around Harry's limp left arm. Eli reached out, grabbed him by the shoulder, and pulled him back. Ryan looked up at the big man, his hands faltering.

The silence in the bunker pressed against my ears.

Eli stared me down. "Before we help any further, you are gonna tell me exactly what the fuck just happened."

"Other than us saving your ass yet again?" I pressed past Dennis and got in Eli's face. I glared up at him, with only my anger giving me courage.

"Regular firecracker, you are." Eli didn't smile. "We've kept you safe, kept your bellies full, and you've done absolutely nothin' but complain. Try to leave. Ya know, I had some high hopes for you."

I nearly spit in his face.

"Annie?" Ryan brought a hand to his forehead, perplexed, unable to rouse Harry. "What the hell's happening?"

"Oh, he's right." My words tumbled free. "They've kept us down here under lock and key, nice and safe. Been feeding us, too, and letting us sleep off whatever Tristan's slipping into our food."

The big man's eyebrows shot up. "Okay. I'd hoped we'd do this the pleasant way but fuck it."

Before anyone could react, Eli grabbed me. His big fingers wrapped tight around my throat. He slammed me into the cabinets, the doors shuddering. Pain shot through my back and skull.

Martin finally stopped examining Harry. Brow furrowed, he stared at the floor with a clenched jaw. My body tingled with adrenaline. I stared up into Eli's pale eyes. Dangling helplessly in his grasp, I clawed at his hands with little effect.

Dennis lunged forward, face tight with fury.

"Stop." Eli backed up and tightened his hold, bringing stars to my vision. "Her neck is all sorts of delicate."

Dennis didn't listen. He pushed past Martin. I expected my spine to be snapped right then, but Martin sprang into action. He surged forward and roughly pulled Dennis back.

Ryan whirled from Harry. He threw a fist at the podiatrist, who feinted to one side, narrowly missing the blow. Martin shoved Dennis into his brother, then backpedaled until he was between Eli and the brothers.

"Please." Martin held up his hands, looking between us all, his face full of uncertainty. "No one needs to get hurt. Eli, come on. They stopped the wraiths. They saved us."

The big man's grip on me loosened. He lowered me down. The moment my feet touched the concrete floor, I tried to throw a punch of my own, but Eli easily caught my arm and pushed it behind my back. Seconds later a slim pocketknife flashed. Light glinted off its blade as he whipped it up and pressed it against my throat.

"Y'all best start spewin' some truth," he growled, his hot breath caressing my cheek. "Or I'll open her up."

Twenty-Eight

Harry
2020

Equal parts nausea and agony crashed through my body. I struggled to sit up on the hard, flat surface upon which I lay.

"Whoa, take it easy."

I squinted up, searching for the owner of the familiar voice.

Ryan Breckner stood next to me, his face set in enmity. He reached out to aid my attempt to rise. My vision cleared to show a scene that I struggled to comprehend.

Eli chewed the side of his cheek, his jaw working back and forth. The stare from his hard, unblinking eyes brought chills to my stiff back, but the blade he held against Annie's neck shook the very essence of my soul.

"So, you're an Evo?" The big man licked his lips.

I met Annie's fearful but defiant gaze.

"Aye. I suppose so." My voice was weak and tremulous. I attempted to quell the roiling in my stomach and took a quick stock of my health. I did not note any broken bones or any scrapes, merely an upset stomach and deep ache in my chest.

Eli scoffed. "From the past."

Horrified, I looked over the faces of the brothers who stood on either side, their stances protective. Ryan's hateful gaze could have melted steel; Dennis was gritting his teeth, standing on the balls of his feet and flexing his fists. He gave me a sad, apologetic glance, but neither spoke.

I slowly nodded. "I was born in 1819."

Martin inhaled softly, but I stared hard at the weapon Eli held near Annie's neck, looking for any twitch of his fingers.

"Right." Eli's jaw kept moving. "And you're here to help us in present time by doin' what you just did to the wraiths."

"How could you possibly get them all?" Martin asked, arms crossed, his black hair ruffled. A long red scrape along his forearm nagged at the healer in me, but I dared not rise.

Mind flying, I settled on revealing the most threatening part of the truth: "Because these types of things, they're drawn to me somehow. And I can call them."

Eli let out a short laugh. "Oh, 'course you can."

Annie's wide eyes watched me. Her fists were clenched but she stood absolutely still against Eli.

Unperturbed, I pushed myself up, sliding off the table and lowering to my feet. I stepped between Ryan and Dennis. Staring hard at Eli, I lifted my chin. "It's why I was taken from the past. To draw the wraiths, eliminate them."

"Right." Eli's eyebrows rose. "So instead of goin' back and stopping them in the first place, instead of savin' family and loved ones, they go get you."

Annie's eyes fell shut. I knew her thoughts: there was no point in trying to explain how the time traveling worked, as Eli would never believe it.

"Stephens." The big man looked over a shoulder at the podiatrist. "Lock 'em up."

Martin pushed past Dennis and pounded on the door.

"Move away," he shouted, his deep voice level and firm. "We're comin' out."

The door opened to reveal a large crowd of colonists, each watching carefully. They stood in a tight semi-circle, poised to lunge forward at command.

"Whatever it is you are, son," Eli growled, his eyes boring into me, "it ain't safe. I thought you'd be a good addition to my little colony. But now that I've seen what you really are, well…y'all will stay put until I know what to do with you."

I held up both hands. "We'll go willingly. Please, release Annie."

"Y'all go first. She'll follow if there's no violence."

It took a bit of hushed convincing on my end, but the brothers reluctantly turned and followed Martin into the hallway.

The crowd parted as one to let us pass. I met Annie's gaze, willing her to know I would burn Heaven and Earth if any harm came to her. Her eyes softened slightly. I stepped out of the medical quarters.

Ryan hurried after Martin. "Hey. You helped us with the wraiths," he hissed, voice barely audible. "Help us now. Get us out of here."

The podiatrist shot an amused look over his shoulder and snorted. "Hell, no."

The colonists followed us. They again moved as one. No one spoke. Eli pushed Annie forward a few yards behind us, watching us, still holding the knife too close to her throat.

"My back's bleedin' like a stuck pig." He grimaced. "Hurry up, Stephens."

The moment we reached our room in the south hall, Martin yanked the keyring from his pocket. He twirled it around one finger, pulled open the door, and stood aside with a smug, contemptuous smile. Ryan shouldered into him as he went into the room. Dennis followed close behind, glancing back at Annie instead.

I watched Martin a moment, not moving. He did not look away. His dark eyes were flat, emotionless, but I recognized something in them. Something I'd seen in the eyes of the mutinous men in the Arctic: recalcitrance. I gave no sign I'd noticed and entered the room behind Dennis.

Annie was finally released. Eli shoved her inside and she stumbled against me. I pulled her close and lifted her chin to inspect the reddening indentation along her neck; the knife had not broken skin.

The stare I fixed on Eli churned with hatred. I willed him to feel the rage within me, to feel how close I was to testing the limitations of the power I now understood. Instead, he wiggled the knife at us, grinning, and then walked away. Martin stared at me a moment before quietly shutting the door and locking the four of us in.

Ryan instantly rounded on me, shoving me into the closed door. "What the *fuck did you do*?"

"The hell?" Annie croaked.

He ignored her and came at me again. Dennis backed away against the far wall by the bathroom door. There he stayed, arms crossed, chewing his thumbnail, watching his brother but making no move to stop him.

"You think you can just take Annie and bolt?" Ryan pushed me again. "What did you do to her? Why'd you make her leave the bunker?"

Unable to retreat, I opened my mouth to protest, but Ryan didn't give me a moment to speak.

"We save your damn life, and this is how you repay us? How you repay Annie?" Ryan's brown eyes were bloodshot and nearly wild. He grabbed the front of my wrinkled shirt, shaking me.

"Enough!" Annie shoved in between us and pushed Ryan away. He stumbled back, the rageful trance broken at the contact.

"We came back to a broken gennie, and you...you were just gone," Dennis said quietly. His eyes were very wide and round. He wouldn't look at me.

"Please," I said. "I did no such thing."

Annie pushed Ryan again. "I told you exactly where we went in my note! That we went north, to that gas station. We got stuck there and had to spend the night."

"What fuckin' note?"

She hesitated. "The one I left outside of the bunker door."

Dennis shook his head.

"I watched her leave it beneath a large rock," I added. "We tried to find you, but the wraiths came. That is when Tristan arrived. He rescued us, brought us here, and that is all."

Ryan's upper lip twitched. "No, that is not fucking all. Do you know what it felt like to come home and find someone you care about just...just *gone?*"

"Aye, I do, and I'm sorry this transpired. But we are together again and all in good health."

"We were nearly torn apart," Annie said quietly. "Maybe the wind took the note, or a fucking wraith, I don't know. We wanted to come back but these people, they're—"

I touched the back of her hand. Eli was no doubt listening, and we could not risk giving away what Martin had shown us earlier; the podiatrist was our only hope now.

"Don't look back," I muttered.

Ryan slapped my hand away. "They're what, Annie?"

"Like I told you already," she looked up at him. "Locking us in here, not letting us leave. I'm fully convinced I saw Tristan grinding up some plant that was some sort of sedative. We keep sleeping, all the time. Day and night."

"Why would they do that?" Ryan's face was blotched with red. "Why would they save you just to drug you, lock you away? That makes no sense."

Neither Annie nor I responded. The image of my headless diagram came forth in my mind.

Dennis finally spoke. "We fixed the gennie. Water got into the fuel line I'd replaced before, made its way into the fuel tank. That's why steam was billowing. It was an easy fix but getting to it wasn't fun. The second that was done we went looking for you two. Every day. Even for just a sign."

Ryan dropped heavily into the armchair, its frame groaning underneath his weight. He stared down at the ground.

"I'm sorry I snapped," he said at last. "And that I pushed you, Goodsir. I was so scared we lost you, Annie."

She went to her friends, pulling them into an awkward yet fierce three-way embrace. "I'm so, so sorry, too. You have no idea how badly we wanted to come back that same night, but Harry advised against it. I'm damn glad he was with me, because I would have tried to come back and been out in the open when the wraiths attacked."

I felt a soft tug on my heart. "And I would have certainly perished without Annie; I never would have known where to go or hide without her."

Her smile told me more than words could have. I knew the fondness I had developed for her was blossoming, and that she felt it, too. Not wanting to intrude, I started with my own plan.

I scooped up Annie's iPod from the nightstand, then picked up my long coat and dropped the device into the front pocket. The metal water bottles I fished from Annie's pack were cool to the touch. Twisting their caps free, I slipped into the dark bathroom and filled both with water from the shallow sink.

Ryan spoke too quietly for me to hear when I headed back through the room. Annie and Dennis listened with rapt focus. I replaced the water containers in her colorful pack, careful of the strange teeth along the edge of the pack's opening. I draped my coat over the top. My fingers brushed the front pocket and felt the familiar bulk of my diary.

"I'm sorry, Harry, but what the hell are you doing?" Ryan asked.

Annie stood and shuffled to the bed. She dropped onto the mattress and tied her hair back. Dennis moved to sit along the far wall with a long sigh.

"Just…tidying," I said, not wanting to share my true plans for the whole bunker – and Eli's cameras – to hear.

Ryan shook his head and sat back in the chair. He stretched out his legs and crossing his ankles. I leaned the pack against the nightstand next to the bed.

"Sorry we got pissed at you." Dennis finally met my gaze.

Ryan said nothing.

I nodded wearily, sinking to the edge of the mattress next to Annie. "I would never hurt any of you."

"We didn't know…couldn't have known what happened." Dennis let his hand fall.

We sat in silence for a long moment.

"So, do you know something we don't?" Annie asked in a whisper, nodding at the pack I'd filled.

"Just a hunch," I whispered back.

I kicked up my feet, pushing back on the bed until I felt the cool surface of the wall behind me. Annie lay down on the mattress on the other side, facing away from the room, from us. The brothers were silent. Each stared at different spots of the grey floor. I eyed the bulge of my diary, then withdrew it.

After a moment's consideration, I slowly opened to the first page to see my own handwriting, faded on its thin pages. Memories of my friends and all the horrors of our Arctic journey came back to me, fresh and full of sadness.

I recounted my three-year journey that started on the HMS *Erebus* with Sir John Franklin and over a hundred men. My comrades. Men I had treated, healed, befriended. My throat tightened as I read in silence.

Halfway through, my writing ended with the final entry I'd written soon before Annie arrived. I glanced down. She had fallen into a deep, exhausted sleep while I read. A few locks of hair covered her cheek. I reached down to gently brush them aside. My fingers stroked the soft skin of her face, but she did not stir.

Ryan grunted. He stared at me for a long moment before resting the back of his head on the wall. He closed his eyes. Dennis, however, did not look away, but continued to watch me with redness slowly blossoming high in his cheeks. His eyes had grown hard and unfriendly.

I dropped my gaze, unsettled, and dropped my hand into Annie's pack to withdraw a pen. Clicking the nub at one end, I settled back and began to write.

Twenty-Nine

Annie
2020

Someone was watching me.

A tall figure stood over my bed in the dark, room. Adrenaline soaring, I rolled and collided with an unmoving Harry. I let out a choked shout.

"Shh," came a whisper.

Light flared. I flung an arm over Harry, frantically trying to find a pulse or feel his breath.

"Mmph." He shifted in his sleep. "Annie?"

My eyes painfully adjusted to a sudden glare of bright light. I found myself staring up at Martin Stephens. He dropped a hand from the light switch and held a finger up to his lips. In a fluid movement, Harry sat up.

"Annie?" he asked again.

"What the hell do you want?" Ryan had fallen asleep in the chair but now bolted to his feet.

"Keep your voices low." Martin held up his hands, backing up towards the door. "I'm here to bust you out."

"Huh?" Dennis rose from his spot on the floor, blond hair tousled. A long, deep crease from his sleeve lined one cheek.

Harry rubbed an eye and nodded. He bent to pick up my backpack and slipped his arms into its loops.

"How do you plan on doing that?" he asked.

"Wait." Ryan stood, rubbing one eye. "You knew he was coming for us?"

Harry smiled at Martin. "A hunch."

"How do you expect us to trust you?" I slid off the mattress and stood between them.

The harshness in Martin's eyes faded away. "Eli's keeping me down here, too. Lured me down here with a job promise a few months before the wraiths showed up. I didn't know how sick he was until after the end, and if I'd tried to escape then, I had zero chance of surviving outside. So, I stayed. Better to be a well-fed captive with a safe place to sleep than killed by the wraiths. Your arrival changed that, though. I want to get the hell out of here. We can help each other."

"Why is he holding you? Why are all the others okay with what's going on?"

Martin shot a look at the door. "Look, we have zero time to talk about it, but I'm happy to explain everything once we're clear of this damned place. But we have to go. Now."

Harry lifted his chin. "I assume you have conditions?"

Martin's brow furrowed. "I want to go with you, obviously. Additionally, when we get to your home, I want to see this time machine."

Harry nodded.

"And I want to use it."

Ryan let out a barked laugh. "Fuck, no."

Martin watched Harry with sad eyes, a sudden shift in his cold demeanor. "Those are my only requests."

"Accordin' to the machine's instructions," Harry said, "this request poses a great risk to all our lives, includin' your own. Nothing can be changed or altered, and you can't return to a time between when you were born and now. Usin' it may not give you the same results you desire."

"I get it." Martin nodded eagerly. "I won't. You have my word I won't."

"Right." Ryan threw his hands up. "There is zero chance of this happening."

"It's the only way I'll let you out." Martin crossed his arms. "And won't raise an alarm."

Harry turned toward Ryan, one hand gripping the fabric of the pack's shoulder strap. "I think we take the risk."

"Of course, you do."

"Isn't…aren't they listening?" I shot a look at the ceiling.

"I gave Eli an extra dose of pain meds." Martin gave me a grin. "Okay, I tripled it. No one will be awake for hours, and I'm on watch. But dawn is coming. I need your protection, and you're not getting past this door without me. I want to help you. A safe outside world means that I can be free. And once the wraiths are finally gone, if Harry can do that, well, that's what I'll do. I'll go."

"Go where?" I asked.

Martin gave me that transforming smile again. "Home."

Weighing our options, I realized that the jerk was right. He was our best option for survival, for getting out unharmed.

Slipping on my shoes, I sidled up next to Harry. "We're in."

"Excuse me?" Ryan stepped toward me.

"Harry's our protection," I pointed out. "And we can take the canisters."

Martin nodded quickly. "I've already readied three."

"What canisters?" Ryan demanded.

"I'll explain on the way." Martin looked at the door. "But we really need to move."

Dennis stepped forward. "If this is the only way to get out of here, then I say we do it."

"Unbelievable." Ryan fumed, glaring at the podiatrist.

The five of us fell into quiet contemplation.

"I want tae risk it." Harry took my hand, his fingers warm and soft. "Those creatures oot there won't be defeated unless I step up and do somethin'."

"Fine." Ryan sucked on his teeth, staring over at Harry. "If anyone dies, it's on *you*."

Harry nodded once but did not back down.

"All right." Martin's eager voice lowered. "I'll make sure the hallway's clear. The second we leave this room, follow me closely. Do not stop for anything. I brought three canisters to the front door, for us to take with."

I pulled Harry close to me while Martin cracked open the door. The four of us held our breath for long, silent seconds.

"Now," Martin hissed.

The four of us snuck single file behind the podiatrist. I held my breath as we went. The skin of my arms prickled, and I couldn't shake the feeling that we were being watched.

The bunker was deathly and eerily quiet. We hurried along the hall. There were no shouts, no calls; nobody ran after us.

Martin whispered the basic workings of the liquid nitrogen canisters to Ryan and Dennis as we passed quiet doors on either side. I fully expected one to fling open at any moment, but they all remained shut.

We arrived at the entrance without issue. Dull light glinted off the three metal canisters near the concrete steps. Martin handed the brothers one each, whispered a quick how-to, and turned toward me with the final weapon.

I took the cold metal canister and pulled the straps onto my shoulders.

Martin glanced around a final time, then pulled the keys free and ascended the stairs. He shoved the largest key into a lock on the right of the door, twisting it with a grunt. When he spun the dials in the door's center, it silently shuddered. The suction from the air-tight seal releasing, however, echoed loudly through the nearby corridors. Martin surged forward and shoved the door up with a shoulder, lifting it high.

The sky was clear and cloudless. Pre-dawn light was just emanating from the horizon through the barren trees that surrounded us. No wind stirred through their bare branches.

Harry helped me out of the bunker, turning to do the same for Ryan and Dennis. Martin slowly and quietly lowered the door, the muscles of his arms straining against his short t-shirt sleeves.

"Which way?" he asked in a soft voice, eyes on Ryan.

"We came from the southeast." Ryan stepped past the rest of us, facing east. "Follow me."

As quietly as we could, we made our way to the tree line. I scanned the skies but saw no movement. I'd given up counting the tallies the brothers marked on the wall back home, so I had no clue what day or even what month it was, but the air was cool.

Dead leaves rustled and crunched underfoot. Unseen twigs broke with sudden snaps. The sky shifted from a light grey to a bright blue as we all quickly traversed the desolate land in a tight knit group. The rising sun started to warm my skin, a pleasant contrast to the constant cool of either underground bunker.

Long minutes later, the gas station where Harry and I had sought refuge in appeared. We passed the small building at a slow jog. The sight of it made me remember how I'd cowered in fear with Harry, expecting to be slaughtered. Another glance at the clear sky above did nothing to stop the chill that dropped down my spine. A few minutes later, we stopped for a quick breather.

"So, Martin," I said in a low voice that sounded dead and flat. "What the hell was Eli planning for us, exactly? What were those diagrams on the wall? Whose room was that?"

"That was what he called his studio." He sidled up on my left and shoved his hands in his pockets. "I don't know what he uses those drawings for. It's probably just a sick thing he likes to do to entertain himself. I'd only been in that room once before, and back then, there weren't as many."

"Back then? When he lured you with a job promise?"

Martin's eyes dropped to the water-desperate dirt. "I had recently lost my license. I was quite despondent. He said he had a group of people living off the land who desperately needed a doctor."

I slapped at layers of brown dust that caked my clothes. "That didn't sound like a cult to you?"

He didn't respond. Ryan waved his hand and we started off again at a fast walk. Harry came up on my right with a smile. Martin stayed near, thoughtful and quiet.

"Why you?" I asked after a few minutes. "How did no one else have medical experience? There were tons of people down there."

He walked in silence for a moment. His face had softened since we'd left, as had his voice. He no longer held tension in his shoulders. Running a hand through his neat, black hair, he sighed. "Annie…no one else *is* down there."

"What are you talking about?" I reached for Harry's hand in the growing light, but my fingers found only empty air; he had stopped walking.

Harry stood frozen a few paces back. He rubbed his chest. His eyes were unfocused. "They can sense me."

"Shit." Ryan started to jog. "Come on."

Harry watched the sky through the trees. He crouched low and sidestepped to avoid a long branch in his way.

We jogged through the woods for nearly three hours, now only stopping to take small sips from the water bottles Harry had filled the previous night in the bunker. The sun crawled above the tree branches, its warmth and light making our tense escape easier but more obvious.

"I can…" Harry breathed suddenly. His pace had gradually slowed, and his face had paled. "I can feel them. Please, wait a moment."

Martin shot a scared look toward the sky. "We don't have time."

I followed his gaze, but all remained quiet and clear.

"We're almost there," Ryan panted. He pulled Harry along, hopping over a large dead log.

We all broke into a sprint. My feet pounded on the hard-packed dirt. I slowed only to help Harry when he stumbled.

Finally bursting out of the trees, we all sped up our frantic run, aiming past the familiar destroyed building with no roof. I stayed close to Harry, but he was struggling, clutching his chest and gasping.

"Here! Here!" Ryan leapt over the dirt mounds we'd never investigated. He skidded to a stop and pulled the small key from around his neck.

"Hurry," Martin urged. His dark eyes searched the sky.

The wailing finally reached our ears, raw and etched with loathing.

"How the hell do they always come for us?" Dennis spun in a slow circle, his dirty sneakers kicking up dust.

"Whenever I went outside, they were called to me," Harry gasped. "They couldnae sense me when I was below ground but flocked here, then waited until I emerged again."

"How do you know?"

He shook his head, curls flopping. "I can…I can hear them now. Their existence. Their hate."

Dennis grunted. "Well, tell 'em the feeling's mutual."

No one laughed.

Harry's eyes were full of horror. "It is as if I communed with them. When I trapped them outside of Eli's. And now, they are aware of this escape attempt."

"Oh, shit." I gripped his arm, scanning the sky.

"There's thousands." He blinked and swallowed. "Annie, whatever's left, they're coming. All of them."

The door clanged open. I clambered down into our bunker, pulling Harry with me. One after the other, Dennis, Martin, and Ryan followed.

"Fuck." Ryan pulled the door shut behind us, throwing the bolts into place. He coughed, slapping dust from his clothes and wiping his eyes. The five of us watched the door seal.

I quickly pulled free of the metal canister, relieving my back of the added weight, and lowered it down to the floor. I turned and stepped up to Harry, hugging him tight.

"Thanks," Dennis said. He reached out and clapped Martin on the shoulder. A puff of dust rose into the air.

Ryan coughed and stepped back. "We need to get this plan in motion as soon as possible. Can you stand, Harry?"

He pulled off my backpack and nodded. "They're out there. They can't find us down here, but they'll keep searching this area. Most were already nearby. A great amount sensed me when Ryan and I went outside nearly a week ago. More came this way during my flight with Annie to the gas station."

"Did you really, like, mind meld with them?" Dennis asked.

Ryan helped Harry down the hallway and into the medical room before he could respond. Once they retreated inside, Martin spoke.

"Thank you." His dark eyes locked onto mine. "For trusting me."

"Yeah, well, thank you for busting us out," I said.

Dennis regarded the podiatrist with uncertainty. "Yeah, I'm not sure I can trust you after that shit yesterday."

"Nice to meet you, too." Martin rubbed an arm interlaced with shallow scratches.

"He has a point." I shrugged. "You want the time machine. You're technically a threat."

Martin dropped his gaze, shaking a dead leaf from his hair. "You talk like I'm going to steal it. I don't want the thing, I just want to use it."

The bunker door thudded, shaking in its frame. All three of us jumped. I leapt back, colliding with Martin, who held me steady with both hands on my shoulders. We all stared up at the door.

"The hell was that?" Ryan poked his head into the hallway.

"I'll check the monitors." Dennis jogged away, leaving me with Martin. We didn't follow. My hand hovered over the nearby canister by our feet, but the sound didn't come again.

"Was that them?" Martin whispered, still holding onto my shoulders. "The wraiths?"

I shrugged out of his grasp and stepped away. "I don't think so. Why stop with one hit? *Can* they hit things that hard? I've only seen them claw shit."

"That was the first time I'd seen them in person. When Harry saved us, I mean. I'd seen them during the initial outbreak, but only watched on the cameras at Eli's. We all did. It's the only time I was ever glad to have been trapped down there."

I blinked up at him. "What the hell was that place?"

Martin finally broke eye contact. He glanced down at his scratched arm again, clearly uncomfortable.

"You're gonna have to start talking if you're switching to our side."

He let out a long sigh. "I will. Once we regroup and we are all in one place and not running or fighting for our lives, I'll tell you anything you want to know. You have my word."

"Hey." Dennis had returned. He shook his head and shot me a nervous glance. "There's nothing outside. I checked all the cameras."

"Maybe they scattered already." I turned and hurried down the hall toward the medical room.

Harry sat, back straight, on the exam table. Ryan peered into his eyes with a bright slit lamp.

"Are you all right?" I wanted to go to him but stayed in the open doorway.

Harry nodded, disrupting the examination of his eyes.

"I don't think you have a concussion." Ryan stepped back, dropping the instrument. "You seem okay now."

"The influence of the wraiths seems to drain me. I already feel back to normal, though. Just a bit chilly."

"Well, you need to rest."

Harry slid off the table. "They're here, they're close. I say we carry through with our plan now."

Ryan frowned. "You of all people know the toll that took on you yesterday. And you could barely get here."

"Because of the pain, aye." Harry pulled on his coat. "It is intense, but I can ignore it best if no one else is at risk. When I fight it, the pain worsens."

"No," I said sharply. "Harry, you don't have to do this right now."

Harry smiled, the corners of his eyes crinkling. "It should be now. If we wait, we run the risk of some wraiths leaving; I may not be able to get them all."

"I'm not confident in your power." Ryan reached into the sink, washing his hands and drying them on a nearby towel.

"As I said, if no one else is in danger, I will be able to focus on the task at hand. And as a precaution, we will close the bunker door before I call the wraiths. If I face the same issue and cannae hold them again, none of you will be at risk."

Harry looked into my eyes for a moment, his own gentle and searching.

"We still need to question him." I gestured at the podiatrist, desperate to stall the inevitable. "Figure out if we can trust him, and what to do about his demands."

"Martin has been of great help already. He can assist with this as well." Harry locked eyes with the other doctor.

"I want to prove myself." Martin didn't drop his gaze.

I stubbornly refused to acknowledge my heart, which had begun to beat harder the moment Harry said it was time. This had been the plan all along. We had brought him here to save the world, but now that he was ready to do it, it was the last thing I wanted.

"So, what are we doing?" Dennis led us toward the back of the bunker. "Trapping the wraiths inside the platform room? We need to move the Zapper if we are."

"We had a better idea." Harry followed close.

I tried to keep my voice steady. "While reading the Franklin books, a few mentioned a huge winter storm in the late winter months of 1848. The rescue party that came after was told about it by the Inuit people they came across. It's noted in more than one book that many feel this storm could have been what wiped any remaining Franklin survivors."

Harry and I shared a look consumed with unspoken fears. "Knowing cold can freeze them," I continued, "we could put him back in the Arctic at that time. I know for a fact at least two books mention the date. If we send him back to then, he can let them out there. They all freeze, and we pull him back to us."

We passed through the little study then into the control room. I couldn't help feeling on edge as Martin gazed over at all the things we'd been hoping to protect, but we had to keep up our end of the bargain, whether or not I liked it – or him.

"Was it cold enough, though?" Ryan studied the monitors, especially the one showing the outside view of our bunker door. Nothing moved. "Liquid nitrogen is, I dunno, negative two hundred or more."

"It's about minus three hundred twenty Fahrenheit." Martin glanced around the sparse room. He had little interest in the screens, but he eyed the control panel nearby. "The Arctic is nowhere near as cold."

"Nae." Harry pulled my iPod out of his coat pocket, then slipped it into my hand. "However, the winter temperatures were enough to freeze my breath to ice droplets in the air."

Martin thought for a moment. "Water freezes at thirty-two degrees. I think that it'll will work. We don't know what the wraiths are made of, but if it's as cold there as Harry says it is, they should still freeze, even if it's eventual."

I glanced at Ryan. "Do you have the Zapper ready?"

"If we're putting him back where we found him, all the info is still entered." He was watching Harry, distant concern in his eyes. "We just need to change the date and time."

"Set it for dawn," Harry said softly. "While the cold of the night still lingers."

Ryan looked as if he was going to argue, but just nodded. "After we send you back, we'll set the Zapper to five minutes later. That should be enough time. I hope."

I flexed my hands, hoping to cover up the slight trembles that had started in my fingers.

"Annie," Harry said. "They weren't able to hurt me at Eli's yesterday. They tried, but their claws simply passed through me. If I go out alone, I will know the rest of you are safe. I'm sure I can hold them. Once I'm confident of my hold, I come back to the bunker and straight to the platform room. The cold will kill them. All right?"

My smile felt too wide on my face. "Okay. Let's do this."

Thirty

Harry
2020

I stood at the foot of the stairs leading to the bunker's door. My heart hit against my ribcage in a steady, stressful beat.

"All right," I said. "Dennis is watching the cameras. Annie, you, Martin, and Ryan stay back at the entrance with the canisters. Since the wraiths cannot hurt me, you protect the bunker at all costs. Be ready to shut and seal its doors if anything goes wrong, even if I'm still outside. Once I've trapped as many as I can, I will come back, but I may need assistance. Dennis will inform the three of you if that is the case. It is of the utmost importance that you must be ready to shoot if any break free."

Annie stood close, holding down a button on her device to allow Dennis to hear, an ability which shocked and confused me.

Ryan stared down at the metal canisters by our feet. "I still think I should be outside with you, Harry."

"He's right," she said. "You could barely stand yesterday."

Their fear was understandable. Their concern for my safety touched me, which made hiding what else I knew so much worse.

"Dennis will be watching." I gestured at the device Annie held. "He'll know if I fail, but you must shut the door if that happens. As I said, I will be fine. Can you do that?"

Annie would not look up.

I refrained from reaching for her, turning instead to Ryan. "If I am unable to hold the wraiths, they will merely stay near me while I recover. They can attack all they like; it will not make a difference."

Ryan gave a grim nod, hefting a long metal pry bar in one hand. "All right. And you still refuse a weapon?""

There was a crackle from the walkie talkie at his hip.

"Harry *is* the weapon," came Dennis's voice.

I smiled, but no one else did.

Ryan unclipped the small device, bringing it to his lips and pushing the side button. "We all clear, Dennis?"

"Nothing's moved out there, sky or ground, since you stuck me back here."

Ryan climbed the four steps, pushing his shoulder against the bunker's door. He paused and looked back down at me. Martin stood off to my left, a canister already secured to his back, nozzle in hand.

"Do not worry." I reached out and took Annie's hand, noting the quivers in her slender fingers, the tears she held back. Her face had paled considerably, which caused her freckles to stand out.

"You're coming back to me, Harry Goodsir." Her strong voice contrasted with the emotions playing across her face.

A warmth grew in my heart. With eyes only for Annie, I took her gently by the waist, leaned down, and kissed her softly on the lips. Her body pressed against mine. I trailed a thumb along her cheek, then broke away. I nodded at Ryan.

He pushed upward, eyes averted, and shoved the bunker door open. Early afternoon sun shone bright inside, bringing with it a stagnant heat. I climbed the stairs, not looking back.

A moment of grief and despair nearly overwhelmed me. I paused, wishing I'd had such a full grasp on the ability I possessed years ago. I could have stopped the ice demons. I could have saved my friends.

My scuffed boots crunched across dirt and small stones. I stood between the bunker and ruined building, keeping my eyes forward, refusing to turn back to safety.

I allowed myself to relive the kiss I'd shared with Annie. The memory of her lips on mine warmed me, lessening the chills dancing along my arms despite the heat of the day. I'd already begun to sweat, but I dared not remove my coat; once the wraiths were trapped inside my center, I would feel as cold as the Arctic itself.

A glint in a nearby tree showed me the camera through which Dennis watched. I lifted a hand, knowing I might not see him again. That I might not see Annie again. But they all had each other, and I knew that should I not survive the next hour, if I could at least destroy the wraiths, then they'd be safe.

The three could rebuild. With Martin, too, if he chose to stay. He had everything to lose, including his life, and risked it to free us. I trusted him with the others and truly hoped he remained.

The wraiths' claws couldn't hurt me. Not on the outside. But when they were trapped inside at Eli's bunker, the pain that tore through me had been searing and unbearable. If I had shared this with Annie, she would have never let me face the wraiths, so I had withheld the agony of the wraiths tearing me apart from the inside. I also had chosen not to disclose the mental turmoil that came when I merged with the creatures.

The ice demon of the Arctic had been different. When I'd trapped it, there was discomfort, but its mind had been calm, and at a strange sort of peace.

The hatred, the fury, the pure madness of the wraiths, however, had nearly dragged me to insanity.

It could consume me this time. It was the true reason I had decided to do this as far from the bunker and my friends as they would allow.

I stood quietly at the edge of the trees, putting the camera to my back. My friends were safe. I glanced at the sky.

It was time. I was ready.

I wiped my trembling hands on the front of my old wool shirt I'd been wearing when I had arrived in the future. Ryan had washed it, and I inhaled the faint, pleasant aroma. Oh, how I would miss the trio.

Letting my body relax and head tip forward, I released my power, mentally pushing it outward. The consciousnesses of each wraith quickly latched onto my mind. I could feel them turn towards me with eager triumph.

Within moments, their wails reached my ears.

They were coming.

A soft rustle sounded ahead. I released my hold, turning my gaze to the tree line beyond the crumbled building. All was calm and still. There was, however, a pale swatch of flesh on the ground, just barely visible from where I stood.

I stared at what could only be a woman's limp arm, the rest of her shrouded by the plethora of dead bushes and leaves. In a moment of panic, I took three steps forward before catching myself; it could be a trap.

But was it? She lay buried in the trees on the opposite side of the trampled path we had arrived on hours earlier. None of us would have seen her if she'd been there. What I could see of her skin was quite red from sun exposure; not the pale white I so often saw of the dead.

The howls of the wraiths drew nearer.

Black, undulating masses appeared in the distance, dotting the sky on all sides. A harsh wind kicked up the ends of my naval long coat, whipping the fabric around my calves.

Turning back toward the camera, I made a few sharp motions with both hands that I hoped Dennis interpreted as a command to stay inside. Without another thought, I bolted toward the unconscious woman.

I stepped into the dead forest with care. I ducked beneath long branches and picked my way over scraggly roots, eyes searching for the injured woman. Tall brown grass reached past my knees and hid large rocks that made me stumble. The air was dusty and hot, and smelled of copper.

"Miss?" I said, startling myself with the cracks in my voice. I cleared my throat and tried again. "If you need help, please call out."

The woman was gone.

I spun in a slow circle, peering around to no avail. Had I truly even seen anyone out here?

A soft sigh came from my left. It was followed by a groan and cough.

"Miss?" My voice was barely a whisper.

Bare branches rustled as she slowly pushed herself to her feet near a break in the trees mere yards away. She held her arm, which was bent at an odd angle, close to her body. Dead twigs poked out of her mussed yellow hair, and dirt streaked one cheek.

"Who are you?" She sounded weak.

I stepped through the trees toward her, holding both hands before me as best I could. "Please. I'm a doctor. I can help you."

Her eyes were cautious and full of suspicion. She watched me approach without a word, backing up into the open area behind her.

The wraith's wails peaked. They pierced my eardrums, and I winced. The woman let out a yelp and flinched downward. Her gaze snapped up toward the sky.

"They're coming this way!"

Glancing to the heavens above, I nodded. "Aye, they are. We must get you to safety before they arrive."

She didn't respond. I dropped my gaze to find she'd simply vanished.

"Miss?" I called over the din of the creatures.

There had been no rustling, no footsteps running away. So where had she gone?

A shiver traced its way down along my spine. The hair on my arms raised, pressing against the sleeves of my coat. The wind, growing in ferocity, whipped my hair into my eyes. I spun again, looking for any sign of life other than my own.

Nothing.

I pushed out of the trees and into the small clearing where the woman had stood. The sky began to darken. Nothing attacked me. I flexed my power, calling the wraiths again.

The spreading sensation made its way through my chest and up into my throat. The creatures increased their speed, churning like angry storm clouds. Fear seeped through my courage. I thought of Annie, trying desperately to recall the warmth of her lying next to me, the sound of her laugh, the flashing determination always held in her pine green eyes.

"Miss, if you're out there, the creatures will be here soon. I can take you to safety, but you must call out now."

Still no reply.

I pushed my power harder than I ever had. It flushed out of my body. My energy dropped momentarily; I fought against the inevitable exhaustion. My reach expanded further than I had thought it could, shooting out in all directions, an invisible beacon to the demons.

A beacon that would also act as a net.

Something hard and quite cold pressed against the base of my skull and startled me from my focus. My power snapped and faded.

"Don't fuckin' move, son," growled a familiar drawl.

My eyes dropped shut a brief moment; it had been a trap after all. I kept my voice soft and forced myself to stand still. "Eli, this is a mistake."

"Maybe. But you folks have a time machine. A damn time machine. Who gives y'all the right to keep it for yourselves? Now, stop those wraiths so we can negotiate."

The chill in my blood deepened. "I said I could call them. I never said I could send them away."

He grabbed my shoulder and spun me around to face him. I found myself eye level with the gun Annie had discovered before our close encounter at the gas station.

I held his gaze, still fighting fear not of my safety, but for my friends.

"The injured woman?"

"She's one of mine. Knew you'd come runnin' if someone was hurt."

"You broke her arm intentionally?" I asked, horrified.

Eli shrugged. "Had to be believable, didn't it?"

"You conspired with Martin, then?" I asked. "Had him lead you to us."

"Martin?" Eli snorted and wiped his nose with the back of his free hand. "God, no, that shit didn't help me. He didn't need to. You think I didn't see his face when your crew told us about the machine? He double crossed me so he could take his chances with y'all."

I squinted against the wind that whipped past us. "You held him prisoner. What did you expect?"

"Yeah, well, I needed him."

I didn't argue. The nose of the gun wavered. If I could keep him talking a bit longer, the wraiths would be upon us.

"If Martin was telling the truth, you were drugged when we left. How did you find us?"

"Yeah, he sure tried, but like I said, I saw right through him. I spit that shit out the second he left, pretended to sleep, then watched you fucks run off."

The cries of the wraiths increased; they continued to draw near.

Eli scowled. "That asshole. I took him in, gave him a job when he was too ashamed of himself, and this is how he repays me."

Realization dawned on me. "It was you at the bunker door. After we sealed it."

"Wasn't as fast as y'all." He patted his gut with one hand. "Y'all were too preoccupied starin' at the sky instead of back the way you'd come."

I had been too concerned with the lethargy that had tried to consume me, too convinced Eli had truly been drugged, that I had not even thought to ensure our retreat had gone unnoticed. I took a step backwards, ashamed at my utter stupidity.

Eli snapped the gun up and pointed it between my eyes. He waggled it, gesturing at me to move toward the trees.

I stayed where I stood. The gun Eli held did not scare me; my weapon, my defense, was much more powerful. And it was nearly here.

"I won't bring you to the machine," I said as I again reached for my power. My voice shook despite my efforts to remain in control. I could only hope Eli mistook it for fear.

"You will."

I called to the approaching masses of wraiths. Instant, hot adrenaline slid through my core. The beasts were hungry. They wanted blood. I clasped my hands before me and shook my head.

"I'm not taking you to it, and you won't shoot me. I'm the only thing that can stop the beasts from tearing you apart."

He grinned, a madness sparking in his cold eyes. "I'll drag you if I have to, you fuckin' dirty Scot."

"Do as you must. The wraiths will come much quicker than you can pull me to the bunker, and they can't tear me apart the way they can you."

I began to draw my power back in, trailing as many wraiths along its path as I could hold.

Eli paused, his hand just about to grip my shoulder again. Caution spread through his twisted expression.

A sudden, loud rustling behind him drew our attention. We turned to face the dead woods just as Ryan leapt past the tree line, brandishing a metal pry bar. With a grunt of anger, he slammed it against Eli's back, directly on the bandaged claw wounds.

The big man let out a howl of pain and staggered down to one knee. Bright blood burst along the fabric of his shirt, his stitches torn free. I stumbled to one side, fearful of his gun discharging, but the weapon merely clattered along the dirt.

"No! Get back!" I shouted at Ryan.

He didn't respond, didn't look at me. His face set in hard anger, he threw a fist into Eli's jaw, driving him flat onto the ground.

I pushed my power outward again in a desperate attempt to slow the wraiths, but they kept coming. Their shrill screams made my ears pulse painfully.

Ryan hit Eli again. When the big man fell flat on his back, Ryan drove a knee into his large stomach with such force that Eli merely flailed in the dirt, choking for breath.

"Take the weapon and flee," I shouted. "The creatures are almost here!"

He didn't listen and drove a hard kick into Eli's side. I was torn between facing the wraiths and leaping forward to pull Ryan away. If I could break his vengeful trance, perhaps he still had enough time to get to safety.

Three sprinting figures among the trees decided that for me.

Carrying the metal containers we'd stolen, Annie, Dennis, and Martin charged through the trees and toward the fight. Horrified, I turned and sprinted away from them, desperate to put as much distance between them and me as possible before the wraiths attacked.

With my focus distracted, pain and pressure accosted my chest. I gasped at its ferocity and stumbled. The piercing cacophony of wails grew fierce. Full of rage and malice and hate, the creatures flew toward me. I saw with relief they were angling away from my friends as I ran.

The sounds of Ryan and Eli battling each other faded. I raced away until all I could hear was my boots slapping in the dry dirt. Only then did I slow and risk looking back.

The distant figures of Dennis and Annie were side by side. They aimed their nozzles at Eli, holding him at bay. Martin stood off to one side. He stooped and snatched something metal from the ground.

The revolver. I skidded to a halt, my heart pounding, mouth and throat dry.

Suddenly, Tristan, Gloria, and over two dozen colonists from Eli's bunker appeared out of nowhere. Quite literally. They simply blinked into existence and sprang into action, running toward the battling Eli and Ryan.

I couldn't move. My mind could not comprehend what I had just seen.

Ryan spun away from the big man on the ground, narrowly dodging an oncoming Tristan. Dennis raised his nozzle and fired without hesitation.

The liquid nitrogen spray caught Tristan in the chest, and he shuddered to a stop, then toppled backward. He vanished before hitting the ground.

"*No!*" Eli feinted left in the dirt and attacked, shoving Ryan into his brother. Both toppled over.

Annie slammed the handle of her nozzle against the back of Eli's skull. Almost half of the colonists flickered, then vanished inches from their intended targets. Those that remained stopped and backed away.

Martin lifted his nozzle and shot the nearby Gloria. She fell back with a biting scream and vanished. He shot two other colonists and they, too, flickered from existence.

Annie hit Eli again, harder. He fell forward onto his hands and knees. Martin stepped forward. He pressed the gun's barrel against the big man's temple. The colonists vanished.

My relief was short lived. Wraiths swarmed me. More shot past, mouths hanging wide to let out their chilling screams.

"No!" I forced my power out in a surge then pulled back, yanking them toward me and away from my friends.

Most froze in the air, struggling against my hold. They tried to whip around and slash at me. But there were too many. Some slipped free.

I watched in horror as they streaked toward the others. Toward Annie.

Praying they were able to destroy the creatures I'd lost, I made myself focus on the rest. Those I still held shuddered in my grasp as I used my power to pull. They quickly began to fly backward and painfully into my core.

I sank to my knees. Choking on dirt and my own broken breaths, I tried and failed to scream. Ice cold claws raked but did not pierce my flesh. The mass of wraiths, more than I had thought I could handle, melded into me in a furious, deafening whirl.

It felt as if my entire soul opened itself up. I lost all grip on everything around me, on my mind, on time.

My insides burned in a gruesome agony. I couldn't breathe. My muscles spasmed and twitched and convulsed. Bright white clouded my vision entirely.

Two gunshots cracked over the screeches of the monsters. Startled, I lost my concentration and collapsed forward, just barely catching myself in the dirt.

Martin was on the ground, scrambling away from Eli who had somehow gotten the revolver from him. He raised it, aiming it at the podiatrist, but Annie charged. She slammed her shoulder into Eli's and knocked him aside. The weapon flew wide and discharged at the ground in a blast of dry dirt.

The excruciating pain in my chest throbbed in time with my racing heart. I turned and scanned the sky while flexing my hold on the creatures within me.

The wraiths I'd lost my hold on earlier were nowhere to be seen. Had the others already killed them? Nothing glinted in the dirt at their feet.

I fought the pain and forced myself to hurry back to where my friends battled, covering yards in moments. Lowering my shoulder and gritting my jaw, I ran at Eli just as he rose from the ground.

A sudden surge from the wraiths I held sent blinding pain through my core. It seared bright and hot, and I tumbled to the dirt before my attack could connect. The knees of my trousers shredded against small stones. I coughed a spray of blood that decorated the dirt below my boots.

My body shuddered, a quick, involuntary motion. The pain inside worsened. I swore it was slicing me open. Rage and hate also yearned to flood my mind, but I desperately held it back, letting the pain overwhelm me in place of going mad; I refused to let the wraiths take control.

Through my blurred vision, I could just see Ryan wrestle the gun free and point it between Eli's eyes. With the wraiths inside, everything was in black-and-white but crisper and clearer than my own sight.

Annie noticed me huddled on the ground. She started to run over but froze. She whipped her eyes skyward.

The searing throbbing in my breastbone told me the rest.

With a flick of my consciousness, I dug into the minds of the wraiths inside me, reading them as I'd learned to do. Their wide-open minds told me they'd left groups of others behind in hiding, knowing their numbers weren't enough against the liquid nitrogen and me combined. They'd waited, hiding, acting as backup to attack once I'd been weakened.

Struggling to my feet, I turned and braced myself just as a fresh onslaught of wraiths, more than what I'd lost control of prior, flew down towards us.

I narrowed my eyes and threw out my power, reaching out for as many as I could. Nothing happened.

I tried again, but the howling, writhing creatures flew past me without a moment's pause. I couldn't stop them. I could barely hold the giant mass of them already trapped within me.

A sudden flare of cold shot past me. Dennis stood behind me, Annie on my other side, both spraying liquid nitrogen in quick arcs. Martin ran forward and joined, standing a few yards back, trying desperately to spray the creatures the other two didn't catch. Ryan held Eli at gunpoint, but it was clear that his focus was on his younger brother.

Wraiths froze in batches and fell to shatter in the dirt. More soared past me, faster than the three holding canisters could follow. I tried again to reach out with my power, but unless I released my hold on the hundreds I'd already trapped, I had no control of the rest.

Eli took his opportunity. He shoved Ryan and bolted away, heading toward our bunker. Ryan landed on his back in the dirt and the revolver flew from his hand. He scrambled to his knees, reaching out for the weapon. His fingers brushed the barrel just as wraiths flooded over him. His shriek was that of pure torment.

Dennis screamed, dropping to his knees and letting go of the canister's nozzle. His spray of Arctic air sputtered and died. He gawked at the teeming mass of demonic creatures slaughtering his brother, his face and hands slack. I nearly lost my hold on the wraiths inside of me.

Ryan's howls stopped short. The wraiths that had attacked him now flew after Eli. He barreled through the trees but was much too slow. They quickly enveloped him and brought the big man down in a bloodied frenzy.

Martin, his eyes still trained on the few remaining wraiths, took hurried steps backwards. He brought his nozzle up, his mouth set in a grimace. Annie did the same, but her wide eyes were solely focused on Ryan's unmoving, flayed form.

Once Eli's flayed body had finally stopped twitching, the creatures separated into smaller targets and careened around toward the podiatrist. He cried out and backpedaled as fast as he could. His heel caught in his haste and he went down hard, dropping the nozzle. His skull thudded against a large stone protruding from the dirt and his body went limp.

"Harry!" Annie's scream was loud and raw. Hers was the only spray that remained to defend us.

I shot my power out but couldn't gain enough of it to trap the remaining wraiths without letting the ones inside of me free. I could feel their glee, feel their impatience. Sensing the opportune moment to attack, the wraiths descended in a great surge.

They reached for Dennis, who crawled in blind grief toward his brother's bloody remains.

They reached for Martin, who was shifting on the ground, holding his head, unaware of his impending death.

They reached for Annie, just as her nozzle sputtered and her spray evaporated.

Something inside me snapped.

My power surged with sudden ease.

The tearing pain in my throat told me I was wailing long and high, not unlike the wraiths. Annie's scream joined with mine. I threw myself to the ground, digging my fingers into my hair. Tears of pain streaked down my face.

Unrelenting nightmares flashed through my mind. Captain Crozier hauling a sledge boat on his own and brandishing a severed human arm. Dr. Stanley from *Erebus* performing an autopsy on a still-living Lt. Le Vesconte. My brother Robert on a boat, clutching a blood-soaked letter addressed to me. Captain Fitzjames pushing the barrel of his pistol deep into the soft tissue of his eye and then pulling the trigger. Annie wrapped in seal furs and nothing else, smiling and holding out her hand. Her features hardened and grew long, shifting into those of the ice demons in the Arctic. Its long fingers plunged into the center of my chest and ripped out my beating heart.

Rage and fury and despair and madness flooded my mind. The consciousnesses of the wraiths brought me to the brink of insanity and held me there. Screaming my throat raw, I clawed at the dirt. Tears streamed from my eyes.

My breath returned in a sudden force and I inhaled deeply. I stared up at Martin's narrow, sweat-streaked face. Blood stained his neck and right shoulder. He recoiled when he met my gaze, his expression twisting to one of shock and fear.

I struggled upright and mentally probed within myself. The wraiths squirmed in their impossible cage, furious and wild, outraged that I had bested them all. I ground my jaw and reached out for Martin.

He shied away. "Y-your eyes."

"Come here." My voice was a death rattle, my words hard to decipher.

After a moment's pause, he leaned toward me, allowing me to check the back of his head. Hot blood stained my fingers.

"I'll be fine," Martin grunted. He stood and helped me to my feet in a quick, rough gesture.

I gripped his hand in mine a moment, thanking him with my eyes. He nodded and wiped sweat from his forehead. A weak lament sounded from behind him. Annie and Dennis huddled on the dry ground close to Ryan's torn corpse.

A quick spasm in my spine drove me to my knees again. I shoved my power inward, keeping my hold on the wraiths firm. I ignored Martin when he bent and gripped my bicep. Pushing him away, I crawled over to my friends.

Ryan's sightless eyes, speckled with dirt, stared up at the clear sky. What little was left of his face was pale in fear and death. Annie sobbed into Dennis's chest. He gripped her by the shoulders and just stared at his brother. Tears slipped from his eyes, but I could see the disbelief written across his face.

I forced myself to leave them, pushing myself up on weak legs and lurching into the dead trees.

Eli's body was barely recognizable. Both his throat and stomach were torn halfway open. His intestines glistened in the sun. I felt no satisfaction in the big man's death.

I turned away to make my way back toward the bunker, desperate to finish what I had started. After only a few unsteady steps, my hold on the teeming mass of wraiths suddenly slipped. I crouched and shut my eyes tight. I slowly counted to three, solidifying the tight invisible cage, then rose back to my feet.

I wished beyond all else that I could remain and comfort Annie and Dennis, but if I didn't release the wraiths soon, they would slaughter me, body and mind. I tripped through the trees, using large trunks nearby for balance.

Rough hands grabbed hold of me. Martin grunted to my right, pulling my arm over his shoulders.

"Did you get them all?" he breathed.

Sight swimming, I lurched and nearly vomited. After a few heavy breaths I reached inside. The fury of the wraiths told me that I had the entirety of their numbers locked away, at least for now. Their obsession with my presence in this time had been their annihilation. I nodded at Martin. He shifted under my weight, and we struggled forward.

"Harry!" Annie was crashing through the trees behind us, but I did not turn.

"I have…have to get back. Now." I coughed and spit blood to the dirt. "If I lose the hold, I won't be able to stop them again."

Martin pulled me along faster. Annie gripped my arm and took some of my weight. Blood stained her hands and shirt.

Frantic, I tried to let go of Martin to check her for injuries, but she only went faster, shaking her head.

"I'm fine. It's not mine." She trembled violently. Tears fell from eyes large and glassed. "Martin, what the hell was that back there? Tristan, and Gloria, and…and…?'

I lurched forward, trying to move as quickly as I could. Air seemed to escape my lungs faster than I could breathe. My eyes fell shut for a few moments.

"Eli's like Harry. An Evo." Martin grunted, half-pulling, half-dragging me through the dead woods. "I was going to tell you after all this, I swear."

She swerved to the side, skirting us around a large tree. "So, what, he could teleport people?" she asked, her voice throaty with emotion.

Martin shook his head. "None of the people in the bunker were actually real. He could…I don't know the right word for it…conjure living, breathing people. Ones that could be touched, be hurt. Killed. All he needed was a piece of their original body. He'd lure people somewhere, kill them, and make replicas. Copies that he could fully control. Tristan, his oldest…he sent him out for supplies after the end. He found plenty of survivors that way."

"Oh, God."

"It's been a long while, though, since anyone new came through." Martin choked on his words a moment, his dark eyes troubled. "I'm so sorry I couldn't find a better way to warn you, but through the cameras or his creations, he was always listening. I knew I had to get you out before Eli did the same to you."

I took in a shuddering breath. "Why did he not turn you into one as well?'

Had I spoken? Had they heard me? I could not tell. Pain flooded through me in quick waves and made it too difficult to comprehend what was happening.

"We were…we used to be friends. Before the end. Long before he held me hostage." Martin's deep voice softened, as if he was talking to himself. "Before he went mad."

Annie grunted from my other side. "Why didn't you drug him earlier? At least try to stop him from killing people?"

"Look, can we talk about this later?" Martin's chest heaved. "Maybe when we're not constantly running for our lives?"

Annie and Martin pulled me along faster just as the pain took over.

I could just make out Martin and a heavily bloodied Dennis carrying me. I looked past them at the clear sky and a beautiful array of dead tree branches. The taste of metal seeped along my tongue. I tried to turn my head but couldn't move. Blood trickled from between my lips.

The wraiths were killing me from the inside.

I grabbed a hold of my power again, relishing how simple it finally was. With a weak grunt, I tore inward and shoved them back with a brutal flare.

My consciousness snapped back. I choked on a mouthful of thick blood.

"We're almost there," Martin grunted.

I turned and spit crimson onto dead grass. A glint of metal behind the podiatrist caught my eye. The sight of the bunker door was all that calmed me. We were going to make it.

Annie pulled the door wide. Martin and a silently weeping Dennis carefully carried me down the steps into the bunker. Natural light gave way to the fascinating bulbs I'd barely gotten the chance to examine. I made a mental note that they would be the first thing I focused on if I returned.

Finally lowered to my own feet, I met Annie's gaze. No. The light bulbs would come second to her.

A shudder rippled through me. The wraiths clawed at my insides.

"Now," I rasped. "It has to be now."

Martin and Annie supported me as we hurried through the halls. Our scraping footfalls and grunts of exertion were all that followed us through to the back of the bunker.

Annie helped me up onto the platform. Her flushed face, streaked with tears, turned up toward me. I stared into her green eyes, longing for this to be over.

Almost.

Dennis jogged over from the shelving unit. Moments later he slapped an electrode below my neck, beneath my loose wool shirt.

Everything was happening so fast.

The wraiths surged in me, threatening to burst out at any moment. I fought back as ferociously as I could. After a few deep, steadying breaths, I looked up at Dennis.

"I'm so very sorry about your brother," I managed to rasp. Despite our urgency, I pulled him into a fierce hug, swaying on my feet.

Dennis choked on words he couldn't form. He pulled away. Martin took his place, helping Annie pull my old, bulky cold weather slops over my clothes. She tightened my long scarf, then slipped thick gloves over my hands.

Thoroughly bundled but trembling, I reached into my core, searching. I pushed the wrath of the wraiths away and just focused. I no longer felt Annie and Martin holding me up.

Everything faded to black.

My friends now watched me from beyond the room's large windows; I hadn't even realized they'd left me alone with the Zapper. They stood in the control room, with Dennis at the panel by the screens.

I fell to my hands and knees.

"Do it," I rasped.

Dennis slapped the red button. A hot, piercing agony shot through my body. It joined the excruciating torment that already raged through my core, and I was ripped apart.

Thirty-One

Harry
1848

The Arctic storm hurled raw glacial power.

Deathly frigid air seared my lungs the moment I was able to breathe again. Hard pellets of snow were flung into my eyes before I could flinch away. The loose sides of my slops whipped and snapped in the harsh wind. My two layers of thick gloves did nothing to stop the freezing bite of the ice underneath my hands.

I'd been taken from the future and placed back near the mouth of the river with a simple press of a button. I wanted to marvel at such a feat but could not.

This is where I had died.

A gust of harsh wind knocked me sideways, kicking more snow and ice against my back. I curled into a tight ball and tried desperately to cling to my sanity against the roiling forces of the wraiths.

Dull yellow light glimmered faintly to my left, but the ever-whipping snow and ice of the howling storm blocked the sun from view. I had no clue which way was which; the tents of the camp had all vanished. The men had moved on.

My breath left my lungs, leaving me gasping through the tight scarf. I had nearly forgotten the excruciating cold; the weeks I had spent in Annie's time had spoiled me.

Annie.

I couldn't give up, not now. It was nearly the end. All I had to do was let go of my control.

I pushed off the loose shale stones I had never hoped to see again. Unable to rise to my feet, I settled on my knees and focused on Annie. On the time we spent listening to music, on her warm embrace enveloping me. The memory of her honed my focus.

The utter beauty of each shade of blue and white and grey swirling before me was the last clear thing I saw before I did what I'd been chosen to do. Releasing the hold at my core, I let my eyes fall shut and finally released the wraiths into the raging Arctic storm.

The countless souls recoiled in fury. They shot out of my body with ragged wails that deafened my ears.

I screamed with them.

Unimaginable pain shot outward from my breastbone and seared up through my neck, through my stomach, down my quickly freezing arms and legs. They were tearing me apart, clawing and fighting their way out of me to streak up through the whipping snow.

Mouth open wide against my scarf, I kept screaming.

Once free, the wraiths whipped around and started to fly back, reaching for their executioner. Claws raked toward my upturned face.

Nothing they did hurt. The unending blasts of Arctic wind, however, already began to numb my extremities and face regardless of my layers.

After long minutes attempting to slaughter me, the wraiths finally began to freeze. Their strange mist turned to droplets and shattered on the ground. More wraiths poured from me. They, too, met the same fate.

I could not revel or rejoice; the horrible pain was the only thing keeping me upright and awake. I had never felt such torment. Not slowly starving to death, not from the burning inclemency of the Arctic as we'd trudged from ships forever stuck in the ice. Memories of Annie, of music, of a full hot meal, vanished as my mind surged toward madness.

And then it was over. The pain abated.

Gasping in air that froze my throat and lungs, I covered my mouth with violently trembling hands and toppled forward amongst the glittering ice crystals that had once been the wraiths. The monsters that had killed Annie's world were defeated.

My throat was raw. The bitter tang of hot blood flooded my mouth. I squinted against the whipping snow, too exhausted to stand.

I'd survived.

I had no idea how long had passed. I reached up, fingers grazing the small lump of the electrode. My lips managed a smile. I was going to see Annie again after all.

Shivering so hard my spine popped, I curled up again. The feeling in both feet and hands had fully fled. I pushed my scarf higher, covering my eyes and blocking out the stinging snow, the frigid air.

An ache began to form in my chest. It wasn't the familiar pressure that signaled nearby spirits.

I waited. Any moment now, my friends would whisk me back to the warmth of the bunker and back to the arms of the woman with whom I'd fallen in love.

In a brief moment of panic, I shifted on the rocks only to find my face had frozen to the stones. When I pulled it free, I did not feel any pain.

I could no longer feel my legs.

My shivers began to subside.

My body slowly relaxed on its own, unfurling prone along the stones.

Soon. They'd bring me home soon. I just had to hold on a little while longer.

A strange heat began to overtake me. I didn't notice when my eyes fell shut, but they must have, for my vision blurred and then faded away.

I breathed slowly now. Each long second seemed a little bit easier, a little bit warmer.

Through violently chattering teeth, I quietly began to sing the words to "Here Comes the Sun," thinking only of Annie.

Thirty-Two

Annie
2020

A small explosion, epic in the confined bunker, shook the concrete foundation and rattled the thick shatterproof glass of the windows. I cursed and stumbled back into Martin.

Darkness shrouded the entire room.

I pushed away from him, stumbled, and landed flat on my back. I flailed, unable to see anything. My fingers grazed someone's arm.

"What happened?" Martin's voice was next to me.

"The main breaker blew." Dennis sounded far away, as if he was on the other side of the room.

Martin's fingers slipped down my arm. He squeezed my hand. "Don't move. Let Dennis fix it."

I stilled. The air around us turned claustrophobic. My heart thudded a heavy staccato against my ribcage. Long seconds ticked by. I could feel his narrow shoulder against mine and hear his quickened breaths.

The lights came back on in a silent glare. I scrambled to my feet, pulling Martin with, and stared through the windows in horror.

Thick, grey smoke filled the platform room. It blocked my view, roiling against the glass, reminding me of the wraiths. But this was different. Thicker. Slower. Devoid of claws and skeletal faces.

Unable to form any words around the huge lump in my throat, I sprinted to the large metal door separating the two rooms.

"Don't!" Dennis reappeared. He ran to the controls, thighs slamming into the long table. The small stack of monitors wobbled. Hunching over, he flipped through the instruction manual, then slapped a few buttons.

The smoke billowing in the platform room swirled and flew upward in a violent funnel. It disappeared seconds through the ventilation shaft in the low ceiling.

Pressed against the glass again, I peered into the platform room, desperate for any sign of life as the smoke cleared.

Harry was gone.

Now that the smoke had been vented, we could see the Zapper. It had been thrown to the middle of the room with the force of the explosion. It lay crooked on the floor, small and pathetic, with sparks flying high from a gaping hole in the metal casing. Grey tendrils billowed and twisted from its depths.

"No..." I sprinted into the platform room before Dennis or Martin could stop me.

My eyes instantly teared up. I coughed, blocking my nose and mouth with one arm. More coughs wracked my chest, but I surged forward, relentless, only stopping at the ruined remains of the Zapper.

Dennis appeared next to me. He carefully prodded the case of the Zapper with the toe of one sneaker, flinching back at a fresh onslaught of sparks.

"What the hell happened?" I shouted over the hum of the ventilator, voice muffled against my sleeve.

He pulled the front of his shirt up over his nose. "The only thing I can think of is that sending Harry back with all of the wraiths at once killed the Zapper and tripped the breaker."

"We have to fix it."

Dennis looked over and met my gaze. We shared a silent, hopeless moment. He shook his head, turned, and left the room.

I screamed into my hands. Martin stood a few feet away, staring at the remains of the Zapper, his face filled with a deep despair.

A fresh surge of nausea bubbled low in my gut. My knees gave out and I sank to the cold floor. The air was clearer there, but I still couldn't breathe. My heart shattered as the reality finally hit me: Harry was gone.

"Annie." Martin's voice was a low rasp. He crouched beside me and lay an awkward hand along the back of my neck.

I crumpled into him, clutching the front of his shirt. "He's gone."

"He did it, though." Martin murmured. "He saved us."

Dennis appeared again, arms full of Franklin books, face miserable and slick with tears.

I pulled out of the awkward embrace with Martin that was nowhere near Harry's comfortable, loving one I craved. The thought of him back in the Arctic, alone, surrounded by the wraiths and in impossible cold, sent me into a fresh wave of despair.

I snatched one of the Franklin books from Dennis, opening it at random. I flipped through marked, dog-eared pages I'd marked well before I'd met Harry.

My eyes fell on a heart-wrenching sentence: "*The remains initially thought to be Lt. Le Vesconte's were recently confirmed as those of Harry Duncan Spens Goodsir, the assistant surgeon aboard Erebus.*"

I threw the book.

I pulled another toward me, then another.

"*...was found near the mouth of the Peffer River. Harry Goodsir's remains were brought back...*"

"*Free of lead poisoning and scurvy, it is now thought Harry Goodsir perished due to exposure and a tooth infection in his upper jaw...*"

Harry had suffered again. He had died again. He had risked life and limb for strangers of a future he'd never experience.

He'd frozen to death, waiting in vain for the moment we'd pull him back to safety, to warmth. How long did he survive before death claimed him this time? How long did he linger? How much pain had he endured again?

"How could we do this?" Dennis stood behind me, holding one of the books I'd dropped. "He did nothing but help us, and we fucking killed him."

The backs of my eyes pounded in time with the crushing vice-like pressure in both temples. I left the books and made my way back into the control room. Both Dennis and Martin followed but I didn't care. I could only think of Harry. I stared at the red button that had taken him away from me.

He'd never see the sun rise again. Never see its light glinting off of nearly invisible city windows, or over waves of green grass with snow-crusted mountains on the horizon. He'd never lay in a bed so soft he'd swear it was a cloud.

He'd never hear music again.

He'd never be warm again.

The Zapper was broken, and I couldn't save him. Not this time. He had died alone because of me.

Dennis, his eyes unfocused and dull, lowered into one of the rolling chairs with a heavy sigh.

"We need to go move the…" He waved a hand. "We need to bury…"

I wiped my nose on my sleeve and just walked away, turning my back on the controls, on the Zapper, on my friends. I left the control room and shuffled through the bunker in a numb state of shock.

Something caught my eye when I passed the open door of the medical room. Harry's journal was on the counter, black against stark white. Guilt crashed into me, so fierce I bent at the waist, clutching my chest. I took the journal and held it tight in both hands.

I carried it to the first bedroom, where Harry had slept. My eyes took in the tidy piles of sketches Harry had drawn, the narrow mattress, the sheets he had folded and tucked that still held remnants of my peach shampoo Harry had used. It all weighed me down with heavy grief. I sat on the bed and stared down at his journal.

The piece of paper that I'd been using as a bookmark had been moved. I pulled it free and ran a thumb over the small photocopy of Harry's black and white picture.

His eyes held excitement, anticipation, curiosity and confidence. It had been taken just before the voyage had sailed; he'd had no clue how much he was going to suffer.

I lowered the photo aside and stared at a new entry. It had been recorded in ballpoint pen.

Dearest Annie,

I'm writing this with the full knowledge that I most likely won't survive the coming hours. Even now, as you sleep one last time next to me, I can feel the calling of the wraiths deep within my core.

The pain, which used to be unbearable, is almost welcome now, like a necessary weight of what I must do in my final moments of life.

Do not grieve. This is my true purpose. I was given this ability upon birth and, while I did not know how to use it to help people sooner, I can use it now to save the future of the world we briefly shared.

I pray I am wrong. That I release the wraiths in the Arctic and am able to come back to you.

In all my short years, I have never found anyone to love. I delved into my studies, prideful of my accomplishments prior to leaving for Franklin's Expedition. Annie, you have opened my eyes and my heart to more than I could have dreamed. I will cling to the beautiful memories we've shared to keep me warm, to keep me sane.

I do not fear death, for I have found life.

I love you.

Forever yours, in eternity,

Harry D. S. Goodsir

Thirty-Three

Annie
2020

Tears finally fell. They coursed down my face and splattered on the freshly disturbed dirt at my feet. Dry heat warmed my skin. I said nothing, just held Harry's journal to my chest and stared at Ryan's grave.

I barely heard Dennis start to speak, his voice cracked and hollow.

"I don't know what to do without you." He wiped his wet eyes. "You were such an ass. Such a stubborn ass. I know I fought back. A lot. That's what younger brothers do, right? But you looked out for me anyway. You were always there, always making sure that I was safe. That I was happy."

My throat closed. I slipped my hand into his.

"You could be a jerk," Dennis went on, "but all I ever saw was how much you loved me and Mom. Even after it was just us and Annie, you somehow always kept us grounded. But if it hadn't been for you, Annie and I would have probably blown ourselves up by now. You helped me see different sides of stuff I didn't even think to consider. How am I…I just…you're gone, and now who's going to make sure we have everything in proper order? Patch us up? How are we gonna know when to charge into something and when to stay back and listen?"

Dennis sniffled and wiped the back of one hand along his reddened nose. "You looked after me, Ryan. Always have. Kept me from doing anything stupid, and now, without you, I'm fucked."

"No, you're not," I said, and squeezed his hand. "I'm here. We'll get through this next chapter together. We'll look after each other. Got it?"

He didn't respond. Silence stretched on for long seconds. I shared a look with Martin. The sun glared at me from over his shoulder, making him a dull silhouette. I glanced away, but my mind had already started making connections I didn't want to think about, not right then: He was a level-headed doctor, and quick to act under pressure. He was a huge asset.

I looked back at the dirt; despite everything, he could never replace Ryan.

Martin cleared his throat, then spoke.

"I don't know what happened," he said softly. "I drugged Eli to the teeth; he should have been asleep for hours. I'm so, so damn sorry."

Dennis let out a long, weary sigh. "We don't blame you, man. You risked everything to help us, and we're grateful."

"Years ago, Eli was discovered by the people making the Synths." Martin's voice was distant. "The ones you learned about in the files. They wanted to take his DNA in exchange for a shit ton of money, but he didn't want it. Instead, he asked for a secluded place to live. Just wanted to just be left alone with his creations, didn't want to deal with the real world. They were his family."

"These people didn't care he killed to create his people?" Dennis asked. "That's sick."

Martin shook his head. "He already had some when he was found. No one knew how he did it. Not even me, and I had to live with the crazy fuck. I didn't find out they were fake until after the wraiths killed the planet. Eli got careless one day. He wanted new faces, more people to fuck with. That's when I realized nobody in the bunker was real but me."

"But they *were* real." I shuddered. "I interacted with them, touched them. They were solid, breathing human beings."

"I still don't fully understand how it worked. But I do know they all had a small part of Eli's consciousness. That's why

I could never communicate with you. He could control them, even watch through them if he wanted, but it would leave his real body undefended. So, for the most part, he let them just hang out. He liked to see how they interacted. He kept them for company, or to perform certain, uh, duties for him. Guy's fuckin' nuts."

The silent dead woods wrapped around us. I listened to him, uncaring, trying to block out as much emotion as I possibly could. My grip on Harry's journal tightened.

Martin wiped his forehead with the back of one hand. "The bunker was built for him with the express agreement that he was to never leave. Him or his creations. That was the deal he made so they could take his DNA. If he did leave, they'd kill him without question.

"Supplies were regularly delivered, but once the rest of the world died, it didn't matter anymore. That's when he began to send Tristan out on runs."

"You said he'd been doing it his whole life?" I looked at Dennis. "I bet he's the little boy in the video we found. The one that got pulled forward in time during an experiment."

Martin's head snapped toward me. "What video?"

"We'll show you. It's how we even knew what the Zapper did in the first place."

"Aw, hell." Dennis's eyes welled. He turned, staring up at the clear sky and blinking back fresh tears.

I slipped my hand into his and rested my head against his shoulder.

"We studied those files over and over." Dennis said with difficulty. "I don't remember seeing Eli's name on the list of Evos."

"Maybe he changed his name," I offered.

"No clue. He was an adult when I met him." Martin wiped his brow again.

"And where did you come in?"

Martin's eyes were full of churning emotions I did not expect. "I'd met Eli years before, but Tristan actually found me one night. After some conversation, he let on that he knew Eli. Tristan got excited, said they needed a doctor, so I went with. I had been so desperate. They took advantage of that.

"You have no idea what it was like down there. How it felt to discover you were surrounded by nothing but fake people every waking moment. Eli bragged about it openly soon after I found out. He used it as a threat. Once the wraiths took over, I knew for certain I was trapped. Where could I have gone? Safe was better than dead, so I just stayed."

He turned his dark, piercing gaze on me. "Then you showed up."

I lowered to the ground and hugged my knees to my chest. The slowly setting sun warmed my back; its light filtered through the naked tree branches.

"I think we could fix it." Martin's words broke the miserable silence. "The Zapper, I mean."

"How?" I crushed a dry clod of dirt in one hand. "It's fried. Where would we even get new parts to a time machine?"

"Yes, there's only one Zapper, but the wraiths are gone." Martin raised his eyebrows, dark hair shifting in the breeze. "Now that it's safe to be outside, we have an endless amount of time to loot from science labs and universities. What if we lock up the bunker and go looting for parts? Hell, the machine is small enough to transport. We could bring it with, repair it over time, and come back here for the controls once we're ready."

"We can't save Ryan." Dennis didn't look away from his brother's fresh grave. "We can't go back to a time that we already—"

"Exist." Martin nodded, frowning. "I know. But we can go back for Harry. Save him before he dies."

We all fell silent. I mulled over the seemingly impossible task, not daring to hope. I looked up to the sky once more, but not for the danger of wraiths. I looked toward the slowly setting sun. Orange and pink light painted the sky behind the bare, gnarled tree limbs, a beautiful background Harry would have marveled at for hours.

"It could take years," I said softly.

"Which wouldn't matter," Martin replied. "We can go back to any time in the past. We could go back to seconds after he arrived in the Arctic."

"We might not even finish it." Dennis knelt in the dirt and drew a cross on the loose dirt atop his brother's grave. He wiped at his red eyes, smearing dirt along one cheek.

I slipped an arm around his shoulders. "Or what if we just messed it up worse?"

"Then we'd be in the same place," Dennis muttered. "But then we'd at least know. I think Martin's right. If it actually worked, we could save Harry again."

Martin nodded, gently touching the injury on the side of his head. It had stopped bleeding, but his shirt was still stained crimson.

"We should at least try," he agreed. "We need to, for all he did to save us."

Could it be done? None of us knew anything about making a time machine or how it worked, aside from what was in the instruction manual. I couldn't let myself believe. Even if we did fix it, how could we be so sure going back to save him would work? That there wasn't some stupid rule we didn't know about, one that could get more of us killed?

But still…

I stood to face the slowly setting sun. I thought of Harry's kindness, his determination, his passion for doing the right thing even in a strange new time surrounded by strangers.

My hands flexed on Harry's journal. Hope kept struggling to combat the misery flooding my soul. Slowly, I let it begin to grow.

"Harry's dead," I said, "but maybe not forever. Let's go get him back."

AUTHOR'S NOTE

Those who die are never truly gone - not if we have anything to say about it. They live on through us, and that's why it's so important to remember. To continue their legacies, their ideas, their passions.

I didn't write this book for me; I wrote it for Harry D.S. Goodsir. None of the men on the Franklin Expedition deserved the cruel fate that awaited them, but the moment I saw the photo of Harry, I knew he was to be the focus of this series. This connection I felt only grew stronger as I researched the kind of person he had been. It's important to me that he, and the other men, be remembered.

This was also written for everyone who was taken too soon, before their lives were truly finished. My dad, who was my hero and greatest friend, and who I miss every single day. For my father-in-law, Bob. For Kyle. For Brett and Mike.

We live on, and it's crucial to carry their memory with us. Despite the pain and horror, it's still a wonderful life, and we only get one.

HARRY GOODSIR'S CHANGED FATE TRILOGY

In Eternity
Homeward
Torn Apart

ACKNOWLEDGEMENTS

I also didn't write this book alone. Huge thanks go to my editor, D.W. Vogel, good friend and a personal hero. I've never met such a badass. Without her, I wouldn't have even written my first book, and I most certainly wouldn't have become the author I am today.

Kenny MacDonald, manager of The Proclaimers, deserves a huge shoutout. I emailed him on a whim, asking for dialect help. He took a chance on a person he'd never met before, never heard of, and agreed to help me perfect Harry's Scottish dialect. Since then, he has continuously helped with my research, sending photos and information from Edinburgh I'd never be able to get on my own. Kenny is also one of my beta readers for *In Eternity* and has lent ideas and that have helped make this whole series unique while staying historically accurate. Above all else, Kenny has become a cherished friend.

Speaking of music, that's another thing I couldn't have written this novel without. The idea came from hearing "Rosanna" on Pandora after researching a bit into Harry's character. I remember wondering how he'd react to our music today, which led to imagining his reaction to other modern things of our time, and it just took off from there. I started listening to and picking out songs until a sort of book playlist formed. And, while writing, I spent many hours writing with music blasting, especially that of The Proclaimers, who, by the way, are still a band and a damn good one at that (apparently the US doesn't know this). Thank you, Craig and Charlie, for your amazing music and for your support of Harry's books. Please never stop creating.

Another, more obscure soundtrack I turned up to eleven while writing the most intense scenes in this book was actually Cirque du Soleil's *La Nouba.* I was taken to a live performance of the show when I was a child, and the music and how it affected me never left. To this day I'm in awe when I watch those three little girls toss up their big yoyos and impossibly catch them with ease. Or when watching the man who could fly by merely touching silk. And let's not forget that insane act when the monster battles the live flame amidst soaring, tumbling people on a trampoline power track. Much of the music from *La Nouba* inspired the intensity of *In Eternity.* I can perfectly describe the scene where Harry, Annie, and Tristan flee the gas station choreographed with "Urban." Check it out. I've never seen such talent anywhere else, and although the show itself is no longer touring, its music is still inspiring, and I owe those artists a big thank you.

Another wonderful connection I've made while writing this is with Michael Tracy, Harry Goodsir's last living relative. He generously helped with not only the accuracy of Harry's past and his family throughout this series but has also been a supportive and encouraging friend.

I also would like to thank the distinguished Dr. Russell Potter. I came across his reviews on *The Terror* television show and discovered he was a leading authority on the Franklin Expedition. He helped with Harry's 1848 chapters, which in turn ensured I maintained accuracy with the ships, the men, and the entire voyage itself.

It was also crucial for me to research other things for this novel, especially since I have never lived underground for three years. I wanted to make sure every real thing in this book was accurate, right down to the generator in the trio's bunker. That's where Nicholas Peterson from Critical Power Products & Services LLC came in. He helped me look at different generators available in 2020 that could power the bunker and was quick to answer any questions that often arose as I wrote. It was his assistance that helped bring the bleak bunker to life.

And of course, I want to extend a huge, heartfelt thank you to my husband, Derek. He was an excellent beta reader who read through this novel more than once to help with content and story flow. In addition, he graciously put up with knowing that when my keys were clacking away, it meant I was on a roll and in the zone. He would quietly bring me coffee or food as he knew I wouldn't eat for long stretches while writing. I can't thank him enough for his endless support as I continue these journeys of mine.

Ultimately, I wrote this series because I wanted to bring Harry Goodsir back to life. I haven't done that in this book; I've only told you about his death.

Now, let's go save his life.

HISTORICAL NOTES

Michael T. Tracy

In the Kingdom of Fife along the Firth of Forth lies a town: Anstruther Easter. It has an excellent harbor which to this day shields vessels overtaken by storms in the Firth of Forth and was one of the first fishing stations in Scotland. A short distance from the harbor on Backdykes Street is a rather large residence known presently as "The Hermitage." It was here that Henry Duncan Spens Goodsir was born and raised, the third son of Dr. John Goodsir (1782-1848) and Elizabeth Dunbar Taylor (1785-1841).

Harry, as he was known, was named after his paternal uncle, a military surgeon of the 82nd Regiment of Foot. As Harry was growing up, the Firth of Forth played an important role not only in his upbringing but also in his career. He could see the body of water from his residence each day and from its shoreline he, along with his older brother, John, would collect the abundant marine life that was deposited in their paths, thus cementing an interest in marine biology for the rest of his life.

His parents both played significant roles, with his father encouraging his studies at school. From his mother, who possessed great artistic powers, Harry learned to draw exceptionally well. He lost his mother when he was only twenty-one, and her death would have a deeply profound impact on him. The significance of his older brother John would not only shape his medical studies at the University of Edinburgh but also his career.

Harry followed in the footsteps of his successful brother as he succeeded him as the Conservator of the Royal College of Surgeons of Edinburgh Museum. It was John who was one of the earliest to bring the compound microscope to Edinburgh, and who offered to similarly equip Harry if he sent him ten pounds to cover the cost of the instrument. [i]

Harry was awarded his Licentiate in Surgery in 1840 and immediately set out to work by assisting Dr. John Reid in the Royal Infirmary in Edinburgh. He also returned to native Anstruther Easter to assist his ailing father with his medical practice. He would also be called upon to assist John in conducting autopsies; one a notable and esteemed doctor in Edinburgh.

Harry was also a rising pathologist and morphologist in his own right and great things were expected from him. [ii] He wrote numerous scientific and natural history papers which were all well regarded; additionally, in 1845 he co-authored along with his brother John: *Anatomical and Pathological Observations.* It provided important confirmatory evidence to cellular theory.

Fate, be that as it may, intervened for the young surgeon and naturalist when Harry was offered a position as Acting Assistant Surgeon and Naturalist on HMS *Erebus*, a Polar expedition that aimed to chart the elusive maze of the Northwest Passage. Harry was the only member of the crew not from a naval background. He was thrilled, however, for the opportunity meant he could immerse himself in marine biology (when the *Erebus's* dredges were deployed and brought up various creatures of the deep, he was exuberant).

One has to only read the surviving letters Harry wrote home to clearly capture an accurate picture of his personality. His great powers of artistry began in earnest on a table provided to him by Sir John Franklin in his own quarters.

Even Franklin himself was clearly impressed with his Acting Assistant Surgeon and Naturalist, writing: "Everyone, officer and man, is happy to collect for him, in fact, he is a very general favourite on the ship." [iii]

Harry gleamed with joy while being one of the first members of the crew to climb on his first iceberg and was perhaps the custodian of the expedition's daguerreotype apparatus. He was not only the ship's possible photographer, but he was also the ship's librarian, and, before vanishing, he compiled an Inuit vocabulary dictionary. He did this by observing their characteristics, and he even wanted to make casts of their heads and faces. [iv]

It is my strongest conviction that Harry was true to the spirit of the Hippocratic Oath; simply put, to help all of the officers and crew that he possibly could. This one attribute was embodied by him as he traveled in his own death march. In the face of the extreme weather and with dwindling food supplies, Harry put the interests of his fellow crew members first and provided them with the encouragement and yes, the hope to keep going forward. In the face of these many arduous extremes, with death all around, watching as the crew one by one succumbed to starvation, tuberculosis, scurvy, and pure madness, possibly brought on by lead poisoning, and eventual cannibalism, Harry continued to administer medical treatment, comfort the disenchanted, and reassure the dying.

No penned words of mine can adequately address the absolute bleakness, despair, and pure horror that must have gone through the minds of those gallant men as they walked forward along the western coast of the island, each on their own personal death march.

In closing, there is one thought I would like you, the reader, to remember: this was one of the world's greatest naval voyages of discovery of the nineteenth century and remains to this day the greatest single loss of life in polar exploration. It furthermore has mysteries that continue to haunt us today.

As a result, I cannot overstate that this unparalleled loss of life had far-reaching consequences as a result of Harry Goodsir's disappearance and eventual demise. His family would never be the same again. The never-ending waiting for a letter or an answer that never came; this grief-stricken family never fully recovered – ever.

I recall before Harry's brother, Robert, sailed to search for him, his sister Jane entrusted to him a letter, bordered in mourning black, to give to Harry of the painful tidings that befell the family while he was gone. Harry never got that letter. The tragedy of the Goodsir family was shared equally by the one-hundred-twenty-eight families of the lost crews of the *Erebus* and *Terror*.

Names such as Franklin, Crozier, Fitzjames, Gore, Le Vesconte, Fairholme, Irving, Reid, Hartnell, Little, Peddie, and Hickey are also the heroes of my long-ago youth and are eternally etched in the recess of my personal memory.

For those interested in more, Dr. Russell Potter, a leading authority of the Franklin expedition, will lead you further into the expedition. He is a person for whom I have the greatest esteem and admiration. His writings will inspire the reader.

ALSO BY JENNIFER REINFRIED

GRIM SERIES

Grim Inception (0.5)
Grim Ambition (Grim 1)
Grim Misfortune (1.5)
Grim Judgment (Grim 2)
Grim Resentment (2.5)
Grim Vengeance (Grim 3)

HARRY GOODSIR CHANGED FATE TRILOGY

In Eternity
Homeward – coming soon
Torn Apart – coming soon

OTHER WORKS

The Souls of the Lash

CPSIA information can be obtained
at www.ICGtesting.com
Printed in the USA
FSHW022208180620
71228FS

9 781087 882161